'*Guess Who* is a fresh take on the locked room murder mystery. The plotting is intricate, the characters well drawn, and the pace never lets up as it drives headlong to the surprising end'   David C. Taylor

'One hotel room. Six strangers. One corpse. Good fun'
                                                    Cavan Scott

'Phenomenal. An utterly compelling and fiendishly clever read – it blew my mind ten times over'
                                                Francesca Dorricott

'Chris McGeorge has a knack for conjuring up the biggest of mysteries in the tightest of spaces. Dark and claustrophobic in all the right places'   Robert Scragg

Chris McGeorge lives in Durham and is a graduate of the Creative Writing (Crime/Thriller) MA at City University. He loves film and acting in an amateur theatre group. His debut novel *Guess Who* was picked for the WHSmith's Thumping Good Read Award.

Chris can be found on Twitter at: @crmcgeorge

By Chris McGeorge

Guess Who
Now You See Me

Inside Out

CHRIS McGEORGE

ORION

First published in Great Britain in 2020 by Orion Fiction,
an imprint of The Orion Publishing Group Ltd
Carmelite House, 50 Victoria Embankment
London EC4Y 0DZ

An Hachette UK Company

1 3 5 7 9 10 8 6 4 2

Copyright © Chris McGeorge 2020

A CIP catalogue record for this book
is available from the British Library.

ISBN (Paperback) 978 1 4091 8756 1
ISBN (eBook) 978 1 4091 8757 8

Typeset by Input Data Services Ltd, Somerset

Printed and bound in Great Britain by Clays Ltd, Elcograf S.p.A.

MIX
Paper from
responsible sources
FSC
www.fsc.org   FSC® C104740

www.orionbooks.co.uk

'Sometimes you just have to accept where you are and embrace, however unwillingly, that there is no way back to where you were before . . .'

ROBIN FERRINGHAM, *Without Her*

A ringing. Loud. Too early for the alarm. Must be his phone.

He opened his eyes and reached over in the dark. A 12-44. Couldn't be real. But he had to check.

He got up, got dressed, turned the window on for a moment. There was an avalanche outside. Lovely. He turned it off again.

He left his bedroom, slipping his Cuff on as he went down the corridor into the control room.

Continell was at the desk, watching all the monitors, a half-drunk cup of coffee forgotten next to her.

'Harper,' Continell said, as he leant on the desk. She sounded worried. 'One of the Cuffs just went off. No life signs.'

'Which one?' Harper said.

'FE773 Barnard.'

'That's Lockhart's cell? You got A/V on it?'

Continell didn't even need to press any buttons. She already had it up on the screen. An overhead of a cell, two beds with two women sleeping. Then the cameras went to static.

'A/V is lost for 12.3 seconds,' Continell said, 'and then . . .'

A sound. Loud. Like a roar ripping through the static. Gone as soon as it hit his ears. And the camera clicked back on. One of the women was still sleeping as before. The other was draped over the bed, head falling to the floor. Some kind of substance was flowing onto the floor from her forehead. Harper was glad the camera was black and white.

'What—?' He couldn't say anything. 'What happened?'

'That sound,' Continell said. 'I heard it. Not on the cameras. I actually heard it. From two floors away. I think it was a gunshot.'

'You checked the records on the door?'

'No one went in or out. No prisoner. No guard. Lock wasn't disengaged. Records are one hundred per cent, no one can change them.'

'One hundred per cent?'

'One hundred per cent.'

Harper picked up Continell's coffee without asking and downed the rest of the contents. 'Wake 'em up. Tell them to suit up. 12-44.' He started out of the room.

'Who am I waking up?'

Harper paused at the door. 'All of them.'

Ten minutes later, they were all at the lifts. All in their armour. All carrying their service weapons.

They got in the lift. Went down two floors.

Harper paused them all at the entrance to the Unit. 'This is the first time we've dealt with something like this. Krotes has signed off on the weapon usage, but no one is firing unless absolutely necessary. Let's not be trigger-happy.'

'Don't need to tell me twice, Chief.' Anderson smiled, pumping his shotgun. Why the hell had they given him a shotgun?

At least the others appeared more apprehensive. 'OK,' Harper said, 'me and Abrams take point. Truchforth and Anderson take the rear.'

They went through the double doors into the Unit, and down into the Pit. Prisoners were waking up, shouting questions through their cell doors. They ignored them. Got to the cell they were here for.

Harper took a long breath, nodded to Abrams and the others behind him. Then held up his Cuff. The light on it went green. And so did the light above the cell door.

They rushed into the dark. Abrams had a torch and she found Lockhart's face. The young woman was still asleep, or doing a damn good job at pretending. And then the torch went down to the puddle of blood on the floor, and then to Barnard's face. A hole in the middle of her head. Her eyes open, forever.

'Jesus,' Harper said.

Then the lights clicked on. And they all saw.

Harper found himself frozen. As Anderson and Abrams rushed to Lockhart, woke her up, got her in cuffs. She was gibbering about not knowing what was going on. And then she saw Barnard, and was gibbering about how she didn't do it.

Something was wrong.

Truchforth was scanning the cell, searching for it. He completed the quick search. 'There's no gun in here.'

Just a brief look-round. He could be wrong.

Lockhart was being dragged out of the cell. All three of them were restraining her, taking her off to the Hole. But Harper couldn't move. All he could do was stand there, looking and thinking. About something . . .

'Harper.' Continell, in his ear. 'I've been looking over the footage.'

He looked up at the camera.

'12.3 seconds the camera was down,' Continell said. 'I layered over the before and after images, on either side of that cut.'

'What about it?'

Continell paused a little before speaking. 'Lockhart doesn't move. She doesn't move even a millimetre. The images are identical.'

'What are you saying?' Harper asked.

But she didn't need to answer. Because Harper was thinking it as well.

Was there a possibility that Lockhart didn't do it?

PART ONE

Welcome to North Fern

1

39 days earlier . . .

They came for Cara in the middle of the night – barged into her cell and told her to get her things. No time for goodbyes. No grand sending off. Nothing but a pair of cold handcuffs and a delirious walk down a mostly sleeping cell block getting prodded in the back by a guard's finger, until she emerged into the freezing night air of the yard. A van was waiting. As were two other prisoners with their own guard. The guards were both in SWAT vests.

The three of them were bundled into the van, each put into their own sweatbox – basically a cell inside the van. The guards went out of sight, to sit out of sight.

No one told her where she was going. She didn't ask.

That's how their journey started. That seemed like a day ago now.

The van was driving along at a steady speed. Were they on the motorway? If so, how long had they been on there? Not worth thinking about it when it didn't really matter.

There was a soft constant weeping coming from the

sweatbox next to hers. The woman inside it was crying. She had been for the last few hours – so much so that Cara had almost completely tuned it out now, except for the odd louder wail.

A wail came then, along with words, 'Where are we going? You shouldn't be allowed to do this. I should've been able to see my boy, tell my family . . . Where are we going?'

Silence, for a few seconds. And then a minute. And then ten. And then it became the norm again – the question left hanging, almost visibly, in the air. Sometime after that the sobbing from next door started up again.

And equilibrium was restored. For an hour or two.

Suddenly, the van swerved sharply, hurling Cara into the sweatbox wall, and moments later, the road became bumpier. The van rocked along for another hour, giving no respite in its erratic movements, until finally it seemed to drive onto a consistent road. Not concrete, but a fairly well-worn track nonetheless. They definitely weren't on the motorway anymore.

Finally it stopped. In a great triumphant motion, the van was still.

'Hey, driver?' one of the guards said, banging on what sounded like the mesh between the driver's cab and the body of the van. 'Sitrep?' But none was given.

Instead, the radio and the engine died. And then nothing.

Cara nervously glanced around her four white plastic walls, hoping she would find at least some clue as to what was happening. But of course there was nothing.

There were voices outside. The sound of a gate being opened. The engine again. The van moving in a low gear for about five hundred metres. Then nothing.

Cara couldn't help feeling the impatience one felt when a plane landed and the seat belt sign seemed to be stuck on. And you always felt it was a fraction of a second more than it should have been before it turned off.

Then the back doors swung open. Dull sunlight flooded the van, and she blinked away sunspots, seeing the shadow of the driver on the wall of the van.

'We're here,' the driver said, rather unceremoniously. Not to her.

And then the two guards were rustling. They unlocked her box last, leading all three of them out of the van one at a time. Cara jumped down to see that they were in an enclosed loading bay, and the sun was disappearing inch by inch as a large shutter closed behind them. As the shutter reached the ground, she had a strange sense that she might never see it again.

She looked around to see that her peers were thinking something similar. Her neighbour from the van, the crier, was still sobbing, wet tracks down her cheeks. She realised she knew her. From New Hall – her wing. The other woman was trying to hide her discomfort, but it came through. She seemed tough – black hair, black mascara (which must've cost a pretty penny in New Hall), and a haircut that wasn't in style when Cara was incarcerated, but could be now – a buzzcut on her left side, and long hair on her right swept over – but she couldn't hide her worry. 'What's going on here?' she asked.

At one point, it would have been Cara who had the courage to speak up. But now all she saw was the point-lessness of it. And it was indeed pointless. The question left, unanswered.

The driver wordlessly turned and started to walk towards a towering red door that appeared to be more like a door into some bunker. The guards seemed to take the hint and pushed her and the other two prisoners to follow them.

At the door, one of the drivers knocked – a great booming THRANG that smashed into her ears.

Nothing. For a minute.

Cara looked around, and her eyes fell on the clos-est body in the strange huddle they had created. The younger guard was looking at her, and as their eyes met, his eyes quickly darted away. He looked scared of something – he was even shaking slightly. Why was he scared?

For the first time, Cara felt unsafe.

The driver seemed to be waiting for something, like he was counting in his head before he decided to knock again. But eventually, he did.

Finally, the door swung open to reveal a burly man – black with a greying goatee. His muscular frame was not complemented by his guard's jumper, embroidered with the name Harper. He held a tablet, looking small in his firm hands. He assessed each of the group in turn – a strange picture they must have made. 'We have FO112, NH597, and FE773?'

Cara felt the older guard nod behind her.

'And we have new guards . . . let's see, Dale Michael and John Anderson.'

The older guard grunted. 'Thanks.'

Harper sighed, 'Relax, Mr Anderson, they're not exactly going to add you on Facebook, are they?'

Anderson mumbled something under his breath, not best pleased.

Harper didn't seem to care. 'OK, residents follow me. Guards, follow your drivers to the main entrance.'

A shuffling behind Cara. She looked to see that the younger guard, Michael, was moving away with the drivers, but Anderson was standing his ground behind his quarry. 'I'm sorry, but my job was to deliver the prisoners to their new cells. Not just to the front door. I have a duty. And I intend to carry it out. I can't just leave these women on the doorstep – they are dangerous.'

Harper frowned, 'And if you do not adhere to policy here, I assure you so am I.'

Anderson scoffed but turned away and followed Michael and the others.

Harper watched them go and then did something bizarre, something Cara would question whether she'd actually seen for days to come. He winked at her and smiled.

'Ladies, please follow me.'

'The guards are getting transferred here too?' the woman with the parting asked, as the three of them followed Harper down a white corridor with a hideous grey-striped carpet.

'Guards Anderson and Michael have chosen to help build this new establishment, yes.'

'And what the hell does that mean?' Parting whispered in Cara's ear.

Cara shrugged.

The other woman had stopped sobbing, but had started chewing on a strand of her auburn hair. She met Cara's eyes for the first time, as if in agreement with the others' wonderment.

They were taken to a desk that appeared around a corner – two women were standing there in uniform, one middle-aged and blonde, one older and greying. Cara didn't have time to look at the names on their jumpers. They had a whiteboard and, at the appearance of the three, started writing on it.

'FO112?' the blonde guard said.

They wondered amongst themselves, before Harper came to their rescue. 'You'll have new IDs here. Such is the new initiative. FO112 is Moyley.'

Moyley – that was her name, Cara remembered it now. Moyley was the crier, and her wing-mate. Parting turned round.

The two female guards wrote some things down on the whiteboard. And told her to pose with it against a lined wall. They took a photo. A mugshot.

It was much like what had happened when Cara had arrived at New Hall. Just the usual welcoming party. But now she was – 'NH597'. 'NH597. Lockhart. 12th June 2020'. A mantra. A talisman. This was what she was. She held the sign up. They took the picture. Awesome.

Next, they ushered her, without waiting for Parting to get her photo taken, into a cubicle. The older greying guard stayed watching as she was commanded to strip, which she did without a moment's thought. Now it was almost second nature. She bent over while the guard searched her. She tried to switch her brain off as she rummaged around inside her.

Then it was done. She was told to turn around and was given a fresh pile of clothes to wear – her new wardrobe. It comprised of two T-shirts, two pairs of nylon trousers, some bras and pants, a purple static jumper, and a beige pair of canvas shoes.

'OK,' the guard said.

Cara waited for a second, then realised that was it. The guard wrote something on a pad and then glared up at her. Perturbed, she nodded to a door behind her.

So Cara went through it. It wasn't exactly like she had a choice.

She came into an interview room, with a man in a white coat sitting at a table. 'Ah, hello, Ms Lockhart, I am Doctor Tobias Trenner. I just have to ask you a few questions.'

She sat in the chair facing him, with a camera on a tripod pointed at her.

And the questions began, jumping wildly from mundane to fantastical. 'Your full name is Cara-Jane Lockhart, yes?' was juxtaposed with 'Have you ever thought about taking your own life?' 'And you are 23 years of age?' countered with 'How many sexual partners have you had?' and 'You fully acknowledge why

13

you are here? You are of sound mind?' drowned out by the absolutely ridiculous 'Is there any possibility you may be pregnant?'

After the taped conversation, the greying guard came in and Cara was moved around again through another door and to a desk, where she got her picture taken on a webcam and was asked to hold out her wrist. She was given a metal bracelet that seemed to be a slightly thicker version of a handcuff. It clicked around her wrist and a blue light throbbed on it.

'This is your Cuff,' the guard said. 'It acts much like an ID card, with a built-in vital tracker. It will automatically open any doors that you are allowed to go through, and restrict you from the ones you're not. It also has a tracker, so we can see where you are at all times. If you somehow manage to get somewhere you're not supposed to be, the light on your Cuff will turn red. You have 30 seconds to return to where you should be before the Cuff will emit an electric shock much like a taser.'

Cara opened her mouth to say 'What?' but someone got there before her. She turned around to see Parting had been dropped off behind her.

The guard asked Parting to hold her wrist out.

'No.'

The guard said nothing, just raised her eyebrows.

And Parting, who must have seen the futility of the situation, put her wrist out. A Cuff closed around it.

'You may find things a little more high-tech here than New Hall. This prison is the first of its kind after all.'

'What do you mean?' Parting said.

But Cara was focused on something else. The guard had a Cuff of her own. With a pulsing blue light just like theirs.

Harper interrupted them, appearing out of nowhere. She automatically looked at his wrist. He had a Cuff too. So the guards were being tracked as well? 'Are these two ready, Continell?'

The guard, Continell, nodded.

'Good, I'll take them along, you and Abrams can manage to bring Moyley, I assume. Tobias is taking a little longer with her. She's a gusher.'

'Of course,' Continell said.

With a curt nod, Harper guided Cara and Parting through another door, to a long white corridor. At the end of the corridor, they came to a black marble wall with three lifts. It looked like something from a hotel, only adding to the patchwork nature of the building she had seen from the outside.

Harper stepped forward and pressed the call button.

The left-hand lift doors opened and although Harper stepped forward, another male guard and a female prisoner lurched out. The woman was wide-eyed, scraggly ginger hair waving around in clumps. She was chewing on the sleeve of her top and emitting a strange moaning sound.

The guard just dragged her out. 'Come along, Ray.'

'But it wasn't him,' Ray, presumably, said.

'Yes, yes, yes,' the guard muttered. Pulling her out of the way of Harper and his deliveries.

'It sounded like him, but it wasn't him,' Ray wailed.

'We're going to see the doc and he'll clear this right up.' He started pushing her down the corridor, unlocking another door halfway down and propelling her into it. 'Come along.'

'But—' Ray started and then the door shut, cutting her voice into a muffle.

Cara and Parting looked back around to Harper. He didn't seem willing to give any answers.

Prison was an acquired taste – some people just couldn't hack it. Cara once thought she was one of those people – that she was destined to drive herself crazy, pacing up and down, mumbling about how she shouldn't be there and this wasn't what her life was supposed to be. The days were so long, the meals were so tasteless, the showers so humiliating. But . . . then something happened. One day she woke up. One day she realised that all she could do was carry on. So she did – and the days went by a little quicker after that, the meals had more flavour, the showers . . . well, no, the showers were still the showers. But, somehow, somewhere, she'd found some peace.

She'd given up.

And she couldn't be happier she did. Although it wasn't the same happiness she used to feel. This happiness was soaked in grief.

Harper led them into the lift and pressed the button. A mere ten seconds later, and the smoothest lift ride ever, the doors opened onto a scene much like the one downstairs.

A white sterilised room, with white tiles and white

floors, with a currently unmanned guard's station in the centre. Harper led them past it, through a set of double doors.

The noise was the first thing to hit them. It sounded like a public swimming pool when the children's floats came out. The noise was so massive and echoing and triumphant, it was hard to conjure up any coherent thoughts. Like a tremendous school of fish snaking and winding towards one goal, voices disappeared into one another to make an uncontrollable din. It was, unfortunately, a familiar sound – New Hall was exactly the same.

Therefore, Cara was hardly surprised when she got through the double doors and was greeted with an equally familiar sight. They were on a metal balcony looking into a long rectangular hall lined with cells on either side, and a mosh pit of flowing bodies in between.

Women were standing, sitting on plastic chairs, leaning on tables, playing board games, lounging on a ragged sofa, ducking and diving between tables, draped over the metal stairs.

Some of the women down in the Pit quickly realised they had company, and were pointing upwards and sneering. Some others just stood motionless. While more still were telling their friends. Soon most of the women were looking up.

'Hoah,' one shouted, 'new ones.'

A few more heads looked up and around at the alert. Most didn't bother.

'Pay them no mind,' Harper was saying as Cara

hurried to keep up with him walking across the gangway, 'they're mostly harmless.' They reached the nearest
staircase, and Harper had started to descend. Into the
sea of women. Cara wanted to do anything but. As
she stepped back from the staircase, a hand gripped her
shoulder. Parting's.

'I've got this, Butcher, I'll go first. Let me through,'
she said and smiled. Before going down first, two steps
at a time – almost like she couldn't wait.

Butcher.

Parting knew who she was.

Butcher. The name New Hall had picked out for her.
Her reputation preceded her. And all these women
would know who she was too.

Nevertheless, she found it somewhere within her to
start the slow way down the steps. Harper was at the
bottom now, and some women came to meet him – shouting incoherent things and gesturing in incoherent hand
signals.

'Ladies, come on, please. It's not the first time you've
ever seen new arrivals, is it?'

Harper started to walk forward and the women began
to part. She and Parting were the last to set down in the
Pit, and they stayed as close to Harper as they could.

Now, they could hear individual shouts, and some of
the women were recognising Cara as she went past.

'It's the Butcher! It's only the damn Butcher.'

'You're gonna fit in right well here, Butcher.'

'Careful, the Butcher's about. And she's got an
entourage.'

'The Butcher's on the prowl tonight,' one woman, lost in all the faces, sang. 'So get your loved ones hid.' The song, the song they'd sung at New Hall. 'We may be the scum of the Earth. But at least we . . .' How did she know it? Was someone else from New Hall here?

'Shut up,' a booming voice erupted.

The women stopped, wheeled around. Cara and Parting did too – it was hard not to. A woman in prison attire was descending the stairs they had previously walked down.

'What the hell is going on?'

Cara felt her shoulder being grabbed, and then Harper was pulling them both through the crowd.

'I was at the hairdressers, and I come back to this!' the woman shouted. She was short and stout, and took one step at a time. Then Cara's head was jostled around and she lost sight of her. 'What is going on in my district?' She almost sang it out like a gospel singer.

Cara didn't really care. She just wanted to get through the throng of women as quickly as possible and if this new woman was able to distract the crowd, so be it.

It worked. And they were free to follow Harper over to a white door on the left side. There was a light above it. Red. But as Cara and Parting stepped forward, it turned green.

'Only the two of you and the guards in this unit can access your cell,' Harper said. 'You are not permitted to go into anyone else's cell. No one is permitted to come into yours. Likewise, you will be permitted to go elsewhere in the Unit at certain times of day – the yard, the dining room, the laundry, the showers, et cetera – accessing the various doors just as you have done now. To make sure no one is where they shouldn't be, these doors always lock behind you and cannot be kept open. This way, we know where every prisoner is at all times, and you are protected from anyone else. Any questions?'

'Why do you have a Cuff?' Cara said.

'We have Cuffs for much the same reason as you,' Harper said, holding up his wrist. 'It unlocks doors, and keeps track of our vitals. But we also have key cards for overrides in communal areas.'

Cara and Parting looked at each other. Parting shrugged. She didn't seem bothered by it. But something about it bothered Cara. Like the guards were prisoners too.

An awkward silence for a moment.

Cara was sure she'd have plenty of other questions in due course, but none came to mind in the moment.

'So everything you need should be in there,' Harper was saying, 'you both have a washbag on your bed with the appropriate necessities. And you have your wardrobe there, I see.'

Cara looked down at the unimpressive bundle of muted fabric in her arms.

Harper checked his watch. 'It's half four. You must be starving. We're going to keep you separate from the other residents today, because well . . . they get a bit excited by new arrivals, as you've seen. I'll bring you some dinner after it comes out, around six. Then, tomorrow, we can see about incorporating you into life here.

Contrary to how it looks, it's not that bad. Come along now.' Harper guided them into the room backwards. 'Welcome to North Fern.'

They stepped through the open door. Harper stayed on the outside of the room. The door shut. The mechanical lock clicked.

Parting sighed and looked around. 'What the—?'

This made Cara finally turn and take in her new home. The cell was small, cramped, but not unbearable. There were two bony-looking beds, one on each side – plastic mattresses and rigid purple duvets – both made up, with a small washbag placed on each pillow. In between the beds was a sliver of floor leading up to a shared bedside cabinet.

The last detail of the cell was a small alcove, where there was a toilet and a sink, shielded by a waist-high wall. Although a normal person would have baulked at the audacity of it, it was a level of privacy she hadn't been afforded in quite some time.

But no, it wasn't the last detail. As Cara looked at the wall above the beds, she saw there was no window. She had never been claustrophobic, but the lack of a window really seemed to irk her. Maybe it was what was put in place of a window that was affecting her so much. A thin rectangular screen set behind glass was showing what seemed to be rolling green hills under a blue sky – not unlike a PC desktop wallpaper. Framing the window were bars of light, which were pouring into the room. It didn't feel artificial, the room felt just as if there was a window, as if this were a normal room in the middle of the afternoon.

It didn't help though, in fact it made her feel worse.

Parting seemed transfixed too. 'Well, isn't this lovely?' she said, stepping forward and tapping the glass in front of the screen. 'And decidedly weird.' She sat down on the right-side bed, seeming to claim it. Cara didn't mind. 'You OK?' Parting said.

Cara gave a half-smile. 'I'm fine.' She sat down on the left bed – *her* bed. As it adjusted to her weight, it gave a plasticky scratching sound. It sounded about as comfortable as it looked.

'Are you sure?' Parting asked. 'Because you're shaking.'

Cara raised her right hand to see that she was indeed shaking, her hand slowly vibrating to a silent tune. She balled it into a fist, and put it back down on the bed. 'It's been a long day.' Hoping it didn't sound like the empty excuse it was.

'That it has, I would have slept in the truck if Moyley hadn't been so . . . gushy.'

'We used to call her Niagara,' Cara said. 'Never stopped crying.'

'Huh, you were on the same Unit then. Back at the Hall.'

'Yeah.'

'Seems like I'm the odd one out then. And as I obviously know who you are, I better introduce myself.' Parting raised a hand, bridging the gap across the beds. Cara took it. 'I'm Stephanie Barnard.'

2

Cara and Barnard talked for another half an hour or so. Barnard was an ecologist in a past life, having been at New Hall for five years. She didn't offer up an explanation of what had landed her there in the first place, and Cara didn't ask. Barnard talked about her family, her ex-boyfriend, her dogs, barely giving Cara a chance to participate herself. But that was exactly what she wanted, and something in Barnard's tone and looks towards her made it seem that her cellmate knew. Barnard was trying to make her feel better. And she was endlessly grateful for that.

As Barnard talked, Cara studied her Cuff. The pulsing blue light was already annoying her. Was this going to be on her wrist forever?

After some time, a hatch in the bottom of the door opened and two trays slid into the cell. Each had a bowl with a plastic spork sitting in it, propped up by some brown mush, a cup of water, a stale biscuit and a napkin.

Barnard jumped up ravenously and grabbed her tray. 'Finally, I'm absolutely starving.'

Cara, a little less enthused, got hers. They both slumped back on their beds and Cara prodded at the greying brown mush. It looked like a stew, with chunks of some non-descript meat and slivers of something transparent, all soaked in sauce.

Cara looked up at Barnard, who had already started shovelling sporkfuls into her mouth. Her face erupted in pleasure. 'Did they know I was coming?' she said, mouth full. 'My favourite.'

'What is it?' Cara asked with trepidation.

'Liver and onions,' Barnard replied, chewing. 'Just like my grandmother used to make. Perfection.'

Cara's stomach churned, and she looked down into her bowl. The chunks sat there, and she poked at one. Liver and onions. The mere thought of eating it made her feel sick, but she was agonisingly hungry. She pierced one of the chunks as best she could and lifted it to her mouth, biting down before she could think. She chewed. It tasted meaty, with an underlying almost-irony taste. She swallowed.

'There,' Barnard said, who'd stopped to watch her, 'not so bad, was it? And it's great for keeping your strength up.'

Cara managed a smile, before her cheeks begin to fizz. She felt her stomach roll over and prepare to erupt. She had no time to think. It was all she could do to make it over to the toilet before she made an involuntary retching sound and the entire contents of her stomach went flooding into the bowl. That was it. Everything. But she stayed there for a few minutes, kneeling in front of it, to make sure. Eventually, when the moment had well and truly passed she shakily got up, flushed the toilet and went over to the sink to wash her face.

When she was done, she looked around at Barnard, who was clutching her own empty bowl. 'Does this mean you're not going to eat yours?'

And despite everything, Cara laughed. And Barnard laughed too. And the rest of dinner was spent in high spirits. Barnard traded Cara's bowl of liver and onions for her biscuit. And Cara found that even though the biscuits were indeed stale, they managed to line her freshly empty stomach, and even made her feel a little better.

When they were done, they put the trays on the floor. And soon, the hatch in the door opened up again and Barnard slid them through. 'Compliments to the chef,' she said.

If the guard on the other side of the door found it funny, he didn't show it – merely taking the trays and slamming the hatch shut.

Barnard tutted, throwing herself back on her bed. 'Wish I had a book or something.' She turned her attention to the bedside cabinet between them. It had two drawers – presumably one for each of them – and a small night light on top embedded into the wall. She flipped a switch and the light came on, then flicked it off again.

Cara stifled a yawn as Barnard looked in the drawers. How long had she been awake? She couldn't even guess. All she knew was that her whole body yearned for sleep, but at the same time she knew, right now, that she couldn't achieve it.

'Bingo,' Barnard said, 'doesn't look like a page-turner, but here we are.' She pulled out a laminated, ring-bound collection of pages. She held it up to Cara. A picture of a sunny, grassy hillside – the same as the one that was displaying on the screen – and at the bottom, in thick black letters, 'Welcome to North Fern'. A prison handbook.

Barnard sat back and started to read. Cara found herself sliding down her bed, until her head was on the pillow. It was rock-hard. Standard. But, still, it supported her. The bed was full of static, plastic sheets and duvets. Flame-retardant. She was used to all of this. And she took a little bit of comfort in it. However different this place was to New Hall, the beds felt the same.

She stared up at the ceiling, listening to the muffled voices of prisoners and guards outside in the Pit. She couldn't make anything out. But the voices were almost soothing, oddly. She closed her eyes . . .

BLARRP.

Her eyes snapped open and she sat up.

Barnard jumped, although she didn't know if it was at the sound or her movement. 'Steady, Lockhart,' she said. It looked like she had finished the handbook as it was lying on the end of her bed.

'How long was I—?'

'An hour, maybe an hour and a half,' Barnard said, picking up the handbook. 'You need to read this. Some weird stuff in here. Like how no one gets visitors.' She placed it on the bedside table.

But Cara didn't really hear. She was looking around, trying to see where the sound had come from. Her eyes finally found a small speaker in the corner of the room.

BLARRRP.

Cara frowned.

Barnard nodded. 'Not the most appealing of sounds, huh?'

The cell was a little darker, and she took a moment to realise that the screen behind her, and the lights around it, had turned off.

'Lights out in five minutes,' a voice boomed over the speaker.

Outside had grown noisier. It sounded like women were still congregating in the Pit, and this warning was for them to get back to their cells.

'Night one in a new place,' Barnard said, at least appearing to be worldly and full of experience. 'Like breaking a new bed in. Never know how it's going to go.'

She was right. Cara remembered her first night in New Hall all those months ago. She didn't think she got even a second of sleep. It was deafeningly loud on her block, not unlike here.

Barnard started to clean off the top of her bed – putting her folded clothes into the top drawer beside her, and peeling back the plastic duvet.

Cara did the same, still listening beyond their cell. It was starting to calm down, become quieter and quieter, as the women went back to their cells, and Cara was starting to wonder if she might find out if she could sleep in silence.

They were both in bed under the covers, by the time the klaxon went for one minute to lights out.

'What kind of prison has no visitors?' Barnard said, to the ceiling.

'What?'

'North Fern has no visitation. Says so in the handbook. Only phone calls and written correspondence.'

Cara looked at her own little patch of ceiling. No visitors. It's not as if it really affected her – no one would visit her anyway. But others? Was this prison max security? It didn't feel like it. But then—

Barnard stopped her thoughts before they got out of control. 'No use wondering about it now. We've got enough to contend with tonight. Let's worry about it in the morning,' she said, resolutely. 'Maybe it was a typo or something,' she added, slightly less so.

Cara nodded, although Barnard wasn't looking at her. She was right. They just had to focus on getting to sleep.

'Goodnight, Lockhart.'

'Goodnight,' she said.

And, as if on cue, the central light in the cell's ceiling went out. And, thank God, that bloody light on their Cuffs went out too. And they were plunged into complete darkness. A resounding cheer came from the other cells, and for about an hour afterwards conversation sparked from cell to cell. The window warriors, akin to the ones in New Hall. Cara just lay there in the dark, throwing off her plastic duvet, and waiting for sleep to claim her.

Soon, the thrum of voices became strands, and then nothing, and there was total silence. Precisely what she had been afraid of. But, against the odds, she found herself welcoming the absence. She settled into her pil-low, creating a crater for her head as best she could. And closed her eyes.

And, soon enough, the world became less concrete. Wispy. Falling down and down into sleep.

And, as always, she dreamt of them.

3

BLARP.

Cara's eyes shot open — already sick of the klaxon. Light smashed on at the same time as the sound. Her Cuff glowed. Morning. She still felt incredibly tired. And the toxic aftertaste of her nightmares was still on the tip of her tongue. She got up, pulling the sweaty duvet off her which had claimed her again at some point during the night. She flexed her back. It hurt, but she hadn't expected anything less. Her wrist was itching, under the Cuff. But she couldn't get at it.

Barnard was already up, sitting on her bed. She was rooting through the handbook, having snatched it up as soon as the lights came on. Cara remembered what she had said the night before and opened her mouth to ask, but there was a loud rap on the cell door.

'Are you decent?' a familiar voice said through the door. They both dressed quickly — North Fern clothes, and just as Cara finished, the door opened to show Harper standing there. 'Thought I better escort you ladies to breakfast this morning.'

Outside the cell, women were slowly making their way past to the back of the Pit, where there were a set of double doors. They didn't seem to care about the new arrivals anymore, led by their stomachs through the double doors. The light above pulsed green every time someone went through.

The room beyond was far smaller than Cara had thought it would be. The room looked like a school canteen — an open space with lines of tables and chairs. At the end of the room, along the far wall, were a row of steel hatches where a group of hungry women were already lined up. The space was a lot lighter than everywhere else, and Cara glanced up to the ceiling, to see it was covered in the lamps that emitted the near-natural light she had seen from the similar bulbs in the cell.

There were four guards, all male, posted at intervals around the room. Cara was a little shocked to notice Dale Michael, from the prison van, standing in one of the corners of the room, blankly watching. He didn't notice her.

Once they were in the room proper, Harper nodded to them and went to join the guards by the wall.

Barnard got into the queue and Cara followed. Her cellmate seemed to be hungry again as she was staring intently at the front of the queue. Luckily, it seemed all the other women were just as hungry, as no one even glanced at Cara.

She just waited and kept her head down and when they got to the front of the queue, she was handed a tray with a bowl of Weetabix, a browning apple and a tin cup of milk, by a woman in the same uniform as her. The woman, in her fifties, with a somewhat fresh scar down her left cheek, making her look like the antithesis of a dinner lady, glanced at her with no recognition as she handed it over.

Cara stepped out of line and into Barnard, who was assessing the tables, most full of women already halfway through breakfast, but some tables were free – either with a few women sitting there, or some completely empty. Barnard seemed to be thinking intently about where to sit.

'First day of school,' she muttered. And Cara understood the sentiment. Where they sat would likely inform the rest of their time here at North Fern – at least it felt like it.

Cara did her own scan of the tables and, at a table at the very back, set away from all the others, she saw a familiar flash of reddish hair. A woman was sitting, her arms crossed on the table, blankly staring at her breakfast. She seemed, unsurprisingly, like she'd been crying.

Niagara - or rather Moyley. She had been transferred to the same unit.

'We should go and sit with her,' Cara said, and nodded towards Moyley.

Barnard looked over to the table and sighed. 'Waterworks is here – lovely. She doesn't look like she wants company.'

Cara had to agree, but sometimes the most important time to have company was when you didn't want it. She said as much. 'She needs a friend in here.'

Barnard rolled her eyes. 'OK then.'

They slalomed through the maze of tables, Cara trying

not to look anyone in the eye, until they got to the back where Moyley was sitting. They stood there awkwardly as Moyley stared into her bowl, scrunched up, trying not to cry. She had no idea they were standing there.

Barnard cleared her throat, noisily.

Moyley looked up and her eyes widened, glistening with tears not yet shed. 'You,' she said, looking at Cara.

'Can we join you?' Cara asked.

Moyley seemed to shrink away. 'You . . . you were on my truck.'

'We both were,' Barnard said, sitting down.

Cara felt awkward standing, so took her lead and sat down too. Moyley jumped and stood up.

'How dare you?' Moyley said, picking up her tray and looking down at Cara. 'As if I want to associate with you. You make me sick.'

'I told you,' Barnard said to Cara.

'I hope they kill you,' shouted Moyley. And she spat at Cara.

The globule flew through the air and splattered on Cara's cheek. She recoiled and almost fell backwards on her plastic chair.

Moyley looked at her, smugly, and then skulked off towards the exit, nearly colliding with a group of women standing by a table, talking. Cara recognised some of them as the welcome mob from the previous day. She wiped away the spit rolling down her cheek with the provided napkin.

Barnard looked unimpressed, but whether it was with Moyley's outburst or Cara's offer of friendship, she couldn't tell. 'Why don't we just eat our breakfast?'

Cara agreed. They sat in silence, while she scraped up her Weetabix, which had never been especially appetising to her, and drank her milk. She wondered if she could manage to keep her head down and avoid any scenes like the one the previous day. She was used to it – but being a new arrival always made it worse.

She remembered when she had arrived at New Hall. With all the press and public attention, every single person in the prison knew who she was. There was almost a riot the day she got there, so much so she was placed on the medical wing for a week for her own protection.

'May I join you, ladies?' a voice said, cutting through her memory. She was glad it did – what came next was when she got shivved in the middle of the night – the scar on her abdomen still throbbed with pain whenever she thought of it. So she didn't.

She looked up. As did Barnard.

Standing there was the woman who had descended the stairs the previous day, the woman who had seemed to have some power over the others, the woman who had rescued them. She was about fifty, plump, with short curly brunette hair. She looked motherly, with kind eyes and a soft demeanour – someone who seemed very out of place in a prison cafeteria at the crack of dawn.

Barnard gestured to the seat opposite them, but the woman had already started sitting down anyway. 'I thought I'd try to smooth over some of the misconceptions you must have from yesterday's little spectacle. Give you a proper welcome.'

Cara stayed silent. There was something about the woman – she was as genteel as a cloud on the surface, but Cara couldn't help but feel there was thunder inside. She also couldn't ignore that, around them, the cafeteria had grown a little more subdued, as if everyone else was keeping one eye on proceedings.

'Some of my girls can get a little overexcited at newcomers,' the woman smiled, looking from Barnard to Cara. 'I'm sure you understand.' Then, a beat. 'They said you were coming. I didn't quite believe them. You don't look like a Butcher.'

'No, I suppose I don't,' Cara said.

The woman reached out her hand, over the table, to Cara. 'My name is Minnie Marple.' Cara took her hand. 'No need to tell me your name, Miss Lockhart.' She moved her hand over to Barnard. 'And you are . . .'

'Stephanie Barnard,' Barnard said, her mouth full of Weetabix. She didn't offer her hand and Minnie just withdrew hers, a look of disappointment, but understanding, flashing on her face for a millisecond. 'You wouldn't be the same Marple from the Marple Murders, would you? I've read about you.'

Minnie smiled. 'In the papers, no doubt. You wouldn't believe how mad the press went over having a murderer called Miss Marple. Well, Mrs Marple at the time, but that didn't seem to stop them. My old place had a field day too, before I got transferred here, I mean. About two months ago now.'

'You were transferred too?' Cara asked.

'Well, we're all crooks,' Minnie said, pushing her

bowl away and taking up her mug instead, 'we all get transferred from somewhere. Especially when this place is younger than my son.'

Cara didn't quite know how to respond to that. So she said instead, 'Was there a reason you were transferred? I wasn't given a reason.'

'Well, the government does what it wants, don't it? Too many crooks here, move them somewhere else. But, yeah, I suppose you could say there was a reason. My cellmate tried to kill me, so I hit her over the head with the top of the toilet cistern. Strictly self-defence, you understand. Intended to knock 'er out. But I'd never actually hit anyone over the head with the top of a toilet cistern before, and turned out I did it a little too hard,' Minnie said, plain as day. 'So she's dead now, and I'm here.'

Cara couldn't help a quick glance at Barnard.

'Don't worry,' Minnie said, laughing, while Cara sized her up. Even though she was much older, if Minnie wanted to, she could overpower Cara about five times over. But the woman still looked awkwardly kind. 'I've calmed down a lot now. Had a lot of anger back then.'

'You said it was only two months ago,' Cara said.

Minnie made a *pfft* sound. 'Look around Lockhart. The walls. You see any clocks, or timers, or any indication of time passing? No, you won't. You know why? Because it doesn't matter. Not here. Time is as useful a concept as freedom at North Fern. Two months ago could be five years, or this morning. The only things we have are breakfast, lunch, tea, and Illumination. That's all we have to structure ourselves here. Two months. A lifetime. Interchangeable. Especially when you were the first one here.'

'The first?' Barnard asked, finishing her Weetabix in a grand swoop of her spoon.

Minnie smiled. 'Well, North Fern being this grand new venture – stands to reason there had to be someone who was the first one here. It was just me and a guard for a while. This whole unit – just two of us. I was un-supervised a lot of the time, because, well, what could I do? There wasn't really anything *to* do. So I walked this place, I learned its secrets, if you will. Places to hide things, places the cameras don't reach, places to gain the upper hand. And finally, when girls came to join me, I was in the perfect position to, well, assume a role.'

'A role?' Cara queried.

'Yes,' Minnie replied, 'a role of . . . matriarchy, let's call it.'

'Ah,' Barnard said, pushing her tray away, 'so this is *that* speech. You're mother. And you're here to tell us not to step out of line.'

Minnie chuckled. 'No, no – you misunderstand. I'm here to extend a courtesy. Anything you need – any-thing at all – I am here to make these first few days as painless as possible. Now—'

'This is low, Minnie. Even for you.' A shout echoed through the room, silencing the last few conversations that were happening.

Cara wheeled around to see a blonde woman strutting towards their table from the small gaggle of women who had accumulated in the centre of the room. A few steps behind her was Moyley, who was standing watching with morbid fascination.

'Is this really the company you want to keep?' the woman asked.

'Liza, this is not the time,' Minnie snapped, her face shifting into something more serious.

'I think it's perfect,' the blonde woman, Liza, sneered, stopping a few feet away from the table. 'The Butcher. Here, in the flesh. And you're sitting down to breakfast with her.'

Cara felt a cold sensation wash over her. She knew it well. Shame.

Liza was continuing, talking to the room now. She stood up on a chair. 'One thing. Just one thing. We are all prisoners because we've broken the law, but some of us have broken more than that. They've broken human nature.'

There was a groan of support from the women in the room. They were all joining the group in the centre. The guards were starting to take notice. Most of them stepped forward from the edges of the room. Cara looked around to see Michael nervously advance too.

'We have one of them right here,' Liza announced, and pointed to Cara. 'Miss Cara Lockhart. Little Miss Butcher. From the news. How about it, ladies? Do we want to share our air with scum like her?'

There were murmurs of 'No,' from practically all of the women. Moyley screamed it. The guards were getting closer now.

'We're all lifers,' Minnie said, calmly, remaining seated 'we're all the punished, we're all broken. And we are – I'm sorry but we are – all in this together. Liza.'

Liza got down off her chair and advanced towards Minnie. And Minnie finally stood, turning to Liza, with a barely annoyed expression, like one may look at a pesky moth basking in the light of a television set. Minnie was far bigger than Liza, a more menacing presence. It wasn't much of a showdown. But she tried. 'She your little pet now? You get horny for Butchers, Minnie?'

And suddenly the mass of women was advancing, but not towards her, towards Minnie and Liza and they fell out of sight. Barnard stood up too, and joined them, shouting something Cara couldn't quite make out. The guards moved quickly, trying to calm everyone down.

Cara got up and stumbled backwards, turning just in time to stop herself colliding into Harper.

He looked alert and ready, but apologetic. 'Sorry, I really think it would be best if you left.'

'I think so too,' Cara said. And started for the door.

Harper went ahead of her, but no one was watching her anymore. They were all in a clump in the centre of the room, surrounding Minnie and Liza. They still appeared just to be talking, but everyone else seemed game for a fight. The other guards were attempting to get into the centre of the scrum.

Harper held the door open for Cara, and she went out into the corridor, staggering to a wall. There was a spreading emptiness in her stomach that wasn't just the lack of any substantial food. Maybe it was the realisation that this was it. This was where she was going to stay. There was always a chance she would get transferred again, but she knew it was highly unlikely. Everything about North Fern told her that this place was for keeps. This was the setting for the rest of her life. This was where she was going to grow old. This was where she was going to die.

'Are you OK?' Harper said, concerned but still keeping his distance.

Cara held up her hand. 'I'm fine.' It hadn't been like this at New Hall. She had shut down there. She had pretended she didn't care – but was it possible that she actually did? There was still a teenage girl inside her hoping for the best. Hoping for something that would never come.

'I'll help you,' Harper said.

'No,' Cara replied pointedly, 'I'm fine.' But she took two steps and stumbled.

Harper went to catch her but stopped himself, and she righted herself anyway. Even the guard that liked her seemed to be scared of her.

She started across the empty Pit, and Harper followed at a safe distance. 'Look,' he said, 'I know this may not be the best time to mention this, but you're not going back to your cell.'

Cara stopped and turned. 'What?'

Harper smiled sadly. 'The Governor has requested to meet with you.'

'What if I refuse?'

Harper thought for a moment. 'I don't really think that's an option.'

Cara scowled at him.

'I'm to take you right away,' Harper said. He reached to his belt and brought out a pair of handcuffs.

Cara scoffed but offered up her wrists. The cuffs clipped under her other Cuff.

Harper led her past her cell, up the steps and out of the Unit. All the way, Cara listened to the thrum of the ruckus still happening in the dining room. At least the place sounded more like New Hall now.

It almost sounded like home. And she hated that.

4

Harper took Cara to a room that looked like a doctor's waiting room with another door that seemed to be the entrance to the Governor's office. He uncuffed her and left her alone. The door's light throbbed red when it shut.

Cara sat in a chair. She reached out and picked up a magazine from the table. She used to love trashy gossip magazines – *OK. Closer*. Anything about celebrities. She used to spend hours poring over them, mostly while consuming similarly trash TV, like *Jeremy Kyle* and *Resident Detective*. She was so concerned with other people's lives, she mostly forgot about hers. She guessed that was the point.

What a waste.

There was a clock on the wall – she'd never been so happy to see one . She waited for half an hour. She wondered if she should do something. She waited another five minutes and then couldn't take it anymore. She stood up, stepped forward towards the Governor's door, and reached out for it. It squealed open.

The open door revealed another room, much the same, only bigger. Mahogany bookcases, filled with books of all shapes, sizes, and colours, lined the left and right walls, leading up to a desk at the far end of the room. There was a woman sitting there, but Cara couldn't pull her eyes from what was on the far wall. A window, stretching from floor to ceiling. A real window, looking out into a real murky day, nothing like the fake image on the screen in her cell.

The woman at the desk was slender and elegant, her head down reading a blue file. She was tall and athletic, wearing a deep blue suit and crisp white shirt. Her face looked kind, and when she saw Cara, she smiled – her mouth stretching across her face. She had wrinkles around her eyes, masked by faint mascara. She had thin rectangular spectacles on her nose, her shoulder-length brown hair tucked behind her ears, helped by a hair clip, and through all this was an ostentatious air of youth that seemed almost alive in itself.

She stood, putting the file on the desk, and sliding her glasses up her nose with one long finger. 'You must be Cara Lockhart. I have been so anxious to meet you. Welcome to North Fern.'

Cara didn't quite know what to say. The woman's elegance seemed to be tripping her up. She had never known anyone so out of place in a prison, since . . . well, since herself. 'I was waiting outside,' she stammered eventually. She knew it was a stupid thing to say. But it seemed better than the silence. She was wrong – the remark seemed to be a barrier between them, almost tangible.

The woman broke the silence, strangely, with a

chuckle. 'Please sit.' She gestured to the plush armchair in front of her desk.

Cara sat.

The woman just looked down at her in amusement before sitting too. 'My name is Madeleine Krotes. I am the Governor here at North Fern.' Her words draped around Cara like a satin scarf. She had a very faint French accent – so faint Cara almost thought she imagined it. But, no, it was there. As if this woman needed any more help to be enticingly beautiful. 'I have been waiting your arrival here in Buckinghamshire.'

Cara almost didn't even hear that – the answer to one of the questions she had been asking ever since she arrived. It almost slipped away, but she caught it. 'Buckinghamshire? That's where we are?'

'Yes. East Buckinghamshire to be exact. You were selected to be part of a new prison programme – North Fern. Do you like it?' Krotes seemed actually to be asking.

Cara didn't bite. 'And you're the Governor?'

Krotes held up a slender palm. 'Guilty as charged.' And then laughed – a small tittering sound that was far too pleasing to the ears. 'I am rather thrilled to make your acquaintance.' Her words sounded genuine, and her face looked so too, which is why Cara felt so unsettled. Anyone who knew her, knew her name, would not be pleased to see her sitting in front of them, much less to 'make her acquaintance'. There was something about Madeleine Krotes – she was too beautiful, too enticing, too enigmatic. She wasn't like any governor Cara had ever seen.

'You're in charge here?' Cara said, careful to show nothing.

'Well,' Krotes said, 'I suppose you could say so, yes.'

'Suppose?'

'You see,' Krotes began, leaning forward, 'this being a private enterprise, even I have someone I answer to. Although that is the way of the world, isn't it? Hierarchy just keeps going up. You can reach the top of the mountain, only to find someone's built another on top.'

Cara didn't know what to say to that. So she didn't say anything.

Krotes left the topic alone too. 'How are you getting on with the other residents?'

'You mean prisoners?' Cara said.

'Well.' Krotes ran her tongue over her top teeth. It was disconcerting. Her teeth were incredibly white – almost like they weren't real. 'Yes, prisoners. But we prefer the word "residents".'

'Doesn't really matter what you call us though, does it?' Cara said, bluntly. 'Given that the definition's still the same.'

The Governor leant back in her chair and regarded Cara with those glistening eyes, so much so Cara had to look away 'They did tell me you were clever.'

She decided to waive the compliment. 'This is a private prison?'

'Yes.'

'Then who's paying to keep us here?'

'Much the same as any other private prison – the government.'

45

'OK. But I came from New Hall. A *public* prison.'

Krotes chuckled. She got up and walked over to the bookcase, where a jug of water and a hip flask sat. Cara got poured a glass of water, which she took. Krotes, of course, got the golden liquid in the flask.

'We could go round the houses all day talking about prison reform, Cara. And you'd probably find it marginally more interesting than even I do. But you've been out in the world relatively recently. Did you ever hear them discussing the well-being of prisoners or the institutions themselves? They have bigger fish to fry, or at least they like to think they do.'

'So the private sector steps in?' Cara said.

'Exactly. Just as regulated, just as observed, just as safe – but a bit nicer, if you catch my drift. We can afford the better facilities, the state-of-the-art lock system, the increased manpower. The screens that you see in your cell and all around that pump in not only natural light but better air – that is all made possible by the private sector.' Krotes wandered over to the window and looked out as she swigged the liquid in her glass. 'It's a cold, hard world out there, as you exemplify, Miss Lockhart. We wish to contain that coldness, that hardness – to make it a little bit brighter for everyone else.' She turned to Cara. 'Surely, you must see that this is noble?'

Nobility. That made her crack. 'Why the hell would you care what I think?'

Maybe the old Cara was still in there somewhere after all.

Krotes sat down again, tucking herself into her chair.

'I suppose it's personal. I'm endlessly fascinated by your case. I don't know quite what it is, but I just think that there's so much more to know about it. There are so many angles, so many layers. And yes, every case has that. But yours . . . yours is . . . different. Different . . . somehow. I just can't seem to get enough.

'You see, I'm a little bit of an amateur sleuth myself. That's how I fell into this field of criminals and prisons. I read all the cases, I watch the news, I draw conclusions. And you, you seem as guilty as sin, you *are* as guilty as sin, but there's just something I can't quite articulate. A question maybe. Or maybe an answer in need of a question.' She paused and stared into her eyes. It was almost sickening. 'You are an enigma, Cara Lockhart.'

Cara felt uneasy. The power had shifted almost in an instant, like they had both tipped a pool table so all the balls rolled down her end. The conversation had been with the Governor of North Fern, Madeleine Krotes. But now, Madeleine Krotes seemed like a . . . No, it was too absurd. But as she looked at Cara, almost panting at the prospect of meeting her, she knew it was true. Madeleine Krotes was a fan. And that was far worse than anything else.

'I would like to go back to my cell now please.'

Krotes held up a palm. 'Soon. Soon. First I need to ask you a question.' Cara knew she wasn't going to like it, but surprisingly Krotes said softly, 'Have you seen *Rain on Elmore Street*?'

Cara was starting to wonder if Krotes wasn't a little insane herself. And she was more than done playing her little game. 'What?'

Madeleine seemed to relax once again. 'I watched it at the weekend. In my chair – a little tipple of Macallan Scotch, not unlike this one.' She tipped her glass with a sliver of the liquid in, as if she were giving a toast. 'On comes one of those old movie musicals. Curt Americans, proper Englishmen, and droll dames. From the forties or something. Unbearably dull. Unpalatable by today's standards. Big song and dance, at the expense of the audience's sanity. A proper time-sink. Because it's long too. Even without inane advertisements, it's one hundred and forty-six minutes. And you can really feel it – it stretches on and on, as some primped-up protag sings about love, or something equally incongruous. But it's the kind of thing you can't stop watching. And it keeps going and going and going and going. But still, you are there watching – you don't want to, it's almost like you need to. You're locked there in front of the screen, praying to a movie God that it will cease. Funny, those types of movies. The type that you just have to see through to the end.'

Cara opened her mouth to say something, anything – why did this matter? – but before she could Krotes continued - 'The musical's on now in the West End apparently, people actually choose to go and see it. And, I looked it up, on stage it's even bloody longer. Anyway, I did indeed see it through. And then, as the credits finally started, I got to thinking about time. Rather a grand concept to come from such rubbish, I know, but I did. I got to thinking about what could be worse than sitting and watching *Rain on Elmore Street* and how many times I could watch *Rain on Elmore Street* before shattering my glass of whisky and cutting my own throat with one of the shards.' She laughed – a sound that pierced her much like one of the shards would have.

'Seems to me being in prison is rather how I view watching that movie. You have nothing but time – you're staring at your own mortality just ticking away – second after second.

'I can't stand *Rain on Elmore Street*, seconds passed by like hours, civilisations could have risen and fallen for all I knew. I couldn't stand it even once and I don't think you could either.'

'Why are you telling me this?' Cara asked. What on Earth was she on about?

Krotes smiled. 'Because after the film, in the warmth of my consumed glass of Macallan, I did some calculations. Do you want to know how many times you, Cara Lockhart, get to watch *Rain on Elmore Street*?'

No, I don't. But she couldn't say it.

'You would get to watch it two hundred and fifty-two thousand times. Two hundred and fifty-two. I don't think I could do it. I don't think many people could. I wonder how long you'll last.'

Cara tried not to look fazed – that was Krotes' intention after all – but she was slightly. Once again the woman had done a complete U-turn – her joviality turned to ash, her smile turned upside down, inside out. She had thunder in her once-inviting eyes. And it took great will for Cara to sit tall.

But she couldn't help but think of what Krotes had said. She hadn't thought of her prison sentence quite so

49

granularly. When you distilled it down to those sort of metrics, a lifetime did seem almost unbearable. A lifetime of fearing closing your eyes. But what pulled Cara through, what kept her from breaking down, was the simple fact that she didn't want to give this strangely enticing woman the satisfaction. Krotes was a mermaid, this speech, this performance, were the rocks that could sink her. Cara could tell this was just one of the perks of her job, the part she enjoyed most. Well, she wouldn't get her satisfaction today.

And it showed on her face, as Cara said again, 'I would like to go back to my cell now please.' There was just a flash of it, but she saw it. Disappointment.

Krotes instantly went back to smiling. 'Very well. But before you go, I have to inform you that I have referred you to our prison doctor for psychological treatment. I believe you have already met Tobias Trenner.'

'I don't want treatment,' Cara said, through gritted teeth.

'This is non-negotiable. No matter what the courts say, you clearly have some deep psychological issues. Someone of clarity would not do what you did. Would not dream up this – what do you call him – No-Face?'

Every muscle in Cara's body tensed at the mere utterance of his name. She wanted to scream at Krotes to shut up, to stop, to think about what she was doing. But she knew exactly what she was doing.

A flash of him. Coming down the stairs. Slowly. His face – or rather where his face should've been – looking down at her.

'You see,' Krotes said, looking far too pleased with herself. 'You need help. You may even thank me for it.' And without time for Cara to respond, she yelled, 'Harper?'

The door to the office opened and Harper came in. Even the great hulk of a man looked small under Madeleine Krotes' gaze.

She presented a dazzling smile, once again running her tongue over her top set of pearly white teeth. 'Miss Lockhart is ready to go back to her cell.'

'Ma'am,' Harper said.

Cara stood up, her breath hitched and she held it.

It was not until Harper had led her halfway down the corridor that she allowed herself one quiet, long, shuddering breath. If Harper heard it, he said nothing.

The longer they walked, the calmer she became. Madeleine Krotes was without a doubt the strangest woman she had ever had the misfortune to meet. A woman she never, ever wanted to see again.

But with each step, a grim realisation occurred. That that was wishful thinking.

5

Barnard wasn't in the cell, but the screen was on, displaying – of all things – a snowy mountainside. The lights around the frame were on as well, but were decidedly more blue than the previous day, no doubt to match the theme of the picture.

Cara wondered where Barnard could be, hoping that she hadn't got hurt or reprimanded for the dining-room incident. She hadn't seen her or Minnie as she had rushed back to her cell, although she admittedly hadn't been looking because she was too unsettled by her fair Governor.

She went to sit on her bed, but something scrunched beneath her. Cara pulled a piece of paper out from under her, and saw that there was one on Barnard's bed too. She looked down at hers, turned it over and read the finely typed message:

CARA LOCKHART – Laundry/Sanitation

You will report to work every weekday at 8 a.m. Your job is to collect all prison uniforms, wash them in the machines provided, dry them, fold them, and return them to their original owner. This will happen on Tuesdays and Fridays. On days where washing does not occur, you are to clean the laundry room, the telephone area, and the yard. You will earn £2.50 an hour to spend on sundries available in the prison shop.

What followed were very rigid and boring instructions of where to report for work. It seemed there was another corridor off the dining room where the laundry room and the telephones were. Cara didn't really know where the yard was – there was a vague diagram that showed it was between the laundry and the dining room, but that didn't seem to make any sense. Surely the yard was outside.

She shook the thought off – it didn't matter right now. She must read the prison handbook at some point. But the most important thing was that she had been assigned to the laundry. It wasn't a glamorous job, not that anything was in prison, but it was simple. She could live with it, and it was enough work to keep her brain occupied.

That was the only way she was going to get through this. Life. Her life. Behind bars.

Over the page, there was a crude timetable of the rest of her life. It was pretty much the same as what she'd learned to expect at New Hall, except Association was replaced with Illumination. She scanned it:

Monday – Friday
7 a.m. – LIGHTS UP
7.30 a.m. – BREAKFAST

8 a.m. – WORK/EDUCATION
12 p.m. – LUNCH
1p.m. – WORK/EDUCATION
3 p.m. – ILLUMINATION/YARD
5 p.m. – DINNER
6 p.m. – EVENING ILLUMINATION
9 p.m. – LOCKDOWN
9.30 p.m. – LIGHTS OUT

(Dirty uniforms are to be put out in the hampers provided on Monday and Thursday nights. The library and post cart will come round every Tuesday morning. Telephones are allowed to be used at any time during Illumination hours.)

Saturdays and Sundays
8.30 a.m. – LIGHTS UP
9 a.m. – BREAKFAST
9.30 a.m. – MORNING ILLUMINATION
12 p.m. – LUNCH
1 p.m. – ILLUMINATION
5 p.m. – DINNER
6 p.m. – EVENING ILLUMINATION
7.30 p.m. – LOCKDOWN
8 p.m. – LIGHTS OUT

(Saturday evenings are extended for MOVIE NIGHT. Residents may continue their EDUCATION on weekends if they wish).

Today was Saturday, so tonight was Movie Night. That was something at least. Cara hadn't expected anything that could be construed as fun to be on the timetable. But at least, once a week, she could look forward to some form of escapism. She had never been a massive movie watcher – she hadn't seen many of the classics, or the nerdy things that everyone else went crazy over – but she would take what she could get.

And also there was a library cart that came around every week. It sounded very primordial compared to the high-tech nature of everything else – almost quaint. Maybe she would get into reading too. On the outside, all she read was trashy biographies, and even trashier romances – maybe she could get into literature. Maybe it wasn't so bad.

As if in response to this, the door opened and Barnard came in. Cara looked up to see that her cellmate was a little worse for wear than the last time she had seen her. She was sporting a scratch down her left cheek, and a patch on the collar of her uniform was wet with blood. She looked positively miserable, although her eyes lit up when she saw Cara.

'Where have you been?' she asked, going over to the sink and looking at herself in the small mirror. She turned the tap on, cupped her hands, and splashed her face with water.

'I had a meeting with the Governor,' Cara said.

Barnard looked round. 'Really?'

'Yep.'

'What's she like?'

Cara wondered how to describe Krotes and settled on, 'A horrific Barbie doll.' It wasn't perfect, but it would do.

Barnard mimed a shiver. 'Ouch. Well hopefully I never have to meet her. Or maybe I should – I have some questions for her.'

'What do you mean?'

'You still haven't read the manual, have you?' Barnard said. 'While you were meeting with Sindy, I had a scout around. There's no visitation room. I also talked with this girl, Peter. She confirmed it. No one comes and goes in this place, except the guards. We're totally closed in.'

'What about the yard?'

Barnard actually laughed. And then beckoned to her. 'Come on, we're going for a walk.'

Cara was annoyed with herself at how sick that suggestion made her feel. Going out there, into the Pit, into public – she had seen what happened at breakfast because of her, the damage was visible on Barnard's face – she didn't really want a repeat of it so soon.

But Barnard ended up saying what her brain thought. 'You can't spend your life in this room. You're going to have to face the other women here eventually.'

Cara reluctantly nodded.

But first she held up her piece of paper. 'You read yours?'

Barnard beamed. 'Yeah, they assigned me to the kitchen. They're going to quickly reverse that decision when they see I can burn water, let alone dinner.'

56

Cara laughed. She couldn't help it. She felt unusually at ease with Barnard, already. Getting a new cellmate was always a dangerous gamble, but she had pretty much lucked out. It could have been much, much worse. Her stomach turned at the mere thought of having to share a cell with Liza, or someone like her. She was betting she would look a lot worse than Barnard did right now.

'Come on then,' Barnard said, 'we haven't got all day . . . well, I mean, we do . . . but . . .' she trailed off purposefully.

Cara rolled her eyes just as purposefully and got up, following her cellmate out into the Pit. She tried not to look around too much as she followed Barnard to the dining-room doors. They passed a group of women who seemed to be playing a very competitive game of Scrabble at a table, where profanities scored double for some inexplicable reason. She only barely recognised the faces as women who were in the dining room that morning but had merely been onlookers. Some of them looked up as they passed but didn't seem interested in them, fortunately.

Barnard got to the dining-room doors and scanned her wrist. So did Cara. And they went through into the quiet and almost empty dining room. It seemed like the dining room was open to the prisoners – residents – during Illumination as well, as some women were just milling around not doing much. There seemed to be a lot of that going on – in prison there wasn't always much to do, most of the day was intended to make you think about what you'd done, like a petulant child made to sit in the corner of a classroom.

Barnard made her way to the left side of the dining room, where Cara saw a small, non-descript door that she hadn't noticed before. It was almost like it didn't want to be found, and the fact Barnard was leading her to it made her feel a little uncomfortable. Barnard held up her Cuff and the door unlocked. She glanced back at Cara, raised her eyebrows and went through the door. Cara followed.

A narrow, white, vacant corridor unfurled beyond. Barnard was striding down it, seeming to know where she was going. 'This is the other end of our unit,' she said, 'I saw it in the manual. And on that piece of paper left in our cell. And I had to see for myself.'

Barnard turned a corner and Cara found another corridor almost identical to the one they had just been in, except there were only doors on the outer side, and instead of cells, the rooms were the kitchen ('This is where I'm working I guess,' said Barnard), the laundry ('And this is you'), an office, something that looked like a waiting room, and a single door that didn't have a light above it.

Cara was about to ask what where the door led, but she looked around to see Barnard had disappeared down another corridor. She rushed to follow, trying to work out where they were in relation to the rest of the Unit. It felt like they were doubling back on themselves, skirting around a bigger inside room. And then she remembered the big room on the diagram on her job paper – the yard.

But how was it in the middle of the Unit like this?

This new corridor was a little wider and a little lighter, and there were a pair of wide, red double doors nearby that stood open. Barnard waited by them and beckoned to Cara. 'First stop on the tour. Coincidentally, it's also the last.'

Cara came to a stop next to Barnard and looked inside to see a vast room – the size of an Olympic swimming pool. It looked like a sports hall, with mats and equipment at the side and a varnished wooden floor, with lines marking two tennis courts side by side. At one end of the room, there was a mass of gym equipment – three or four treadmills, a few cross-trainers, a rowing machine, and plenty of free-standing weights. There were two women with purple trousers and tops tied around their waists already attacking some of the weights.

Cara looked across the airy room to see another set of double doors. She thought they must connect back to the Pit. She was starting to get a mental map in her head of how the Unit and the surrounding areas were structured.

Something about the room was inviting. Maybe it was the spaciousness of it – after being led down cramped corridors and stuffed into efficiently packed rooms. But she didn't think it was that.

The room was very light – a different kind of light to the corridor. A more natural light, but there were no bulbs or strips on the walls, so she couldn't see where it was coming from. 'Why does it feel so airy?' she mused, mostly to herself.

But Barnard prodded her, and led her inside − their shoes squeaking on the buffed floor. Barnard pointed, and Cara looked up the tall walls to the ceiling. Up to see the bright morning sky through segmented panes of glass.

'What?' Cara said, looking confusedly at the ceiling, then back at Barnard, then back at the ceiling. 'What? But? Are we on the top floor?'

'Not even close,' Barnard replied, almost sounding like she was getting some delight from Cara's confusion. She had already figured it out. 'Look closer.'

Cara did, craning her neck upwards; it was so high, it must have spanned two or three floors of cells and everything else that encompassed the Unit. But it wasn't the height that startled Cara, there was something about the sky − it was almost too perfect, the clouds drifted across pane to pane and the sun was high in the sky. Cara understood before she could voice it. 'The sun. It's in the centre of the sky. But it's not midday. And it looks pixelated. But . . .'

'While you were out talking to the Sindy doll, I was watching the sun. And I'm pretty sure that sun you are seeing there above us never moves. It's stuck like a fixed point. Like time has stopped. I'm pretty sure that's the intention.'

'It's another screen,' Cara said, looking closer to see that, indeed, yes, it was. She could see the almost too perfect renditions of clouds. It was like another one of those stock Microsoft desktop images, except this one was moving. No doubt this was another Krotes

60

manufactured idea. Just like her speeches – this was a gross joke.

'It's lots of screens,' Barnard said, 'knitted together, keeping us looking up at a painted sky.'

'But where's all the natural light coming from?' Cara asked. 'I don't see any light like that in our cell.'

Barnard pointed up and ran her finger across where the ceiling was about forty feet above. 'That's all part of the illusion. Look at the seams, there's strips of lights hidden in them, and there are lights hidden in the walls.'

'This is fantastical,' Cara said, almost in awe of it all.

'Yes, I rather thought so too when I saw it first. But now I don't think it fantastic. I find it rather sickening.'

Cara had to think a moment, and look past the spectacle of it, to see Barnard was right.

'You get it, don't you?' Barnard asked.

'Why go to all this trouble?' Cara said, bluntly.

'Bingo.'

'Why not . . .' she said, trailing off. She gawked up at the ceiling – up at the digital sky, made of multicoloured pixels changing from cloud to sky when needed. What was this – why was this? What was wrong with normal prisons, with proper yards that looked up to the real sky? Making one of those would have been far less effort.

Someone – maybe Krotes, maybe someone higher up – really wanted to hide her and these women away. Put them in a building with no windows, tuck it away in the landscape, so everyone could forget about them. After all, that's what prisons were, she supposed – ways to cordon off the undesirables, like the murderers, and the cheats, and the villains, and the monsters. So they couldn't hurt anyone else – the normals of society. North Fern was an extension of that – the natural evolution.

She'd thought it when she first arrived and she was right – *a woman in a box.*

A box, sealed from the outside and the inside.

6

Cara couldn't keep looking up at the sky – no, at the fake sky. She felt dizzy. She looked down and brought her hands to her face, staggering slightly. When she had recovered and brought her hands down again, Barnard was watching her.

'Are you OK?'

'Yeah,' Cara said, 'I'm fine.' Although she didn't know if she really was. She didn't know if she would ever be again. 'It's just . . . I don't know . . .'

'A lot to take in?' Barnard finished and Cara nodded. 'There's more too. I walked this place because I couldn't believe there was no visitation. But there's not. No special rooms, no link to the outside where visitors could come in, nothing. We are entirely enclosed here – no in, no out. Apart from the way we came in. No contact with the outside world except a few telephones just beyond the doors out in the corridor. And get this, they're currently out of order. No idea where we even are.'

Cara's head was swimming. 'Krotes, the Governor – she said we were in Buckinghamshire.'

'And what do we have to prove that?' Barnard said, throwing up her hands in disgust and gesturing around the large hall. 'We didn't even see anything outside when we were dropped here. We sure as hell can't see outside now. And Buckinghamshire? New Hall in Wakefield to Buckinghamshire. What is that? A three-hour drive at most? We were on the road for seven, eight, nine hours at least.' Barnard was spinning out. But Cara couldn't help her — because she was making too much sense. She looked up at the sky again — a perfect encapsulation of the problem. Anything could have been put there. They had no way of knowing where they actually were. They only had the word of people they were supposed to trust. *Supposed* to. 'Peter?'

Cara looked around. Barnard was marching towards a small mousey girl who was sitting on a bench at the side of the room. She looked reasonably young, but her slightly dishevelled appearance made her look beyond her years. Her clothes were dirty, her face stricken with scratches and acne, her frame gaunt. She was hunched over and fiddling with something. She had thin, cheap-looking headphones draped over her wiry dull-blonde hair. As Cara caught up, the girl looked at them to reveal she had been peering at a portable tape player. She had a smattering of tapes that she had lined up on the bench beside her, and she appeared to be deciding which one to listen to. She took her headphones off (wired, they were allowed?) as the two of them approached her.

'Can you please tell Cara some of the things you told me?' Barnard said, and then to Cara, 'This is Peter.'

'I'm Peter,' Peter said, in a small voice staring up at them.

Barnard rolled her eyes.

'I'm Cara.'

'I know,' Peter said. 'The Butcher.'

Cara's heart couldn't help but sink, as it always did. Even after all this time. Even after the thousands of people who had called her that. 'I don't like that name.'

Peter shrugged.

Cara didn't know what else to say, but Peter looked expectant. 'Um . . .?'

Barnard shifted uncomfortably. 'I'm gonna go search for the showers.'

Barnard left, and Cara felt the uncomfortable urge to go with her. Peter was surprisingly intense.

There was silence. Cara sat down next to Peter. And awkwardly asked, 'What are you listening to?'

Peter looked at her tapes. 'Nothing yet. Too much choice.' Cara looked down at them, but Peter quickly started gathering them up. 'I can choose by myself.'

A silence fell as Peter scrabbled around and put all her tapes back into a bumbag. Cara almost felt like she needed to ask a question to stop this weird lack of anything. So she said, 'How long have you been here?'

Peter finished up and simply fiddled with the zip on her bag. Cara thought that the girl wasn't going to answer, but eventually she muttered, 'A few weeks. I was the new one in here before you.' She looked at Cara. 'I didn't like it. Thank you for coming.'

'No problem, I guess,' Cara said and nervously smiled.

Another silence fell, but this time Peter broke it. 'I killed my boyfriend.' She said it like it was nothing. A fact. A fixed point in time. Something that had happened – and was nothing to do with her.

'Oh,' Cara replied. 'I see.'

'I stabbed him fifteen times. He was sleeping. I got him seven times in the chest, three times in the leg, four in the arm, one in the eye. That adds up to fifteen. There was a lot of blood. I was soaked. He deserved it though. I think.' Peter said it with such a throwaway tone that it seemed like she was talking about some random, unimportant fact. She didn't elaborate on why her boyfriend deserved it and didn't look like she was going to any time soon.

'Right.' Cara looked around for Barnard, willing her cellmate to come back, but she'd disappeared.

Peter smiled. 'I just thought because I knew what you did, it would only be fair that you knew what I did.'

Cara actually smiled a bit too, against everything. It made sense. 'Thanks, I guess.'

'How did it feel?' Peter asked, fascinated – her eyes becoming globes and almost spinning. In fact, her irises were spinning. It was almost hypnotic. 'Mine felt good.'

Cara said nothing, tearing her gaze from those eyes.

'It's OK. You don't have to tell me,' Peter said. She looked around and then shuffled her bottom closer to Cara. 'I've never met anyone famous before.'

'I'm not famous,' Cara said. At least not for anything good, she thought.

'Still. Will you be my friend?'

Cara mulled this over for a second. Peter seemed a little shaky. The young woman seemed to normalise murder like it was nothing, but then this was a prison. Sometimes Cara thought that if people could accurately see her shock every time she heard that someone had committed murder – and more so were generally unperturbed about it – it would be enough to prove she didn't belong here in itself.

She thought of *them*. Of the thing . . . and the stairs.

Cara shoved the thought out of her head. And gave a weak smile. She didn't ever think she would be friends with a person who stabbed someone fifteen times. It wasn't really something someone aspired to. But in this place, she had to take what she could get. 'Sure. I'll be your friend, Peter.'

Peter smiled. 'OK.'

'Do you have many other friends?' Cara asked.

'Not really. People don't like me. That's why I don't mind being friends with you, because they don't like you either. People like us have to stick together.'

'Sure,' Cara said. It wasn't wrong, it was just that Peter was summing up something that she hadn't really wanted put out there. People like them did have to stick together.

She felt a little shiver in the base of her spine, a cold feeling that spread.

People like *them*.

'How are you finding it here?' she found herself asking, before she could think any more about it.

'It's OK. Better than I had it at my last place. At least the guards are nice here. Well, pretty much all of them.'

'How many guards are here?' Cara asked.

67

'About ten, but usually only about five at once, and they rotate around. Truchforth's the worst – he's a short stocky old man who likes to perv over everyone. He's in the perfect job, sexist as they come, and entirely useless. He's only really good at looking at our tits. And he never gives us any leeway. It's like we're second-class citizens, and being murderers, or arsonists, or con women has nothing to do with it. Luckily some of the other guards have a shred of decency and don't let him come near us when we're showering. You seen the shower block – just over there? 'Bout ten showers in there – only privacy is a few flimsy curtains I'm afraid, but we've seen it all before, haven't we?'

Cara nodded but really didn't want to talk about showering. She didn't mind anyone leering at her any-more, but that didn't mean the act of showering with other people was anything less than horrific. You just shoved your terror in a little compartment in your head and tried to forget about it. 'What about the other guards?'

Peter thought. 'Largely forgettable, really. Harper and Abrams are probably the best, but they can still have their bad days. Most of them – like Continell, Georgeton, and Hamish – just do their job. They don't make it easier for any of us – I mean why should they – but they don't exactly make it any harder either. They're just in it for the pay cheque, I think. Aqua said she saw Harper's pay cheque once – a lot more than a guard should usually get, apparently. Probably something to do with this place.'

'Who's Aqua?' Cara asked.

'Oh, just another lass on the Unit. Usually keeps herself to herself. You'll know her instantly, has blue wavy hair, like water.'

'And she's called Aqua.'

'Someone nicknamed her that.' Cara made a face and Peter responded, 'We're prisoners not poets. You've met Liza, haven't you? She gave her that name.'

'I've met Liza,' Cara replied.

Peter laughed. 'I guess you have.'

Cara was suddenly struck by how much Peter had changed over the very short time she'd known her. The small, shy girl who had introduced herself and stuck her head back in her bumbag, now she was forthcoming and confident, as if each second she had known Cara was more like a year of loving friendship.

Peter got up, picking up her bag. 'I'm going back to my cell,' she said bluntly.

Cara got up too, looking for Barnard. She still wasn't around. She must've found the showers and Cara really didn't feel like braving them today. Eventually, she'd have to – sooner rather than later – but not right now. And that decision was enough to make her feel a little better. 'I'll come with you.'

Peter shrugged, not appearing to care either way, but accepting it nonetheless. They both made their way out of the yard, scanning their Cuffs, and starting back towards the dining room.

Two women Cara hadn't learned the names of – in their purple uniforms – passed them in the corridor. They looked at Cara with no recognition at all, but when they saw the unkempt wiry frame of Peter, they gave both of them a wide berth. Was it possible that Peter had not been shy but tentative? Peter had said she had killed her boyfriend – but was it possible there was more to it than that? Because why had those women seemingly been indifferent to the Butcher but dismayed by a pissed-off girlfriend? She followed the duo with her eyes, until they disappeared into the yard. She wondered, for the first time of many, why Peter had stabbed her boyfriend fifteen times. That factor had been skated over.

'Have you wrapped your head around Illumination yet?' Peter asked, clearly not aware of what was going on in Cara's head.

'I guess,' Cara said as they rounded the corridor corner.

'I still don't get it. Those screens in our cells. The "windows". It's just odd, isn't it? I think, in some sick way, they think that it's some kind of treat. But it's really so we don't get pale. They turn on the natural lights, and think it's some great kindness. And I guess it is. For people who don't leave their cell especially. Don't venture as far as the yard. Like Aqua, in fact.'

Cara would hardly call the yard 'far', but she was pretty confident that she had seen the entire Unit now, and she supposed that it kind of constituted the label. They scanned their Cuffs and were back in the dining room, which was now entirely empty – apart from one woman, who seemed to be cleaning with a mop.

'They decide what's out the window of course,' Peter said somewhat jovially, skipping across the dining room.

'A field. A desert. One time it was a cat daycare. One time it was the Statue of Liberty. But from high up – it made no sense. Made me dizzy.' With this, she started into the Pit. Cara followed, and couldn't tell if Peter was joking, but from what she'd seen of the Unit so far, she'd guess she wasn't. Peter clapped her on the back. 'You get used to it.'

The Pit was busy, and incredibly loud. Echoed voices bounced off the walls and created an oppressive wall of noise that hit Cara at once. She almost staggered back. But Peter carried on. The girl seemed intent on getting to her cell, so much so that she didn't wait for Cara and stalked off.

Cara tried to follow her, but Peter disappeared into a crowd of women who were standing around the same table that had housed the Scrabble game earlier. Cara couldn't see what was happening on the table now, but after a moment listening to them – although it was difficult through the din – she realised it was still going and had attracted an audience. 'Bye,' she said, not particularly loudly. Just for herself. 'I guess.'

Cara started through the crowd back to her own cell. But stopped a few steps later. She felt eyes on her, and looked around. Surprisingly, no one seemed to be interested in her. The women who had screamed at her the day before when she had arrived were amongst her – passing her, sitting or standing near her – and didn't care. They just enjoyed the spectacle of fresh meat, no doubt. It was little comfort that they were at least accepting of her, but it was enough.

She stepped towards her cell, but on instinct, she looked up, out of the Pit, to where the entrance to the Unit was. The gangway at the top. A figure was standing there, watching her, with a great beaming smile on his face.

Anderson.

They locked eyes. What was wrong with him? She had never met him before the van and now he seemed unreasonably interested in her.

Cara tried not to look as scared as she was, as he formed his fingers into a gun and pointed it at her.

He winked. And pulled the trigger.

7

Cara spent the rest of the day in her cell. She missed lunch – she couldn't go out there, with Liza and Anderson. She needed a break. It was too much. So instead she busied herself with sitting back on her bed and reading the prison handbook. She didn't really glean much more information than she'd already got from her prison-mates.

Illumination was described as an 'enriching' and 'freeing' experience that was at 'the forefront of prison technology'. Cara put the handbook in her lap and found herself drawn to the window on the wall. It was just a screen and some lights. She couldn't help but feel that this 'enriching' and 'freeing' idea needed some more time to percolate. So all the residents of North Fern were guinea pigs. That was fantastic.

She skipped through a few pages, which were variations of what she had got on the job paper. There were descriptions of every job available at North Fern, which didn't really matter, seeing as they got assigned one without their input anyway. There was another timetable, which was slightly different, explaining why she had been given an updated one. There was a list of things that were sold at the shop, as Barnard had said. She scanned the list, and made a mental note of some things she would want: soap, shampoo, toothpaste, deodorant, et cetera. Essentials. And she even made a note of something she'd like if she had some extra leftover: Rice Krispies and Chilli Heatwave Doritos. Maybe her life wouldn't be so bad if she had those two vices to satiate her.

What a strange existence. Where even the thought of those two things gave her an unrivalled swell of joy.

The rest of the handbook proved rather dull. There wasn't really anything useful – droll paragraphs of prison regulations written in almost incomprehensible language. It seemed that North Fern was pretty much the same as any other prison – or at least they abided by the same regulations.

She gave up in the end and flipped over the page to the back, and found a short paragraph on the subject of contact with the outside. It read:

Contact with the outside

North Fern is an entirely enclosed institution, and therefore visitation is deemed impossible. This decision has been debated and fully signed off by all regulating members of the prison service. Contact with the outside world is highly monitored and kept at a minimum even for staff. Contact with loved ones can still be enjoyed through telephone calls (telephones situated in D corridor next to the yard) and written correspondence (via the librarian, who will collect and deliver letters once a week). Small packages are permitted to be delivered into the Unit, but they will be thoroughly screened before reaching the resident. No other contact, including personal, is permitted or possible.

Cara read it, and reread it, and reread it again. How was this possible – how was it allowed? No visitation. No one from the outside world could even get inside North Fern. This facility had to be the highest of high security. But at the same time, the 'residents' were allowed to walk around the place almost unguarded. It didn't line up.

The laminated pages didn't really seem to offer any answers. It was all a lot to process. This place – it was too much.

She put the handbook on the bedside table, slid down the bed so her head was on her pillow and closed her eyes. She needed just to rest a moment, and before she knew it, she had fallen into a doze.

When she next opened her eyes, Barnard was standing at the sink with wet hair applying some mascara. She glanced down at Cara and smiled. 'Shop was open. Got you a present.' She threw a box at her and it rested on her stomach.

Cara picked it up. Tampons.

'Don't worry, they're free for all. You coming to dinner?'

Cara reluctantly agreed.

Dinner was a sloppy-looking shepherd's pie that did at least taste a lot better than the liver and onions of the day before. Cara and Barnard sat by themselves on a table. Peter came to join them but didn't talk at all. She was listening to something on her tape player. All of the other residents left them alone and Cara was starting to believe that maybe she could have a life here. This place was so strange, but at least it seemed safe.

For the time being.

After dinner, Cara and Barnard returned to their cell. And Cara spent more time lying around – there was going to be a lot of that in her future. Lying around and thinking about the events that led her to this moment. Barnard was lying on her bed too, staring up at the ceiling. She wondered what events had led Barnard here.

There was a rap on the door – four quick knocks. Without a thought, Barnard got up and opened the cell door. It was Minnie.

'Hate to be the bearer of bad news, girls,' Minnie said, 'but it's almost time for Movie Night.'

Cara smiled and got up. A movie. She hadn't seen one of those in a while. Something to take her mind off this. But why did Minnie sound sad – almost fearful? 'I don't understand.'

'I don't want to tell you, don't want to break your spirit.'

Barnard looked back at Cara, raised her eyebrows and shrugged.

Outside, there was a mass migration. The whole Unit was being escorted down the Pit by the guards. Minnie, Barnard, and Cara joined the flow of women to the dining-room doors, which were unusually propped open.

Movie Night appeared to be mandatory. Cara walked with Barnard and Minnie, trying not to look anyone in the eye.

About halfway down the Pit, Anderson came out of a cell, dragging a blue-haired inmate. This must be Aqua. 'Please no,' she was saying, 'not again.'

Anderson shoved her out into the flow of her fellow prisoners so she could do nothing but follow everyone else. He was smiling. 'You know the rules, Blue.'

Cara followed the others, through the dining room, down the corridors, until they all filed into the yard, which was now incredibly dark, and had a large thin, wobbly screen drawn across one wall. There were rows of plastic chairs, that had appeared since that morning, and Cara just followed Barnard, who appeared non-plussed by the whole situation and was going with the flow, and sat next to her in the centre of the room.

Minnie sat down on Cara's other side and gave her a sad smile.

Cara just frowned, confused.

They sat there for a few minutes as the room filled up. Five minutes later, the seats were mostly taken and there was an odd silence in the room. Women were talking, but they were hushed conversations, as though they were actually in a cinema. Guards filed in to the room – Michael (who still looked tentative and out of place), Harper, the two women she had met the day before, and others – and stood around the walls.

Conversations ceased and then a shouting started up from somewhere beyond the yard. It grew louder and then finally Liza burst through the double doors. Followed by a very angry Anderson.

'I'm not doing this again. I can't do this again. You can't make us.'

'Bite me,' Anderson said. He seemed to have integrated himself into North Fern life incredibly quickly, and, what was more, he was enjoying it a little too much.

Liza snapped her teeth together and laughed. 'Don't tempt me, dickhead.' She half lunged at Anderson, a fake-out but a convincing one.

Another guard rushed forward, but Anderson held up a hand, and, sure enough, Liza stopped before she got to him.

'Sit down,' Anderson said firmly.

And Liza cackled. 'You'd like that, wouldn't you?'

'Very much . . . yes.'

'Liza,' another voice, more authoritative but also somehow friendly. It was Harper, from across the hall. 'Please would you sit down. We do this every time, and, if you can recall, the outcome is always the same.'

Liza looked at Harper and then back to Anderson, who was doing his creepy smile at her. 'I assume the outcome,' Anderson said, 'is you sit down and watch the bloody film.'

Liza backed down, but she mumbled and groaned all the way to a seat, left empty at the end of one of the front rows, as though not only the guards had known this performance would happen, but also the other prisoners. She sat down, with a great THWUMP that must have hurt. This was a common occurrence then?

Cara turned to Minnie and whispered, 'What can be that bad to go through all that?'

Minnie looked at her. 'If you don't know, you haven't been listening.'

And just like that, the lights went off.

The screen came alight with a fuzzy projection, and the words 'North Fern' hovered on it slightly haphazardly. The picture was widescreen, but the actual film was in 4:3, leaving cavernous black bars at either side. The 'North Fern' logo disappeared as the programme cut to the actual film. A ton of small white words on a black background saying that this reproduction had been licensed for showing in a public place.

And then a crescendo of music, and a black and white scene came up on the screen. An old New York street in the thirties, with old cars and even older outfits on people passing by. The camera panned up as the music swelled and fell on a street sign poking out the side of a building.

Cara's mood instantly dipped – why hadn't she realised as soon as she'd heard of Movie Night? How could it be anything else?

The street sign was joined by loopy letters and some small print underneath denoting copyright notices, to complete the title.

Rain on Elmore Street.

'Every single week,' Minnie whispered in her ear, and Cara almost jumped – she was so transfixed. But not in a good way. She couldn't really believe this was happening.

And as the film began, with a plucky opening number that included all the passers-by bursting into gleeful song, Cara found that actually it wasn't the film that was creeping her out so much, it was the segment of numbers in the corner, denoting hours, minutes, seconds, and even milliseconds.

A timer ticking up.

8

The film felt longer than it was – even first time round. These old-timey films were all the same – wooden sets, wooden acting, wooden songs. When the film was over and Cara had fully experienced the love story between Eugene, the lowly doorman of a fancy hotel, and Miss Giratina, the highly-strung businesswoman who learns to reconfigure her world view and blah blah blah . . . the prisoners (now all extremely irate, yet happy to be able to talk again) were all shuffled back to their cells, Barnard and Cara muddled in with them.

And as she thought about the film, something felt familiar. She hadn't even considered it when she was in the moment, but now she had seen it, she had the strange feeling – she'd seen the film before.

Cara didn't speak as they went back to their cell. She was still trying to make sense of what she'd seen – not the things that happened on the screen, but the things that had happened off-screen – the Unit. All funnelled into a room and forced to watch that film, once a week too. No wonder Aqua and Liza had put up such a fight.

'You realised yet that there wasn't actually any rain on Elmore Street?' Barnard said, flopping on her bed in disgust. 'I think that's the thing that winds me up the most. It never bloody rained. Not one shitty drop. Why was it called that? What does it mean? Why not Sun on Elmore Street? Or Slight Overcast-ness on Elmore Street?'

'Maybe it was a figurative rain? Like the rain of emotions?' Cara said, half-jokingly.

'Shove off,' Barnard said, only half-jokingly too, and not quite as friendly.

Cara laughed anyway. And relaxed — if that was the right word — on her own bed. She stared up at the blank ceiling — there was a thin crack snaking across the white stone. 'I understand Movie Night now.'

You've seen it before. Somewhere. Why is that important?

Barnard laughed. She was in high spirits. She'd just seen a bad movie, and she was riffing. Cara almost didn't want to burst her bubble, but knew she had to. When Barnard finally calmed down, Cara told her about her discussion with Krotes and what Minnie had whispered to her. But she didn't need Minnie to tell her — she had known. She had known the second that movie started.

'You're kidding right?' Barnard said. 'We have to watch that every week?'

'I think so,' Cara replied.

Barnard was silent for a moment. 'Well that's not happening.'

Cara looked at her and laughed, although there wasn't much humour in it. 'I don't think we have a choice.'

'What kind of place uses an old musical as a form of torture?'

Cara shook her head. She had no idea. There was so much that seemed wrong, it was hard to focus on anything else. She longed for the simplicities of New Hall – a prison that was just a prison, with windows and normal locks and no movie night, and, above all, a governor who didn't chill her to the bone.

'At least we have a week to recover,' Barnard said.

And Cara felt an overwhelming gratitude. Barnard was looking on the bright side – something that she should've been doing but couldn't. She wondered what Barnard was like on the outside – whether she was as strong and witty and compassionate. Or if the situation was bringing out the best in her.

BLAARRP.

'Second night,' Barnard said, 'it feels like we've been here a lifetime already.'

It did. Cara felt like she was sinking. North Fern was wrapping around her, constricting her, so she couldn't see anything else. It was like that in prison – at some point it was impossible to convince yourself you ever had a life outside of the four walls around you. The difference was it usually took weeks, months, maybe even years.

At North Fern, it had been two days.

She thought back to what Krotes had said. The 252,000 instances of *Rain on Elmore Street* that comprised her sentence. How many times had it been so far? How many times had she seen that opening, suffered those songs, seen the credits. She didn't want to know the answer.

The lights next to their cell door changed to red, and the lock clicked.

83

BLARP.

'We're going to have to work something out . . .' Barnard said to the ceiling.

The lights went out.

'. . .Because if I have to watch that film every week for the rest of my life, I'm going to shoot myself . . . right between the eyes.'

9

The next morning, Harper came for her. She had expected to be left alone, seeing as it was Sunday, planned a day in bed feeling sorry for herself – her body ached with the unbearable knowledge of time yet to serve. Some days she just needed to keep herself to herself, regroup mentally and fix her defences for the week ahead.

But no, that wasn't on the cards. It was time for her first session with Doctor Tobias Trenner. Great. Harper escorted Cara wordlessly out of the Unit, and they retraced their steps towards Krotes' office. Harper took her down yet another corridor and stopped outside a glass door, with frosted glass. The plaque on it read Tobias Trenner, Resident Doctor. Harper knocked and a voice shouted for them to come in. Harper opened the door and let Cara in, pausing to unlock her handcuffs. With a little smile and nod at her, Harper left her alone with her new psychiatrist.

Cara turned into the room. Dr Tobias Trenner was sitting at his desk – he smiled. His office was very clean and minimalist, compared to Krotes'. The walls were a baby blue colour, with a feature wall being pure white. His desk was uncluttered and simply had a laptop and a file on top of it. There was a real window behind him, with three potted plants on the sill – two cacti and a sunflower. There was one small bookcase with a smattering of medical books in the corner, and a round table with two comfortable-looking armchairs in the other corner of the room. Atop the table was a square box of tissues – one pulled most of the way out and ready to catch any tears that may fall. On his desk was a framed photo – himself, a woman, and a girl. A happy family. The kind that she'd never have.

'It is nice to see you again, Cara,' Trenner said, genuinely.

And Cara felt her own expression – a pointed scowl – softening. Something about the room, and the doctor, was infectiously calming. She couldn't help but feel at ease, no matter how she tried. The sun was even shining through the window.

'Would you like a glass of water?' Before she could answer, he got up and went to the bookcase. On top of it was a jug. He poured two tall glasses of water.

Cara went to sit at the desk, but Dr Trenner held up a hand.

'No, no.' He gestured to the comfy-looking chairs and the ominous tissues.

Cara sat, sinking into the chair as Dr Trenner placed a glass of water in front of her and sat down with his own.

When they had briefly met before, Cara hadn't realised how young Trenner was. He didn't look much older than she was.

'I know, for all intents and purposes I am Doctor

Trenner, but please, at least while we are in this room, call me Tobias. In fact, call me Toby. Only if I annoy you should you call me Tobias.'

'Tobias then,' Cara said bluntly.

He laughed.

'How are you finding your first few days at North Fern?' Toby asked, taking a sip of water and relaxing into his chair.

For some reason, Cara felt compelled to lie, as though she almost wanted to impress this man in front of her. But she didn't. Instead she relaxed too. 'Not great.'

Toby smiled. 'No, I would have thought there was something wrong with you if that wasn't the reaction. I heard what happened when you arrived and what happened in the dining room. The argument. Liza was it? It often is, I'm afraid.'

'It's not because of that,' Cara said. 'In fact, that's the only normal thing that's happened since I've been here.'

Toby considered this. 'You mean to say that you think you deserve it?'

'What?' Cara said, incredulously. 'No. I'm saying North Fern is—'

'Ah, yes, beg your pardon. I've worked here since North Fern's inception, and that means sometimes it's easy to forget it is an odd facility at first sight. But trust me, that it does get easier.'

'I don't want it to get easier,' Cara said. 'I want to understand where I am.'

'Well, in the broad sense, you are in prison. But North Fern is slightly more than that. I'm sure you have heard the pitch from Ms Krotes. To combat overpopulation, and the rise in violence because of that, North Fern was created to house the most likely to incite trouble. Krotes calls the residents the worst of the worst, which is rather crass, but it is a saying that gets the job done.'

'Does that mean we should be shut off from the world? No visitation, no sky, no fresh air? Phones that are out of order?'

Toby thought about this for a moment. With the air of choosing his words very carefully, he said, 'I know this may be hard to hear, but from the view of the greater populace, and the view of the government . . . yes. And North Fern houses you all in the most humane way possible. The natural light, the "windows", the jobs, and the tasks you are given to activate your mind, the education classes you are offered . . . they're all for your benefit. To help you grow and rehabilitate.'

Cara scoffed. 'I have two life sentences in prison. You've read my file, you've read the papers – you know I'm never going to get out. Why the hell would I need to "rehabilitate"?'

Toby smiled, against everything. 'Because I think there's more to you than just the crime that's hanging over your head. You're not that person – at least not entirely. You were a promising journalism student, you had friends, you were an asset to the community – and then one night, in that house in the London suburbs, you did what you did. You're a therapist's puzzle if ever I've heard of one.'

'So that's all I am. That's why I'm here. For your

88

enjoyment, your academia. You want to write a paper on me or something? Have you already booked your TED talk?' Cara spat.

'No, no, no,' Toby said, holding up a palm. 'Maybe I got a little carried away. Madeleine referred you to me for your benefit. We – you and I – are going to work together to make sure you can have the best life you can. We are going to look into your past, your present, and your future. And, by the end of our sessions, hopefully you can see that North Fern is not the end, but rather a new beginning. Even if it is admittedly a different beginning from the one you would rather have.'

'You know all about me,' Cara said, 'you know my plea?'

'Yes.'

'Are you here to convince me I imagined everything?'

Toby straightened up, scratched his nose a little awkwardly. 'It's not about absolutes. It's not about saying you're wrong and we're right. You know the phrase "Let the chips fall where they may"? Well, we are beyond that. The chips have fallen. Where they landed is where we are. We need to see where we are going to go from now.'

Cara understood. But that didn't mean she liked it. She was boxed in – she couldn't go back – if she turned around she would see a barred wall. But every step forward felt like a betrayal to herself. Every step was an acceptance of where she was. And she was stepping further and further away from who she had been. Maybe Toby Trenner's guidance was exactly what she needed, maybe acceptance was not a dirty word. 'OK,' she said, before she even realised she had opened her mouth.

'OK,' repeated Toby. 'So this session, I would like to keep things light. You probably have many questions about North Fern, so I invite you to ask,' he looked at his watch, ' . . .some of them now.'

'Where are we?' Cara said quickly.

'I don't understand,' Toby said, leisurely taking a sip of water as though this conversation was not at all taxing to him. 'Didn't Ms Krotes tell you?'

Yes, but I don't trust her. But Cara didn't say that, instead she just rephrased the question. 'Where are we in the country? Really?'

'We are in Buckinghamshire. Really.'

'Oh.' She believed him.

Toby studied her for a moment. 'You see sometimes answers are just totally unsatisfactory. More than that, they're absolutely needless.'

'I'm just not coping with the secrecy.'

'I think you're confusing secrecy with redundancy. Why would you need to know? In fact, the rise and fall of emotion you experienced – the disappointment at a simple answer – is precisely why you're not told. There are no visitors at North Fern. There is minimal correspondence. There are no "field trips". The fact that we are in Buckinghamshire is quite simply irrelevant.

'And I don't know if you are being very fair saying we are being secretive. You are given a handbook in your cell, which I trust you've read, and judging by the look on your face, Ms Krotes told you where North Fern was located. Secrecy is not the same as choosing not to believe the answers. I don't blame you for being untrusting, but we can only do our best.'

Cara was annoyed at that, but at the same time could understand what he was saying. So she moved on. 'Why is there no visitation? What category is this prison?'

Toby cleared his throat, took another sip of water. 'We don't work with categories here. Being a private prison, it can be run how Ms Krotes and the management wishes, provided they meet a benchmark standard that the government implements. The lack of visitation is to satisfy both the higher-ups and the government. North Fern is a special case, I suppose you could say. But you can rest easy that every bottom line is being met.'

'I don't care for myself – no one would visit me anyway,' Cara said, 'but I came here with a woman called Moyley. She has a young son. Is North Fern really going to deny her seeing him?'

'Hmm,' Toby said, 'wasn't Moyley involved in the altercation against you in the dining room? You're still concerned for her.'

'Don't make this about my empathy,' Cara replied, angrily, 'and just answer the question.'

Toby was mostly a friendly presence, but she could already tell he couldn't walk the line between therapist and actual human being very well. He looked at her like he almost understood his own shortcomings. 'Fair enough. The lack of visitation is going to be solved eventually. I have heard that Ms Krotes and the benefactors of North Fern are looking to create a unit where visits are possible. This institution is still very young, things are still being sorted out. When this unit is built, it is likely Moyley will be transferred there.'

'Who are the benefactors?'

'There is mainly one, but I have never met him.'

'What's his name?'

Toby thought for a moment and then looked at his watch awkwardly. 'Does that really matter? Cara, our time is limited today, and there is rather a lot I would like to get through. But if you have one last question, I will answer, and then it will be my turn.'

Cara didn't like the sound of Toby's 'turn' but cycled through some questions in her head. There were still so many. Toby had given answers, she even believed he had been truthful – or as truthful as he was allowed to be – but he hadn't really helped. But there was one question she seized on. 'Why are there no windows in the units? You're allowed them, I see.'

'Windows?' Toby looked back at his own. 'Ah yes.'

'I don't understand why there's not more.'

Toby sniffed and got up to refill his glass of water. He had already drunk the entire tall glass, at some point. 'North Fern was built on two principles – economy and punishment. The lack of windows – real windows – rather satisfies both. You build a prison and, by mere design, not every cell can have a window. They can't all be on the outer wall – that would be ridiculous. So, from a psychiatrist's point of view, I guess – which is the only view I can have – if not every prisoner can have a window, why should any?'

Cara thought about that for a moment. Opened her mouth. And then shut it. It made an annoying kind of sense.

Toby poured more water and paused by his window, looking out on a blue Sunday sky. 'Anyway, then there's the punishment side. The lack of windows demonstrates a special kind of confinement, a kind that I'm not particularly a fan of, but a kind nonetheless. And the screens help. That was my contribution to North Fern.'

'Your contribution?'

'Yes,' Toby said, gesturing to the window, which didn't help, seeing as his was real. 'They consulted me when building the place – a doctor's point of view. This is a prison, not a torture chamber. There is a base of human rights; North Fern is not Guantanamo Bay. I advised that there had to be sources of natural light to help general nutrition, circadian rhythms and mental health. The "windows" are there to provide stimuli. A trick of the mind – sometimes you may even think of it as a window. The brain sees what it wants to see – so any prompts it's given can lead it to the desired results.'

Cara understood, but didn't like the sound of it. It was the way he said *the desired results.*

'I'm quite proud of the "windows" and I hope that once you settle in, you learn to appreciate them. The yard is always bathed in this natural light, and I set up the daily process of Illumination to help the prisoners who like to stay in their cells. It may seem odd, and it very much is – I'm not disputing that at all – but see it as better than nothing. And, in time, you may even see it as better than the real thing.'

'But why—?'

'I'm afraid,' Toby said, sitting back down and replacing his glass, 'you're out of questions for now, Cara. Now I would like to talk about you.' He smiled.

Cara stopped. This was what she had been dreading.

She remembered in another life, she almost revelled in talking about herself, when she was at school and college. She used to talk about stupid things, like make-up, and television shows, and male celebrities. Now, whenever she talked about herself, she had to go into trials, blood, and murder. And sometimes she could even talk about how she didn't do any of it. But it never helped. Never.

Toby looked expectant.

'What do you want to know?' Cara said, through gritted teeth.

10

Over the next hour, Dr Tobias Trenner asked Cara about all aspects of her life, aspects that she didn't really want to delve into, but wasn't given any avenue to refuse.

She was asked about her parents. Toby seemed very interested in her mother, which wasn't something she particularly wanted to talk about. Martha Lockhart was not someone who needed to be talked about. She was a fine enough mother, until she went and got herself killed. Cara knew it wasn't her fault, and it definitely wasn't something she strived to do – but she left Cara alone. And the more the days, and weeks, and months, and years went by, that fact that she was alone seemed more important than all the love of the times before. It all seemed like a distant memory, almost a foreign one – like it had all happened to somebody else.

And in a way, it had. A different version of Cara Lockhart.

Next, Toby wanted to know about her father, which was altogether a shorter chapter of the conversation. She only had one real memory of her father and that was of him walking out the door when she was in a toddler crib.

Toby just sat and listened. He didn't write anything

down, but his expression was so constant and knowing that Cara got the impression he was internalising all the information. Next, he wanted to hear about anyone else close to her before what happened. Friends, boyfriends, teachers – any significant relationships. He asked about her education, how she was accepted on the course at the London School of Journalism, how her future was bright. She started to talk about the events that led up to *that* day – how she had to take a job to make ends meet and how that led her to 358 Dayes Drive on the night of 5 September 2018.

But Toby stopped her before she could even start.

Cara was surprised by this – was pretty sure this was going to culminate in her having to recount the fateful night again, but no.

'This is not the session to begin delving into that. I'm sure you don't wish to relive it, and currently I don't need to hear it. We will get to it. But for now this is about you.'

So Toby skipped over it and wanted to know about what she had been doing at North Fern since she arrived. And finally, Toby wanted to know about Cara's nights – how she slept and what she dreamed and whether she felt rested after she did. But before Cara could say much, Toby stood up.

'I'm going to prescribe you some medication, to be taken daily.' He went into his desk and brought out a green pad. He started writing on it.

'Wait, medication for what?' Cara said, standing up with anger.

Toby laughed. 'Don't worry, it's just a mild sedative to get you through the first few weeks. It can be hard to sleep in a new place and specially in North Fern.'

'I don't want to take medication,' Cara said firmly.

'It'll be beneficial,' Toby replied. 'Trust me.'

That was just the problem. Cara really wasn't sure if she did. Toby was part of the hierarchy of North Fern, and in Cara's mind, that gave him a label of mistrust.

'Can I—?' Cara started, but then there was a sharp knock. It was so sudden, both Cara and Toby's eyes shot to the door.

'That is my next appointment, so we have to finish up,' Toby said. 'I'll give this prescription to the pharmacist and you can start your medication tonight.'

Cara started to say again that she wasn't going to take it, but Toby ushered her to the door, without another word.

He opened it and smiled. 'Ah, hello. I don't believe we've been introduced.'

Cara looked around to see who it was, and her mood instantly dropped.

'Phillip Anderson,' Anderson grunted, 'you're the quack?'

Toby gave a curt laugh. 'Well, I suppose I am.'

'This is yours then,' Anderson said, pulling a woman into view. It was Peter. She looked dazed, and as she saw Cara, there was almost no recognition in her face. Cara smiled. She did not.

'Peter, hello,' Toby said.

Peter mumbled something.

'Shall I take this one back?' Anderson said, nodding to Cara.

Toby's smile disappeared and he made a deep sigh. 'Cara Lockhart, Mr Anderson. You can say her name.'

'I know I can,' Anderson said, giving a wicked smile.

Toby sighed again, but conceded. 'Come in, Peter.'

Peter made a real effort to walk into the room. Cara crossed her into Anderson's thankfully figurative open arms. He took a pair of handcuffs and seemed to take great pleasure in slapping them on her wrists.

Toby went to shut the door, then thought again and opened it. 'Oh, Mr Anderson . . .' He crossed to his desk, picked up the green pad, ripping off the top sheet. He returned with it in his hand. 'Seeing as you're going that way, would you give this to the pharmacist?'

Anderson took the prescription and looked at it like he had just been handed a dog turd. 'Fine,' he said.

Toby turned to Cara. 'Cara, please take the medication. It will really help you settle in.'

Cara said nothing. The door shut.

Anderson pocketed the prescription, muttering something, and took Cara's arm, using too much force to pull her along the corridor.

They rounded a corner, and as they were about to go past Krotes' office, the door opened. Madeleine Krotes stood there in the doorway, in a dazzling blue jacket and skirt. She looked like a movie star – almost like she had walked off the screen while *Rain on Elmore Street* was playing. As she noticed Anderson and Cara coming, she paused, watching them. She smiled – not at Cara, but at Anderson.

Cara glanced at Anderson. He had a goofy, almost boyish smile on his face, watching his governor with lustful eyes. But that wasn't what Cara was looking at.

Because Krotes had done something else – given Anderson an almost imperceptible nod.

Anderson nodded back.

And Cara spent all the way back to her cell wondering what the hell that meant.

11

That night, just before lights out, Cara and Barnard were talking about nothing in particular. Barnard was mulling over the idea of buying a television for the cell. It was a nice thought. Cara could imagine relaxing on her bed, and watching *Homes Under the Hammer* with Barnard. She surprised herself by actually wanting that.

A knock on the door cut through the fantasy, and the cell door opened to show one of the female guards.

'Lockhart,' she barked, standing in the doorway. Finally, Cara could see her name on her uniform. Continell. 'Come with me to the guards' station please.'

She'd been expecting it, but she still didn't want to. With one look at Barnard, she could do nothing but follow Continell across the emptying Pit, as women went back to their cells for the night, and up the stairs. Continell took her through the double doors at the entrance and led her around the semicircular desk that was the guards' workstation.

Continell went behind the desk and started busying herself with some paperwork, and Cara was just forced to stand there and watch. Continell got out a folder, and signed something, before disappearing below the desk and pulling out a yellow cabinet on wheels. It was chained to the bigger desk and had drawers in it. Continell checked something in the folder before getting a bunch of keys from her belt and unlocking the top drawer. She brought out a packet of medication and popped one blue pill into a little paper cup – one of those cups that looked like those you pumped fast-food condiments into. She put it on the desk in front of Cara without a word.

Cara regarded it. The little pill seemed a lot larger than it really was – most likely because of what it represented. Toby said it was a sedative to help her, to get a good night's sleep. But if she took this, she was conforming, she was giving in to Toby, and, more so, she was giving in to North Fern. Maybe it would help her, but maybe it was just a symbol.

'I don't want to take this,' Cara said, looking down at the little pill.

Continell put a glass of water next to the tablet. 'You don't have a choice, Lockhart. Doctor Trenner marked that this was mandatory. You aren't going anywhere until you take it.'

'No,' Cara said. 'I won't.'

Continell looked at her with annoyance – something about her gaze was so painfully dismissive. Cara was a small nuisance to her. Continell had her own life, full of her own problems, with a real future. Continell was free, Cara was not – and her gaze somehow communicated this perfectly. 'You will take the pill or you'll be forced to take it.'

101

Cara opened her mouth to object, but a guard came up behind her and touched her shoulder. She knew who it was before she turned to look. There was only one person it could be. She smelled a mixture of body odour and something else she didn't wish to know about and heard the thick breaths of the guard who made her shiver.

Anderson. Of course.

Cara shrugged his hand off her shoulder and scowled at him.

'Is there a problem here?' he said, in such a slimy way that it made her wince.

'Lockhart here will not take her medication,' Continell said.

It took only another second of Anderson's presence for Cara to pick up the paper cup and swallow the tablet whole. She washed it down with water. It was only a sedative – one day wouldn't hurt, and she could fight the decision at some other point. For now, she just wanted to get as far from Anderson as possible.

'Ah, you see,' he said, laughing, 'there's a good girl. Now open your mouth.' Cara almost vomited right there and suddenly a look of something like shared revolt passed between her and Continell.

'Why?' Cara said.

'Well, we have to make sure you've swallowed.'

Continell reluctantly nodded. Cara opened her mouth.

'Tongue,' Anderson said, gazing into her mouth.

Cara lifted her tongue up, thinking how easy it would be to unleash a mouthful of spit on the disgusting guard's face. But that wouldn't help anyone, least of all her.

'Good, have a lovely night, Lockhart.' Anderson's smile was like a bucket of ice water to her.

When Continell unlocked the unit doors for her to go back in, she almost ran to her cell.

Feeling Anderson's sticky eyes burning into her back. Every step of the way.

12

The laundry was a thin, long room with big silver industrial-sized washing machines on one side and similarly big silver industrial-sized dryers on the other. In the middle were wooden benches as if this were a public launderette. Cara couldn't help but think of the launderette from *EastEnders*, especially when the woman explaining how the machines worked and what her job was looked a little like Dot Cotton. She was definitely just as old.

'So we take the uniforms from these baskets, which go around the cells a week before we get them,' the woman said, who was not in fact called Dot, but actually Deidra. 'We check the pockets and make sure they're ready to be washed, and then we put them in the washer. Now, this is very important, we have to put them on a forty-degree wash for one hour thirty-seven minutes. Not a minute more, not a minute less.' She stopped and stared intensely at Cara.

Cara nodded.

'When they're done, we then transport them to the dryer and put them on a full dry. While that is happening, we are also responsible for the sanitation of this room and the yard, so usually I pop out and do some cleaning while waiting for the uniforms to dry. After they are finished, there are some irons and ironing boards at the back of the room. We only iron the towels mind you – no ironing nylon – fold them and they are ready to go back. We place the uniforms back in the same baskets and they are returned to their owners. It is very simple, see.'

The fact that Deidra had to explain it in detail and enunciate specific words meant that she didn't think Cara would find it so easy.

She ignored the feeling of being talked down to, thanking Deidra and getting to work.

At one point she had hoped to be a world-famous journalist, maybe a foreign correspondent flying all over the world – reporting from dangerous warzones, lands devastated by natural disasters, trying to help people. Now, she was washing and ironing (dear God, not the uniforms though) and folding it so it didn't crease, inside a prison facility.

Still, however, she ate lunch that day with a sense of actually having got something done, and then she returned for the afternoon shift. By the end of the shift, she was in a surprisingly good mood and walked back from the launderette actually a little tired from a hard day's work. Although, compared to her old 'normal' life, she hadn't really accomplished much, she still felt a sense of satisfaction at having completed something.

She walked through the dining room, looking around for anyone she knew. There was hardly anyone in the room, and no one she had been introduced to. Two women were sitting at a table at the far end of the room, seemingly collectively reading a newspaper. She went through the dining-room door, scanning her Cuff and started into the Pit, which was getting busy now that the jobs had finished. As she walked, the *BLARRRP* signalling afternoon Illumination sounded. Cara dodged the crowd that had started to form around the games table and skipped behind the stairs towards her cell. But what she saw made her stop.

Barnard was standing in the doorway of their cell, and someone else was standing with her. It was Minnie, and she looked incredibly angry. They were talking heatedly. Minnie was gesturing wildly, her face red, while Barnard was standing tall and strong, towering over the matriarch, and trying to remain calm.

Cara looked around, but none of the other residents had noticed. She wished she could hear, but the usual swimming pool-like echoed din was assaulting her ears and all she could make out was the end of sentences.

' . . .family,' Minnie shouted.

Barnard actually laughed in her face. Cara couldn't believe it − she would never have the nerve to do that to Minnie. ' . . .you,' Barnard shouted back. Cara was pretty sure there had been an expletive.

Cara had to move closer. She had to hear what was going on. But getting any closer would mean she'd have to step out from under the stairway, and she'd be easily spotted if either of them looked around. Thankfully, two women went to their own cell door in front of them and Cara was able to use them as cover to move up slightly.

Barnard was speaking again. 'I don't know what kind of "girl" your tactics work on, but I can assure you it's not me. You've been nice to me, you've welcomed me and thank you for that. But just know that I don't think I owe you anything.'

Minnie jabbed her in the chest. 'Don't make the mistake of portraying my efforts as a kindness, Stephanie. I run this unit and I will not allow you to trounce all over it. If what I heard is true . . .'

'It's not. It's hearsay. No, even worse, it's fourth-hand hearsay from an unreliable source. And you'd believe him over me.' Barnard pointed right back.

Him. Who was she talking about? If she'd said 'her' it could have been anyone, but 'him'? That really narrowed down the list of suspects. But Cara had no idea what they were talking about.

Minnie laughed. An empty sound wrapped in malice. 'This conversation's over. You know where I stand, now it's time to decide where you do.' She started away across the Pit.

Cara waited a few seconds and then headed towards Barnard, before hearing, 'I would hate you to get hurt, Stephanie.' Minnie calling back as she walked away.

Barnard stared daggers at her.

'What was that about?' Cara asked.

Barnard looked after Minnie, scowling. Then she looked at Cara and her expression softened. 'It was nothing.'

'It didn't look like nothing.'

Barnard reluctantly smiled. 'I just want to relax and

forget about it. I've been peeling potatoes all day.'

'Sure,' Cara said, as Barnard disappeared into their cell. She watched Minnie stalk away across the Pit. *I would hate you to get hurt.* She wondered about it for the rest of the night, even as they went for dinner. She was so preoccupied, she didn't even notice that there were no potatoes for dinner.

13

The next day after work, Cara decided to force herself to go to the yard for a while, and to use the showers for the first time.

Barnard refused to go, lying on her bed and tossing a crumpled-up piece of paper into the air and catching it again. She had been unusually quiet since her argument with Minnie, and she wasn't telling Cara anything more about it. She said she was waiting for the library cart, which was due, seeing as it was Tuesday – so at least the excuse checked out.

The showers were a horror show – with open cubicles covered only by purple, almost transparent curtains. Cara finished up as quickly as she could, dumping her towel in a hamper of dirty ones, which she knew she might indeed be washing and drying in the week to come, and went back to her cell. Barnard was still waiting.

The Pit was unusually quiet and there was an almost palpable air of expectation, and soon enough they both heard a rickety trolley in the distance. It was a strange sound, in the midst of all the high technology around them.

Barnard sat up and listened intently, but it was a good

half an hour until the trolley finally stopped outside their door.

There was a tentative knock and a small man in guards' uniform fumbled with the door as he wheeled in a cartful of books of all shapes and sizes. Some were even piled on top of the cart, and they shook as it went over the small lip at the bottom of the cell door frame. The guard quickly grabbed for them as the door shut behind him, but they toppled to the floor.

He went to go and pick them up. Barnard jumped to help. She handed him some of the books, and he thanked her, straightening to finally show his face. It was Michael.

'Hello, ladies, would you like to . . . borrow anything from the library cart?'

'Michael?' Cara couldn't help but say.

Michael smiled at her but couldn't meet her eyes. 'Yes.'

'I . . . Are you the librarian now?'

'I am in charge of the library cart, yes, And the post. It's an important position.' He couldn't even say it like he believed it. Michael had always seemed a little less imposing than the other guards, but now he looked even worse. He looked . . . broken.

'What's . . .' she was about to say *what's wrong*? but she happened to glance at Barnard, who was quickly shaking her head at her. And then Cara understood. Michael had suffered an indignity already being given this job – he didn't need the pity of a convicted prisoner, let alone one offering comfort.

'You have any horror?' Barnard said, filling the silence.

Michael looked thankful at something to do and went behind the cart to look. 'Yes.' He recited what they had and Barnard picked a dog-eared copy of a Stephen King.

'What about you, Lockhart?' Michael asked.

Cara smiled. 'What would you recommend for a first-time user?'

Michael looked blank and so did Barnard.

'I don't really read,' she conceded.

Michael looked up and down the cart and got her a canvas-bound copy of *Catch-22*. 'It's a classic,' he said, handing it over. 'I'm afraid neither of you had any post this week,'

And Barnard gave a sarcastic gasp. 'Shocker,' she said.

Michael laughed. And started the awkward process of reversing the cart out of the cell. 'Goodbye,' he said clumsily, as he disappeared around the corner, his cart shuddering and wobbling. The cell door shut.

Cara assessed her book, still wondering why they had given Michael the job. It had to be a demotion – from prison guard to librarian. If they hadn't wanted Michael as a guard, why did they transfer him here?

She looked over at Barnard to see if she was thinking about it too, but instead she found her cellmate smiling and tucking into her book. There was something different about her that Cara hadn't noticed before. She was wearing foundation, whereas usually she just wore mascara and eyeshadow.

'Did you know he was coming with the cart?' Cara asked, narrowing her eyes. 'Michael?'

Barnard blew out with her mouth incredulously. 'What? No. Don't be stupid.'

'You did, you knew.'

'OK, Ms Conspiracy,' she laughed, getting up and putting the book on the cabinet. She was almost a different person – happy and sunny. What the hell was happening? 'You coming to dinner?' She didn't wait, leaving Cara to rush after her.

The dining room was abuzz with a strangely positive energy. Dinner was a grey stew full of mushy vegetables and flavourless chunks of meat. Not that it mattered. Even though she had no mail, Cara's own mood was lifted by everyone else. She could rest easy knowing no one would be giving her grief tonight. They were all busy – reading scraps of paper and some even unwrapping parcels.

Peter came to dinner proudly holding a chocolate bar, which had to be melting given how tightly she was clutching it. She sat down next to Cara, with her tray, placing the bar next to her cup of water and her apple, with a massive grin on her face.

'Every week my mum sends me my favourite choco bar!' she said, gleefully, without need for prompting. 'A THWAMP! Every single week without fail.' When she had finished her dinner, she unwrapped the chocolate bar and consumed it in two quick bites. She emitted a kind of satisfied squeak that Cara had never heard come from anything before, let alone a human.

Across the way, Minnie was sitting alone at a table, reading a letter on paper that looked like a night sky. It was dark blue with stars on it. Her letter seemed to span multiple pages and she was alternating between smiling and silently sobbing.

For the first time, Cara was glad she didn't have any post.

'And that's when I turned to the study of amphibians,' Barnard was saying. It was the next day. She'd been incredibly talkative since Cara got back from taking her meds, which were again imposed upon her by a virtually salivating Anderson. Well, in reality, she'd been in a good mood since the library cart came around the previous day. Her book lay on the bedside table, finished. She'd read an astronomical amount of pages in such a small amount of time. But Cara didn't think Barnard would be one just to skim read. She thought that the bookworm was just incredibly fast – still managing to absorb every word. 'But I was never meant to study frogs.'

BLARP.

'I don't understand,' Cara said.

'I was meant to come here. Destiny's a bitch,' Barnard said. 'Destroy it.'

'What?'

'Talk more tomorrow,' Barnard said. 'Right now, I've got a date with some sheep going over a fence.' She laughed.

And Cara laughed too, as Barnard closed her eyes in

preparation of lights out. Even though she couldn't help wondering how her cellmate came to be here. She almost needed to know at this point. The hunger for the knowledge was so great that her breath practically caught in her throat whenever it seemed that Barnard might slip and tell a crucial detail.

Cara shook herself — it was time to forget about that and unwind. She got up out of the relative comfort of the bed — it annoyed her how used to it she was already — to go and shut the cell door, which was ajar.

She happened to glance out into the Pit. It was deathly quiet — all the women must have already retired as all the doors were shut except hers. She looked down the length of the Pit — no guards either. That was a little odder. Unless they were inspecting the rest of the Unit for any stragglers. It was almost like she was entirely alone.

She turned and tilted her head around, looking down in the direction of the dining room. No one there either. And almost utter silence. All she heard was a soft moan of conversation coming from a few of the cells.

A clatter behind her.

She looked back the other way. And then up to the gangway at the front of the Unit. Nothing. But—

A blur of movement.

An uncontrollable shiver burst through her like a painful fizz.

Someone had been there but had moved so quickly, dashing for cover across the gangway, she hadn't been able to focus on it. But she saw some details — the boiler suit, the hooded jacket, the face – or the place where the face should be.

No – no, no, no, it couldn't be. It was impossible. Just her imagination.

Her feet moved independently of her, bringing her out into the Pit.

'What are you doing?' Barnard asked. In another universe. An echo. As the door shut behind her.

Because all Cara could see now was the Pit and the gangway. She stepped out into the centre and saw something in the top corner of the gangway. The very small hint of a blue-sleeved arm around the corner on the top floor – hiding from her. She didn't want to – she had never wanted anything less in her life – but she stepped forward. Starting down the Pit. For her sanity, she had to see. She had to know that what she thought she saw wasn't there – couldn't be there.

She stepped forward on uncertain legs but couldn't stop. She knew if she was to stay here, she had to confront the notion that this thing could, or couldn't, be here. She focused on that little shred of blue she could see upstairs, hoping it would just dissipate, proving itself to be a hallucination. But it didn't. Every step she took, it seemed to grow stronger.

A few more steps and she was at the metal stairs up to the gangway. And it was still there. The muttering around her had stopped completely – all she could hear was her own hitching breath. And – another person breathing. Strong, swift breaths. It was coming from behind the corner. This was real.

She rocketed up the stairs, knowing that as soon as she was at the top, she could look around the corner and see it. See him. See . . .

She got to the top and stopped. She braced herself, held her breath and forced herself to look around.

She let her breath go.

Around the little corner at the top of the stairs, next to the first cell was a chair. And on the chair one of the guards had draped a jacket

Nothing. There was nothing – no one – there.

The piece of blue she had seen was a sleeve of the jacket visible around the corner.

But no – she had definitely seen . . .

She wheeled around, her eyes flitting across the gangways, down into the Pit, everywhere. She had seen him – she wasn't tired, or delirious. What she had seen – the figure duck behind the corner – had been so real, so strong. But the more she stared, the more she began to doubt herself. There was not even a hint that anyone had been there. No boiler suit. No No-Face.

But she had seen him.

No, she couldn't think that – she *thought* she saw him.

She sighed and shook herself.

'Lockhart!'

She jumped out of her skin and turned around to see Anderson standing there directly behind her. He seemed to notice her distressed state and was a little amused by it, a wicked smile playing across his face.

'Get back to your cell. Now. Lights out!'

Cara obeyed, trying not to run down the stairs.

She couldn't have seen him. It wasn't possible. This was North Fern, a prison. And the worst thing about prisons was also a good thing. No one could get out, but equally no one could get in. So what she'd just seen was simply a trick of the mind. She was suffering from a lack of stimuli – maybe she should try to go to the yard tomorrow, walk around more, engage more. Stop her mind from inventing. Because that's what it had just done – it must have.

'What the hell did you think you were doing, Lockhart?'

She didn't even hear him.

'I'll have to report this, you know.'

No-Face couldn't be here. She repeated it to herself as she walked, hearing Anderson's footfalls behind her. Their two sets of footsteps almost complemented each other.

When she got to her cell, she saw Barnard looking confused. Cara stepped inside, chancing one last look back down the Pit. But all she saw was Anderson, shaking his head and chuckling to himself, as he slammed her cell door.

15

The days stacked up like playing cards in a deck. Rhythm was an awful thing. You woke up, you ate, you worked, you ate, you worked, you rested, you ate, you talked, you went to sleep. And all the time you thought about how your life was being wasted, about how human beings weren't meant to be caged up, about how your existence was just the same as everyone else's in here, about how you would die and you wouldn't even be a footnote in history, about how if you died now, you'd actually be better off.

Cara had already lost concept of days – she had arrived on a Monday, hadn't she? Or was it a Tuesday? But then equally it could have been a Friday, come to think of it. So today was . . . Well, it could have been any day of the week and she supposed in most ways, it didn't matter.

BLARP.

Cara woke up next to Barnard. Her cellmate was usually already up, applying her eyeliner in the mirror. They went to breakfast, which was often Weetabix and fruit. They went to work, Barnard in the kitchens and Cara in the laundry.

Cara came to hate the laundry. Whereas at the start,

she had welcomed the distraction, now it was too monotonous. Collect the uniforms, wash the uniforms, dry the uniforms. Oh, and don't forget to check the pockets.

Some days, she was allowed to go and mop the yard. Most days, she just had to sit and watch the clothes tumble around in the machines. Some days, she found something interesting in a pocket – a small note to another resident, an odd amount of fluff or multiple chocolate wrappers. Most days, she found nothing.

She had exhausted all conversation with the older women who worked with her, so now she laboured in silence. At least, it made getting off work exhilarating. Sometimes she couldn't even seize consciousness. Like it was something she had to grab constantly flailing in front of her face. Even if she could catch it, she didn't know whether she would.

She went to the dining room. Sat with Peter while she ate her breakfast. 'I've been thinking a lot about sudoku. Everything in its rightful place, you know,' Peter said, starting to launch into a conversation Cara didn't have to be a part of, but it progressed nonetheless.

She felt like she was sleepwalking.

In a fog.

She went to the yard. Basked in the sun.

No. Not the sun. Not at all.

An artificial light. A sunny day – made up. Manufactured.

Somehow, that had started not to matter. She liked it, nonetheless.

She had a shower. Didn't even bother to pull the curtain. She didn't really care.

North Fern had her now.

She went back to her cell for Illumination. The screens showed a New York skyline. A place she would never go.

She lay down on her bed, fell into a restless sleep. Maybe she would tell Toby she wanted to sign up for some of the activities.

Sessions with Toby continued. They never talked about that night.

The rest of her life stretched out in front of her.

On Saturdays, everyone was shepherded into the yard, transformed into a makeshift cinema, and *Rain on Elmore Street* played for its long runtime. Every time, she tried to think of where she'd seen it before. It seemed important – it probably wasn't.

Once a week, Barnard became a different person – lighter and happier. That was when Cara knew that it must be Tuesday and the library cart was coming around. Each time, Barnard became slightly more flirty with Michael and she also seemed to, without fail, take one more book than the last time. Once, Michael handed her a book and Cara saw that it had a little note inside – when Barnard saw, she almost swooned. Cara didn't know whether to think it was romantic or kinda weird.

She took her medication without any pushback. She did sleep better. At least she thought she did.

And she never repeated the evening look-around for the non-existent No-Face. He wasn't here in the Unit – it was ridiculous even to entertain the idea. But still, there were a few moments, when she turned around quickly, where she saw some movement behind her. She always felt like someone was following her – her footsteps echoing and duplicated. But she suppressed the feeling. And as the days went by, she forgot about it and came to realise it was just a trick of the mind.

One day, Barnard asked if Cara would give her some money, and she gave it to her without much fight. Barnard disappeared for a while and came back with a box television that looked like it had come straight out of the year 1995. Cara didn't care – she was so excited. They propped it in the corner on the stool that was usually under the sink. They always had the TV on from then on, watching all the throw-away daytime television they could. It was odd that a television could go so far to making North Fern, unfortunately, begin to feel like home.

But even so . . .

Cara just existed. Keeping inside her little bubble of people. Trying to keep away from Liza and Moyley. Hanging out with Barnard and Peter, and sometimes Minnie when Barnard was away, and one time even Aqua joined in the mix. She carved out a little life with the tools she was given. Unfortunately, unbeknownst to her, she was travelling on a course that was edging her ever closer to disaster.

16

'Cara, Cara . . .'

Cara opened her eyes. 'Barnard?'

Barnard looked about ten years older than when Cara had last seen her. She seemed to have more wrinkles, darker bags under her eyes. Her hair had lost its strong colour and now looked grey. The fire in her eyes had been extinguished. 'Cara, I found it.'

'What?' Cara said, jumping up as Barnard swayed.

She caught her, and guided her to bed.

'I don't know what you mean. You look exhausted. You have to rest.'

A guard banged on the door. Anderson. Cara looked at him with hatred. 'In your bed, Lockhart. Lockdown's in less than thirty.'

Thirty seconds.

Cara got back in her bed. Took her shoes off. Her trousers. And slipped under the crackly plastic covers.

'This place, it's not what we think.' Barnard. Almost like she was talking in her sleep.

'What?'

'You didn't do it.'

Cara held her heart where it was meant to be. Here. It

didn't soar any more. Wasn't allowed to.

'You didn't do it, just like I didn't do mine. Chocolate bars and star-bound wishes.'

'How . . . What?'

'Show you. Tomorrow.'

Heavy breaths. She was asleep.

And the doors swung shut. The impenetrable electronic locks clicked on.

And the lights clicked off.

Cara continued staring in Barnard's direction. Even though she couldn't see her. And then as her eyes adjusted, her form crept out of the dark.

Thoughts running through her head. A mile a minute.

She thought she'd never sleep.

She looked at her cellmate for as long as she could.

And eventually she felt sleep forcing her eyes shut.

So she gave in.

Show you. Tomorrow.

Within five minutes, the day caught up with her and she was asleep.

Her final thought was one of a sliver of hope.

17

She didn't dream of them that night. Her dream was confusing – full of loud noises and contorting shapes. And in the centre, a great CRACK of a sound, like a whip snapping at her ears. So real.

Her eyes shot open.

And the real scene in front of her was somehow even more confusing.

The cell's lights clicked on. Abrams was there, holding a torch, but she wasn't wearing her usual uniform. She was in riot gear.

'What?' she squeaked. Barely audible.

Another guard came into her vision. Harper – also in riot gear. He looked shocked. He had a pistol in his hand. And at her gaze, he raised it slightly.

And then Abrams and Anderson were rushing at her, getting her up, putting her hands behind her back. And she didn't understand.

'There's no gun in here,' a guard behind them all said. Sounded like Truchforth.

Gun? What?

And then she was being dragged out of the cell, her bare feet scraping across the floor.

What was happening? They couldn't do this. She hadn't done anything.

Harper was talking to someone on his headset as she got wrenched out into the Pit.

She twisted her head round till it hurt, so she could look over her shoulder. Truchforth's back standing over Barnard's bed, blocking it.

'I didn't do anything.'

She knew before Truchforth stepped aside.

But that didn't stop the shock of the sight of . . .

The sight of the blood.

Barnard was slumped over the side of her bed. Her eyes were open, a look of blank revulsion painted on her face. Her head was resting on her arm, which was hanging down to the floor, providing a suitable pathway for the estuary of blood to flow from the bullet hole in the centre of her forehead.

She was dead.

PART TWO

Chocolate Bars and Star-bound wishes

Twenty months ago

'Peekaboo!'

Kelvin squealed with glee, clapping his pudgy hands together. It was the sixteenth time in a row that Cara had fooled him, and the small toddler didn't seem to be any the wiser about where she went when she put her hands over her face. She almost felt jealous of his earnest igno-rance, but nonetheless she still felt more kinship towards him than the two formalwear-toting adults dashing from room to room.

She was sitting in a living room that was at least three times bigger than her entire student apartment. She had biked to the house, and couldn't quite believe her eyes as she entered the cul-de-sac. It was a gated mansion – she'd been buzzed in. She'd never been anywhere so fancy.

'We've left our number on the fridge,' Mrs Stoker, dressed in a red satin gown that Cara could admire but would never wish to wear herself, said for the umpteenth time. 'And you know where the nappies are?'

'You've already shown me the nappies . . . three times actually,' Cara said, laughing.

Mrs Stoker didn't laugh. Just stared at her.

Noted. Not a woman with a sense of humour.

'Your number's in my phone too,' Cara said, flatly.

'Of course,' Mrs Stoker said. 'Good.' And she disappeared again.

Cara suppressed a sigh for Kelvin's benefit. *Your mummy's a bit of an arsehole, little dude* . . . And scooped him up from his makeshift hammock on the floor. She rested him on her shoulder, bouncing him ever so slightly and slowly revolving, until Kelvin was looking out of the glass patio doors into the night.

Kelvin laughed, proclaiming 'Pink!' at the top of his little voice.

Mr Stoker came in wearing a tux. 'Did I hear someone talking gibberish?' He was smiling and decidedly less stressed, although he was trying and failing to do up his top button.

Cara wondered where they were going looking so fancy.

'Don't let her play that all night,' he said. 'Rots her brain.' Cara looked around to the sofa, where eight-year-old Tilly was silently jabbing a Nintendo Wii controller at a large plasma screen. She seemed to be guiding some kind of ball around a maze with her movements.

'Sure,' Cara said, as Kelvin gave out a cough, and Tilly made the ball go the wrong way and exclaimed loudly.

'Dad, I'm trying to concentrate.'

'Sorry, hunny-bun,' he laughed, kissing his daughter

on the head, and looking to Cara. 'I've moved Kelvin's cot into Tilly's room for tonight. My wife doesn't think we need to, but he usually sleeps with us, so I did anyway. Just don't mention it before we leave or she'll make a thing of it.'

Cara nodded.

Mr Stoker looked at his watch and called, 'Dear, we need to go.'

Mrs Stoker came back in the room, looking like she'd run a marathon since last being present, but also managing to still look radiant. 'Right, OK. I think I'm . . . OK. Now, you're sure you have everything?'

'I have everything,' Cara said, careful not to show any emotion.

She got no emotion back.

'Thank you for doing this at such short notice,' Mr Stoker cut in. 'Our usual sitter's always very reliable, but we couldn't get hold of her.'

'No problem,' Cara said as Mrs Stoker came and kissed Kelvin. She got a whiff of sickly-sweet perfume that made her want to throw up and, as she came over, she saw that Mrs Stoker's beauty was offset by a row of crooked teeth.

As his mother kissed Kelvin, he squirmed in Cara's arms, as though he was already getting embarrassed by affection. Next, Mrs Stoker took two steps towards Tilly, and then stopped. Cara watched as her expression changed from love to something darker. Something more like annoyance. They must have fallen out. As soon as her expression had changed, it snapped back.

'We'll be back by 11.30,' Mr Stoker said, and Cara nodded, cradling Kelvin's head.

The parents went to the front door, but Mrs Stoker paused and looked back, wordlessly staring at Cara, once again assessing the scene. She seemed to accept Cara as a worthy keeper of her children – as though Cara's spotless BabysitterVIP rating was inconsequential compared to the ruthless gaze of a mother.

Mr Stoker opened the front door and his wife waltzed out into the night. He looked after her with something that looked a little like weathered disdain, before he followed her.

Cara went to the front door with Kelvin, careful to shield him from the harsh October evening, to watch the black-as-night BMW reverse out of the driveway.

'Say goodbye to Mummy and Daddy,' Cara whispered in Kelvin's ear, and he looked around to watch as the car peeled away. 'Say goodbye now.'

'Got no face!' Kelvin said, pointing off into the dark, seemingly onto some other track of his mind.

'I guess that'll do,' Cara laughed, going back into the house, and shutting the door with her leg.

Over the next few hours, Cara played with Kelvin while letting Tilly play on her games a little longer than she probably should have. Kelvin only filled his nappy once, so she chalked that up as a win, and Tilly was no problem at all, bewitched by the television.

By the time Tilly was nodding off on the sofa, her controller poised to bowl a digital ball in a digital bowling alley that was cursed never to be bowled, Cara decided she had better put them to bed.

She carried Kelvin upstairs first, checking the clock: 8.30 p.m.

Cara went through the door with the pink, sparkly, cut-out letters spelling 'TILLY' emblazoned on it, to find an equally pink, sparkly room. Kelvin's cot had already been dragged in and placed at the end of Tilly's bed, as Mr Stoker had said, so Cara put him down inside, giving him his favourite green dinosaur plush to sleep with (another curt instruction).

Cara felt a chill, and didn't locate where it was coming from, until the flowery curtains billowed with a gust of wind from outside. The window was ajar and she quickly shut it with an involuntary shiver.

She turned away from the window, and then, thinking again, turned back and looked out into the night, into the quiet cul-de-sac. Everything was silent, still. Where she lived, there'd be at least one gang of young people smoking and causing a ruckus on the corner. She was always unsettled by that, but the silence of the Stokers' street was unsettling in its own way too. She shut the curtains, with another small shiver that this time had nothing to do with the wind.

Kelvin made a spluttering laugh, and Cara went back to his crib, tucking the blankets in under him.

She went down to get Tilly, and found that she was so soundly asleep, she had to be carried upstairs too.

With both children tucked up, Cara headed back to the lounge, turned the Wii off and started searching for a film to watch. The Stokers had all the film channels, nothing like her paltry selection at home, and she curled up on the sofa and settled on *Friday the 13th Part 2.*

It didn't take long for her eyelids to start feeling heavy and sleep to become inevitable. Her eyes closed and . . .

A clatter. Her eyes snapped open, sleep now gone. The clatter came from the kitchen. Her senses heightened. No other sound apart from the television. The second victim had just fallen to Jason. She muted it. And got up. What had made that sound? And why did she have that feeling – the feeling you feel on the back of your neck. The feeling of someone who shouldn't be there watching you.

She took a deep breath. Swung round. And went to the kitchen doorway. The door stood open. Inside was dark – the ghosts of a breakfast bar, a countertop, cupboards, and something in the corner, by the window. A mass illuminated by the moonlight. She didn't even wait to let her brain wonder what it was. She flicked on the light.

And breathed out. The room was empty. The mass was a pink backpack on the windowsill. A plastic cup lay on the floor, must have fallen from the counter somehow. That was all. Too many scary films. Her nerves relaxed.

And her eyes fell on a sideboard where there was a bucket of ice and a bottle of white wine chilling in it. There was a note by it:

FOR WHEN THE KIDS ARE ASLEEP
from the STOKERS

Cara smiled. She'd never had anyone let her drink wine on the job before, let alone actively encourage her. She briefly wondered whether this was a test, whether BabySitterVIP were going to hear of this and her rating was going to go plummeting. But she was bored and thirsty, and one or two glasses couldn't hurt. She wasn't a complete lightweight – she could probably finish off the bottle and still be OK when the Stokers got back.

So she started opening cupboards, until finally she found a wine glass almost as big as a fishbowl. The sounds from before were out of her mind now – she even absent-mindedly picked up the plastic cup and replaced it on the counter, wondering only half-heartedly how it fell off in the first place.

She brought the glass to the table with the wine and unsheathed the bottle from its icy scabbard. Like pulling the sword from the stone. It was her favourite – Banbroad Castle, Sauvignon Blanc. What a coincidence – but now she almost had to drink it. It was like it was fate. Or how could they have known otherwise?

She shook the thought out of her head, went back to the sofa, pouring herself a glass, and turned the volume back on the TV. She rested her head on a plump, velvet pillow, took a deep sip of cold fruitful wine, and watched the group of teens dwindle. At some point, it was their fault for sticking around. If a deranged killer was on the loose, surely the first thing you would do is run. Just go, get the hell out of Dodge . . . Don't stick around and scream, and barricade yourself into a small building or run out onto a pier or leave the group and go off alone.

You couldn't do any of these things and then complain when you got murdered.

Cara yawned. There was something incredibly homely about the house, even despite its size. What she would give to live here, instead of her pokey little flat – and even then when that lease was up, she would be back with her aunt, sleeping on the sofa. Maybe she should have been born a Stoker. These kids would never know what it was to eat beans out of a can, or work two jobs on top of studying, or be afraid to let anyone see where you lived.

She yawned again, and this time her eyes drooped. She hadn't realised how tired she was. She slid down the sofa, and put her feet up. Bloody hell, this was the comfiest sofa ever. But then, of course it was.

She tried to focus on the film, drank some more wine, and then put her glass on the table. She lay back and closed her eyes listening to the last victim plead for her life. It didn't do much good – her screams indicated that she was definitely getting stabbed to death, the killer escaping. Ready for another go-around in a few years when the movie studio ran out of ideas. The credits started and the surprisingly soft music was soothing. If this kept up, she could almost see herself going to . . .

Her eyes snapped open but she didn't quite know why. A sound? Must have been. How long had she been asleep? She felt around her for her phone but couldn't find it. The television was now showing some kind of black and white musical – it looked like it was set on a New York street and was about a hotel bellboy.

She straightened up and looked around, rubbing her eyes. Her wine glass was empty but the bottle was still two thirds full. Lucky she hadn't drunk any more really. At least the Stokers would see she was a responsible drinker.

Cara got up and put the wine bottle in her backpack. She took the empty glass into the kitchen and rinsed it, putting it in the glass cupboard.

A creak. And then another.

Right above her.

Like someone was walking around upstairs.

The back of her neck exploded in tingles, as there was the sound of a door closing. Someone was in the house. She had no idea how, but someone was upstairs. With the children.

Was it the Stokers? No. Why would they leave her asleep? They'd surely wake her up, chastise her for sleeping on the job. No, it couldn't be them.

Maybe a neighbour who had a key? But why? And again, why leave her on the sofa?

This had to be an intruder. And she was the only one who could protect the children.

She felt for her phone to call the police, and remembered she hadn't found it. No time for that.

She pushed herself to go back into the lounge, as quickly as she could make herself. She had to go upstairs, and she rounded the corner to the staircase, reached out for the banister and looked up to the landing.

Her world splintered. She froze, looking up at the landing. She knew in that second that what she saw would be etched in her mind forever. Her hand tightened around the banister, her only connection to an evil world.

There was a figure at the top of the stairs. Shrouded in darkness. It was a tall, hulking human. Holding something in its left hand – something shiny. The figure was still. As still as Cara herself. They stood regarding each other.

The figure had something on his head. A mask. At least she hoped it was. Because under its hood, Cara could see no face – just pink skin where a face should be.

Cara's breath hitched. She knew she had to move, she knew she should be hurtling up the stairs, but she was stuck, motionless.

But the figure was not. Its head snapped to the side, as though it was regarding Cara. And then it took the first step down the stairs.

Cara's heart lurched – powerless to watch as it took another. And then another. And slowly the figure came into the light.

She couldn't tell if it was a man or a woman. The figure was wearing a boiler suit, masking its build. And the hood around its head came from a jacket it had over the suit. And the face – the . . .

No-Face. Kelvin had said it before, when they were waving the Stokers goodbye. Had he seen this person? Had they been waiting all this time? No-Face. The little boy described him perfectly.

Every step, No-Face seemed to grunt. Cara felt sick as her eyes slid down to what the figure was holding. A gun – a pistol – with a long snout of its own. Glinting in the light.

As the figure stepped ever closer, Cara thought only of one thing. Not her own safety. Not the encroaching danger. She thought of the children.

It was halfway down the stairs now, and Cara hadn't moved a muscle. She willed herself to break out of her fear, but she couldn't, and the more she tried, the more she seemed stuck, as though she were standing in quicksand.

Closer and closer it stepped, until they were face to face. Face to – to No-Face. No-Face twisted in front of her own, and Cara closed her eyes, waiting for the pain, as a bullet pushed its way through her skull.

But it never came. There was just another creak. She felt something press into her right hand – she didn't know why, but she gripped. And then Cara felt the presence move away.

She waited five seconds and opened her eyes.

She was alone.

And she was able to move.

She looked around. The patio door was open. No-Face had gone. She looked down at her right hand and instantly let go. The pistol. It clattered off the bottom step and left her field of view.

The children.

She took the stairs two at a time, and went to the closed door of Tilly's room. There was a smear of red across the white satin paint. No. God no. This can't have happened. This wasn't possible.

She opened the door.

And it all came tumbling down.

No.

No.

No.

NO.

NO. The scene, laid out in front of her like some sick present just for her, burned into her retinas. The bed. The cot. The red.

The entire contents of her stomach lurched out of her throat as she vomited into her own hands. She staggered and slipped, the sick being followed by a deep and guttural yowl.

'NO,' she screamed. 'NO, NO, NO.'

Red.

The . . .

The children . . .

Why . . . would . . . but . . . gone . . . dead . . .

Why?

She felt the urge to be sick again and tried to get up, but slid on her own vomit and slammed her head off the wall, before going sprawling. She cried and screamed into the carpet until she had no energy left.

She knew she should get up, call the police. But what would she say? How could she ever even start to describe what she saw? She didn't want to, she shouldn't have to. And she had no energy to get up anyway.

So she just lay there. And at that moment, she wanted

to die. And if willing made it so, she would have.

The house was silent. There was no one alive in here to make any sound, except her. And was she really alive anymore? No – at least not in the way she was before walking up those stairs, opening that door.

She lay there for seconds, minutes, hours, days, months.

It didn't matter.

Nothing mattered anymore.

The world was wrong.

And, in some far away universe, Cara heard the familiar sound of keys in a front door.

1

How long?

How long had she been here? Darkness. Not even her Cuff lit up anymore.

And, more pressingly, had she ever not been?

'What are you doing?' she had said, as Anderson and Abrams dragged her down the Pit – not out of the Unit, but further into it. Into the dining room. But they didn't go towards the corridor and the yard. Instead they went to the opposite wall, where Abrams felt around on a certain tile, while Anderson wrestled with her.

'What are you doing?'

She got no response.

Abrams finally found what she was looking for, got her fingers behind the tile and pulled. A hidden door opened up, and revealed a corridor beyond, much like the one mirroring it on the other side.

'What—?'

They hoisted her down the corridor. She tried to resist, but there was little point. They passed many sealed doors.

'I didn't do it. I didn't kill her.'

'SHUT UP,' Anderson shouted at the top of his lungs.

'You were locked in. There were only two of you in the cell. Can you tell us why we would think anything other than you killing her happened?'

They got to the end of the corridor. A dead end. With just one door. This door looked like it was from a prison of the past. In fact, they all had, all the ones in this corridor. It was like getting a glimpse down a staff corridor in Disneyland. Behind the magic.

'There ain't many places you could have stashed that gun, and when we find it, you're over, Lockhart. Even more than you were.'

Abrams took out an old bunch of heavy-looking rusted keys and put them in the lock. The door creaked open. They took her inside – her Cuff blinking off across the threshold. It was a cell, but even smaller. There was only one bed and it looked ancient and decrepit – the mattress stiffer even than hers. There was a toilet, but it had no seat, and the sink had no mirror above it.

'What is this?' she said.

Anderson smiled. 'Your new home, Butcher.'

'No,' she said, looking around. Abrams relinquished her grip and stood back, but Anderson's seemed to tighten. 'You can't do this, I didn't do anything.'

Anderson let go, shoving her further into the cell. He stepped back out into the corridor, as Cara stepped towards him.

'I didn't kill her.'

'Sure you didn't,' Anderson said, smiling. 'We'll have to see what Krotes wants to do with you.' He slammed the door shut. And the room was plunged into the complete darkness she now knew well.

If she had to guess, she'd say that was about twelve hours ago.

But who knew?

There was absolutely nothing to indicate what the time was, or how much had passed.

Even less than outside of this room.

All she knew was that she was getting hungry and thirsty, and no one had come to give her any food or drink.

She would have run her mouth under the tap, if she knew exactly where the tap was. She knew it was towards the back of the cell, but she didn't feel like reaching around in the dark like an idiot trying to find it.

The only light in the room was a small strip under the main door – a sign that there was life outside this room, a reminder. Sometimes the light faltered, a shadow flicked across it – as someone walked along the corridor. But the shadow never stayed, as if they'd thrown her in here and forgotten about her.

The shock gave way to tears, and then gave way to shock again. What was happening? What was happening out there? The guards were combing her cell, no doubt. Trying to find a murder weapon that couldn't possibly be there.

You didn't do it. You didn't do it. You didn't do it.

BANG. Like a whip-crack. Twice. In her dream.

Gunshots.

Had those sounds been real?

Had she heard the gun that killed Stephanie Barnard?

How had she not woken up if that was so?

And how had someone else got into her cell?

You didn't do it. You didn't do it. You didn't do it.

But who else?

Someone else.

You didn't do it. You didn't do it. You didn't do it.

Not her.

You didn't do it. You didn't do it. You didn't do it.

And somehow, she found she had a few more tears to shed.

2

A daze. A state of consciousness where she thought, if she wasn't careful, she could tumble off the edge of existence.

The only thing that kept her tethered was hunger. Roaring hunger. It hurt. But it was also comforting. It was something to focus on that wasn't the sight of Barnard draped over her bed – that cavernous hole in the middle of her forehead oozing blood down her arm, pooling on the floor. Or the sight of No-Face ducking around the corner. Or the sight she was presented with when she opened Tilly's blood-spattered door. Or the sight of the judge and jury as they convicted her of Kelvin and Tilly Stoker's murders.

Four images that would never leave her – that would define her forever.

Was she mad?

A wrenching sound of metal on metal, and Cara looked towards the door. The sliver of light on the ground had become much larger. A tray was shoved through the slot – with a bowl and a mug. Cara got into a sitting position, as another slot opened further up the door. Harper's face appeared in the opening.

'I'll be back in half an hour to collect the tray,' he said, lifelessly – as though he were directing some words at an object that couldn't talk back. 'Whether you've eaten or not.'

'Harper,' Cara said, standing up, and going to the door, 'Harper, please, I just want to know what's going on.' His face was in front of hers now – the air from the corridor playing on her face. She could feel the sticky tear tracks down her cheek. 'I need to know.'

'I'll be back in half an hour to collect the tray,' Harper said again. Such a small viewing slot but he still found it hard to meet her gaze. 'I'll leave this open so you have light to eat by. Don't want the cell getting any dirtier.' Matter-of-fact, cold, calculated – a different man to the one she knew.

'Please, Harper, I just . . .'

And then he was gone, and all she could see was the corridor. She went right up to the slot and looked either way – the corridor was empty. She cursed under her breath.

A secret corridor – so at least she was safe from the other prisoners. But she still had to deal with the guards – looking in, gawking. Looking at the Butcher and her sad little life.

But she would have to deal with the other prisoners at some point. News would get out about Barnard's death – hell, Anderson was probably spreading that news like hot butter on toast, with a smile on his face. When they let her out of here – whatever they found – she would be Public Enemy No. 1.

Cara shuffled back from the slot quickly. As though someone – Liza or Minnie or Peter or Aqua – had shot their hand through, trying to strangle her. Exactly what would happen if they knew where she was. But they wouldn't know – they couldn't possibly know about that hidden door.

As she stepped back, the rectangle of light from the corridor was cast on the floor, coincidentally where the tray had come to rest. Cara went to the tray. She picked up the mug and swallowed half the water before realising that she should probably savour it. So she slowed down.

She picked up the bowl and jabbed at what was in it with the spoon. It was brown mush. With chunks of something.

Her stomach lurched, as if it itself was disappointed, as she realised what it was.

Liver and onions.

As though they'd seen her picking at it the first day – not eating a bite.

But then she thought of something even worse.

Liver and onions – Barnard's favourite meal.

She would have vomited then, if there was anything in her stomach to come up. She threw the bowl down so some onions slopped on the cell floor.

And then the hunger took over, and she quickly scoffed up the pieces of liver, swallowing them before she could even chew. When all the chunks were gone, she ate the onions and the sauce, with somewhat more enjoyment, liking the taste of the thick gravy and the slippery onions in her mouth. She finished too quickly – and she put down the bowl in disappointment. She was still very hungry. The portion size had been half of what she'd got in the dining room. And her eyes fell on the small pile of gravy and onions that had slopped onto the floor.

No – she couldn't . . .

Could she?

Not this early on in . . .

But she did.

She took the spoon and scraped the onions off the floor, stopping them with her finger. She ate them, and then went back for the sauce. She felt slightly ashamed, but not ashamed enough to make sure she got everything she could from the patch on the floor. It was strange, but those few extra onions filled her up more than the entire bowl. Maybe because she felt a little sense of triumph.

You thought I was too high and mighty to eat off the floor, well I showed you.

She laughed – a hollow sound. With nothing to it.

She threw the spoon into the bowl and leant back against the bed – as full as she could hope to be, but still craving more. She went to finish the water and saw that she had forgotten something on the tray. A small tablet. Her sedative. At least they were still giving it to her. She took it with the last of the water and then went to the sink and filled the mug up with water again.

She thought she should use the toilet, while she had some faint light. So she squatted over the bowl and tried to pee. She supposed, quite soon, she would have to try and do something worse, but she only had to pee now. She did it, flushed, and realised for the first time that there wasn't a shower in the cell. She already stank, with the cold sweats and the crying. And now she couldn't wash – she couldn't even have that liberty. At some point, they would have to let her wash, surely? But then, she wouldn't put it past them not to.

Harper appeared in the hatch. 'Push the tray along the floor. You can keep the mug.'

'Thank you,' Cara said, and instantly felt a thousand times more ashamed than she had when she'd eaten off the floor. 'Please tell me what's going on, I need to know.'

Harper looked at her and opened his mouth and then closed it again. And then opened it, but all he said was, 'Push the tray along the floor. Through the slot.'

'Harper . . .' Pathetically.

Harper paused. 'I don't understand what's happening. I just don't. Please just push the tray through the slot.'

'Harper . . .'

'NOW.'

She started, silently went to the tray and pushed it along the floor, through the slot and out into the corridor. Harper's face disappeared, as he picked it up, and then he was back.

'Please . . .' Cara began, but Harper pulled the viewer shut.

Plunging her into darkness once more.

3

She wasn't asleep.

But she wasn't awake either.

The mattress felt like she was resting on a granite slab, and the thin sheet didn't keep out the cold.

She'd had dinner shoved through the slot in the door a few hours ago – or was it a few minutes ago – or even a few seconds?

She was perpetually in night. And always in day.

How long would she be here? Until they figured out she hadn't killed Barnard? What if they never did?

After all, they'd never worked out that she hadn't killed Kelvin and Tilly Stoker. They'd gone for the easy option – blame the babysitter, but then all evidence had pointed to her. It – No-Face – had seen to that.

Who had framed her this time – and to what end?

She had lain down and taken it before – the injustice of justice wrongly carried out – but she wasn't going to do it again.

If no one else was going to prove her innocence, she would have to do it herself.

Yes.

She felt slightly better just thinking that. She would

show them that Cara Lockhart wouldn't be taken twice.

Hmm. Very good. She almost believed that. Very confident.

But she couldn't exactly do anything from inside this room, now could she? The Hole.

'Detective Lockhart in the Hole,' she said, laughing for a bit and then crying. She cried for herself. And she cried for Barnard – a nice, clever woman who had only ever shown her kindness. And, after, Cara curled up in bed – eyes shut.

Could the brief conversation they had had before lights out be the reason for her death?

This place, it's not what you think. Was someone protecting the secret?

Something moved in the cell. Her eyes shot open but were presented with no more visual information than when they were closed. But she could hear something – someone. There was someone in here with her.

How was that possible? It wasn't. But there it was – a fact. There was someone in the corner.

She looked to the only bit of light in the room – the thin strip under the door. It was interrupted twice – a strip with two breaks in it – where it used to be whole before. Two legs, standing there.

Her eyes raised to where the person's torso would be and their head. She saw nothing – just blackness – but she knew they were there. Beyond her vision. Standing there, watching her.

Cara took in a deep breath and then held it, listening for something, anything. A set of breaths, maybe. Or a shuffling. But there was nothing. But still she knew. And after a few more seconds, she knew who it was. Because she knew how it felt to be under this presence's gaze. It was him.

No-Face.

Standing there.

Like something from a cartoon.

Just watching her with no eyes. Haunting her.

'Go away,' Cara said, or maybe she thought it. She supposed it didn't matter either way. 'You can't be here.'

But what if he was? What if it was No-Face that had killed Barnard, shot her in the head and framed Cara? Again. But why and how? Could No-Face walk through walls, a locked cell door?

No-Face watched her. She couldn't see him, but yet she could. He was there all right, his lifeless gaze all encompassing, his pale featureless face accusing. What was he doing? Or was he doing nothing – and was that entirely the point? To faze her.

'Get out of my head,' Cara said. 'Get out.'

At that, the thing shifted in front of her – she imagined him twisting his head around as he had that night – regarding her with blankness. And then it stepped towards her. She heard it – a distinct footstep, but it wasn't just one. It was two, and the footstep sounded like a *clop*.

Ridiculous. This wasn't happening. But just because it wasn't didn't make it any less terrifying.

'You're not there,' Cara whispered harshly. 'YOU'RE NOT HERE. You can't be.'

And there was a grunt in response – a small grunt,

easy to miss, but it was there. Or was it?

'What are you doing?' Cara tried.

And there was another grunt. And then a click. A dull grey light lit up the cell and he was there. No-Face – standing before her, the front of his head just a stretch of pink skin. But this No-Face wasn't wearing a mask, he actually had no face. The absurdity of the sight was what made it so absolutely abhorrent. As she looked, a tear formed at the bottom of where one of No-Face's eyes should have been – a red viscous tear, that trailed down its hollow face.

In the squalor of the cell, he was all to see. Or nothing. And he was less than an arm's-length away.

Cara shut her eyes. And opened them again. He was still there, in the dull wavy grey light. Standing tall in that blue boiler suit. She screwed up her eyes again and opened them. Still there. He had something in his hand – something long and plastic. And he was pointing it past Cara. It was a television remote.

The light was coming from behind her. She tore her eyes from No-Face to see where he was pointing. He'd clicked the button and that had turned something on. And she saw. On the back wall, there had been a screen, that she hadn't been able to see before. And now it was on. And that grey wavering light was the opening shot of a black-and-white New York street. One she knew quite well.

'No, no, please,' Cara said, and looked back at No-Face.

She started. He was gone – mask, suit, even remote, disappeared into thin air. Like – no, *because*, he was never there in the first place.

But the screen was still on, and the camera was panning up to the street sign and the title of the film appeared. *RAIN ON ELMORE STREET.* Copyright notice. The timer was in the corner, ticking away – and in the darkness of the rest of the room, it bore into her. The camera went back down to fall upon Eugene, and she stopped watching, as he started to sing 'Revolving Doors'. She had spent so long wanting some light, and something to focus on, and now she had it – she felt almost ungrateful when she shoved her pillow over her face and willed herself to sleep.

At least it wasn't that loud, and it would be over soon enough.

Three hours later, Eugene and Giratina went off on their honeymoon on a cruise ship and a choir bade them farewell. Cara was still awake – the pillow was thick, but somehow she could still see the grey, putrid light of the film.

She took the pillow off her head to delight in seeing the loopy letters return and read 'THE END'. The screen clicked off and she was plunged into darkness.

She actually laughed in exaltation. It was over.

She put her head back down and closed her eyes. It was peaceful – silent and dark. She was silly not to want this.

There was a click.

And even through her closed eyelids, she could see the light. The grey light.

She knew what she was going to see before she opened her eyes. But she didn't want to believe it. And anyway she could hear it. The swell of an orchestra. She looked to see the New York street on the screen.

'No . . .' Cara said desperately, 'no, no, no, no, no.'

The camera panned up from the street.

The words with the street sign.

Copyright notice beneath.

'No, no, no, no, NO.'

Pan down to Eugene, the doorman outside of the fancy hotel.

'NO.' Cara jumped up and clattered over to the door, slamming her fist against it, again and again and again. 'You can't do this. You CAN'T do this. Let me out. Let me out!'

And behind her, on the screen, Eugene took off his cap, bowed low to Miss Giratina entering the building, and started to sing about the life of revolving doors.

4

The film didn't stop. It never stopped. And days passed.

Cara had something to measure time by now, and she had something to focus on. And Madeleine Krotes was right – one showing of *Rain on Elmore Street* was a lifetime, one hundred and eighty minutes of a lifetime which stretched on forever. And it wasn't a good life – it was one of no colour, and crispy sounds, and bad rhyme schemes.

It was hell.

Cara lost count of how many times it had played at about number seven, but then she thought that was probably all to the good.

But things weren't going well. She had started singing along a few days ago.

But now she wasn't just singing along, she was talking along with most of the lines. It was an involuntary action. Somewhat comforting – like a conversation echoed. But, at the same time, it was torture. She was vicariously living a life already mapped out, and it included at least a few redundant musical numbers.

The next time dinner was shoved through the slot, only the bottom one was opened. She greedily dived onto the tray and started eating before she realised what it was. Liver and onions – again. It wasn't the same menu as the dining room – they must have been making liver and onions especially for her. Just because she hated it. She chewed the liver this time – it felt old, tasteless, and as rubbery as an old tyre. She still swallowed it – every chunk, but she didn't enjoy it and was sure she could feel every bit sitting in her stomach. She left the onions and sauce until the end, so she had something to look forward to. If that was the right phrase.

She finished and pushed the tray back through the slot so hard she heard it clatter against the other side of the corridor wall. She spent the rest of the day thinking that maybe they had made a mistake giving her liver and onions again. Yes, that must be it – tomorrow would be better. Tomorrow they would right their error.

They didn't. Seven showings of *Elmore Street* later and a tray was shoved through the slot. Liver and onions. She ate, washed it down with water that didn't taste like it was filtered through the devil's intestines, and shoved it back. She couldn't bring herself to complain – even in her head.

She had to wash. The smell of herself had almost become another physical presence in the room. The stink of her actually stung her nostrils, and every time she lifted her armpits, now less stubbly and more just hairy, a waft of body odour filled the room. So she just stopped doing it – in fact she tried to move as little as possible. She could almost feel her muscles atrophying as she lay there.

So the task of washing, although disgusting, was welcomed.

Her tray always came with two pieces of kitchen roll, folded over into one. She took it and went over to the sink, wetting the paper as much as she could without it disintegrating. Then she took off her top, and her vest, and washed as best she could – under the arms mostly, but also everywhere else. She didn't know how much it would help, but at least it felt a little better – the cold water on her skin, even from the rough paper.

When she was done, she balled up the now rather smelly rag of paper and slopped it into the empty bowl, before kicking the tray through the slot with her foot. Five minutes later, someone – she didn't know if it was Harper or not anymore – came along and audibly gave a groan of disgust. Cara actually laughed, genuinely.

The slot closed.

There continued to be no rain on Elmore Street despite being called that. Barnard had said that to her, hadn't she? Yes, she had. And now Barnard was dead and she was trapped in this endless limbo. She didn't know which of them had it worse. She wondered what Barnard would have said – and knew she would probably have chosen death. Well, looks like Cara drew the short straw.

You didn't do it. You didn't do it. You didn't do it.

But she didn't really have to think that over and over. She knew. She did not kill Barnard. Who had framed her this time – and to what end? And who would want to kill Barnard – her only friend in this abomination of a place. Barnard had seemed to be well liked, not having arguments with anyone. Apart from maybe Minnie, but even that squabble had come to nothing.

She had lain down and taken it before – the injustice of justice wrongly carried out – but she wasn't going to do it again.

If no one else was going to prove her innocence, she would have to do it herself.

Yes.

Wait . . .

Wait a second . . .

Hadn't she thought that before? All of that – she'd thought it before, hadn't she? Word for word. Was she repeating herself?

Her mouth opened and before she could stop herself, she croaked, 'Detective Lockhart in the Hole.'

And then she laughed.

Why did she do that?

She hadn't even been thinking—

Had she?

She looked at the screen. Eugene was there, doomed to do the same thing over and over and over. A revolving door. Sometimes it was nice to dream for more, but he would always go back to his revolving door. What did that song mean – was it just about his character, as it seemed at first, his life? Or was it something more? To her, as someone who'd watched this dozens of times, it seemed about the life of a film character, doomed to a real-life Groundhog Day, but one that never changed. Did Eugene know that? Did he stare out at her, feeling forced to say and sing the lines, just as she had said the one she knew she had said before. Was he looking out at her with longing, or with relief he wasn't her?

Wait . . .

No.

She croaked. 'Stupid.' And that was an understatement. Absolutely ridiculous. It was a film. Eugene wasn't real – he was played by an actor called Roger Steyford, who was no doubt long dead, and not trapped inside a film.

Cara really needed to talk to someone, see someone – she was going crazy.

She looked at the screen, and saw Eugene cue up for the first musical number.

He looked at the screen as he always did.

But this time, she didn't feel like he was looking out at the entire audience.

This time, he was looking at her.

5

Seven tips of the hat and some more liver and onions. Then seven revolving doors and some more liver and onions. Things became routine. The only thing more certain than a breath following a breath was that ten-second period between *Rain on Elmore Street* ending and *Rain on Elmore Street* beginning. Cara lived in that moment – the peace and quiet, the only ten seconds where she felt like she could change things.

But the only thing that was changing was her sanity slipping away.

And on it went.

What was that about sanity?

She sniggered.

Sometimes she thought she heard distant footsteps coming from beyond the door, a muttering. No-Face. Out there. It didn't make any sense. She hadn't been framed by a monster that could walk through walls, into a prison. She had been framed by a man in a mask.

Still, it terrified her. And that was when she focused on the film.

They seemed to look at her more now – the characters

— with every viewing in fact. Eugene's eyes lingered and even Giratina occasionally glanced at her with disdain.

Sometimes she smiled at them.

She liked Mr Mogul though — he never looked at the camera, never looked at her. He was too wrapped up in how amazing he was to notice anything else, even the pathetic sack of human bones she had turned into on the other side of the screen.

Mr Mogul was gearing up to do his big song. Inviting Giratina into his premiere suite. Pouring her a glass of champagne at ten in the morning. And then talking to her about his business until he leapt up, straightened his bow tie, and began:

'I can sell a Q-tip, a U-bend or manure
And everyone will come and lap it up
But you see now change is a concept that is strange
And barely even worth—'

The film cut out. The cell went dark.

Was this it?

Was it done?

Was she saved?

She practically basked in the dark, soaking it in. Already managing to think the worst.

Was it just a glitch?

Would the film come back on in a few minutes, a few seconds?

Right then, right at that moment, she didn't care.

Five minutes went by. She knew, she had an internal

clock now. The film played in her mind, almost as clearly as it did on the screen.

A scraping sound. She'd heard it before. Was it the shutter? She opened her eyes – no, it was still dark. Another sound – it was coming from the door. The locks. She kept staring upwards – not wanting to believe what she was hearing. She felt that if she moved, she might break the illusion – realise that this was actually a dream, she had succeeded in falling asleep. But then the cell was flooded with light, and there was the sound of the door swinging open.

Cara shot up and looked around. Dr Toby Trenner was standing there in the open doorway. He looked exactly the same as he had the first time they'd met, like he too was repeating himself. Same suit, same smile, same tussled hair, same kind eyes.

He looked at Cara with a friendliness that, now more than ever, seemed out of place.

Cara stood up on shaky legs. 'Are you real?'

Toby's smile widened, even though that didn't seem possible. 'Probably not the best opening line to say to your psychiatrist.'

It was a joke.

Cara didn't laugh.

Unsurprisingly.

Toby gestured back to the bed Cara had just got up from.

'Please have a seat, Cara. We have a lot to discuss today. Seems like you've been a busy bee.'

6

The cell lights flickered on as Dr Toby Trenner stepped into the room. It was almost as if his presence alone had illuminated the room.

Cara sat down on the bony bed and watched as Toby looked around and then saw he would have to sit on the bed too. He sat on the opposite end, rather delicately closing his folder and perching there.

'Well,' he said, looking around, barely able to hide the disgust on his face, 'this is a sorry state of affairs I find you in. You know, I didn't even know this place existed. A hidden wall in a dining room. Obvious now you've seen it. Funny the things the mind just skates over, isn't it?' He gave out a little chortle.

Cara couldn't relate. Her mind was now wired in such a way that she picked out every little detail. All those viewings of *Elmore Street* had made her hypersensitive to everything, as though she were replaying the real scene over and over in her head even though it was still happening. There was a stray thread on Toby's cuff that was annoying Cara. And she paid particular attention to how Toby's smile had faltered ever so slightly as he had sat down on the lumpy bed. And the way his nostrils flared for the smallest of microseconds as Cara's body odour wafted to him.

Cara very much hoped this state would pass – it seemed to slow down real life. And she had no desire to be a real-world Sherlock Holmes. 'Can you please, just . . .' she gestured to Toby's cuff.

The good doctor looked down and picked the thread off with two fingers acting as tweezers. He tossed it out into the room. 'Thank you.'

'Don't mention it,' Cara said, gruffly – without a single emotion towards what that phrase actually meant.

Toby got a pen from his top pocket, clicked it and opened his folder. He clicked, with the click of the pen, into therapist mode – his eyes seemed to show some more emotion – something that was almost . . . what was the word? Friendly. That type of concern that only a true friend could conjure up.

She'd forgotten the word 'friendly'. Great.

'Are you all right, Cara?'

Cara shook herself from the memory and focused in the present. And then finally on what Toby had just said. 'What?'

'Are you OK?' Toby said again.

Cara scoffed, shook her head at the audacity. 'You know what, Doctor, I'm just peachy.'

Toby didn't smile. He just shuffled a little, no doubt adjusting to the discomfort of the bed, which he seemed to be slipping off by the second. 'I thought it best, under the circumstances, that we do continue our sessions. I thought you might appreciate the presence of another human, if only for a little bit.'

Cara didn't say anything.

'I thought we could maybe talk some more about your mother.'

Cara laughed – a strange squawk. 'You thought – what?'

'Your mother. There's just a couple of things that . . .'

'You know why I'm here,' Cara hissed, 'you know what those idiots out there are just assuming I did. Again. Again, I'm locked up on assumption. Guilty until proven innocent – if anyone can be bothered to find out. Where's Poirot? Ahhh, he's on holiday, so we'll just lock Cara Lockhart up, I guess. They've kept me here for 76 hours, 14 minutes and 27, 28, 29, 30 seconds, with no shower, barely enough light to eat and piss and shit by, the worst form of torture imaginable, water that tastes like it's been passed through a kettle about ten times and the worst bed I have ever felt. And you come in here and you want to talk about my MOTHER. How does this suit? NO. No, I am not talking about my mother. Not to you. Not to anyone in this place. Never.'

Toby remained silent, but his gaze seemed to soothe, even though he had looked a little taken aback by the outburst. Cara felt herself calming.

Eventually Toby said, 'OK, we don't have to talk about that. But we do have to talk about something, or the guards outside will drag me out. I had to bend a few arms to get in here.'

Cara said nothing.

'What would you like to talk about?' Toby asked.

'Nothing.'

'Cara.'

'I never believed in God,' Cara said, surprising herself even more than she visibly surprised Toby. It was just like when she spoke into the dark – like there was some unseen force writing her lines before she said them. It was like she had just moved onto Elmore Street. 'I never believed in God,' she said again, as if to test whether she had any control at all, 'but now I think I do.' She stopped and looked at Toby.

At some point in all that, he had put his folder down, his pen back in his pocket. 'OK, we can talk about God. Go on, Cara.'

So, without knowing where she was going, she started the journey – 'I grew up in a nice enough way, but I can't remember my father. My only memory of him is his back walking out the door. When I was a little girl, a 4x4 slammed into my mother's car on a country road pinning her inside and she exploded while the Ranger was speeding away. Police didn't seem that interested – no witnesses, treacherous road, no idea whose fault it actually was. Case closed, but not the good way – the shelved way. I went to live with my aunt until she decided to up and leave too, because, frankly, she didn't like me. Still, bit of an overreaction to move to Canada, right?

'So I'm eighteen, alone, and I think I won't use the last of my mother's money to buy a place and set myself up for life – no, I think I'll go to university and try to help. Help people. Help society. So I do a political degree at Huddersfield and then I realise that's not for me, so I transfer to doing journalism in London. Student accommodation in London isn't cheap, so I know I have to use all my free time at work.

'Got one job in a stupid souvenir shop in the Camden Mall, selling teapots and plastic statues of Big Ben to tourists who were just high on the holiday of everything and didn't realise they had no need for that tat, and on nights – on nights – I babysat. Got my profile up on this new app, BabySitterVIP, and for a while it was good. I enjoyed the work. I liked the kids, if not so much the parents, but luckily a babysitter's job description pretty much dictates that the parents will piss off at some point. Parents rate the babysitters at the end of their shift, a star rating – the higher your average star rating, the more clients you get and the "better off" clients you get. I used to pride myself on getting the highest rating every single time. And one day I got offered a lot of money to babysit two children for an upper-class couple in the suburbs. That couple was the Stokers.

'You might have heard of them.

'I doze off on the sofa in the Stoker house and a freak with No-Face shoots the children to death in Matilda's room. I see him— it, coming down the stairs and I can't move, I have to close my eyes. And the thing presses the murder weapon into my hand and leaves. Finally I can move and I go upstairs and— They're dead. They're both dead. There's blood and – stuff – everywhere. And all I can think is why and what and who – who would ever do such a thing?

'The world asked that same question, but it looked back at me and said, "You. You would do such a thing, Miss Cara Lockhart. Now empty your pockets. And look into the camera. And press your fingers into the ink, and then onto the page. Strip off while we hose you down and make sure you haven't shoved anything up your vagina."

'I'm called every name under the sun, and that's only in print. The people who see me manage to come up with worse things somehow, like they're just inventing things on the spot, but I know they're horrible. And by the time you're paraded in front of all the cameras and all the vultures and all the guys in wigs that really are an outdated tradition and are kinda just plain bloody stupid now, prison is almost relief.

'And then this place. And then this. My only friend in here is dead. And everyone outside this door thinks I killed her. And the worst thing is, sometimes, I can't even blame them.

'Look at me. Cara Lockhart – once I was at least. Broken. Rewritten. And for what? Why? I didn't kill Barnard any more than I killed Kelvin Stoker or Tilly Stoker. But here I am. Paying for it all. And the only thing I ever wanted was to be a good person.'

Cara paused, sniffed. Toby had watched her intently through it all, her expression showing nothing. Cara almost wanted him to say something but he didn't, so she continued herself.

'It's a funny thing when everything changes. A revolving door that comes off its hinges, spins out of control.

171

How can everything you've ever done, everything you've ever worked for, everything you've prided yourself on – prided yourself on being – how can all of that not matter one bloody iota?

'It's funny really. If you think about it. Have you thought about it? Because I have – I've had a little time to think, you know. And it is just incredibly, massively, ecstatically hilarious. We're taught that we should be good people, like we're earning points in some kind of invisible morality game, but we're not. Good will never trump evil. Bad acts, or even the accusation of bad acts, can wipe out everything good you've ever done. And sometimes, don't get me wrong, that's a good thing. But sometimes, my time, it's not. It's just really really really funny, isn't it?

'Because there's no way back for me. Ever. They can't unprint those red tops, they can't unclick those keyboards, they can't unsay those words any more than they can change the perceptions in their heads. It's almost like someone just decided that it was my turn to fall. Maybe one day, I drew the short straw in some kind of celestial game.

'So, yes, now I do think there is a God. And I think sometimes maybe he gets a little lonely. And a little drunk. And a little mean. And he likes to have some fun. And he picked me.

'People talk about God and the Devil, but they don't realise that they're the same being. Just on different days.

'So if God is up there right now . . .

'Then screw God.'

7

Dr Tobias Trenner was gone. Had been for seven minutes and thirteen seconds.

After the God stuff, Toby had just got up and produced a small paper cup. Cara knew it well. Medicine. And a bottle of water.

She took it and although she didn't want the tablet, she did want the water. So she swallowed the tablet and upended the water bottle into her mouth, drinking it all at once. By the end, she was wheezing, but she felt momentarily better.

Toby said nothing except, 'I know it seems dark, Cara. But even in darkness, you can find the smallest light.'

What great advice.

Not really.

Toby had slammed on the door till it opened and left.

Rain on Elmore Street had just clicked back on. In the exact same spot it had stopped. Mr Mogul in the middle of a singing line.

Weirdly, Cara actually enjoyed it for the next one and a half viewings. It was a return to normal – the film was bad, but at least it wasn't whatever had just happened.

That whole speech she'd given to Toby. It came out

of nowhere. Like someone else was saying it – *or writing it?* she had thought at the time. Her life was very specifically spiralling out of control, and it was hard not to think that someone was targeting her.

Maybe they are.

Not God. No – maybe someone down here. No-Face, or whoever was beneath it. That was an interesting thought. But what had Cara ever done to deserve being framed for two separate crimes – three murders? Ridiculous – but was it more ridiculous than Cara coincidentally being framed twice? Like someone just wanted the Stoker kids dead and Barnard dead and Cara was the easiest scapegoat? So which one was it – each with more questions than the other.

The tablet was making her drowsy and she didn't want to think about this right now. She'd have to figure out how to get out of this cell first before she could even begin to worry about finding the answers to those questions. This cell was her prison, and then she remembered out there she was still in prison, and that made her burst into laughter. Genuine and erratic laughter.

What was it Eugene sang in his second song?

'The world may seem topsy-turvy, upside-down, inside out

But there's always a good way to look at things
A way to put a smile on your face
So just straighten up your suit and put your tap shoes on
And get ready to put the world in its place.'

'Jog on, Eugene,' Cara said, through choking laughter, 'because Detective Lockhart's in the Hole.'

She laughed her way through the credits of *Elmore Street*, but by the time it started up again, the laughs had turned into cries. She cried for half an hour and, at some point, the film paused again and a tray slid through the hatch, but she was so distraught that she just kicked it right back. She wasn't hungry anyway. The hatch closed straight away.

She just wanted to sleep.

She collapsed onto her bed, and wiped her face and nose with the duvet. And put the pillow over her face, wanting to sleep so much, but thinking that it probably wouldn't happen. But the tablet helped her mellow, and the noise from the film became incoherent and soothing, and she got pulled down into the dark.

And she was glad.

8

A slide and a clang. In the middle of the night. A sort of *Ssshuph-bing*.

Cara opened her eyes. Her mind was still away somewhere else. It was like when you woke up from a terrible dream to slowly recall that everything was OK. Except this was the reverse. Because what she saw was her dank, putrid cell, in the micro-light.

Still here.

Still in prison.

But *Elmore Street* wasn't on. She looked down to see that the far wall was pitch black. In fact, it all was.

But – light? From the door? Maybe she'd imagined it.

Ssshuph-bing.

The noise was real. She hadn't imagined it.

She raised her head. Her back strained against the skeletal bed, promising to ache in the morning. Where was the noise coming from? It sounded close.

Ssshuph. A little square of light appeared on the floor beside her bed, and then *bing* it was gone.

This was almost too much to comprehend and Cara pulled herself out of her sleepy daze. The light? Could it be – the corridor outside her cell?

Yes. And the sound? The shutter where the guards looked in.

She looked up at her cell door just in time for the *Ssshuph*. The shutter opened so a stream of light came through. The door was at an angle where she couldn't see who was looking in. For some reason, she felt incredibly thankful for that.

Bing. The shutter closed.

What was this?

One of the guards being a prick? In the dead of night no less. Maybe one of them had got drunk and decided to play some sort of game? Peter said that the night guards drank, but Cara hadn't believed her. Until now.

For the first time, since the incident anyway, she wished she was in a cell with someone else.

Ssshuph. The drawing across of the shutter. The little rectangle of light shining down onto the floor. And then – *bing*. Gone. Done.

After it happened a few more times, Cara decided she had to see who it was. She had to look through the shutter to see who thought it was a good idea to do this to her. Her heartbeat seemed to double every time that infernal sound completed.

Cara tried to slow her heart, and listen. In between the sound. Trying to hear beyond the door, to who was moving the shutter. Over and over. Again and again. Why would anyone do that? Why would anyone want to bother? All she knew was that it definitely wasn't another prisoner. It had to be a guard, or . . . well . . . or someone else.

She threw her legs over the side of the bed, and touched the cold floor with her bare feet. The connection made this feel real; it wasn't some sick auditory hallucination brought on by sensory deprivation.

Sshuph-bing. Sshuph-bing. Sshuph-bing.

It was getting faster. And faster.

She stood up on shaky legs and stepped towards the door. She could see the shutter opening and closing, opening and closing. But she still couldn't see who it was through the small slit to the corridor outside.

She stepped forward again. As the shutter opened and closed with startling violent motions, all she saw was the corridor. The door to the next cell across the corridor.

Sshuph-bing. Sshuph-bing. Sshuph-bing.

Another step. What was this?

Sshuph-bing. Sshuph-bing. Sshuph-bing.

Another step. She was basically in front of the door now. She reached out and ran a hand over it. *Sshuph* . . . At her touch, the shutter stopped. Open.

Still just the corridor. Cara craned her neck, moving her head forward so she could see more of the corridor. But still nothing – no one. She looked as far left as she could and then right. There was a supreme calm, that seemed to drape over everything. And she started to think that maybe, in some weird way, she had overreacted. There was no one here. Was it possible the shutter was loose and there was some kind of draught? It sounded stupid, but no more stupid than some guard doing this?

She reached out to the gap in the door as though her

touch would solidify this whole situation. But the shutter quickly shot closed . . . *bing*.

And reopened. *Sshuph* . . .

And Cara stepped back as icy-cold shards broke through her heart. It was there. Looking in. She knew instantly what it was, even before it snapped its head around and revealed that blank patch of skin.

The thing. No-Face.

She didn't know how. But it was here. Behind her cell door. Doing this.

She gasped for breath. But couldn't get any into her lungs. No-Face was there. Staring into the slot – even with no eyes, she knew it was staring right into her soul. It threw around its head and grunted – muffled sentences as though it were actually trying to tell Cara something. This time, the ridge of where its nose should be started to bleed, and then where its eyes should be too, and in no time at all, a stream of blood was flooding down its front.

Cara finally forced out a breath, and then they came thick and fast. 'Go away,' she muttered, and then shouted, 'Go away!'

No-Face peered in at her with recognition, not fear – even though she knew it was incapable of such emotion.

'Go away!' she shouted at the top of her voice.

No-Face just regarded her. And then the shutter closed . . . *bing*.

The cell was plunged into darkness. Cara breathed out. There was something final about it. It was over and—

The shutter slid open again. The place where No-Face's

eye should've been still there. And then it banged shut with incredible force.

Open. Shut. Open. Shut.

Sshuph-bing. Sshuph-bing. Sshuph-bing. Sshuph-bing. Sshuph-bing. Sshuph-bing.

Cara let out a painful cry. 'Shut up!' She turned her back on No-Face. But the noise was still there. Still piercing into her ears. And the light was still perceptible, even with her back turned.

Sshuph-bing. Sshuph-bing. Sshuph-bing.

'Shut up,' Cara muttered, out of breath – beaten. She rested her back against the door – if it tried to get in, it couldn't if she was in the way. 'Shut up.'

She slid down the door, until her bottom reached the floor. And she curled up in a little ball.

Sshuph-bing. Sshuph-bing. Sshuph-bing.

'Shut up.'

Sshuph-bing. Sshuph-bing. Sshuph-bing.

'Shut up.'

Sshuph-bing. Sshuph-bing. Sshuph-bing.

'SHUT UP!'

She woke up in bed, with a gasp. It was still the dead of night. She was drenched in sweat, and threw off the sweat-soaked sheet. She wrenched off her vest, which was stuck to her and didn't leave easily. She breathed in and out – it had felt so real, but it had been a dream. The last thing she remembered had been sitting on the floor, in front of the door, trying to block out the sound of the shutter opening and closing. But it had been a dream, a nightmare – it wasn't real.

She breathed in and out a few more times and couldn't help smiling. It was over. Nothing had happened. Just a bad dream. The worst she'd ever had. No-Face wasn't here, it was stupid to think it was. North Fern was a prison. She was safe. She was—

Cara stopped. And the icy cold fear stabbed through her again. As she looked down to the floor – the section between the beds. To see a rectangle of light.

The unmistakable sign of a door's open shutter.

9

She must have got back to sleep somehow because when she woke up again, she felt well-rested. Or at least as well-rested as she could be. Morning maybe?

She shifted, not wanting to look around.

But she already knew there was someone in the room. No-face? She didn't think so.

The soaked vest she had thrown on the floor in the middle of the night was now dry and draped over her naked torso, and the sheet was pulled up to her midriff. Almost like someone had been taking care of her. Like someone actually gave a crap about her modesty.

Or maybe the sight of her was just so disgusting they'd rather not have to look at her.

She knew she couldn't stay there.

Looking anywhere but where she knew the person was standing.

So she sat up and looked.

Madeleine Krotes was standing in the doorway. Resting her shoulder against the wall. With her arms crossed. She made the pose look like the most glamorous pose in the world.

She wasn't even surprised to see Krotes, and Krotes

didn't seem surprised by her sudden movement. She just looked at Cara through her glasses with her unrelenting but invitingly wide eyes.

'Hello, Cara,' Krotes said. Her faux-friendly shell sounded like it was barely hanging in there, but still it was. 'I'm here to tell you a few things about what has been going on outside of this . . . cell. I thought you'd appreciate hearing it from me personally. And then I'm here to tell you what's going to happen next.'

Cara opened her mouth to tell Krotes to get lost, but realised that she actually wanted to hear what she had to say. But she definitely didn't appreciate the personal touch.

'OK,' she said, pulling her vest on properly, not caring what she exposed even to Madeleine Krotes.

'We can't find it, Cara.'

'Can't find what?'

'What do you think?' Krotes said, her voice raising to, she would guess, the highest it could go, without sounding scary. 'We can't find the gun. Our guards from the unit have been searching your cell, the public areas, everyone else's cell on this entire floor. We've searched the kitchens, the laundries, the infirmaries, the libraries, the yards, the guard areas. The plumbing, the rubbish chutes, the air-filtration systems. Everywhere. Every way in or out of this building. Every nook and every cranny. I knew you were smart, I believe I said as much at our first meeting, but I didn't know you were this smart.'

'You give me too much credit,' Cara coughed, drily.

'No, no I don't. I took this job because I was fascinated

183

by people like you. And now, I'm even more so. How did you do it, Cara? Where is the gun? I don't even care about the case anymore, about the girl – whatever her name was, Stephanie Banbury or something . . .'

'Barnard,' Cara hissed. 'Her name was Barnard!'

'Whatever,' Krotes said, her tongue travelling across her perfect top teeth – her signature move. 'I don't care about that, I just need to know. You could even tell me really quietly, and I wouldn't even tell anyone. C'mon, it's just us here, I'm not recording this, you're not signing anything. Just tell me, please.' Krotes' eyes were fire, which led Cara to actually believe the Governor. She was practically begging, and it wasn't hard to believe this odd, odd woman would actually keep her word.

But she'd already forgotten Barnard's name, which made her angry.

Cara ran her tongue over her lips, almost copying Krotes – but she was doing it for a reason. Her lips now had mountainous, dry cracks in them. 'I can't tell you things that I don't know.'

'C'mon!'

'I don't lie. I'm not a liar, and I am not a killer and I have never been a killer and I never . . .' She trailed off. She was about to say she never would be a killer, but now, that affirmation seemed a little too hazy. The Hole had had a profound effect on her, even for a seasoned detective like Detective Lockhart.

Wait, what . . .

Krotes looked visibly disappointed. She seemed to collect herself in front of Cara's eyes, straighten up even more than she originally was. 'OK, well without a gun, we can't really conclude this case. I mean, there's so much overwhelming evidence, but a murder case is like a nice grammatical sentence. And a sentence is not a sentence without a full stop. The gun is the full stop in this instance, and until we have it, it's going to be very hard to bring any charges against you. So until then . . . Well, I have talked with the benefactor and we have decided it would be best to transfer you to another unit while we continue our investigation.'

'What?' Cara said, not being able to stop it. Transfer. No, she couldn't get transferred. She needed to clear her name and that hinged on being here, in this unit. 'No, you can't do that.' And also what about what Barnard had said before she died? Barnard had seen something here in this place that made her believe North Fern was dangerous. Cara had to find that too. 'You cannot do that. I just got here.'

'You killed someone, Cara,' Krotes said, as calmly as someone saying *Can you pass the salt*? 'We believe, for the safety of everyone here, and, quite frankly, the safety of yourself, you would be better suited elsewhere. We are transferring you to E7 unit, practically identical to this one in every way. It really isn't an issue, and it is definitely not a conversation.'

'When?' Cara asked.

'The soonest we are able to transfer you is Friday.'

Beyond all reasonable thought, Cara laughed. 'You understand that means jack-all to me, right?'

And beyond all reasonable thought, Krotes smiled too.

'Ah, yes, sorry. Today is Sunday. So five days from now.'

That was it. Five days. She had five days – even less. She had five days to find all she needed to find out.

'Until then, you will be taken back to your cell. Your proper cell. You will be allowed to resume life on the Unit, but there will obviously be some restrictions. You will have a guard assigned to you at all times, escorting you where you need to go, protecting you at mealtimes, and outside your cell door at night-time. Your job has been suspended and movement will be restricted as much as possible.'

'No,' Cara said, 'I don't want that.'

'It's non-negotiable. And I think that when you finally get out there, you'll understand why. The residents on the Unit are none best pleased about what you did. It is for your own protection as much as everyone else's. As is transferring you, and as was throwing you in here.'

Cara snorted. 'Well, thank you very much,' she said, making sure to make it drip with sarcasm so she got the point.

Krotes chuckled. 'Once again, you are fascinating to me, Cara Lockhart. A true marvel. Someone who can do what you do with the mind that you have, it may sound silly, but you should be protected – preserved. In the right hands, you could even be useful.'

Cara erupted, 'And, once again, you're really giving me too much credit. I didn't kill ANYONE.'

Krotes winked at her. 'Sure you didn't. We're going to avoid any issues with dinner tonight by keeping you here until then. You'll receive dinner here, as usual. I hear you're having shepherd's pie. And then the guards will come to escort you back to your original cell.'

So only three days really . . .

'The cell where Barnard died?' Cara asked, in a small voice.

'Well, the cell where you killed her, yes,' Krotes said with a smile. 'You say tomato and all that.' She chuckled to herself and turned to the door.

'Wait,' Cara said, as Krotes got to the door, 'I need to ask you why?'

Krotes turned. 'Why what?'

'Why the film? Why the torture?'

'What are you talking about?'

Cara scoffed, 'The screen. You've been playing *Rain on Elmore Street* on a loop in this cell. Forty-six times now. Why would you do that? Isn't that kind of torture illegal or something? Isn't that some anti-terrorism stuff? You should have just waterboarded me.'

Krotes raised an eyebrow. 'I'm sorry, Cara. I'm really not following.'

Cara was caught breathless by her abject lies, being told directly to her face, and without any visual indication she even cared about it. She stabbed at the air behind her with a finger while still looking the glamour model right in her soulless, little eyes. 'The screen. You've been pumping *Rain on Elmore Street* into this cell twenty-four seven to mess with me. To screw me up. How many times have you seen that film? You think you're the expert? Because I'm pretty sure I am now. Want me to sing you a song?'

Madeleine Krotes frowned and straightened her skirt, that didn't need straightening. 'Wow. I've never quite seen such a reaction to suggestion. And, what, you saw it in the yard only a few times. Very fascinating. And you'd never seen it before? Think, because this might be important.'

'I am not doing anything you tell me to do ever again,' Cara said, advancing on her. Krotes stood her ground, looking ravishing. 'You're a liar and a creep and you forgot the name of the victim in the case you're currently investigating because you only care about the thrill of it all. But, right now, that's fine. Right now, I can take that, as long as you just give me one thing – I just want to know why. Why would you do that to someone? How messed up do you have to be to play that on a loop nearly fifty times. And you would probably have carried on right? Because that's who you are. That's what you are. But I'm a person, a human. Even if you think I've done what you think I've done. Hell, even if I did what you thought I'd done, it doesn't excuse it. But no . . .'

'Cara.'

'. . .if you'd found that weapon you wanted to find, you'd have left me in here till the trial, I bet. And Eugene would have tipped his hat a million more times. And Giratina would have walked past him a million more . . .'

'Cara.'

'And the goddamn camera would go up to the street sign a million more times and the name would always be *Rain on Elmore Street*, etched there a million times, despite there never once being a single drop of rain on

Elmore Street. And for a million more times, I would have to suppress the almost painful question about why the hell it's called *Rain on Elmore Street* then? It's not even clouded over, not a single hint of precipitation.'

'Cara.'

'And a million more times there'd be "Revolving Door", and "Right Under My Nose", and "Good Things", and "You Can't Sell Change". And Detective Lockhart is in the Hole. And "Life is Life is Life", and "The Bottom Rung". And that really bad bridge in "Let it All Hang Out" that sounds like the entire orchestra is having a collective aneurysm. And Detective Lockhart is always here in the Hole. And Detective Lockhart has always been here in the Hole. And Detective Lockhart is always here in the Hole. And then it just starts over again. With Detective Lockhart here in the Hole. With the pan. And the hat. And the songs. And a million stupid reprises. And Detective Lockhart is in . . .'

'CARA,' Krotes shouted, holding up a palm.

Cara stopped and realised she was almost crying and hadn't taken a breath since she'd started whatever the hell that had just been.

'Calm down, OK. I promise you that I have not been playing you that film on a loop.'

'Liar,' Cara said, taking another step forward and stumbling to the bed, when she realised her knees were rubber.

Krotes didn't react. 'No, I'm not lying.'

'YOU ARE LYING BECAUSE YOU'RE A LIAR,' Cara shrieked.

'Cara,' Krotes said, as she stepped back, but not because she was fazed, but because she was ready to leave, 'I have not been playing you *Rain on Elmore Street* on a loop and I can very easily prove it to you. Look around, there isn't a television screen in this cell.'

Cara wheeled around to see that Krotes was not lying. The back wall – the wall she knew to be showing *Elmore Street* to her was light now so she could see, and it was the same as all the others. White stone. No screen, no opening where a screen could appear. She staggered over to the wall and ran her hands over the cold stone. Nothing. No indents, no mechanisms hiding somewhere, nothing. 'But . . . I don't understand . . .' She turned back to see Krotes was halfway through the door.

She looked back. 'After dinner, you'll be back in your old cell. For better or worse. And, by Friday, I'm sure you'll be begging for the transfer.'

Cara launched forward at her, knowing – no, hoping – that this had to be one of her tricks, but Madeleine Krotes slipped through the doorway and started to close the door before she could get anywhere near her. She didn't know exactly what she would have done anyway.

As the door closed, the cell was plunged into darkness, but part of it was still illuminated by the light in the corridor, including Krotes' shrinking form. The last thing she saw, before the door was closed, and the dark was complete.

Krotes left behind a stench of rose perfume.

And a promise of darkness ending.

10

Krotes was true to her word.

Dinner was shepherd's pie. And it was delicious. At least to Cara.

In actuality, which she fought to see, it was exactly the same as when she'd had it before – sloppy brown stuff with very little flavour. But at least it was different. And she ate slowly to savour it, even regretting when she had to wash it down with water.

One reason for her improved mood was the food.

Another was the prospect of finally leaving the Hole.

Mere hours away.

And the last was the fact that the film had not come back on.

Elmore Street was over. If it had ever even begun.

Since Krotes left, Cara had thought a lot about it all. And she was still torn. Half of her mind was pretty set on the fact that Krotes was tricking her – she had been playing the film, maybe from some secret projector in the ceiling? But she'd inspected it in the light from the corridor and hadn't found anything, and surely she would have seen the beam of light emanating from a projector in the pitch black if that was the case. Maybe the screen was hidden then – but she'd run her hands over the entire wall more times than she could count and there were no openings. The entire wall would have had to shift, and that seemed to be an impossible task even for North Fern.

The half of her mind that was currently winning thought that she had lost her sanity. The lack of stimulation in this place had made her hallucinate. She had seen No-Face after all, and she had known he wasn't real, but he had started the film. Maybe it was all just one long, long hallucination. And it would make sense that whenever anyone real came close, whether it be the guards with food, or Trenner, or Krotes, the hallucination (the imaginary world) shut off.

But it seemed so real.

It seemed so real. The thing coming down the stairs. But it wasn't. It was you. The thing is only as real as you made him. You killed them. You bought the gun on the dark web just like they hypothesised, even though they couldn't prove it. Because you're smart.

And bat-shit insane.

She stopped thinking about it. That image, the one seared into her brain – what she'd felt when she pushed open Tilly's door and saw *them* for the first time. She knew she hadn't done it, stripping away everything else, just because of that.

She stopped – threw it out of her head. She couldn't see that now.

She was just happy the film wasn't on anymore.

The silence was what she had been craving ever since

the torture had started. And now she had it.

Her meal was consumed in a matter of minutes. And when she was done, she took the paper towels over to the sink and washed herself again. She went to put the soggy smelly rag into the bowl, and then decided against it, turning around and throwing it full pelt at the far wall. It squelched onto the stonework, stayed stuck there for a few moments, and then flopped to the floor. She smiled. She didn't know exactly why, but that felt good.

She slid the tray through the slot in the door.

Then she sat cross-legged on the bed and just stared. She knew that this would only make time go slower, but she couldn't help it.

A watched kettle . . . and all that.

The saying was right.

It was three hours, seventeen minutes, and twenty-nine seconds, timing courtesy of her mind's production of *Elmore Street*, before the guards came through the door, but it felt like a lifetime. Every second reached an eternity and she was reminded of those nights when she was a little girl trying to sleep on Christmas Eve, trying not to think of the amazing day ahead, but failing every second. Equating this and Christmas seemed very depressing, even in her current state – but there it was.

Eventually, the locks on the door jangled.

And the door opened.

And Harper was on the other side. Bathed in light. In his normal guard attire. Not SWAT gear. 'Lockhart, it's time.'

'Let me just pack my things,' Cara said. And smirked.

Harper did not look amused one bit.

So she just went with him.

Detective Lockhart was in the Hole.

Detective Lockhart is now out of the Hole.

Detective Lockhart is very much sans Hole.

And she had to quench an audible laugh.

Before Harper shut the door, she chanced a glance back through the doorway. To see her little home. It seemed much smaller from this angle, but also much bigger. Much dirtier, but much cleaner.

What was happening to her?

Harper shut the door and turned the locks again. As if she had been sharing the Hole with someone, someone they still didn't want getting out.

Someone, or something.

Well, if No-Face is still skulking around in there, good riddance.

Harper led her down the corridor. Everything looked so new and bright and confusing. And big. There was so much space. Even in this corridor. Which she once would have described as narrow. She stretched out her arms and ran both forefingers over either side of the corridor.

'What are you doing?' Harper asked, behind her.

'It's nice to sometimes dream for more,' Cara responded. 'But let's go back to my cell door.' She sang it to the tune of *Revolving Door*.

'OK then,' Harper muttered.

They got to the end of the corridor, and the other

side of the hidden door and Cara felt herself holding her breath. It was time to rejoin the Unit – now or never. What if they were just beyond the door, waiting for her?

Cara could just imagine Krotes setting up Cara being released right at the others' dinner time, so she would pop out of the wall just as everyone was tucking into their dessert. *Hi, guys.* Would they all rush her, gang up on her, fight her? Maybe Krotes was secretly hoping it would happen.

But they went through the hidden door and the dining room was empty. Completely. But just seeing it brought on a wave of emotion. She couldn't stop herself crying as she didn't even know she was. She thought she'd never see the dining room again – she thought she'd never see outside of the Hole again. And now, it was coming into stark relief how much she'd given up.

Harper didn't notice, or didn't care, as she quietly sobbed. He dragged her through the dining room and out into the Pit. It was deserted as well, and through her tears, she realised that everyone had most likely been locked in their cells to allow Cara to be transported without any danger.

Harper escorted her all the way to her cell, like he thought she would have forgotten where it was. And, in actuality, she almost had. She saw her cell door open.

Flashbacks to the night she was pulled from her bed. Taken to the Hole. With Barnard having a very real, very big hole in the centre of her forehead.

A few steps closer, and she was in the doorway.

And there was Barnard's bed. The bed had been made. The sheets changed.

But no Barnard.

The only sign that she had ever existed was a small reddish brown patch on the floor between the beds. Blood that had been sponged and sponged and sponged but still remained.

Barnard.

Harper gently ushered Cara in by placing a hand on her shoulder and guiding her. She fought it, but succumbed.

This was the place where it had happened.

Where she had been given the exciting opportunity to lose her mind.

And where she lost a friend.

But then there was also that slightly selfish voice in her head, marvelling at how big the cell was (bigger than she remembered) and airy and light. Her bed was almost inviting – as she began to remember how much softer and less lumpy it was. And she knew that she wouldn't be able to walk away from this cell – refuse it – not now.

She turned to see Harper watching her. 'I'll be taking first night shift. I'll be right outside.'

And he shut the door, the red light blinking on. Locked.

Cara flopped down on the bed, liking how comparatively comfortable it felt. The cell didn't really look any different, but it did look very empty, lonely. Without Barnard there, it felt quiet, lifeless. Her mind unfortunately went to wondering where Barnard was now – or her body at least. Would it get released to any family she might have? What if she had no family? Would there be a funeral – and would there be anyone there if there was?

What a waste of life.

She peered around, suddenly realising it was very important to find Barnard's books. They had to be here. They were a staple of this cell. She loved her books. *The Stand*. *Needful Things*. *It*. The M.R. Halls that she would never get around to reading, not now. They weren't on the bedside table, so Cara wrenched open the drawers. Empty.

Someone had taken her books.

'She's really gone,' she said, or thought. She didn't really know.

She curled up on her bed, hooking her arms around her knees and pulling them to her. The foetal position. Everyone was gone.

It was only her.

And the fact she'd have to live with herself . . .

. . . for the rest of her life.

11

Sleep came a little too easily. But it was troubled.

Cara had a dream – a nightmare. One of those that was so real you woke up wondering if it had actually happened. In fact, as she thought about it, she couldn't be sure it hadn't.

She had killed the Stoker children, in the nightmare. She had turned to go down the stairs. And stopped. A copy of her was standing at the foot of the stairs looking up, silently shaking. She knew it was herself. Not just someone who looked like her. She just knew. Maybe it was her from another universe. The her downstairs, a picture of confusion, like she was going to shit herself with fear. And she took great enjoyment in slowly descending. At the bottom, as the Other Cara closed her eyes, she pressed the gun into her doppelganger's hand.

And then she woke up.

You didn't do it. You didn't do it. You didn't do it.

She rubbed her eyes.

What the hell was that nightmare?

You did it. You did it. You did it.

She had only got to sleep because of the bed. It was so comfortable.

Perspective was a funny thing in here – not just in North Fern, but in prison in general. The bed was awful – basically a hunk of granite covered with a duvet that felt like cement. But compared to what she had been subjected to in the Hole – it was heavenly. And before she knew it—

Morning. And the feeling she'd just gazed into another life.

Or this one.

The Other Cara – suppose this was what happened – what was the Other Cara? Just a mirage, a symbol of her innocence dying.

Did she really—

NO. NO. NO.

You didn't do it. You didn't do it. You didn't do it.

She. Didn't. Do. It.

A hammering on the door, before the locks slid back – CLANG, CLANG, CLANG – and she was revolted to see Anderson standing there. 'Rise and shine, Butcher Version 2. Get it, because you were called the Butcher when you made those kids into blood fountains. And now you're Butcher Version 2, because you shot the Unit's favourite prisoner right between her soulful little eyes.'

'You're a wordsmith,' Cara said, getting up. She knew Anderson had been looking for something more – something more emotional – so denying him that seemed to be a victory, no matter how petty it was.

'Hope you're ready for your reintroduction into the colony,' Anderson said, smiling. 'This is gonna suck a bag of dicks. Wouldn't like to be you right now.'

Cara glared at him. And suppressed the urge to say what she was thinking.

She actually would prefer to be her than him right now.

Because he had to be the one to stand between her and everyone else. Unless he was planning on turning around and offing her himself.

But there was always something about Anderson – something in his eyes. She had no doubt that he hated her, hated every 'resident' in here, but there was a little spark. Mostly, she could see it in situations like this when she was wearing just her vest and her pants, and her vest was thin and soaking with sweat and she had no doubt that he could see a lot more of her than she would have liked. There was that fire in his eyes, and the way his pupils flitted up and down her.

He hated her. But that didn't mean he didn't spend cold, lonely nights thinking about her.

She shivered at that. And reached for her top, pulling it on. Without taking her eyes from him. Yes – as if to reaffirm what she thought, the spark of fire in his eyes now became a spark of disappointment. She pulled her trousers on.

'Sleeping Beauty's ready for the ball,' Anderson said.

As Anderson guided her towards the dining room, Cara muttered under her breath, 'That's Cinderella, you bloody idiot.'

The Pit was empty, but the cell doors stood open.

No doubt they had saved Cara's awakening until last, so as not to cause too much fuss.

For the first time, as she got closer and closer to the

200

double doors, she wondered whether she shouldn't just go back to the Hole until she was transferred. She was almost sure that if she asked, the guards would gladly sling her back in there until Friday.

But no – she had to be out here in the Unit.

She had to find out what Barnard had been talking about on her last night. And she had to find out who killed her friend.

Both those answers were here, and not in there, in the Hole. She already had an impossible time limit – she couldn't waste it dreaming of the Hole, a place she'd just got out of.

She had no leads. Three days. A whole unit. And a unit full of prisoners who hated her.

Life and death. It was a gamble for her nowadays.

They got to the doors. The light above, and the light on her Cuff, went green.

'You looking forward to this?' Anderson sneered.

Cara truly wasn't.

Suddenly, she wanted nothing less than to go through those doors. She wanted to run – run away, run back to the Hole, get transferred, go and live in E3 or F5, or wherever it was Krotes said she was going, she would even shine Krotes' shoes every morning if necessary.

Just please, please, please – not through that door.

Never through that door.

Please.

Please.

Plea—

Anderson pushed her through the door.

12

Cara crashed and stumbled into the dining room – the doors swinging and banging into the sides of the walls. She heard Anderson behind her give an almost imperceptible chuckle. But she couldn't focus on him.

In front of her – the dining room, and a unit's worth of prisoners sitting, eating and talking. At the sound – that Anderson had made sure to be as loud as possible – they all stopped their conversations and looked up. A total, full, impenetrable silence.

No one talked. No one's gaze broke from her. A sea of faces – confused, contemptuous. No one even seemed to be blinking. Shock.

Cara looked away, to the serving area, and although she wanted to run out of the room, she went over and got a tray. She felt a billion eyes following her, and Anderson hot on her heels.

She got to the serving hatch. Continell was at the hatch in her hairnet.

She waited for the usual grumbled choice – apple or banana (the Weetabix were mandatory) – but the woman just placed the brownest apple she'd ever seen next to her bowl without saying anything.

Cara was about to say that she wanted a banana, had always had a banana, but then she knew that that was probably the reason she'd gotten an apple.

She got her mug of water and Anderson guided her over to an empty table.

Cara tried to keep her head down, but she could feel the eyes on her. And the whispers had started. Muttering she couldn't quite make out – she was glad about that. She heard the word 'Butcher' more times than she could count.

She ate as quickly as possible, and eventually the murmurs were drowned as prisoners started to talk again. Some didn't even talk about her. She just kept her eyes down, looking at her bowl and tried to focus on the fact that the Weetabix actually tasted OK. After a lifetime of liver and onions, it seemed that even gruel proved edible. The water was better though – it tasted fresher than she'd got in the Hole.

Five minutes later, she had finished, but she still didn't want to look up. So she scraped every last bit of sludge out of the bowl. And as she scraped, she heard another scraping – of chairs – as the others started to go back to their cells.

Again, head down, no eye contact. But she felt Anderson step closer to her, and she hated herself that it made her feel a little safer. She had no doubt that he cared more for the safety of his job, than the safety of her, but, at that point, the two things were aligned, so she guessed she should be thankful.

She waited for as long as she could, and then she

chanced a look up. The dining room was mostly empty – there was still a table of purple shirts over in the corner and they were all looking at her, but they also seemed to be playing a game of cards at the same time. Abrams was trying to get them to shift, but they weren't – and she was getting increasingly irate.

'Cara.' She looked up to see Peter standing there. She showed nothing in her expression, but her eyes looked almost inviting, homely. Her other real friend in here. Peter's presence suggested that maybe she wasn't still alone in this. Peter was the very picture of when they'd met – clutching the ends of her sleeves, hiding behind her fringe, biting her lip in trepidation. Cara needed someone on her side and maybe that could be Peter. She needed help searching the Unit for answers.

'Peter,' Cara said, a little too hopelessly.

All of a sudden, Peter's face changed. It contorted in ways Cara would never think possible of the sweet girl. Her eyebrows shot down, and her mouth screwed up into a frown that looked like it hurt her. She lurched forward and spat on Cara's face. The globule landed right between Cara's eyes, and she surprised herself by not flinching. It was an exact repeat of Moyley's action the first morning – but this time it hurt so much more. If the tables were turned, would she have done any differently? It wasn't Peter's fault.

Peter took another look, as the spit ran down Cara's face – regressed back into her timid form and then hurried out of the dining room. Cara just watched her go, feeling an incredible sadness that she hadn't felt in some time. It all seemed to hit her at once – this was it, this was what she was, and this was all she would ever be unless she could try to clear her name. She felt like crying, curling up in her cell and bawling her eyes out, but she knew she didn't have time. And the fact that everyone in the Unit would highly enjoy the thought of her crumpling helped her to stay strong. So she just breathed in, and put her armour on again.

'Thanks for the help,' Cara said to Anderson as she wiped the spit off with her assigned square of kitchen roll. She wished she'd left some water to wash it off with, but she hadn't.

'Hey,' Anderson said jovially, 'she didn't spit a knife at you. She didn't have a weapon on her. I don't have to protect you from propelled saliva, do I? That's not in my job description. If you didn't want the spit, maybe don't kill the favourite of the Unit. Just brainstorming, but I think that might have worked.'

Cara looked at him, trying to hide her hot anger. But Anderson saw some of it, and was amused by it. 'Can I go back to my cell now?' Cara said.

'Of course,' Anderson chuckled. 'I am but your humble servant after all.'

'Why are you enjoying this?' Cara said. 'Did you even care about Barnard?'

'Don't lecture me, Butcher,' Anderson said, putting a hand on either shoulder and wrenching her up. 'No, I didn't care about your stupid little cellmate. At least I didn't when she was alive. But now – well, let's just say I like thriving on a little chaos. For you, it's torture, and it's well deserved, or maybe it isn't and you're telling the truth and somehow you didn't actually do it. But for me, your sorrow is just a way to spice up my day a little bit. So yeah, I'm enjoying it. Sue me.'

Cara just let him guide her back to her cell. Anderson had introduced the possibility that she didn't do it. If anyone else had said that, she would have jumped at them, tried to make them see reason, convince them to help her try to prove her innocence. But it was Anderson, and he was only saying it because maybe he thought it would be more interesting for him if she hadn't done it. He was vile, and the fact that he still hadn't taken his hands off her, even though she was up and following him, leaving the dining room, made her shake with revulsion.

Anderson wasn't going to help her.

Peter wasn't going to help her.

And as they got out of the dining room into the corridor, Cara found someone else who was no longer an ally.

Minnie was there waiting, with Aqua and, surprisingly, Moyley. Like they were lying in wait for her. The others did nothing, but Minnie – ever the leader – launched herself at Cara and grabbed her before Anderson could do anything. In a second, she had pinned Cara against the wall, reached into her pocket and brought out something sharp that she pressed against Cara's neck. 'You goddamn bitch. You goddamn bitch. Barnard was our friend, and you kill her. You act like you're a celebrity and you do whatever you want. You – you do that to her.'

She shifted her weight and momentarily lightened

the grip on her weapon so Cara could see what it was. The arm of a piece of plastic cutlery whittled down into a point. Minnie pressed it back against the softness of Cara's neck and she felt it cut into her.

'Minnie, please, I didn't . . .'

And then Anderson was there, wrestling Minnie off her. The two of them were a mess of purple and black for a moment as they tussled and then Anderson had Minnie's arms pinned behind her back, and he pressed her against the wall. The weapon dropped to the floor with a clatter. Cara felt an urge to quickly pick it up – not to be armed herself, but to keep it out of reach of anyone else – but she knew it would be a bad idea. So she kicked it instead, and it went sliding down the Pit.

'Come on, Minnie Mouse,' Anderson was saying as the muscular woman wrestled under his grip. 'You don't want this to get any nastier. And you definitely don't want to get thrown in the Hole – this one here really stunk it up when she was in there, needs a good deep clean, if you know what I'm saying.' Anderson chuckled.

The threat seemed to work. Minnie relaxed, but she didn't take her eyes from Cara, who just stood there uncertainly. Cara looked around to see that Aqua and Moyley were staring too. Moyley was actually crying – Cara guessed she was the only other one from New Hall, so there was some kind of connection there. 'OK,' Minnie said, 'OK, I'm done.'

'You sure?' Anderson said, in a tone like he was talking to a little girl. 'Because I don't want this to be one of those fake-out situations where I let you go and you just go straight back to cat-fighting again.'

'I'm done, Anderson. Now get your slimy goddamn mitts off me,' Minnie snarled.

Anderson let go with speed, almost as if he was offended by the comment. And Minnie pushed herself off the wall, wiping at her cuffs like he was diseased. She went to pass Cara, but before she did, she leaned in and whispered in her ear. 'Don't think I don't know where you're getting transferred to. And if I don't get to you, they will.' And Minnie flashed a patronising smile at Anderson, and disappeared down the corridor, followed by Moyley and Aqua.

'Bloody hell,' Anderson said, 'that's the deadliest ladies pop group I've ever seen.' And he smiled broadly and maliciously.

Cara didn't. But she did say, 'Thank you. I mean it — thank you.'

Anderson's smile disappeared. He grabbed Cara by the scruff of the neck and spun her round, propelling her down the corridor again. 'Chaos is only fun if it has limits. For example, if Minnie Mouse there had cut you up like a cherry tomato, that's paperwork.' They got to her cell in no time at all. Anderson opened it but held Cara there in the doorway. 'But say if I do something like this . . .'

Anderson thrust his arm forward and upwards, with astonishing strength. Cara found herself propelled into her cell, momentarily airborne, and then saw the cold hard floor approaching too fast. Her body slammed against the floor, and her arm threatened to crunch under her. Her head buckled, ricocheting off the floor and everything suddenly became fuzzy. She looked up at the blurry image of Anderson, and although she couldn't really see anything else clearly, his putrid smile was in sharp focus.

'Yes, now that was fun.'

13

Cara stayed on the floor for as long as her self-worth would allow. She wanted to rip through the cell door and kick the shit out of Anderson – not stop until he was begging her to, and maybe not even then.

But she couldn't – she knew she couldn't.

And the anger subsided.

She was tired. So tired.

And it would be so easy just to climb into bed, and wait for Friday. Stay out of everyone's way, and sleep.

But she couldn't.

And with an enormous weight, that she came to realise was her own motivation, pressing down upon her, she slowly but surely steeled herself to get up. Her neck stung, where the cutlery had slightly pierced her skin. Her body ached from all the shoving around and the beds she'd had to sleep on. And she was just sick of it – sick of it all. But she had to get herself up because this was the only shred of hope she had left – this day and two more, to try to get herself out of this.

She pushed herself up, keeping her eyes shut so she didn't have so much of the dizziness, even though it was still there. She had to reach out in front of her and find the bedside cabinet and steady herself on it. When she was upright, she opened her eyes and looked around, orientating herself and blinking away the fuzziness. In a moment, it was all gone and she looked straight in front of her to see—

She froze.

In front of her – directly in front of her – was the screen, and the screen was turned on. But it was just after breakfast – it wasn't time for Illumination. Not unless it had changed whilst she was in the Hole – it was possible, she supposed. But not probable. This place ran on goddamn clockwork – she would bet her life this wasn't supposed to be happening.

Or maybe it isn't happening at all.

There was always that. She thought back to the endless repeats of *Rain on Elmore Street*. The claim that Krotes had made – *there isn't a screen in this cell*. That hadn't been happening either – unless she was lying.

But no, this was different. She reached out and touched the screen, and it was real.

The screen was showing the field she had seen the first few days – the desktop wallpaper one – just a rolling green field with blue sky. Nothing special about it, rather innocuous. Except—

Cara rubbed her forehead, wondering if this was all brought on by her bump, but there was something new in the picture. There was something in the field – someone – standing at the top of the hill. The figure was tiny – almost a blemish – impossibly small for the rest of the picture. She stepped forward, screwed up her eyes and looked.

And then staggered back.

In the picture, in the goddamn picture, standing at the top of the hill was the figure. In a blue boiler suit. With no face. Her breaths came thick and fast – someone was having fun, a dumb stupid joke.

She looked around as if she'd see someone sitting in the corner of the cell, softly tittering to themselves, but she didn't, and then she looked back at the screen.

And stopped breathing entirely.

No-Face had moved. He was now slightly down the hill and slightly larger. This was silly – he hadn't moved. The picture had just changed. It was just a picture and pictures couldn't move, and what was more, they definitely couldn't hurt you. Ergo, her utter terror was possibly the silliest thing.

But it was still very real. And it felt like it was getting more real by the second, as she blinked and No-Face seemed to lurch towards her again. Closer. Larger. Further down the hill. Towards the camera that had taken the picture. Towards her. Like No-Face was gaining size, gaining reality, getting ready to pop out of the picture and pull Cara in.

Another blink and it had got down to the bottom of the hill. It was hard to tell, but she'd say it was only a hundred or so feet away from her. She hadn't seen it move, it was in the exact same pose as he had been at the top of the hill – hands by its sides, face empty and regarding her – but her brain was filling in the blanks, like she was watching a more fragmented version of a flip book. To her, No-Face was bounding down the hill and trying to appear as though it wasn't moving. Like that game you'd play when you were children – Musical Statues, or Grandma's Footsteps, or whatever it was called.

Blink and it was in front of her, maybe twenty feet away. She could still see its full form – feet, legs, arms, torso, mask – but now it looked almost impossibly large. It still appeared a little lifeless, standing to attention, but he was there.

She kept her eyes open. She didn't want to blink again – she didn't want it to come even closer.

What was this? Why did this thing constantly have to be following her – even if it wasn't physically, it was in her mind. No-Face was like a parasite, and it could leech on her whenever it liked.

She kept her eyes wide and looking at him, but she still felt dizzy and she was already feeling the urge to close them – the dryness encroaching on her eyeballs.

No-Face just stood there in the picture, mocking her. It wasn't going to go away. Not ever. It would always be there. Suddenly, Cara had a vision, crystal clear, of her lifeless corpse in an open coffin in a church, and No-Face standing over her crying tears of blood.

Tears. Moisture. She had to blink. So she did. She breathed in. Close. Open. And breathed out.

The screen was normal. The picture was normal. The rolling green field. The blue sky. The hint of wind blowing the grass. No No-Face. Nowhere to be seen.

She laughed to herself. She was being very stupid – what a thing to get worked up about.

She blinked again.

And fell to the floor. No-Face was right there, looking out of the screen. The field was behind him, barely even visible, behind the blurry big cartoon eyes. 'No,' she said, trying not to shout, 'this isn't happening, no.'

She screwed up her eyes and thought she might never open them again. But still she half-expected hands to grasp at her and No-Face to pull her away with him.

But nothing happened and for a few moments, besides the distant sounds of the Unit, there was silence. Until—

'What the hell are you doing?'

Cara looked up at the screen, as if the voice had come from there and not behind her. The screen was blank, turned off. Only then did she look around to the voice.

That didn't really make her feel better.

Standing by the door, leaning on the wall, looking at her with amusement, was Liza.

14

Cara jumped up onto her bed, turning her back to the blank screen, so she had Liza directly in front of her. Liza was still looking equally puzzled and amused, but she straightened up at Cara's scared expression. 'How are you here? The Cuffs?'

Liza looked down at her Cuff, still glowing blue. It should have been red. She wasn't allowed in here. Liza shrugged. 'Relax, I come in peace, Butcher. As long as you do exactly as I say, but, you know, that's pretty much par for the course at this point, isn't it?'

'How did you get in here?' Cara asked, looking towards the door which stood closed behind Liza. She must have snuck in while Cara was watching the screen. 'Where's Anderson?'

'Well,' Liza said, stepping forward and almost delighting in the fact Cara shrunk back, 'it's morning shower time, so I'm guessing he decided to do some guard duty over by the showers.'

'He's meant to be guarding the cell.'

'Oh come on, Butcher, that's why I find it hard to see you doing what you did. The legend doesn't fit the frankly baffling, real-life figure. You must be really messed up on the inside, Lockhart. Because on the outside you're kinda pathetic.' She flopped down on Barnard's bed.

'Get off there. That's Barnard's bed,' Cara hissed.

Liza propped her head up so she looked like she was lounging like a cover girl. 'I don't see her using it. You saw good and well to that, didn't you?' She laughed. 'I must commend you by the way. I needed to come here, you see, after I heard about what you did. And I want to say good show. Really, I mean it – good bloody show, old girl.'

'I thought you hated me,' Cara said, 'now you break into my cell and offer me compliments.'

'The enemy of my enemy and all that shite,' Liza said. 'Clichés are ever so droll, but sometimes they are dead on.'

'Barnard was your enemy?' Cara asked, confused.

And she was surprised when Liza stuck her tongue out and blew a raspberry with it. 'Barnard. No, Barnard was a mere annoyance. A little thorn in my side. She wouldn't join my alliance, and she would have been such an addition. Don't get me wrong, I am very happy you got rid of Barnyard. I would have quite liked to see her dead body, but they'd taken it away by the time they let us all out of our cells. It was here, wasn't it? On this bed that she lay dead. Was it like this?' Liza lay back on the bed, her limbs sprawled. 'No? What about this?' Liza shocked her by almost doing the pose that Barnard was actually in when Cara woke up – on her stomach, her arm draped over the side of the bed. She looked at

Cara, smiled and then returned to her original position.

How did Liza get that so correct? Was it just a fluke, or did she know somehow what Barnard looked like? Was she just playing around with Cara, like a cat with a mouse? Was she the one who killed Barnard?

The next thing out of her mouth muddied that notion a bit. 'No, I am gunning – figuratively, and hopefully literally, HA HA– for a bigger fish. And it looks like we could be of some use to each other. Judging by the scene out there just now, it seems that little Minnie Mouse is going for you. That bitch has been top of the heap for too long. She even has friends in the other units, just like she told you. Sometimes she loses sight of right here, right now.

'This place – I have to walk through it every day. And it kills me to see it like this. It's not thriving. It's not . . . right. This is the land of opportunity, but every day that fossil is sowing the fields with salt.' She sounded like a viper, her words dripping from her mouth and burning holes in the floor.

'I want to be the Queen Bitch. I deserve it. You help me and I can make sure you don't get hurt and this little Barnard thing is swept under the rug. I'll even see to it that people get off your back – Moyley and those other ones that sneer at you when you're not looking.'

'I'm not who you think I am,' Cara said.

'I think you're a cold-blooded killer through and through. And maybe the most intriguing bit is that I don't think you fully understand how useful you could be to someone like me. I admit, I didn't think it either.

217

Not that first morning in the dining room. I'd say I'm sorry, but I'm really not. But now I'm ready to play nice. If you are.'

'Just tell me what you want,' Cara said, and then added in her head *so I can say no*.

'Word on the corridor,' Liza said, sitting up, 'is that those doughnut-chomping idiots out there haven't found your gun yet. Which means that, beyond all reasonable reason, you still have it stashed somewhere in this unit. Somewhere only you could possibly know. Here's what I want – I want you to get the gun and bring it to me. And then we'll see if Minnie Mouse bleeds sparkles and rainbows, before she has the opportunity to cut your throat in your sleep.'

'That's not possible,' Cara stated, 'because I never had a gun. I never had a gun, and I never killed Barnard.'

Liza inched forward on the bed, reached out and snatched Cara's hands. 'Come on, tell me the truth, just us girls together.'

'Are you not listening? I was set up. I didn't do it,' Cara said to her face.

'OK sure,' Liza nodded sarcastically. 'How did you get it in here? My current theory is that somehow you got it in on the library cart. That's the only thing that we have access to that comes in and out of the Unit. I think that's why they don't let us in the kitchens – apart from the ones who work there of course. And no one who works in the kitchens would have smuggled you anything in, word is you can't anyway. So yes, I think it must have been the cart.'

'I didn't do it,' Cara said again, through gritted teeth this time. 'I didn't have a gun, and I didn't kill her.' But Liza had piqued her interest, if inadvertently. The library cart?

'Right,' Liza said, exaggerating a wink. 'I get it. I get your style. Deny, deny, deny. And all that. Me, I like embracing it. I like holding my head up high and saying that I did indeed slaughter my parents in their orthopaedic bed. I cut their throats with a pair of sewing scissors. I did my father first, smothered him a bit with a pillow so my mum didn't wake up. Then I did my mother and I let her scream the house down. Then I realised my error. I'd been too reckless – it was all about the insurance money, to start with at least. But when it came to the actual act, it was just about killing them. I realised that there was no way I was getting away with it. So you know what I did? I rang the police myself, and sat out on the front step waiting for them. At the trial, they said I was proud of what I'd done. I've never heard anything so true. So maybe try owning up once in a while – it actually feels pretty damn good.'

Cara said nothing. She knew there was nothing she could say to persuade Liza she hadn't done it – either of her alleged crimes – so there was no point in trying. That was what she'd learned over the course of the trial. Some people were at least open to the possibility a fact was not a fact. And some people just weren't.

'So,' Liza continued, letting Cara have her hands back and launching herself up, pacing a little backwards and forwards, 'I hear that they're shipping you out to

219

pastures new on Friday, and our little window of opportunity we find ourselves so gloriously inside will close for good. And you will be thrown to the wolves – or the mice. So you need to get that gun to me by then. And all your problems will go away. And all mine too. You see how gloriously mutually beneficial this is.

'But if you don't get me the gun, you'll have me after you too. And if Minnie's friends don't get you, mine will. You see the quandary you find yourself in – that thing you're doing with your face – is really no quandary at all. On one path, your problems are solved, and on the other, your problems are doubled. I think that's quite an easy one for the Master Butcher to figure out.'

Liza slapped Cara on the leg, laughed and skipped around the cell.

'I can't get you what you want,' Cara said.

'You can and you will.'

'I can't.'

'Have you never watched a self-help DVD? Only damn losers say "I can't".'

'I can't. And in your master plan, what if Minnie gets to me first anyway?'

'Maybe while you're still here you should have this,' Liza said and threw something black and thin at Cara.

Cara caught it, and held it up to look at it. It was the whittled-down piece of cutlery that Minnie had pressed against her throat, the one she had kicked away, and Anderson had forgotten about.

'Keep that with you, for protection.' Liza went to the door. 'Remember, Friday. After you get transferred,

I can't help you. And Minnie's mice will get to you.' She went to open the door and turned back. 'Look at us. Who would have pegged us for unlikely allies, eh? Unbelievable how life works out.'

Liza left, slamming the cell door behind her, her Cuff seemingly just allowing her to exit the cell. Cara relaxed slightly, realising her muscles had been tensed throughout the entire exchange. Now she had yet another thing to worry about – another treat for Friday. But if she happened upon the gun used in Barnard's murder – a gun that no guard in the building had been able to find – would she in good faith be able to hand it over to Liza knowing what she was going to do with it? And that was not even taking into account the logistics of carrying a gun through the Unit? And the morals of saving her own life, in exchange for somebody else's – even someone who wanted to kill her.

Her mind spun with the possibilities upon theories upon probabilities. But she knew she had to stop thinking about it altogether, because it wasn't going to get her anywhere. And her mind finally stopped on the one useful piece of information that Liza had told her.

Less a piece of information, more a theory that actually held some weight.

The only way things could get transported in and out of the Unit. The only things prisoners had access to.

The library cart.

15

As soon as Cara heard Anderson's slimy voice outside her cell door, she banged on it until he opened up. He looked at her, non-plussed. 'Yes?'

'Liza has just been in here. How could you just let her come in here?'

'I had some urgent business to attend to in the yard. As for Liza coming in, your cell is now a crime scene. So it was designated a public area for a spell. I must have forgot to switch it back. Oopsie.' Anderson grinned.

Cara couldn't believe what she was hearing. A public area? Did that mean anyone could come in? Tamper with evidence? Impossible – Anderson must have left her door unlocked on purpose. Had Liza paid him off? Or did he just not care who came in? How could she feel safe in here, ever again?

'Don't worry,' Anderson said, 'it was only unlocked on this side. You couldn't have got out.'

'Liza got out,' Cara spat.

Anderson shrugged.

'Why would you think that would be my concern?' Cara said. 'And that doesn't explain why Liza's Cuff didn't go off.'

'When a lock is disengaged, Cuff rules don't apply,' Anderson mumbled. 'Now if you excuse me, I have a crossword to do while I'm guarding your sorry arse.'

He slammed the door in her face. She looked up at the light above the door. Red. But who knew what the light was on the other side.

At least now she had a weapon. She clutched the makeshift shiv and sat on her bed staring at the door. Flinching at every sound. To take her mind off it, she started thinking about when the library cart came. Yesterday was Monday, today was Tuesday. So it was later today.

Liza wanted the gun – believing just as everyone else did that she had it stashed somewhere. But of course, she hadn't. What were the chances it was still in the Unit somewhere? High, if one of the other prisoners killed Barnard. Low, if a third party did. That was coupled with the fact no one had found it.

Three things: that's what she needed.

The clue that led Barnard to uncover the secret of North Fern.

Barnard's murderer.

Barnard's murder weapon.

All before Friday morning.

That was three things too many.

It was all too much.

Cara lay back on her bed, and closed her eyes. She never wanted this. She never asked for this. Someone had come into the cell and killed Barnard. The sedative made her sleep through. Unless they had used a silencer?

You know, silencers. The court said you knew all about silencers. You had to print off a bloody How-To from the internet about how to attach one. It even dropped off that one time and you spent ten minutes trying to find any bits that may have pinged off it. But you did it. And you went upstairs.

No.

That was a dream.

A nightmare.

She did not kill them.

You didn't do it. You didn't do it. You didn't do it.

She'd been researching silencers for a paper she was doing at university. She didn't deny it. It became a staple of the prosecution's argument.

You didn't do it. You didn't do it. You didn't do it.

Unless . . .

'Shut up!' she said, to no one.

She didn't kill them. This alternate reality was pulling at her, but she knew. She knew. She did not kill them.

Unless . . . maybe you're crazy town banana pants.

'SHUT UP!' She slammed her fist into the wall. She wasn't sure how loudly she'd shouted, but Anderson on the other side of the cell door hadn't seemed to hear.

She couldn't lose her head. Not now.

She couldn't be questioning one crime. When she was trying to disprove another.

She didn't kill anyone. She had never ended anyone's life. Wouldn't know how to conjure up the evil to do it. Wouldn't have the evil to decide to conjure.

Children.

Children.

'I didn't do it,' said Detective Lockhart, in her cell. The weathered detective lay back on her cot but felt no respite. What the hell was going on? Why were all these yellow-bellied punks pointing the finger at her? Such things didn't happen in the Hole of Angels.

'SHUT UP. EVERYONE JUST SHUT UP,' she shouted, and this time Anderson banged on the door.

'All all right in there, princess?'

Cara opened her mouth to say 'I'm fine.' Then realised she didn't owe him anything. So shut her mouth again.

The world fractured before her. She came here, to North Fern, knowing she didn't do it. She didn't kill Kelvin and Tilly Stoker. No, knowing wasn't strong enough.

Adamant.

She had to be adamant.

She *was* adamant. Adamant that this wasn't her. When the whole world said it was, she was still able to stand up and say NO. NO IT WASN'T.

But now . . .

Things were . . . Complicated.

'I just want to . . .' she muttered. She was going to say 'die'. But she wasn't there yet.

So she settled for sleep. Even though she didn't deserve it. The library cart was still a few hours away. She had time to sleep. Even though she didn't think she would.

But, nonetheless, something pulled her under.

16

When Cara woke up, Harper was sitting watching her. He didn't look angry, he didn't look sad – nothing. No emotion. Just staring.

'You know I'm really getting sick of finding someone in my cell,' Cara said, sitting up.

Harper took a second to respond. 'Why would you think it matters what you feel anymore?'

'Why are you here?' Cara asked.

'I've been investigating the case. The case of you killing your friend over there.' He gestured to Barnard's empty bed. 'And I don't understand. I don't understand any of it.'

'You've mentioned that,' Cara said, 'in fact, I think you barked it through a door.'

'You know why we let you out? Didn't just keep you in there?' Harper asked. 'It was my idea. I thought it was a great one, I really did. The criminal returning to the scene of the crime.

'We're watching you, if you didn't already know that. Camera right up there in every cell. We have a control room down in the barracks two floors beneath this one – and we monitor everything. So I watched you. As

226

you came back here. I watched you for every second, for every movement, for every breath. Because I thought you had known we were looking for the gun, and you knew we hadn't found it. But there's only so long a hiding place can be a hiding place.

'I was adamant you would get the gun.

'But you haven't.

'And now . . . now I don't understand.'

Cara waited for him to finish. 'Have you ever considered the possibility that I didn't do it?'

Harper mused over this. He got up, and he paced, and he clutched his head. Like a madman. And then he looked at Cara. 'Every. Single. Second.'

She should have been glad. But she surprised herself by being angry. 'Then why aren't you doing anything?'

Harper resumed pacing. 'Because the logs don't lie. They can't. No one came in or out. And the camera cut out for only 12.5 seconds. Somehow you killed her, stashed the gun, and returned to your original position, to the millimetre, in that time. The only question is how.'

Cara laughed. Harper looked around. 'Bit pathetic don't you think? Coming to the suspect to wallow in the fact you're crap at your job?'

'I need to know, Cara. I'm driving myself crazy here. Just please.'

'Wait,' Cara said, 'barracks? Does that mean you sleep here?'

'Cara!'

'I am tired of explaining to you, I didn't do it. I don't

know who did. I don't know where the gun is because I didn't use it. Get it?'

Harper stopped. Started towards Cara. She couldn't help shrink away. 'But you did, Cara. Don't you see? Maybe you don't remember it, or maybe you're protecting yourself from the memory of it. But you need to let go. You need to just tell me you did it. I need that.'

Cara looked him up and down. 'Pathetic. I didn't do it. Can you leave now?'

Harper seemed to realise what he was doing. He hid his desperation behind the icy stare he wore before. Like he was a different person. 'Bring me the gun, Lockhart. Face up to what you've done. Don't be a coward.' He started towards the door.

'Harper,' she shouted, and he stopped but didn't look around. 'You refuse to see the truth. You refuse to think outside your stupid philosophy. Who's really the coward?'

Harper left the room, but Cara knew he heard every word.

17

Cara sat there seething with anger. She didn't know for how long. But the *BLARP* of work finishing snapped her out of it. Right on time. Anderson hadn't woken her for lunch and she didn't know exactly when Harper had come, but for that she was glad. All she wanted – needed, now – was to wait for the library cart and, presumably, Michael to come along with it. Liza was right – it was the only thing that came in and out of the unit that prisoners had direct access to. Somebody could have smuggled a gun in on it – but would Michael had to have known for that to happen?

She thought about her game plan here, and immediately realised that was a bad idea. The more she thought about what she was going to do, going to say, the muddier it got. Strands of theories and thoughts wrapped around each other and tied themselves into knots.

She thought until she couldn't think anymore. And then just decided to stop. Busying herself with looking out of her window, which was showing an autumnal forest scene.

Wait, window? She meant screen. (How had she got that wrong?)

It was an hour until she heard the cart coming down the corridor.

For one terrifying moment, she wondered if it would skip her cell. *The Butcher multiplied by two doesn't get any books.* Either that or Michael wouldn't be allowed in.

But the cart stopped outside her cell and she heard Michael muttering something to Anderson. Anderson seemed to put up some kind of an argument – Cara heard him muttering all manner of swear words under his breath, some of which she was pretty sure he had made up himself. But finally the door opened and Michael wheeled the cart inside.

He looked at Cara like she was the scum of the Earth. Any semblance of friendliness was gone. 'I need my book back.'

It wasn't what she was expecting to hear. 'What?'

'*Needful Things*. It was left in this cell. Steph— Barnard said she wanted you to read it, so I left it with her. Where is it?'

Cara looked confused. 'I don't know. It wasn't in the drawers. I could look—' She'd already established there were no books in the cell, but Michael seemed so adamant, she thought she had to look. Cara started to get up, but Michael winced, and shrunk away, as though the threat of her hurting him had actually done so already. She scowled at him and looked behind the bedside table. It wasn't there. 'Wouldn't the guards have taken it already?'

'No,' Michael said.

She sighed and slowly got on her hands and knees

230

and looked under the beds. Nothing under hers. And nothing under B . . . No, wait. There was somewhere she hadn't checked. Right at the back in the corner, there was something. She reached in and felt for it, her hands clasping what was indeed a hardback book. Why hadn't the search found it? Maybe they disregarded it?

She pulled it out and got up, her subconscious barely registering a small clatter. She looked up. Michael was staring at her, expectant. 'Here you go,' she said, holding it out to him. Michael snatched it away.

'Thank you,' he said, but he didn't move. He just held it in his hands, while his eyes drifted over to Barnard's bed.

'Michael,' Cara said, and he jumped again like he'd forgotten she was there, 'I need to ask you a question.'

'No,' Michael said firmly, 'you don't get to. I came for my book and I got it – that is all.' He slotted the book back into the cart. 'I don't need to engage with you anymore.'

Cara said quickly, 'Have you ever smuggled anything into a unit for anyone?'

This got his attention. He couldn't help but engage now. 'What? No, I would never . . . What are you talking about? I don't . . .'

'There's a lot of women in here who'd do a lot of things to get their hands on things from outside. Cigarettes, drugs, alcohol . . . even weapons. And you have the only device that goes in and out of the Unit that we have access to. That cart.'

Michael scoffed. 'What do I look like to you? How

can you say that? I have never done any such thing and I would never ask for anything in return. Especially not what you're insinuating.'

Cara almost felt sorry for him. But she couldn't stop now. 'I didn't kill Barnard, Michael. Your first name's Dale, right? I didn't do it, Dale.'

'Don't call me that. You don't get to call me that,' Michael snapped. 'You killed her. You're just so messed up in the head that you think you didn't. I believe you believe it . . . maybe. But you did. And why am I even listening to you, why am I even allowing you to speak? Shut up, just shut up.' He slammed his hands down on the cart and all of the books shook in their makeshift shelves. 'You . . . Why would you do that? Why her? Why would you do it?'

'I didn't kill her.'

'Shut up.'

'I didn't.'

'Shut up,' Michael said forcefully.

'Someone else killed her, which means someone else somehow got their hands on a gun. And, for what it's worth, I wouldn't peg you for a smuggler, but it turns out that I'm not the best judge of character. I mean, look where I am. I didn't kill Barnard, Michael. I would explain it, and try to convince you, but neither of us has time. So I'm going to ask you a question, and I'm kinda sorry – but I have to ask. Did you smuggle a gun into this unit on that rickety little cart of yours?'

Michael laughed but there was nothing but sorrow in the sound. 'Why in the hell would I help smuggle in a gun for someone to kill Stephanie Barnard? Do you know how insane that sounds?'

'From my perspective, this is all pretty insane. So don't hold it against me, if I don't believe you.'

'I don't need you to believe me,' Michael shouted, and they both paused to listen for Anderson outside. There was no acknowledgement of any noise at all, so Michael continued. 'Why am I even saying that? I'm the one who doesn't believe you. This is ridiculous. Why am I still here?' He started to turn the cart to the door and then stopped as though he'd just realised that he had something left to do. He turned back to Cara. 'I would never have done anything that would ever have put Stephanie in even the slightest bit of danger.'

'And why's that?' Cara said.

'BECAUSE I LIKED HER,' Michael shouted. And then immediately snapped his mouth shut.

An immense silence enveloped the cell – Cara felt her cheeks burning hot with shame. She'd known that. So why had she pushed so hard, why had she taken it out on this nice man – barely more than a boy?

'I liked her,' Michael said again, but much softer this time. 'And I know it was ridiculous. And I know it was pointless. And stupid. And all the words you could think to describe something so abnormal. But, somehow, I think she liked me too. I used to start looking forward to coming in this cell for the five minutes that I did every week, and she'd be there, sitting on the bed, waiting for me. Yes, she was out of my league, yes, she was a bloody prisoner, but, for some reason, none of that mattered.'

Michael looked at Cara through tears, and said once more, 'I liked her.'

Cara couldn't think of what to say. She wanted to apologise, but she knew it would fall on deaf ears. Michael was still firm in his belief that Cara had killed his crush. And there was no way she was going to change that. So she just said, as softly as Michael's voice, 'She did.'

'What?'

'I saw it. The way she looked at you, the way she acted when she knew you were coming. She liked you too.'

And Michael's tears warped his eyes. And then there was a spark of anger in his face. 'No. No. No. No, you don't get to do that. You don't get to say that. You don't . . .' He trailed off, wiped his eyes and composed himself. His walls came down almost instantly and Cara knew that she was never going to get anything from Michael, because Michael had nothing to give. And she should have known that.

What had this place made her? North Fern was suffocating her, eroding her – turning her into something she wasn't. Even through all the accusations, all the murder and the bloodshed, she had to stay true to who she was. Otherwise, what was the point of trying to survive. If when you did, you were a different person.

Detective Lockhart in 'The Long Dark Night of the Soul'.

She would rather die Cara Lockhart, than live as the monster everyone thought she was.

Michael turned to go, and Cara didn't stop him, but he stopped himself, at the door. He bent down to the library cart and shuffled a few books around before selecting one. A Stephen King that Cara had never heard of – just a bunch of numbers on the cover, or maybe a date. Michael almost hugged it as he took it over to Barnard's bed and placed it very carefully on the pillow. 'Just got this in,' he whispered softly to the bed. And then he got his cart and left the cell.

Cara looked across at Barnard's bed with the book placed so lovingly on it. And then she remembered that sound she'd heard earlier when she picked up the other book. She got down and looked under Barnard's bed. There was something there – something that had fallen out of the book. Something small, rectangular and white. She picked it up, quickly looking around to make sure Anderson hadn't snuck in or Michael had come back without her hearing. She kept it low, her body blocking it – as she now knew there had to be a camera watching her. And then she looked at it.

It was a card. On one side, it had ridged lines – a little like a barcode but cut into the card itself. The other side was blank, except for a tiny name printed in black – MICHAEL.

A key card. Michael's key card.

Cara remembered what Harper had said the day they arrived. Guards had Cuffs for most things, but key cards to override communal areas.

Had Barnard swiped it from him? And hidden it in the book? Did she leave it here for Cara to find?

There were so many questions, but only one in her head as she slipped it into her pocket.

What did it unlock?

18

'Lockhart needs her medication.'

Continell's voice outside, talking to Anderson. Again, she couldn't hear what Anderson was saying, but she knew he'd be objecting.

Cara had forgone dinner as well as lunch. She didn't want to eat. She just kept fiddling with the key card in her pocket. It had to unlock the secrets Barnard found — it was just a question of where those secrets were. And then, when Cara figured that out, it was a question of getting there.

She had a hell of a headache, thinking about all this, and, what's more, she had started to get incredibly jumpy. More than half a dozen times, she had leapt up out of her bed thinking someone was coming through the door, her left hand gripping the makeshift shiv Liza had given her. But it was just noise from somewhere else in the Unit.

She jumped up now. But this time someone was actually coming through the door. Continell.

'Lockhart, come with me. It's time for your meds.'

Surprisingly Anderson didn't follow as Continell took her out to the entrance of the Unit. They were met with no resistance, as it seemed everyone had retired to get ready for bed. Cara wondered if she could escape from Continell's grasp and go looking for answers – but she had no idea where she'd go, and would probably get caught before she made up her mind. And then she knew there'd be extra security on her – she might even end up back in the Hole.

So she just went with Continell. And, soon enough, she found herself once again standing in front of the guards' station as Continell wheeled out her yellow medicine trolley. She got out her keys and went to put them in the drawer. But there was a strange yelp behind her that made them both jump. Continell wheeled round and Cara looked up.

Truchforth had just come out of the Unit, carting with him a young woman Cara only knew by sight. She was young and pretty, but, right at this moment, her face had gone purple and she was gasping and wheezing. 'Um . . . Rachel? I think this lass is having an allergic reaction.'

Continell cursed under her breath. 'I only gave her aspirin.'

Truchforth looked lost. The girl started clutching at her throat and her mouth, seeming to lose all natural form as she gasped something none of them had any hope of making out. Continell, flustered, flew out from behind the trolley and seized the girl, guiding her and an extremely uncomfortable looking Truchforth into a room just off to the side.

It took Cara a few seconds to realise she was alone. She spun around to ensure no one was around, and, yes, she was totally and gloriously alone. But she didn't know how long she had. She could search the guards' station at least. She looked for cameras in every corner of the small room. But she couldn't see any – not that that meant they weren't there.

She had to move fast.

She rounded the station desk so she was behind it. And it just got better. Continell had left her keys there. Cara searched all the drawers – surprised to find that most of them were almost entirely empty. There was a drawer just full of used newspapers, each open at the crossword, and the crossword was completed on every single one – so she wasn't sure of their use. The other drawers didn't really have anything of any consequence either.

Except the bottom drawer of the yellow medicine cabinet – marked 'Resident Medication'. She opened it, and saw that it didn't actually have the medication inside but, rather, files on all the residents. Most of them were empty – obviously the vast majority of the Unit were not on any medication at all – but she finally found the file marked Lockhart, which had a solitary page inside – along with a dull green prescription. She picked up the page, which looked like the exact form she had seen Doctor Toby Trenner filling out back in his office all that time ago. It was hard to read his handwriting – a true doctor – but eventually she got into the tune of it, and started reading. Most of it was just boilerplate stuff – Cara's name, date of birth, things like that – but finally she got to the medication details. Toby Trenner's notes were:

One sedative to be consumed nightly.

Crossed out to:

Two sedatives to be consumed nightly.

Toby's scrawl of a signature was there at the bottom of the page, but before that there was also a list of what was actually in the tablet she was taking. She couldn't believe her eyes. There had to be some kind of mistake. There was only one ingredient – one drug. Something that turned her stomach.

Codeine.

But that was a painkiller – what was it doing in a sedative?

And she was allergic to codeine. She'd found out when she was four years old and her mother took her to the hospital when she tripped and broke her leg on the kerb outside their house. The doctors had given her codeine and that night she'd had terrible hallucinations of cartoon fuzzy spiders climbing up the walls, and she thought her mother, asleep in the chair next to her hospital bed, was a talking grizzly bear.

But Toby would have had Cara's complete medical history. He must have, if he was allowed to prescribe her medication. So he would have known that Cara was allergic to codeine.

She looked up from the file, trying to process it. Toby would have known what type of reaction she had to the drug. He would have known it caused Cara to have—

No.

No.

There must have been some sort of mistake. Maybe Toby didn't know, maybe it hadn't been included in her notes, there was no way he would have deliberately— Was there?

Why would he give her codeine? To her, a hallucinogen – the allergies saw to that. Unless it wasn't supposed to be a sedative, unless it was there for a different purpose entirely – *that* purpose. No-Face in the cells. The endless loop of *Rain on Elmore Street*. It could have been due to the codeine – and she couldn't disprove the fact that maybe that was the intention.

Cara jumped as the door to her side opened. She quickly put the prescription and the folder behind her back – as though that would really help her. But Continell, who had opened the door, was still looking into the room she was leaving and saying 'Just keep her drinking the water, and make sure she breathes.'

Quickly, Cara put everything back in the drawer, and then swiftly tore off the top layer of the prescription and shut the drawer. She got back around the desk, just as Continell turned.

The guard looked panic-stricken, but recovering. 'Just a tablet caught in her throat,' she said. 'Where were we?'

Cara took her medication, careful not to show anything in her face. The tablet didn't go down quite as smooth as usual – now she knew what it was doing to her. In fact, she rather hoped that it did get stuck in her throat. But it didn't.

After she had shown her open mouth to Continell, moving her tongue around, and she was being escorted back to her cell, she asked as calmly as she could, 'Can I see Doctor Trenner tomorrow?'

Continell thought for a second, and then sighed, 'I'll send a request but I'm not promising anything. You've got me for company tomorrow.'

Continell for an entire day. Lovely.

But also a possibility of finding out the truth.

19

Continell kept her word and after another tense break-fast, she took Cara to Doctor Trenner's office. Cara clutched the prescription in her pocket the entire way. When they got there, Continell guided her into the office – Toby wasn't there – and stayed with her until he arrived.

Toby sat at his desk and Cara waited until Continell had shut the office door to slap the prescription on the desk.

'Why are you poisoning me?' she snapped.

Toby was clearly taken aback. He actually laughed. 'I'm sorry, what?' He looked down at the prescription. She tossed it at him and he caught it.

'This medication – the stuff you're giving me – has codeine in it. Codeine makes me hallucinate – it's why I'm seeing weird stuff everywhere. No-Face. Movies playing over and over. Things out of the corner of my eye. Codeine – and I know my allergies are recorded in my medical notes.'

Toby looked at the prescription for a long time. And finally said quietly, 'What is this?'

'It's the prescription you gave me. It was in my file.'

He turned it over and over in his hand. 'No this can't be. This is signed in my name, but that's not my signature. This isn't even my handwriting. I prescribed you diazepam. And I specifically remember reading you were allergic to codeine, so I chose something that wasn't even remotely close to it. But then,' he regarded the prescription, 'here this is.'

'How can I trust you? How can I trust anyone in this whole place?' Cara jumped up in rage.

Toby didn't shrink back in fear or follow her up in sheepish defence, he just stared at her. Then he said, 'Look I can show you.' He scrabbled around in his desk and brought a pen out. 'This isn't my handwriting, Cara. See?' He wrote something down on a piece of paper and slid it over to her.

This is my handwriting. TT

'Do you see?' He slid the prescription over too. The handwriting didn't match – it was nowhere even close. Cara slumped down in confusion. 'It's incredibly hard to fake handwriting, I'm sure you'll agree.'

She looked at him. He was telling the truth. And he was just as baffled as she was.

Cara put her head in her hands. She couldn't help letting out a sob. 'Someone else. Someone else is poisoning me.'

'I'm afraid it might be even worse than that,' Toby said, taking back the prescription. 'Someone is forging prescriptions. Someone is committing a crime and it had to have happened between me writing the prescription – your true prescription – and it being logged in

243

the system. Furthermore, it had to be someone with authority.'

Cara thought back to that day when Toby initially told her he was giving her some meds to help her sleep. It didn't take long for her to seize on the truth. 'Anderson.'

'Anderson?'

'Yes,' Cara said, 'you gave Anderson the prescription that day. It had to be him.'

Toby got up, scratching his chin, and went over to pour himself a glass of water. He downed it in one, looking very uncomfortable. 'This is a very odd situation. I'll admit I don't quite know what to do.'

Cara went over to him. Again, she was thankful he didn't wince as she approached. 'And what do I do?'

'Well, you don't take any more of the medication, that's for sure,' Toby said, firmly. 'I'll go up to the Unit later today – I'll leave it a few hours, so no one suspects it's because of this meeting. When you put in a prescription, you need to sign off on it – that will tell us exactly who input the data. If it's Anderson, I'll go to Ms Krotes.'

'What do you mean – if it's Anderson?' Cara said, and then she thought back again. And remembered something else about that day—

Anderson pocketed the prescription, muttering something, and took Cara's arm, using too much force to pull her along the corridor. It hurt. She almost wanted to shout that she could walk herself, but every time she opened her mouth, he yanked again and the pain silenced her.

They rounded a corner, and as they were about to go past Krotes' office, the door opened. Madeleine Krotes stood there in the doorway, in a dazzling blue jacket and skirt. She looked like a movie star – almost like she had walked off the screen while Rain on Elmore Street *was playing. As she noticed Anderson and Cara coming, she paused, watching them.*

She smiled – not at her, but at Anderson.

Cara looked around and up at Anderson. He had a goofy, almost boyish smile on his face watching his governor with lustful eyes. But that wasn't what Cara was looking at.

Because Krotes had done something else – given Anderson an almost imperceptible nod.

Cara opened her mouth but saw that Toby was already looking knowingly at her. Then he looked away, out of the window.

Something else had happened.

'You have to go now,' Toby said, 'I have an appointment. Don't tell anyone about this.'

'What's happened?' she said. 'You know something.'

He ignored her. 'We need to keep this between us, until we have more proof. If I check the records, that should be enough for us to work out who did this – who is feeding you a hallucinogen.'

'TOBY,' Cara shouted, and he looked at her, surprised. Cara hoped she hadn't shouted too loud, so as to alert Continell in the corridor. 'Tell me what you know. Please.'

Toby sighed, couldn't meet her eyes. 'I wanted to believe you about Barnard, so I looked at the records of doors locked and unlocked on the night Stephanie Barnard was killed – just as all the guards have no doubt already done. Your cell door was not accessed or unlocked via the Cuff scanner. This means no guard or, potentially – if they found a way to fool it – no other resident went through that door. There was no way anyone else went through that door. Except . . . There's the override.' He grew silent.

'Override?' Cara said. 'Why has no one told me about this?'

'Because it's not widely known. Not just anyone can override the locks – otherwise what would be the point? And if everyone could do it, there'd be anarchy. It's a last resort. There's only one person who has the clearance level to override the Cuff locks, and it wouldn't show up on the logs. Not the guards, not the other staff, only one person.'

'Who?' said Cara.

Toby was still looking at the carpet. 'This is akin to treason. I shouldn't be telling you this.'

'Who?' pushed Cara. Even though Toby didn't have to say anything – she already knew.

Toby's eyes finally rose up to meet hers. 'I can't say yet. Just let me investigate. I promise I'll get back to you. I believe you.'

And Cara found that that was enough.

20

The rest of the day was a washout. Continell revealed herself to be uncharacteristically strict – either that or she wanted to do as little work as possible. She trailed Cara back from Toby's office, and then commanded she go to her cell. Cara had planned on going to search the yard or somewhere – keep her mind busy while trying to process the information Toby gave her – but Continell was having none of it.

'You stay in here,' she snapped as she plopped Cara down on her bed. 'It's better for both of us.'

Cara waited for her to leave – she needed time to process what Toby had said, but, to her horror, Continell disappeared only momentarily to bring in a plastic chair and a newspaper and sit in the corner of the cell, as though she were some kind of suicide risk.

'You really don't need to sit in here,' Cara said.

Continell just looked at her, unimpressed. 'This isn't a five-star hotel, Lockhart. You don't decide what you get.'

Continell stayed there all day, reading her newspaper, and Cara just watched her with frustration and, in time, interest. Continell seemed to be reading the same page over and over. She never turned the page. At one point, Cara wondered if she had fallen asleep with her eyes open, but then she twitched her nose and her eyes started sliding over the words on the broadsheet again – words she must have already read hundreds of times by now.

Time snaked by, and Cara felt an incredible itch to just get up and walk out of the cell. She could overpower Continell – push straight past her – and that was if she even noticed. But then she'd be caught as soon as she left, so what point was there?

To Cara, right here, right now, the answers she had been seeking were just outside the door. They were mocking her, playing hide-and-seek. And she couldn't seek them because Continell was standing guard.

She remembered when she was young, her mum played hide-and-seek with her once. Cara was insanely good at it. She found her mother in, like, two minutes, but she hid for about five hours. When she finally snuck out of her hiding spot, Cara discovered that her mother wasn't even in the house. She had left Cara in the care of the neighbour's daughter, who was lounged on their budget sofa, blowing bubblegum and saying that Miss Lockhart had gone to meet an old friend or something, she didn't care, stop asking her. At the time, young Cara had taken that as a lie – her mother had gone into town especially to look for her because she was so awesome at hide-and-seek. Now, she knew it wasn't.

'Have you ever played hide-and-seek?' Cara found herself saying, to the cell and, she guessed, to Continell.

Continell took a few seconds to look up and glanced around as if there were other people nearby that the question could have been directed to. 'What?'

'Have you—?' And then Cara realised she didn't care in the slightest. 'Never mind.'

'I'm not your chum, Lockhart,' Continell said, going back to the same place in her paper. 'And I don't do small talk. So just shut up and wait to be transferred, so you can stop being such a nuisance to all of us.'

Cara lay back on her bed and closed her eyes.

And soon she had fallen into a doze.

And the day wasted away.

21

Truchforth was due to watch her the next day – the last day. Thursday. She had to assume that she was getting transferred the morning after – Friday. On Friday, she would be taken and the mythical evidence that Barnard had claimed to find would be lost. And what was more, Minnie and Liza would find a way to get to her – kill her, or at least make her wish she was dead.

She'd had a sleepless night.

She started to wonder if Barnard had been telling the truth about this 'thing' that proved her innocence. She started to wonder if she could trust Toby Trenner, and whether he had been truthful when he had said he believed her.

What a way to end the story of Detective Lockhart – if her one and only case had been to chase a magical MacGuffin around the Unit, only to get transferred and then knifed to death in her sleep by lackeys of someone who wasn't even there.

What an end.

Not exactly Reichenbach.

But fitting enough, she supposed.

But then she'd thought about Barnard. Her friend.

And she'd thought about why she would want to lie about something like that.

And she thought about that look in Barnard's eyes when she had told her about it.

Barnard had been telling the truth. Cara knew she had been.

She had to believe in Barnard – even now that she was long gone.

There was a noise by the cell door and she looked up to see she had a familiar caller, but she didn't seem so happy this time. Nice to see her door was still unlocked.

Cara stood up and braced herself. As Liza launched herself at her.

Liza slammed Cara against the wall, her hands clasped around her throat. She gripped hard – and Cara started seeing sunspots. 'Where is it, Lockhart?'

'I . . .' Cara choked, 'I . . .'

'Where is the gun? If you don't get it, I'll get it myself. I might even shoot you with it.' Liza squeezed harder, and then seemed to realise what she was doing, and the fact she wouldn't get any answers if Cara was dead on the floor. Liza stepped back.

Cara's hands shot to her neck and she gasped. 'What are you doing? You're crazy.'

'There's a lot of that going around,' Liza said, slamming her fist into the wall. 'Where is it?'

Cara momentarily forgot what she was talking about. 'Where's what?'

Liza rolled her eyes. 'Very cute. The bloody gun, Butcher. Why have you not got it yet – why have you not given it to me? You haven't got any other ideas, have you? Because I'm here to tell you that it won't go well for you if you try and turn this around on me. You wouldn't be the first person who tried to shoot me.'

'I'm not going to try and shoot you,' Cara said, incredulously – rubbing her neck. 'I haven't got the gun yet because . . . because I haven't had the chance.'

'What do you mean – haven't had the chance? Are you even the Butcher?'

Cara realised she had to get Liza's help. And to get that, she had to persuade her that she could get what she wanted. And, in turn, maybe Liza could help her. Because it took her nearly being choked to death to have a moment of clarity.

She knew where the key card unlocked.

'I am the Butcher,' she said as confidently as she could. 'I've just run into an issue. I have to get to a specific place in the Unit, past the dining room, in the corridor between that and the yard, and I can't do that while there are guards endlessly there, can I? And what's more, I'm being watched day and night. It was easier to hide the gun before, because I had no guard assigned to me. And it was the middle of the night. Simple.

'But now, now the spotlight is firmly on me. And I can't get to it,' Cara finished and knew she had persuaded Liza. The woman in front of her seemed to be ticking, gestating with possibilities. It was almost endearing to watch.

'OK,' Liza said, licking her lips, 'then tell me where you stashed it. I'll go and get it.'

'I'm not going to do that,' Cara said, 'and we both know it.'

Liza considered this.

'Look, just help me get to that corridor and I will get you what you want.'

'You want to go for something else. You want to get there for something else you're looking for too, don't you?'

'Does it matter?'

Liza thought and then shook her head. 'I suppose it doesn't. As long as I get what I want. But if this other thing is in any way some attempt to undermine me, I will find out. And I'll . . .'

'Kill me, yes,' Cara said, actually impressed by how calm her voice was. She sounded more annoyed than terrified. Was this how everyone else saw her? Had she slipped into the guise of what she was perceived to be? What was that old rhyme the bitches from New Hall had made up?

'The Butcher's on the prowl tonight,
So get your loved ones hid
We may be the scum of the Earth
But at least we didn't kill a kid.'

Yes, that was it. Wasn't exactly *Elmore Street*, but it had been catchy enough for a whole wing to chant it over and over and over when she was first incarcerated – led to her cell by two guards that she had already forgotten the names of. What a pathetic state of affairs – to be nostalgic for a prison.

In front of Liza, she was the Butcher now. Confident. Menacing. Definitely not scared. 'You know you should really hand threats out sparingly. Otherwise, the threatened party might start to believe you're full of bullcrap.'

Liza started to launch forward again, and then stopped herself. 'You think you're hot stuff now, do you? I will break you.'

'Another threat.'

'For God's sake, I will tear you . . .'

'Another threat. You see how this is starting to become a little tedious?'

This stopped Liza.

Cara said, 'Now, I need to get to that corridor, without any guards breathing down my neck and I need you to help me. Otherwise, no gun for parent killer. And I'm thinking that you need that gun more than you're letting on – it isn't just a bid for power. I think Minnie might be coming for you too. So what's the plan?'

Liza thought, almost jogging on her feet. Her thinking process unfiltered. 'OK . . . OK . . . OK . . . There's been a schedule change. I don't know why. But it was announced at dinner. Tomorrow in the morning – that's when I'll do it. I know exactly what to do. I can make a distraction – make all the guards come to me. But you have to get me that gun. You have to. Or you know what will happen, and I won't make it quick.'

'What are you going to do?'

'Tomorrow morning, there's a very special film being shown in the yard. I don't suppose you've ever heard of *Rain on Elmore Street*?'

22

The day and night passed extraordinarily slowly. Cara lay there, not moving, just waiting.

She knew why the schedule had changed. She knew why *Rain on Elmore Street* was getting a surprise showing on Thursday morning. It was Krotes – Krotes was tormenting her, giving her a send-off. Maybe Krotes even knew about the threats from Minnie and Liza. Maybe she knew that, come Friday, Cara was getting sent off to her death.

But little did Madeleine Krotes know that the showing of *Rain on Elmore Street* was just what she needed. To get to the one door in the entire Unit that didn't have a Cuff scanner. The door the key card must unlock.

Cara just had to hope Liza would come through. She had told her to keep a low profile until the screening and she couldn't risk running into Minnie, or someone else who only had plans to do her harm. She just waited in her cell, and thought – and the more she thought, the more she knew the answers she was searching for were behind that door in the corridor between the dining room and the yard. They had to be—

Right?

Finally, the *Rain on Elmore Street* procession towards the yard started outside her room. She heard it before Truchforth rapped on her door. 'You're seeing a movie,' he said, his eyes lingering on her frame on the bed for a little too long. 'I've heard it's a musical.' And his old pruned lips stretched into a smile. As if the old bastard hadn't seen *Elmore Street* five billion times before. She supposed it was what he thought of as a joke.

'Good,' Cara said. 'I hope it's *Evita*. I like *Evita*.'

Truchforth didn't like that. He moaned his discontent, and then waved at Cara to get up. She didn't, but when he started forward to help her, she shot upwards.

She didn't want him touching her.

He led her out and she was glad that she found herself at the back of the procession. She chanced a glance down the opposite way, out of the Pit, towards the entrance to the Unit. It was empty. It was stupid, but she half expected to see Krotes there, waiting to foil her plan.

She followed the residents down the Pit, through the dining room, past the hidden door to the Hole, into the corridor and when she rounded the final corner and could see the doors to the yard, she spotted Liza. Thank God.

If Cara got taken into the yard, it was all over.

Truchforth had gone ahead and was standing by Liza at the entrance to the yard. They were already having a heated conversation. Cara inched closer, knowing that she couldn't escape yet. The door – *the door* – was behind Cara now, she'd walked straight past it. She'd done it so many times, it was easy to do it again. Good – it wouldn't look like it meant anything to her.

She studied Liza and Truchforth.

She had to time it just right.

The others were filtering in past Liza, ignoring her, no doubt remembering the fuss she'd caused at many screenings prior. But Cara didn't think that fuss would be enough this time, and Truchforth started to look round for Cara and Liza seemed to agree as she said, 'Did you just touch my arse?'

Truchforth snapped his attention back to the feisty blonde. 'What?'

'You just touched my arse, you creep.'

'I did no such thing.'

'Then why did I feel wrinkly fingers on my left cheek, Scumforth?'

'I have no idea what you're talking about.'

'Harper,' Liza called, trying to attract his attention as she started to step inside the yard, and then she looked directly at Cara and winked. What happened next seemed to take everyone off guard, most of all Truchforth. Liza leapt up, launching herself side first into the yard. She disappeared, and Cara only heard a slam, no doubt as her body hit the floor, and then the scraping of chairs as Liza collided with them. 'He pushed me!' Liza shrieked, and there was instantly a massive uproar from a number of women. 'The bastard pushed me! Scumforth! Assault, assault! The old bastard.'

Truchforth slunk his way into the yard behind the last prisoner, bar Cara of course, and started indignantly proclaiming his innocence. The genius of it was that even though he hadn't actually done it, Truchforth's usual manner and tone of voice made it sound like he was lying through his teeth.

Cara heard other guards pipe up – Harper, Anderson, Abrams, Continell – and the shouts of the other residents as they realised what was going on.

Cara knew it was time to go, before one of them ventured outside the doors, possibly to inspect the scene of the crime, although it sounded like a full-blown riot had erupted, with women shrieking and swearing their own accusations at Truchforth – most of which Cara had no doubt were true.

Cara turned and began walking away, as Liza started up a chant of 'Scumforth! Scumforth! Scumforth!'

23

Cara hurried back down the corridor, past the bend and towards the door – the door without the Cuff scanner. She could still hear Liza causing a ruckus in the yard. The woman scared her to death, but she was good at what she knew – even if that was only being a monster. Everyone was in the yard – including the guards.

One shot.

Cara got to the door, pulling out the key card. She looked at it. There didn't seem to be anywhere to scan it, but she held it up and saw the ridges on the side actually corresponded to a pattern of a rectangle imprint halfway down the door. She pressed the key card into the imprint, lining up the ridges.

The door clicked and there was a mechanical scraping. The door swung open inwards, and with one look back down the empty corridor, Cara slipped into the room.

There was one thing that would screw this all up. But Barnard had been in here, so she thought it must be OK. But still, she looked at her Cuff. Blue. She stepped forward. Still blue. It didn't turn red. She let out a long breath. And looked around.

Everything was dark, more than dark – it was pitch

black. Cara felt around on the wall for a light switch and finally found one. She flipped it and bars of synthetic light flicked on above her.

She was standing in a large room that looked like it was once a classroom but had now become more of a storage room. There was a teacher's desk and a whiteboard to one side, with two smaller desks in the centre. There were bookshelves lining the wall nearest her, with hundreds of books on them. Cara looked and saw with dismay that they were all self-help books – popular ones with titles like *50 Ways to Change Your Life* and *Ways to Cope with Incarceration*. They all had impossibly bright covers for their subject matter. She turned her eyes from them in disgust to see there were two screens, behind the teacher's desk, which were turned off. She really hoped they stayed that way.

She checked the door was completely shut. It was. And her Cuff didn't seem to care.

Over the next two hours, she searched the room top to bottom. She started in the desks, pulling them up completely and upending their contents. There were just papers, files, and more books inside. She searched through them all – the files were nothing special, just financial reports, food rotas, building plans. Nothing that seemed that interesting. Although—

One of the financial reports caught her eye. It was a report on something called The Experiment. A hell of a lot of money was getting siphoned to that project – there was a list of expenses, but all the items were blacked out. But that wasn't all. The Experiment also had income. It was making money. What the hell was going on there?

Cara's mind immediately jumped to the most ridiculous scenario – a secret lab or a space elevator or a nuclear testing site. Something that cost over a hundred and seventy grand at least.

There was a sound outside. Her head shot up to the door, and her hand moved to her pocket where the sharpened piece of plastic was. It was someone moving past the room. They carried on up the corridor.

Cara put the file back in the desk. It was bizarre, but it didn't help her right now. The rest of the contents were unimportant, and the other two desks turned up zero. She turned to the bookshelves next and painstakingly searched every book. She was looking for another bookmark – anything out of the ordinary. But all she found was tips on how to improve her life from some popcorn-eating populists who believed they had something important to offer.

When she was done, she did a lap of the room, looking around. There was a plant in the corner that she even examined – nothing. She went to the centre of the room, slamming her hands on the desk, throwing her head back, screwing up her eyes and letting out a muffled scream of frustration.

This was it? Nothing. She had found nothing – nothing to help her prove she didn't kill Barnard. Nothing to help her prove she didn't kill Kelvin or Tilly Stoker. And just to cap it all off, nothing to help her out of her current predicament.

And she was exhausted. She slammed her back against

a wall and almost fell down it. A book fell off the shelf above her and dropped to the ground next to her. She picked it up, reading the title. *Acceptance and You: How to Deal With A Life Sentence*. She laughed, and laughed until her eyes were streaming with tears. She gripped the book and, with one strong movement, she flung it across the room. It slammed into the opposite wall just above a chest of drawers.

Click.

The wall seemed to fold in on itself, going backwards. There was a little gap of darkness. Cara wiped her eyes, making sure she wasn't imagining it. She wasn't.

Another hidden door. Behind the drawers.

She jumped up, and launched herself at the drawers, gripping them at one end and pushing with all her might. Slowly they moved out of the way and Cara was able to push the door. It was resistant, and took too much effort.

Cara almost gasped as it swung inward, presenting a small dark and damp room, more like the Hole than any other room on the Unit.

Even the Hole wouldn't look this uninviting if bathed in light though. It was a room filled with clutter – boxes stacked up against the walls, shelves filled with folders. Cara would have dearly loved to read every single one, but she knew she didn't have time.

She entered the room, wedging herself between the open door and shelves of what looked like little knick-knacks. Minute metallic models, like pieces of a Monopoly set. A spinning top. A painting. A raft. A radio set. Little trinkets that looked like they came out of a cracker snapped at Christmas dinner and forgotten about by dessert. Everything had a layer of dust on it and she blew it off, sending particles flying into the air. Her eyes stung and she closed them, wheeling around to get away from the dust.

And when she opened her eyes, she found herself looking at a stack of film reel steel containers in the corner.

She crouched down, picked one up and turned it sideways. The little handwritten tag said 'RAIN ON ELMORE STREET'.

Of course it did. It wasn't likely to be anything else, was it?

She cracked open the case, the same sensation as splitting an Easter egg down the middle, with anticipation, and looked at the reel inside.

She'd never seen a film reel before, hadn't been part of that generation, but she prodded and picked at it until she could get a seam free, like Sellotape, and pull it.

She pulled a ream of film out of the reel, already knowing she wouldn't be able to put it back how it was. She kept going until the entire film was out of the container and snaking around her. Good riddance, *Elmore Street* was no more. She held the film up to the light. She saw a miniature version of Eugene on the hotel stairs. It was about five minutes into the film. This particular version of Eugene would never get up those particular stairs. She gave out a cackling laugh, not unlike a fairy-tale villain, before throwing the film to the side.

The film reels were stacked next to a long desk, with

drawers all along the wall, that had an old typewriter sitting on it. A desk lamp was turned on and illuminated a piece of paper in the typewriter. Cara went and sat in the desk chair, looking at the paper. Someone had started writing something, and the more she read, the more she was confused—

My darling Deidra,
How do I even begin to describe how much I miss you?
Every time I go out to the garden, or go to the library, and I see the places we were so happy, my heart aches for you. I know it is not much longer until I see you again, and I hope you are

The letter stopped as if whoever was writing it had been stopped mid-thought.

Initially, Cara thought it was sweet, and then she read it again. Deidra? Wasn't that—?

She tore her eyes from the typewriter and started looking through the drawers. It seemed like every drawer had two things in it – separated by a divider. The top drawer had small green army men by the bucketload and cross-stitch patterns. It was bizarre. The next drawer had pressed flowers and dark-blue boxes of notepaper. The next drawer didn't have a divider – it was full to the brim with chocolate bars. What? The next drawer—

Wait.

Chocolate bars . . .

They couldn't be . . . She opened the drawer again. Chocolate bars in blue wrappers. She picked one up and turned it over – and she instantly felt sick. Big cartoony writing, not unlike a comic book style, said 'THWAMP!'

Peter. Peter's chocolate bars. The ones she got . . .

'Every week my mum sends me my favourite choco bar!' she said, gleefully without need for prompting. 'A THWAMP! Every single week without fail.'

Why would there be a drawer full of . . . But Cara didn't have to finish that thought. Everything was falling into place. And, on instinct, she went into the drawer above to look at the notepaper boxes.

She opened a box and saw exactly what she knew she was going to.

Notepaper that looked like a night sky – black-blue night punctuated with stars. Notepaper she'd seen before. Whenever Minnie opened a letter. She took the lid of the box and turned it over – to see the name of the paper in gold lettering. STAR-BOUND WISHES.

Chocolate bars and star-bound wishes.

She heard Barnard's voice say it again, as if she was in the room, as if she wasn't dead. She had known, she had found it, and she had given her the clue to find it. Barnard had unlocked the secret of North Fern.

And now Cara knew it too.

Even though she wished she could lock it up and throw away the key.

24

Cara's heart was pounding so hard she thought it might smash her ribs and burst through her chest. They were faking the letters – no one was actually receiving correspondence from their friends, their families.

It was all a lie.

Every time the Unit received letters, every Tuesday, lies were being spread to everyone. Peter's chocolate bar was not being sent by her mother but whoever was using this typewriter. Minnie's son wasn't using Starbound Wishes paper to write to her – this person was.

What the hell was North Fern?

What was going on here?

Cara had been wrong all along – ever since she'd got here, she'd been thinking about how much trouble *she* was in. But they were all in trouble.

Barnard had found that out. And now she was dead. Did Krotes discover she'd been in this room and had to silence her?

This was too much. This room was dark, evil. She had to get out.

With a THWAMP! bar in one pocket and a pad full of Star-bound Wishes-branded paper in the other, she left the room, not even bothering to replace the chest of drawers in front of the door. She didn't need to cover her tracks – by the time the person who used the typewriter returned to the hidden room, everything would be different anyway.

Cara walked through the classroom and switched off the light, before opening the door just a crack. Residents were walking past – *Rain on Elmore Street* must have just finished. It was hard in her panicked state to realise how lucky she was – she'd come out at just the right time.

The crowd was thinning and it looked as though the majority of the Unit had already gone past. She waited for a quiet moment and slipped into the corridor. She could just pretend she was going back too.

'Lockhart.' A shout and her stomach dropped. But as she looked back, she saw it came from someone around the corner, so someone who couldn't possibly have seen her leave the room. Truchforth came around the corner, with a confused look on his face. 'Lockhart?'

Cara tried to sound as calm as she could, even though her consciousness felt like it was somewhere up in the stratosphere. 'What?'

Were they all in on it? Did they all know what North Fern really was? She had it right the first time – *a box*. A completely sealed box. No in, no out.

This wasn't going to end well.

'How did you get past me?' Truchforth said. 'I was standing at the door.'

Cara shrugged, every movement feeling like she was wading through treacle. 'Maybe you're losing your eyesight in your old age. I walked right past you, Scumforth.'

This silenced Truchforth and he just escorted her up the corridor, towards the dining room.

She was going a mile a minute. If the letters were fake, what else was? Maybe North Fern wasn't even a prison, maybe it wasn't even in Buckinghamshire? But if it wasn't a prison, what was it?

It's hell.

Her inner voice wasn't helping. They got to the dining room, and started making their way across it. Everyone had to know, they had a right to – even if it jeopardised her place here. Of course it would – what would happen to her when she revealed she knew?

You'll end up like Barnard. One popped right between the eyes.

She didn't care anymore.

They got to the doors to the Pit and Truchforth placed her in front of the Cuff scanner. They had to know. But when?

She positioned her finger on the light box until it glowed green, and reached for the door.

No time like the present.

25

Cara rushed out into the Pit. It was full of women coming back from the movie and starting to relax for evening Illumination. They were standing around talking, or sitting, or walking to their cells – but it didn't matter what they were doing, it just mattered that they were all there. She wouldn't have long to do what she wanted to – hopefully it would be enough to get her point across.

She didn't think Truchforth even noticed she'd gone from his grasp, until she had got halfway to the Scrabble table. The usual women were gathered around it, setting up a game, but she couldn't stop to let them know what was going on. She launched herself on top of it, jumping and landing on the board. The residents around the table exclaimed loudly, as Cara kicked over their board and it fell off the table. The more ruckus she caused, the better.

Women started looking around.

'Everybody, listen to me,' Cara shouted into the Pit, her own voice echoing back to her. 'You have been lied to. Madeleine Krotes is a liar. You are not talking to your loved ones. You are not speaking to them. It's all fake.'

Anderson was at the top of the Pit, having walked ahead, almost instantly peering down at Cara and her growing audience. Why weren't they stopping her? He caught Continell, who was walking past and whispered something in her ear. She hurried out of the Unit. He needn't have whispered. Cara knew exactly what he'd said. And she was glad. And now she knew why they hadn't intervened. Because Madeleine Krotes was coming, and Cara could bet she wanted to deal with this herself.

'What the hell are you talking about?' one resident shouted and Cara looked back down. Nearly every pair of eyes in the Pit was on her. She gazed into the crowd and saw the faces she knew, Peter towards the front, Minnie and Liza fighting their way forward from either side, Moyley watching silently, following Liza, Deidra towards the back with a face like a slapped arse.

'Listen to me,' Cara said to the crowd, 'I know you don't have any reason to trust me. I know that you think I killed Stephanie Barnard. And I know that you think I killed two small children. But I didn't. You don't have to believe me about those things. You just need to believe me about this. You are being lied to. And you are being lied to from the very top.'

'Cara,' Minnie said, getting to the front of the crowd, 'what the hell are you doing?'

'Yeah, Butcher,' Liza said, getting there at almost the same time, 'this isn't exactly what I had in mind.'

'Cara?' A voice she hadn't expected. She looked in the direction of her cell and saw Toby Trenner standing there, holding his trademark folder, and looking confused, with a bemused Truchforth alongside him. He had to have been coming to visit her. 'Why don't you come down from the table and we'll talk this out.'

'No,' Cara shouted and she delved into her pockets and pulled out the chocolate bar in one hand and the pad of notepaper in the other. She showed them to the crowd. 'This is important. You can disregard everything I ever say from now on. You can lock me in the Hole, you can beat me up, you can kill me. But you all need to know this.'

'What is that in her hand?' said one resident.

'I can't see it,' said another.

But two people in the crowd looked like they knew exactly what they were.

Peter stepped forward. 'Is that . . .?'

Cara stooped down and handed it to her. Minnie reached up to grab the notepad. They both turned the finds over in their hands. 'Barnard left me a clue. One of the last things she ever said to me – "Chocolate bars and star-bound wishes." She found out that all the letters you were getting, all the presents, they were a lie. I found a drawer full of THWAMP! bars, which Peter thought she was getting from her mother, and reams of the special paper that Minnie gets her letters on, in the room without a Cuff lock near the yard. They've been lying to you. Krotes has been lying to you. Barnard knew it and that was why she had to die.'

As if on cue, a new person joined the guards up on the gangway. Cara knew she'd come – she couldn't not.

'Right on time,' Cara shouted to her. She stood there, looking down at Cara, an initial bout of confusion softening into something more sinister. The crowd was having a time alternating their gaze between the two of them, 'Don't you see. It all fits. Because not only has Madeleine Krotes been lying to you but she also was the only one apart from me who could've possibly killed Stephanie Barnard. She killed her, pinned it on me, and now she's been poisoning me, giving me a medication she knew I was allergic to. Doctor Trenner can attest to that.'

A shuffling as every head shifted to look at Toby Trenner.

Krotes stared down at them all, with an odd look of amusement on her face

'Cara, this isn't the way to do this,' Toby said, 'get down from there.'

Cara pointed at him. Ignoring his plea. 'Doctor Trenner prescribed me a sedative, but he gave Anderson the prescription, and it was changed. Who was the new medicine signed off by, Doctor Trenner?'

'Cara,' Toby said quietly.

'Doctor Trenner?'

'Cara . . .'

'DOCTOR TRENNER?'

Krotes looked expectant.

Toby glanced from Cara to her, and sighed – his humanity winning out. 'It was signed off by Madeleine Krotes.'

A sharp intake of breath from the crowd and then nervous murmuring. Faces were starting to turn and look up at Krotes. She straightened and stared down at everyone, still looking unfazed by the whole situation. It unsettled Cara a little to see her like that, but she couldn't help but be exhilarated by her discoveries.

'So what do you say, Governor?' Cara asked. And everyone seemed to murmur in agreement. Everyone except Peter and Minnie, who were still turning the chocolate bar and notepad around in their hands next to the table. And, of course, Toby who was standing there, not knowing what to do.

Cara looked up at Krotes, over the sea of heads looking at her as well. She had her – she finally had her. Cara had outsmarted her – finally got to the bottom of why North Fern was so bloody weird. She didn't know exactly all the minutiae of what North Fern was, or what its purpose was, but she knew Krotes was at its heart, and she had killed Stephanie Barnard. She had just needed everyone in the Unit on her side to help convict her, and it seemed the plan had worked.

Krotes narrowed her eyes. Then opened her mouth to say something. Then shut it again. She was floundering – and it was oh so glorious to watch. But then she pursed her lips and, with one confident breath, she whistled like a bird.

Cara looked confused. And for a moment, the entire Unit was completely and utterly silent. Then there was a sudden shifting. Waves of faces turned back towards her, and something had changed. Where before they looked confused and receptive, now they just all looked the same – angry.

Cara glanced down at Minnie and Peter. They had

looked up to see what was happening and seemed equally confused by all of it. Toby Trenner was pushed by Truchforth towards them and into the circle occupied by Cara, Minnie, and Peter.

'Moyley, what the hell?' And Cara looked to see Moyley had punched Liza straight in the face and she was staggering backwards towards them. 'What is happening?'

Cara looked up to see Krotes walking across the gangway, passing Harper, Michael, Continell . . . all the guards that were meant to keep prisoners like Cara safe, towards the stairs.

The prisoners, the sea of them, all looking at Cara, stepped forward.

'Krotes, what the hell is happening here?' she shouted as bravely as she could.

'Oh, Cara,' Krotes called as she started to descend the steps. The prisoners who had turned inward were advancing slowly at first, then faster. Minnie, Liza, Peter, and Toby stepped back towards Cara as the circle tightened. Cara looked up to see Krotes laughing. 'This is where it gets a little bit complicated.'

26

That night . . .

He sat in his car, looking out of his tinted windows, munching a Twix and listening to The Stones on the radio.

He'd been there for two hours already, and absolutely nothing had happened. Nothing of any consequence anyway.

The mark, the babysitter, had arrived on her bike (like she lived in some eighties teen movie, for God's sake), and entered the house and that was about it. The man had answered the door and let her in with a baby on his shoulder.

That might be the one, he guessed. Him and the baby actually locked eyes through the patio door when he was scoping out a few minutes ago. He was pretty sure all the little bairn saw was the mask though.

He'd never kidnapped a kid before – usually specialised in hits on more mature targets – but the suitcase of unmarked notes in the car boot said that he was about to change that. A suitcase! A bloody suitcase! Full to the brim. This kinda stuff didn't happen, so when it did you had to grasp the opportunity and not let it go.

At least that was what the self-help CDs he was listening to said.

'You are special. You are important. You are the product of your own past and the arbiter of your own future,' the fruit-loop was saying on the CD. 'The past does not define you. And neither does your future.'

He turned it off.

He popped the rest of the Twix into his mouth and opened the glove compartment, bringing out a half-full bottle of Jack Daniel's. He unscrewed it and took a swig. He usually didn't like to drink and drive – road laws were made for a reason – but he thought he might need something lining his stomach for this one.

He took another swig and looked down at the mask on the passenger seat – odd choice, but for the amount of money he'd got from her, he'd have done the job stark-bollock naked wearing only a BoJo mask.

Actually, that sounded kinda fun . . .

He took one last swig, screwed the top back on and replaced it in the glovebox. Didn't want to get too buzzed.

His phone went off on the dashboard – he turned off the radio and answered.

'Boss.'

He called everyone who paid him 'Boss' because, well, it made an awful lot of sense.

'They're just about to leave the house.'

The woman's voice was cold, harrowing. He'd only ever heard it over a phone line – was kinda grateful 'bout that. He'd got the suitcase from a drop – a hacked

Amazon locker in a Waitrose, so he'd never met her in person.

It seemed she was a little apprehensive of him – when he could have told her it was totally the other way round. He didn't usually ask questions when he got a hit – it would be too easy to go down the rabbit hole.

But this time he almost needed answers.

What kinda cold-hearted bitch wanted this job done? And why?

That was one really big rabbit hole.

'OK,' he said, savouring the sweetness of the remaining liquor on his tongue. 'Here, how do you know all this? I'm parked outside, and I can't see dick.'

There was a silence on the other end, and he knew he'd overstepped his bounds.

'You don't need to know. They are about to leave. Then you should leave two hours for the children to be in bed, and the sitter to be alone.'

'And the children? I've got to—'

'Go upstairs. The room marked Tilly. You are to go nowhere else.'

'Roger, boss.'

'NOWHERE ELSE.'

'I've got it. Nowhere else. Just the room marked Tilly.'

'OK then. They'll be out in five minutes. Then wait . . .'

'Two hours, I've got it.'

He was about to say something else, maybe ask her why, or what happened, but she hung up.

Probably best.

She had a temper on her, that one. And what was

private should be private. He had two million reasons to keep his mouth shut. They were all in a suitcase in the boot.

He checked his watch and, almost five minutes later to the second, the front door opened and a rather stunning woman in a flashy dress stepped out. He didn't know if it was the Jack or the dress or the face, but his knees felt all a flutter at the sight of her. He definitely would have some of that if he'd had the chance. But he'd had a hard life in that regard – not many chances for quality tail.

The man from before came out in a tuxedo this time and paused on the doorstep as he talked to someone in the house. Then he went to the woman, kissed her (lucky bastard) and they both got into the car on their driveway. Illuminated in the doorway was the babysitter (not a bad catch herself) with the baby in her arms.

He slowly got out of the car, picking up the mask and hiding behind the bonnet. He wanted a better look at the house before he went inside. He'd been around the back a few times already, including the zen moment he stared into the little porker's eyes, but he wanted a closer look and he had two hours to kill.

And, to be honest, the Jack was making him brave. He needed a risk to keep him sober. He wasn't worried about anyone seeing him. Neighbours seemed to be away, and there were no cameras on this street. Still, he put the mask on, not loving the feeling of the weird stretchy fabric it was made out of pulled over his face. He put his hood up. And slipped.

He cursed as he lost balance and staggered out from

behind the car into open sight of the doorway.

On the doorstep, the babysitter was saying 'Say good-bye!' to the kid.

The little bastard looked right at him, even pointed, and said 'No-Face' clear as day. He dove back behind the car, as the babysitter turned. Goddamn mask. He tore it off his head. A piece of a morph suit – pink to match his skin, and tight. He'd looked at himself in the mirror – he'd even freaked himself out a bit.

He heard the sitter go back into the house and he chanced a look over the bonnet. The street was empty again. He was beginning to think he should have had at least two more shots of whisky.

'Screw it,' Anderson said, going back for more. You only lived once.

And at some point that night, it all went horribly wrong.

PART THREE

The Prison Experiment

1

28 September 1993

The alarm sounded before Essie even thought she'd gone to sleep. Of course it was set early. She turned it off. Removed her eye mask. And wiped the sleep from her eyes.

She went into the bathroom. Took her sleep-guard out. Looked in the mirror.

First day of uni. Law. Was this the start of something or the end? She'd see soon enough. But it was too early for her dreams to be dashed into the dirt, wasn't it?

She tried a smile to herself. Open-mouthed. Her crooked teeth showed, and her acne. She'd never seen a lawyer with a lopsided grin and a face that looked like a connect-the-dots puzzle. But maybe there was a first time for everything.

She had a shower. Used her face scrub. Tried, as always unsuccessfully, to make her hair look a little less greasy. Afterwards she looked a little better, and felt even more so.

Her mummy and step-daddy didn't talk to her at breakfast. When the car came, they offered a cursory hug. She always wanted to ask them why they didn't lavish their wealth on her – but she never did, because she knew why. Her brothers were the star children – she was the star runt. Her one lifeline was the ridiculous dream that she might become a lawyer.

How did she know it was ridiculous? Because everyone – including her family – told her. But they had paid for this degree just to shut her up. She needed to succeed at this – otherwise they would never let her outside again.

The driver offered more encouragement than Mummy or Step-Daddy. Essie paused as the car drew up. But eventually she got out, and looked at the building. It appeared bigger in reality and more foreboding. Old but somehow modern – with glass doors, but also ancient brickwork. A contradiction made of bricks and mortar. Streams of young people were flocking inside from the pavement, seeming not to notice her. They all looked nicer than her. Yes, her clothes may have cost more than all theirs put together, but you could only hide so much ugliness.

'Don't worry,' the driver said, through the open car window, 'it'll be fine. I'll be back later to pick you up, OK?'

She nodded – although all she wanted to do was crawl back inside the car and go home. Maybe her step-daddy could pay for home tuition – a home degree. That sounded good – and would make her anxieties evaporate into thin air. But university was all about pushing yourself, and she couldn't stay inside forever, with the curtains shut on her head and her heart. She *too* had to push herself, just like all these people, who already looked imposing and confident and well put-together.

She looked down at herself. Her mummy had picked her out a smart and formal dress – a dark blue number, with a collar and short sleeves that stopped at her knobbly knees. Her mother had already taken off the price tag, so she didn't know how much it cost, but she was sure it was incredibly expensive. Even with the expense, it looked strange on her – almost too nice. She still had her acne scars, her bad teeth, her big nose. A contradiction as large as the building in front of her.

She shuffled the books in her arms – she had had to buy more law books than she could count, and, what was more, she was required to bring them to class – to get them into her bag, but the bag slipped from her arm. She swiped for it, the books falling from her hands and slamming into the ground. Her bag exploded – the contents scattering.

She felt her cheeks reddening and turned around – all ready to throw herself back in the car and demand to be taken home. But the car was gone, of course. She was on her own.

She put her head down, using the technique she'd used for twenty years. She bent down, made herself as small and as inconspicuous as possible, and tried to fade away. Her inhaler had skittered across the ground and lay more than an arm's-length away, so she couldn't even use that for comfort. She just tried to steady her breathing using the exercises that her mindfulness teacher had taught her. Slowly, she started to gather up her things.

'Can I help you?' A kindly voice.

She looked up, her neck craning, to see a girl standing over her. She was impossibly beautiful – blonde hair down to her shoulders, freckles playing across her perfectly proportioned face. She was wearing a shabby patchwork shirt and jeans, which looked frayed and as though they had been repaired a few times. It didn't matter though, the girl was captivating.

She bent down before Essie could even say anything and started putting things back into her bag. Essie regarded her, a little tentatively, but then started collecting up her books. In silence. She wanted to say thank you, but the words were catching in her throat.

In a few minutes, they were done, and the girl got up. Essie followed her lead, balancing her books in her arms. The girl went to give her her bag and then thought again.

'Why don't I carry your bag?' she said. There was something in her silken voice, a slight hint of a European accent maybe. 'It looks like we're going to the same place anyway.' She smiled and nodded down to the pile of books. 'Law, right?'

Essie nodded.

'I'm Martha,' the girl said.

Essie smiled a little.

'What's your name?' Martha asked.

Essie's cheeks were on fire again. She pushed out, 'Essie.'

'Hey, Essie,' Martha said, and then checked her watch.

'Come on, we better go and find where we're supposed to be.' And they both started for the front doors, Martha obviously taking the lead.

They found their lecture room in a maze of corridors. It was a large room, and the seats went up steep flights of stairs. Essie and Martha found somewhere in the middle, and waited quietly while the lecture room filled up.

When the final young person sat, almost to the second, the doors opened, and a woman came in, striding to the front desk with a power and purpose Essie had never seen before. The woman got out her laptop, plugged it into a cable coming out of the desk, and cleared her throat for silence before she looked up.

'Good morning, ladies and gentlemen, I am your professor and practising lawyer, Andrea Hughes. You are all here for two reasons – firstly, you have a passion for law, and secondly, you are more talented than the University of Glasgow, but not talented enough for Cambridge.' A titter of laughter, as Andrea looked up at them all, and started to write on the board. 'My condolences and congratulations in equal measure. Now, I'm afraid this first lecture is going to be even more dry than usual, but we need to follow university procedure – and following procedure isn't a bad thing to learn if you want to work anywhere in the legal sector.'

Ms Hughes wasn't lying – the lecture was impossibly dull. Over the next three hours, she outlined the course (hinting at things far more exciting), told everyone of university facilities, how to enrol in the library and how to take out the thick law tomes that it no doubt held.

She told them how much work the course would be, and how they would almost definitely not be getting the full university experience because of how much studying they would have to do. At the end of this bureaucracy, Ms Hughes paused and pulled down a screen over the blackboard.

'Now all that's done,' she said, in a tone indicating she was just as glad that it was out of the way as every other person in the room, 'we can move on to something a little more enticing. Your first assignment. Which I will use to see what I am working with this year. So I am imploring you all to try your best, take this seriously and, for God's sake, don't go on any pub crawls.'

She tapped on her laptop, and some pictures came up of individuals. One was of a man, clearly dead, lying on a post-mortem slab. The other two pictures were less horrifying – of two male children.

'For your consideration: the case of George Jefferies, November 1992, South London. You all read the papers, so I won't bore you with the grisly details. Jefferies was a maths teacher, who was found hanging in his own form room after school hours, by one of his own students no less. The case was ruled a suicide, until a child, of all people, proved that the case was in fact murder. What's more, the child's best friend's father was the murderer. Now, I don't want any hearsay or opinion. What I want is you to examine this case and determine if there was any police negligence. Could they have solved this case? Did they have all the information to catch the killer? Or was this child perfectly poised to solve it himself? Was

this a botch job by the authorities or a case where familiarity . . . breeds conviction?

'Work in threes, see who you're sitting with – that's
your team. You have until the end of freshers' week – or,
as I like to call it "The Shape of Things To Come" week.'

Essie looked at Martha and smiled, then turned to her
left for the first time. A boy was there, cheekily but hum-
bly smiling at them both. Essie felt a twang of something
in her gut – but it wasn't uncomfortable and invasive as
those things usually were. It was warm.

The boy outstretched his hand. 'David. Looks like
we're working together. What do they call you lovely
ladies?'

Essie took his hand, shook it, and had to make herself
let go.

2

31 September 1993

They were slightly tipsy and tossing a small horse plush to each other across Essie's large living room. They needed a place to study, outside of university, and Essie had offered up her house, realising a little too late that it might be somewhat embarrassing. Her mummy and step-daddy were out at one of their many social parties, so she had just suggested it without thinking.

'Jesus Christ,' David had said as Essie led them to her house from the uni bar and they rounded the corner to see her home, 'how big is this place?'

Essie had blushed, saying nothing, and busying herself by going to the gate and inputting the code to open it.

David and Martha had demanded a tour before they even started work, which Essie reluctantly gave, feeling a little more uncomfortable with every new room they came into. She tried to skip past the indoor pool, but David wandered off and found it anyway, exclaiming about it loudly. They resolved they had to come back and use it, and Essie was glad of that at least, because that meant they would come again.

They had found some alcohol, raiding the cupboards and selecting a bottle of vodka they were passing around. They spread out all the paperwork they were collecting on the Jefferies case, and were using the horse plush as a kind of talking point – whoever had the horse had to present a new idea. Of course, with their slight drunkenness (now more than slight for Essie, but she was trying to match the other two), they didn't always catch the horse, which led to much laughter amongst them.

Martha had the horse now. 'So the incriminating evidence was a box that was in an attic. We need to look into the possibilities of the investigation leading the relevant parties to that attic.'

'We need to move backwards,' David agreed. He took a swig of vodka and reached over to give it to Martha. The room was so big they each had a sofa to themselves and he had to stretch to hand over the bottle.

Martha threw the horse at Essie, who caught it just before it sailed into her face, and took the bottle, upending it. She got the last trickle of vodka out and frowned. She turned the bottle upside down and shook it comically. 'We got any more hard alcohol, Essie?'

Essie thought. 'I think there may be some in the kitchen, on the top shelf.'

'Which one?'

'The one above the oven.'

'Which oven?' Martha said, laughing.

'The left-hand one,' Essie replied, laughing too, although she was getting self-conscious again.

'Cool,' Martha replied, and, on unsteady feet, left the room.

Essie and David were left alone, on opposite sofas. Essie couldn't bring herself to look at him, although all she wanted to do was stare and never look away. He had been on her mind ever since they'd met, and having him around was so nice that she wanted this assignment to last forever. Because, after this was done, he would disappear – like they all did. There'd be no need for him to talk to her again.

She gazed down at her hands. And there was silence. And then she felt the sofa depress beside her and she looked up to see David sitting next to her, leaning wonkily towards her. 'You're thinking,' he said.

'What?'

'Whenever you think, you tense and untense your brow every few seconds, like clockwork. You'll get stress wrinkles.'

They laughed together. She had to look away, blushing violently.

'Sorry,' Essie said, fiddling with the horse plush.

'Why would you be sorry?' David said. 'You don't have to apologise for who you are. Not to anyone. But especially not to me.'

'OK,' Essie said, smiling, but she still couldn't look at him.

'No, don't just say OK. I want you to promise. Promise to me. And you'll have to look at me to do that.'

Essie smiled and dragged her eyes up to his face. He was beaming at her – his eyes were so kind, and the slight stubble on his chin was giving him a rugged look that she was absolutely OK with, well more than OK with, in truth. 'I promise.'

'Why aren't you more confident?' David asked, slurring slightly. 'Is it cos your house is bigger than the White House?'

'It's not bigger than Windsor Castle.'

'No, but it's pretty flippin' big.'

Essie laughed. 'Yes. And I guess it is a little bit because of that. I don't feel I belong here. In this beautiful place.'

'Elaborate,' said David, frowning.

'I'm frumpy. I have these scars because I couldn't stop picking my spots. I hate my teeth. I hate my nose. I hate how I can't talk to people without rehearsing what I'm going to say for five hours beforehand. I'm just a bit of a mess.'

David put his hand on her shoulder, and then her cheek. His thumb brushed just under her eye, and she felt herself break out in goosebumps. How could someone like him like someone like her? It was almost too much to take. 'You're far from a mess. And for the record, I think you're beautiful.'

He leant forward. And, before she knew it, his lips were on hers.

And she felt the happiest she'd ever been.

3

15 October 1993

Professor Hughes had given the entire class extra time on their assignment as she was going through a tricky legal case, and most of the class had come to the first real lecture having partaken in many a freshers' week pub crawl, even though they were told specifically not to.

That Friday night, they couldn't go to Essie's house because her mother was hosting a yoga class and absolutely couldn't be interrupted.

So instead Martha said they could go to her parents' house. If Essie had been embarrassed about them coming to her house, she was even more embarrassed when she saw Martha's. This beautiful young woman lived in a small terraced house with no garden and a motorway outside.

Essie tried not to show surprise as she walked in. There were piles of things everywhere – newspapers, magazines, Argos catalogues. Martha waved them away – 'My dad likes to collect things'. But Essie knew it as it really was – Martha's dad was a hoarder. They went up to Martha's room, which was small but relatively relieved of clutter.

David showed up a little late and hugged both of them. He only stayed for two hours as he had a part-time job at the student bar. While he was there, Martha seemed unreasonably happy, but Essie didn't notice as she was too, though he was ignoring her a little bit, but she wouldn't realise until she looked back on the scene. She was just so happy to see him. When he left, it was like the atmosphere itself had changed for the worse.

Martha and Essie kept working for a few more hours – they were making good headway on the case, taking a controversial stance that the police in the Jefferies case actually couldn't have discovered the killer. It had been Martha's idea and she had slowly persuaded the other two – her idea was that even if they were totally off base, they would make a big enough impression to catch Professor Hughes' eye. 'Sometimes,' she'd declared loudly when she proposed her plan, 'the wrong answer is the right answer.' While Essie didn't really agree with the statement, she could appreciate the ballsiness.

When they were done with work, they talked upstairs for a while, Martha waiting for her dad to go to the pub. 'We don't want to run into him right now,' Martha said. 'He's been drinking since 10 a.m.'

When they heard the front door open and close, Martha took Essie down into the cramped and equally cluttered kitchen and sat her at the table. Martha poured Essie a big glass of wine. She couldn't help but notice the wine was the budget kind.

'So I'm sure you've noticed how happy I am today,' Martha said.

'Yes, you're positively glowing,' smiled Essie, who was glad that her friend was just as happy as her.

'Sooo,' Martha said, filling her own glass. 'I have something I just need to share, because I am literally going to burst if I don't.' Martha looked like she was *actually* literally going to burst.

Essie laughed. 'I guess I have something to share too.'

Martha looked surprised. But picked up her glass and held it in the air. 'To somethings to share.'

Essie clinked her glass to Martha's. 'OK, but you first.'

'Good, because I was going to have to go first anyway,' Martha said, taking a big sip of wine. 'Right so . . . uh, where to start, haha . . . so you know we've all been spending a lot of time together because of this assignment . . .'

'Yeah,' Essie said, wondering what it could be that made Martha so giddy. She'd never seen her like this.

'Well . . . something happened the other day . . . and . . . it's been like the best week of my life because everything has kinda fallen into place . . . but . . . (pause for effect) haha . . . I think me and David are in love.'

Essie didn't react. Not outwardly anyway. She felt her entire life had trained her for this one moment. Inside, she was crumpling, everything she'd ever known cracking and crumbling around her.

Martha was just so happy, she didn't even realise. Thank God.

Martha drained her glass of wine and breathed out a long breath. 'So, what was your thing?'

4

The entire law class was staring at her. Essie, Martha, and David were down at the front giving their presentation.

The majority of the presentation went as planned. The overhead projector slides went down especially well – David knew a guy who made them. Their argument was sound – although Essie still didn't one hundred per cent get behind it. They had split the presentation up into thirds, and each of them took one part.

Essie went first – she had asked to. She wanted to get it over with as quickly as possible. She forced herself to raise her head to look at everyone. She talked in a clear, strong voice, and she kept to her script, which she had memorised by going over and over it again.

She was confident and strong and the class seemed to see that.

Something had happened since Martha had told Essie that she and David were in love. First, she didn't mention the kiss at all, to either of them. She felt betrayed, hurt – but above all angry. Essie felt like she had lost everything, so she rebuilt herself from the ground up.

297

She could be whatever she wanted to be. Who said she had to be feeble, and meek, and quiet? Maybe those were just confines that she had given herself. She was always so scared of what other people thought, that she didn't even give them a chance to form an opinion. She thought she was rubbish – and that was the problem. But David had said she was beautiful – maybe she was. And she always had the kiss as a secret. A thing to keep for herself.

David went next, and he was David – funny, charming, and forward. He made a few jokes, showed a few slides and spoke in a way that had everyone hanging on his every word.

Essie chanced a look at Professor Hughes and saw she was feeling exactly the same as everyone else.

They were on track for a good mark.

But then it was Martha's turn. And instantly the air changed – Essie knew it was going to go south before she even started. Martha stumbled, she had cue cards and dropped them. And then she scrabbled to pick them up. Essie thought back to the first day they met, where Essie had been the clumsy one.

Martha got all her cards, stood up, but then was still in a weird fog as she looked at everyone, frozen.

Essie understood what was happening. Martha had been so wrapped up in her budding romance that she had not prepared. David looked at Martha, then at her. And she knew it was her time.

'So,' Essie said out to the crowd, in a strong voice, interrupting Martha. Martha grew silent and just let

Essie take control. 'In conclusion, we take a stance that is a little frightening. We think that there are certain cases where close family or friends are the only ones who could find the evidence to bring someone to justice. I'm afraid, Professor Hughes, we do believe Familiarity Breeds Conviction.'

The room was silent. The class probably didn't think that was the way it was going to go – the presentation had been structured to be very obscure until the end.

Essie stood there looking at everyone and they looked back. A scarce few weeks ago, she would have died if even four people stared at her. Now there were at least sixty.

Slowly a clap started. It was Professor Hughes. And then everyone else joined in. And Essie was reformed in the applause. She looked around at David and Martha, who were staring at Essie as if she were a brand new person. She was. And she didn't need her friends anymore. Essie resolved, just as she once thought Martha and David would do to her, to distance herself from them as much as possible.

5

Essie poured a large glass of white wine. She needed it – it had been a long day, filled with confusing meetings. Her work was going perfectly well – she was hoping for a promotion in the next few months, so she could get off the frontlines and actually get into management. And it was going well.

But something had happened during lunch. Essie had gone to Waterloo station – the *CoffeeCorps* near the ticket barriers. She always got a tuna melt and a latte, and when she had paid, she'd turned and saw David standing there.

She was taken aback – she hadn't seen him in almost a decade, since the course ended and they had all gone their separate ways. He looked as ruggedly handsome as ever, age only enhancing what had made him so appealing in the first place.

They sat and talked for as long as Essie could before she had to go back to work. Essie couldn't help notice that David was wearing a wedding ring. He offered the information, although she didn't need it, she felt it - it

300

was Martha, and they had two children – two girls, one only nine months old. They lived in Martha's old house, moving in after her father died of a stroke most likely brought on by the alcoholism. There wasn't much more for him to tell. He had tried to make it as a lawyer for a while, but when Martha fell pregnant with their first daughter, he knew he had to provide, so he took a job as a risk assessor at a paper company.

Then they talked about Essie. David surprisingly knew that she had landed a once-in-a-lifetime job at Prism, the prison law firm, and she had already been promoted twice. She was on track to becoming the fastest ladder-climber in the company's history – man or woman. She bragged a lot – she deserved it. There wasn't much more to tell – she was very career-orientated these days. Men were few and far between. She couldn't help but notice David seemed a little happy about that.

They left it on a jovial note, with a hug and a promise that they would keep in touch, although Essie didn't think they would. And she returned to work, and thought about the exchange all the rest of the day.

Essie picked up her wine and walked through the empty house. Her mother had died two years before. Breast cancer. With her stepfather long gone, she had inherited the house, and a reasonable amount of money. Sometimes – a lot of the time – it was lonely, but today she was glad of the time alone. She needed to recharge, process. She sat down on the sofa and set about watching the day's news. She always recorded every main station's news coverage to remain unbiased and she'd made it through two programmes when there was a knock at the door. At least she thought there was.

She muted the television, and listened. When you lived alone, in a big house, there were plenty of sounds that you just couldn't account for. Essie was glad she didn't believe in ghosts, otherwise she probably would have run screaming from the house a long time ago.

She was just about to turn the volume back on the television when she heard the knock again. She got up, putting her wine glass down, and went to the door.

David was standing there. And in his arms, there was a baby.

'How did you get through the gates?' Essie asked. An odd first question, but she was so dumbfounded, her brain wasn't working properly.

David looked confused too. 'I remembered the code.'

'What do you want?'

David looked at her and started sobbing. 'I've made an awful lifelong mistake, Es. It's you. It's always been you.'

She almost expected it.

And against her better judgement, she let him in.

6

Early 2009 . . .

Essie sat at the kitchen table. The same kitchen table she had first seen two years ago – small and quaint. The entire kitchen was cramped, and dirty – Martha definitely hadn't coped very well with coming to live on her own. Imagine raising a child in a place like this.

Martha was making herself a cup of tea, which Essie had declined. The cups were probably dirty. And she was avoiding any caffeine, although it was hard. Her bump, stretching out in front of her, restricting her movement, reminded her to forgo certain vices. Sometimes the kicks of the little life inside felt like she was being told it was all worth it.

Martha finally finished making her tea and turned and sat down. The mug she was drinking out of was chipped. 'I know why you're here. And I'm going to sign.'

'Good,' said Essie, getting the short document out of her bag and placing it in front of Martha. She placed a ballpoint pen in front of her too.

'Can't we just chat first?' Martha said. 'We were friends once.' She sipped her tea. Essie couldn't take her

303

eyes from the crack in the lip. The mug had a smiley face on it.

'There's nothing to chat about,' Essie said, 'you just need to sign and I'll be on my way.'

Martha sighed. Even older, after two children, she was still more beautiful than Essie could ever hope to be. Even with the dark bags under her eyes, and the frown lines plaguing her forehead. 'OK,' she said, and picked up the pen.

Just as she was about to sign, there was a sound from the other room. A young girl came running into the kitchen, clutching something. 'Mummy, Mummy, looooook.'

Martha smiled at Essie, apologetically. 'Sorry.' She placed the pen on the table and picked up the girl, putting her on her knee and adopting a lighter tone. 'What is it, sweetie?'

'Loooook,' said the girl, holding up a piece of paper. 'I drew a picture.'

Essie assessed her. 'She looks like her father, but she has your eyes.'

'Yes,' Martha said.

'Muuuuummy I made you a picture. Look!'

'Aww, thank you,' Martha said, placing it on the table so Essie could see too. 'Explain it to me,' she said as it just looked like three different-coloured blobs.

'This,' the girl said, pointing a podgy finger at the biggest blob, 'is you. This,' she went to a slightly smaller one, 'is me,' and then to the smallest one, 'and this is my little sis.'

Essie frowned. She opened her mouth, but she knew the damage had already been done.

Martha just looked down at the picture. For a long time.

Silence.

Until, 'Do you like it, Mummy?'

Martha didn't answer her. Instead she looked at Essie. 'Maybe . . .' She looked at the girl and then at the drawing. And then at the document. And Essie knew. This little freak had ruined it all. ' . . .Maybe I should think some more about this.'

'What?' Essie said, a little too viciously. Martha's daughter, David's goddamn daughter, shrank away. Martha seemed to hold onto her a little more tightly.

Essie should have felt ashamed. But it did the opposite. It made her feel powerful. She remembered when she was the scared, scarred girl sitting on her sofa, not able even to look at the boy she liked. And now she had taken that boy from the woman in front of her. And now she was going to take her child too. And Martha had just been about to hand her over. Not this snivelling horror, the other one. The slightly more cute one. The smallest blob.

The balance had shifted. And Essie wasn't about to apologise for it.

'Why don't you go and watch telly, sweetie?' Martha said to the girl, and she quickly ran out. Martha picked up the picture. 'I was a little hasty. I think, maybe, I don't want this.'

Essie felt like launching herself across the table,

throwing the scalding hot tea in her old friend's face. But instead she just repeated, 'What?'

'I need some more time to think about it.' She slid the document back over to Essie. 'I think I want to at least be in her life.'

Essie said nothing, could only think of expletives. And then it all came out. 'You. You want to be in her life. *You*. The best thing you can do for that child over at my house is sign the goddamn paper. She will want for nothing. I have a good job – I actually used my degree unlike you. David has a good job. She will grow up in the best circumstances. She will go to private school. She will go to Oxford or Cambridge, not second best like we did. She will be happy. What could *you* possibly offer her? Look at yourself. Look at this place. You are an embarrassment. You are a washed-up single mother who no one loves. The best thing for the child is for her never to see you.'

Martha just looked at her, showing no emotion. Most likely because if she did, she would break. Simply, she said, 'I'm not signing.'

Essie angrily snatched up the papers and stuffed them into her bag, getting up so forcefully that the chair clattered backwards. 'You are a disgrace.'

Martha just watched her. Then she said something that would always stay with Essie for as long as she lived. 'It's the blood that binds.'

And Essie stormed back to the front door. She hadn't ever really wanted custody, even though it may have helped to make her think more of the baby girl in her house as her own. She looked into the living room as she went past. Martha and David's first child was watching *SpongeBob Squarepants*.

She hated Martha.

But she hated that hell spawn just a little bit more.

7

It was beginning to get slightly creepy. At first, she saw her out of the corner of her eye, and then she just saw her. Following her. Not seeming to mind if she was seen or not. Martha.

When Essie went out, she was always there. A few paces behind. When shopping, Martha was always in the next aisle. When driving, she was always a few cars behind.

Essie and David had taken the younger child two weeks before. They'd managed to use their contacts to warn Martha off with legal threats. After all, it was clear that Essie and David could take far better care of her. Martha was a mess – but she still had some rights. She would have to be allowed some contact.

Why the hell couldn't Martha just leave them alone? She still had the hell spawn at home. But no, she was so obsessed with this other one. It was clear they would never be rid of her.

Essie felt that now more than ever. It was the dead of night and she had heard something outside. She looked out of her window to see a figure standing by the gate, looking into the complex. No prizes for guessing who it was.

She looked across the bed to see David fast asleep, snoring softly in the way she found so cute. She went over to the crib in the corner of the room to see the little one was sleeping too. Martha and David's second-born.

Would there ever come a point where this child would feel like hers? She guessed it would take time.

Essie took another look out the window. Still there. And then she slipped on her kimono, and went downstairs, stepping out into the night.

As she walked down the driveway, the figure started disappearing into the shadows.

'Stop there, Martha.'

Martha continued to back away.

'DON'T. Let's have this out once and for all.'

This made her stop.

Essie got to the gates, with no intention of opening them. Martha was in a black hoodie, and she took the hood down, seeing as her cover was blown. She looked a wreck – dark bags under her eyes, hair that glistened with grease in the street light, pale skin. Far from the beauty she had met outside LSE. 'What are you doing here?'

'I miss Georgia,' Martha said. 'I miss my baby.'

'You shouldn't be here. Where's the hell spawn?'

'What? She's . . . she's with a friend.'

'Go away.'

'Can I see her?' Martha said, stepping forward and

309

clutching the golden bars of the gate. 'I just want to let her know her mummy loves her.'

'It's the middle of the night. She's asleep. Go away.'

Was this their life now? Three people intertwined together. There had to be an end. David saw Martha follow him too. Although he didn't tell her. There was no way he couldn't have seen her. They all knew. And they were all affected by it.

Someone had to put an end to it.

Someone had to put their foot down.

'I got him in the end, Martha. I may have taken the long way round, but I got him. So stop this pathetic charade and get out of my driveway.'

'Wait . . . you think this is about him?' Martha sounded incredulous. 'I couldn't care less about David. This isn't some twisted game. No one wins. I want to see my child.'

'Whatever it is, Martha, we are done. And if I see you following me around again, I will not be accountable for my actions.'

'Please, Essie. If there was ever anything between us, I need to see Georgia.'

'Oh,' Essie said, enjoying this, 'didn't I tell you? We've decided to change her name.'

Martha let out a horrible weeping gasp. It was delicious. And she shrank away again. 'You . . . Why? What to?'

Essie paused a moment. 'I really don't see how that's any of your business.' Another weep. 'Now get out my driveway before I call the police. Go back to your poor remaining child.'

Martha turned and started to run. And Essie felt like laughing. But she didn't. She just stood there in the dark. And thought. She knew it had to be her to end it.

She had to do something about Martha.

Once and for all.

8

2010 . . .

She looked at the car clock (8.39) as she pulled down the sun visor and flipped up the mirror. 'Yeah, I know. So I told him, I said that this is not the way this relationship is going to go, mister.' She clutched the phone between her shoulder and ear, and started applying scarlet lipstick. 'So I say you can't put your socks in the washing machine if you have not first located both of them and made sure they are together. Because I am sick to death of seeing these lone socks in the drum and I have to – no, the drum, THE DRUM, that's what you call the inside of the . . . yeah – and I have to go about like a sock hunter around the whole house trying to find this one lost sock, and I will not have it, Felicity. I will not have it. I'm up to here with it. I've got two kids already, I don't need a third.'

She finished with the lipstick and got some mascara out of her make-up bag on the passenger seat. As she started jabbing above her eyelids, she glanced at the clock again (8.40). 'I know, I honestly don't know how you manage it with two men, I mean, Jesus, Felicity. Glutton for punishment, ha. Anyway, I've told him I've

312

come to see you tonight, I hope you don't mind . . . No of course not. But if anyone asks, I was with you, girl, OK? You're a star, a real star, a real bloody star, girl. Really, I've gone off and treated myself to a massage, you know, but he'd never have let me with his finances and his spreadsheets and his spending charts, you know.'

Clock: 8.41. She finished with the mascara and looked at herself in the mirror. Beautiful. As always. 'You wouldn't believe how much money I've spent. Gone all out. But sometimes you just need to look after yourself, don't you? Yeah, you're spot on. I just needed a rest from all the sock hunting, you know. Ha. Yeah, anyway, girl, I gotta go. Gotta get to the spa. Yeah, yeah, you wanted to what? Talk about . . .?' Clock. Still 8.41. But surely not for long. 'Yes, sweetheart, of course. But I can't talk right now, darling, sorry. I've got . . .' Staring at the clock now. '. . .I've got an appointment. But we will talk about it, yes. Absolutely.' The clock changed to 8.42. 'OK, honeybun, I've got to go. Yes, we'll catch up soon. Tomorrow? Sure, tomorrow. OK, goodbye, darling.'

She hung up, even though Felicity was still talking, and threw the phone on the passenger seat, rolling her eyes. Ugh. She looked out onto the road surrounded by trees. She was down a dirt track, almost invisible in the wooded area. If someone was to see her, they would merely think she was a glamorous woman, maybe lost, maybe broken down. But no one would see her. She had been sitting here for an hour and no one had gone by. It was almost silent around her, save for the noises of the wind in the trees.

313

So she just sat and waited. For the time.

8.43. And, as if like clockwork, she heard it. The very very faint sound of an engine. That clockwork nature was what had made this possible. She knew her.

She turned the ignition. Pressed down on the accelerator slowly. She didn't want to gun it too hard, so she could still hear the other engine. It was getting closer. And louder. And closer. And louder. Had to be a matter of seconds. She slammed her foot down on the pedal and the Range Rover bucked and rocked under the strain of the power not allowed to be unleashed. Not quite yet.

A few more seconds. But they felt like hours.

And then she saw the lights coming up the road.

She wrenched the handbrake down. The Range Rover sprang forward like a rocket, as the Ford Ka came into sight. The woman driving didn't even notice the huge vehicle practically leaping towards her. The Range Rover collided with the Ka, slamming it off the road and into a nearby tree. The force propelled her upward, bumping her head hard on the roof, before slamming back down into her seat as the Range Rover stopped.

The Ka was in front of her, obliterated – it didn't really look like a car anymore. The woman in the driver's seat was bleeding profusely from her forehead, her body impossibly contorted in the bent frame, but, against all odds, she seemed to be blinking, conscious.

She tried to start the Range Rover. If her calculations were correct – yes, it started. It was OK. She put it into reverse and although it struggled to disconnect from the

Ka, it did. There was a shriek from the woman in the car as she backed away.

She laughed at the shriek, and when she was far enough away, she opened the door of the Range Rover and flopped out onto the road. When her feet touched the floor, a spiky pain shot up her left leg. It was probably sprained or something. She wiped a hand over her forehead and came back with a palm of blood. She would have to deal with that before she went home.

She staggered towards the Ka, looking both ways before she crossed the street. The woman inside had finally seen her, and her eyes widened.

'I told you,' she said, trying not to shout, but not succeeding. No one was around anyway. She'd surveyed this road for days and days. No one ever used it, apart from the bitch in the car. She didn't even know why it existed. 'I told you this would happen, and you didn't listen to me. And now look what you've made me do.' The woman in the car didn't say anything, but she didn't have to. The fear was all in her eyes. 'You think I wanted to do this. I wanted you out of my life and you gave me no alternative.'

The woman was seeming to beg with her eyes. Or was that just her projecting onto her old friend.

'This is it, Martha. This is it. I am going to watch you die.' Her watch beeped. She'd timed all this to the last second, and she looked over the car until she saw it – small, under the hood and just peeking out. A flame. 'You're dead, Martha. This is the worst bit. Because you're in the waiting room. It's mostly happened already, but not quite. You see the fire, Martha? You see what you made me do?'

Martha looked around and saw the flame. And then she did something unexpected – she tried to move. Martha screamed – opening her mouth and spitting out a mouthful of blood – whilst trying to wrench herself free. Every movement Martha made, she seemed to feel, and Martha's eyes rolled.

She reached out to Martha, but didn't touch her, although the sentiment seemed to do the trick. Martha stopped – maybe it was the pain. Realisation was in her eyes – she knew she was going to die, and there was something almost delicious about that look of hopelessness.

Essie stumbled, another shot of pain from her leg drilling up her body into her brain. She had to get away, but she wasn't done. Not quite. She just had to look a little longer – look at what she'd done.

'Why didn't you just leave him alone, Martha? Why wouldn't you just leave us alone? You were my best friend, you bitch. And you couldn't just leave – for me. Like I meant nothing to you. We were friends, but that meant nothing in the face of a boy. How stupidly romantic. Makes me sick. Because you know what – I can't look at him anymore either.'

The flames had doubled. She really needed to go.

'Every time I look at him, I think of you. Every time he kisses me, I taste you on his lips. Every time he's inside me, I think about him being inside you. Him and that little bitch, Georgia. They'll all get what's coming to them. And your little hell spawn too.'

She stepped forward – towards the flaming car – even though she knew she shouldn't. She wanted to be as close to Martha as possible – one last time.

Martha looked at her, coughed up what seemed like a litre of blood, and took a laboured, and almost clicky, breath.

'Essie, please.' Martha opened her mouth, spluttered, and then said one word, 'Cara.'

She beamed and nodded dramatically. 'Yes, Martha. Cara. I'll get Cara too.'

'No,' Martha said, as the flames caught her eye. 'Essie.'

She had to go. 'Sorry, Martha. Looks like we're all out of time. Goodbye, friend.'

She didn't look at Martha again – revelled at the fact she would never have to set eyes on that smug face again. She just went back to the Range Rover, got into the driver's seat and took one last look at the flaming car before she drove away.

She hadn't been lying – she hadn't wanted to kill her. But now – she was feeling something she never thought she would. Exhilarated. Dare she say . . . happy? There had been a problem. And she had found a solution. She hadn't stopped when she thought she was out of ideas. She had prevailed. And the problem was gone. Maybe there were other problems she could solve by thinking outside the box.

In the wing-mirror, she watched.

As Martha Lockhart exploded.

9

Now . . .

Cara felt an icicle of dread pierce her heart, as the circle of prisoners – people she knew, by sight anyway – advanced towards her. She couldn't help but feel happy she was standing on the table, although she felt a bitter regret when she saw Minnie, Liza, Peter, and Toby's looks of utter confusion. They got as close to the table as possible, backing into it, as the prisoners on the frontline smiled awful smiles.

They were getting closer – and closer – and soon they would be on top of them. What happened then? Would they be ripped apart by the bloodthirsty horde? Without even knowing quite what was going on.

The circle tightened, and her peers shrank inward, and she could only look on, as another fierce whistle broke through the shuffling noises. She looked up to see Krotes had got to the bottom of the stairs, and was standing outside the crowd. At the whistle, all of the prisoners stopped and looked towards her. She smiled a gleaming grin, her tongue flitting over her teeth, and then she gestured to them to step aside. The circle parted like the Red Sea, clearing a path for her up to the table.

Cara scowled at her. She was somehow controlling the other prisoners – Did she have something on them? Had she promised them something? – and they were following her like people possessed.

Krotes started to walk up to them. 'This is . . .' she mused, 'troubling, but hey, we can work with it.'

Toby stepped forward slightly. 'Now, look here, what is going on?'

A prisoner stepped forward and snarled, and Toby winced.

Krotes laughed at the little exchange. 'What's going on is this prison is obviously not what you thought, Dr Trenner. And you have been an accessory in the birth of something new. You should be very proud. Now, I could explain more, but you'll all come to know soon enough. For now, let me just demonstrate how screwed you all really are.' She clapped her hands. And the crowd stood to attention. 'You know what to do.'

And the crowd launched forward, infinitely faster than before. Peter, Minnie, Liza, and Toby got swallowed up by the tsunami of purple uniforms, which lapped around Cara's table. Hands reaching for her, and then she was pulled off the table, gripped hard. Pushed and pulled, by so many people. All she could do was let it happen, as she got forced down the Pit towards the dining room.

There was shouting from Minnie. Then Liza. She saw Peter through the sea of purple. And Toby. They were all being taken to the same place.

The doors were held open, and Cara was carried through. Across the dining room. Towards the wall. Through the hidden door. And Cara's thoughts finally caught up with her brain. 'No, no.'

The others were shouting too – Minnie and Peter getting pushed ahead of her, Liza and Toby behind – but she couldn't hear them over the thundering of feet and, more insistently, over the sound of her own palpitating heart as she was carried down the secret corridor.

'No, not there. Please. Please. Please. Anywhere but there. Anywhere but . . .'

But it was on them. Peter was already there, getting thrown in full force. And then Minnie. Swallowed by the darkness. And she was next.

Into the Hole.

10

Darkness. Almost absolute. Just as before. Hands on her.

'Who's that?' Minnie said.

'Cara.'

'Ahhh crap,' replied Minnie, taking her hands off her.

'Just let your eyes adjust,' Cara said. 'This is where they kept me after . . . after Barnard.'

They were all in here. In this impossibly small place. Cara was sitting on the bed. She could feel Peter by her feet, sitting on the floor. Minnie must've been directly opposite by the wall, given where her hands had come from. Liza was next to her. And Toby had been pushed in last, before the door slammed shut, so he had to be somewhere near the door, at least. She could hear them all breathing, thick and panicked breaths. She felt some of them on her skin, awash with goosebumps. She had never felt so hot but also so cold.

'Lockhart.' Liza's voice. Coming from almost where she had thought she was. 'Can you please explain what the hell is going on here? Why the hell did everyone just go all *Invasion of the Body Snatchers* on us? And Krotes killed Barnyard now?'

'It's like I said,' Cara began, into the oppressive

darkness. 'Krotes killed Barnard because Barnard found the room where they doctored all the letters. North Fern is not what we thought it was. As for the others going weird, I don't know. Maybe they're involved. Maybe they knew.'

'But,' Toby's voice, on her right, 'we're talking an entire unit here. How could everyone be in on it – whatever this is? And who doctored the letters? And why? If everyone's in on it.'

'Keeping up appearances, maybe?' Minnie said. 'Or maybe people aren't in on it straight away. Maybe they get turned . . . recruited.'

'What is going on?' Peter said, in hysterics.

'Doc,' Liza asked, 'any ideas? What is this place?'

'I don't . . . It's a prison. It's a developing prison. These are the early days.'

'What do you mean, developing?' Minnie said.

'Well, we're far from capacity. In fact, this unit is the only one that's populated so far.'

'What?' Cara said.

'This is the only unit so far. But there are others ready to be filled.'

'Have you ever been to these other units?'

'I . . .' Toby's voice trailed off. And then defeated, 'No, I haven't. The only places I go are my office, the barracks, and this unit. In fact, that's all I have clearance for at the moment.'

'The barracks? Harper mentioned the barracks. What is that?' Cara asked.

'It's where the security centre is – where the guards

monitor the Unit and the information we get from the Cuffs, and it's where our quarters are. We sleep on site.'

'You what?' Minnie said.

'Toby,' Cara said slowly, 'since coming here, have you ever left the building?'

'I . . . haven't, no. It's not regulation.'

'Doc,' Liza said. 'Could you go outside if you wanted?'

Toby said nothing for a minute. And then, 'I don't know.'

With this, the room erupted in panic.

'Looks like you're just as much a prisoner as us,' Minnie stated.

'How stupid are you?' Liza giggled nervously. 'This dingus just invites himself into a prison.'

'The salary is highly competitive,' Toby said matter-of-factly. 'And it was a chance to be a part of a new venture. A potential new chapter in prison history.'

'Idiot,' Liza said. 'Glad to have you on our side, Doc.'

'Wait, where are we?' Peter shrieked. 'Why are we in here?'

'Calm down, Froot Loops,' Liza said.

Unsurprisingly, this made Peter worse.

Cara wanted to flip out too, but she had to stay strong. 'Shut up,' Cara said, and surprisingly they all did. In a less pressing situation, she would marvel at the new power dynamic that seemed to have descended upon them. 'It doesn't matter right now. First we need to figure out how we're going to get out of here.'

Over the next hour, they started to brainstorm how to get out of the Hole. Initially they talked long and hard

323

about how they could force the door with their joint effort, or find something to pick the locks, or maybe call for someone and trick them, but as the time went by, their dialogue got thinner. And eventually no one spoke for prolonged periods.

And then there was just silence.

For hours.

All Cara heard was four other individuals breathing around her. Minnie and Liza had sat down on the bed, and Cara moved to the floor. She could see vague outlines of them now, and assumed the others could see similarly. Peter had rested her head on Cara's shoulder about thirty minutes ago and was quietly sleeping.

Cara felt like talking, but she had no idea what to say. She was feeling an overwhelming sense of guilt – she was the reason these people were in this situation. If not for her, they would be out there still in the Unit, doing their daily routine. Toby would be in his office. But everyone had to know the truth. Even if the truth led here.

Cara felt her eyes droop, as the in-and-out breathing of five individuals was surprisingly rhythmic. She closed her eyes and felt sleep lapping at her senses.

Ssshup . . .

Light flooded the Hole, so much so Cara could even tell through her closed eyelids. She opened them just as the door swung open. Toby staggered back – he had obviously been leaning on the door, and the others were dazed, blinking away sunspots.

A figure in the door – she stepped forward.

Moyley.

'You, you, and you.' She pointed to Minnie, Liza, and Peter. 'With me.'

'Screw you, Moyley. You snake,' Liza said. 'I'm not going anywhere with you.'

Moyley reached into her pocket and brought something out. Cara didn't realise what it was, until Moyley pressed a button and a jolt of electricity shot between two bars at the top. A taser. 'I wasn't asking.'

A big sigh. Minnie. She got up. 'C'mon, Mona Liza, anywhere's got to be better than here. And there may even be some answers out there.' Minnie looked at Cara and winked. Then she looked to Peter, who was actually still asleep. 'Hey, Peter,' she jogged her and Peter finally woke up. She blinked and looked up at Minnie. The matriarch looked down at her, just like a mother. 'Come on, we're going for a walk.'

Peter looked at Cara, and Cara nodded. That seemed to be enough for her, because she got up.

Minnie and Peter shuffled out of the cell, Moyley stepping aside. Liza reluctantly followed.

'Wait, where are they going?' Cara asked.

But Moyley answered only with a loud bang, as the door shut.

11

It was a long time later. Cara was finding time odd – she was so used to being in this environment with *Rain on Elmore Street* playing on the screen behind her.

No, there was no screen remember. You imagined it. You were hallucinating.

Whatever it had been, she was used to the company. And that was how she had tracked the time. Now that she didn't have that, it was strange.

Toby wasn't talking. She had tried a few times, but he wouldn't. She could imagine him overthinking, his brain working overtime to try to make sense of this mess. Sometimes she could almost feel it overheating. He was clearly freaking out, and Cara couldn't help but feel responsible – Toby had a lot on the line. His family were out there, waiting for him to come home. Cara needed to help him get back to them.

But they couldn't exactly do much stuck in the Hole.

She wondered what was happening out there – whether Minnie, Peter, and Liza were even still alive. Why did Moyley take those three specifically? What did Krotes want with them? Would she ever see them again?

Cara rested against the wall, putting her head on

the bed. She breathed in and out, trying to slow her breathing down. She was doing everything not to lose it herself. There were so many questions, so many things that didn't make sense. And there was no guarantee of answers.

They might even die in the Hole. Maybe Krotes had a sense of humour, and had dragged her out of the Hole once, just to put her back in.

Cara shut her eyes, though it didn't make any difference.

And at that point, the door squealed back. Her eyes shot open to see Minnie and Liza getting shoved into the cell by Moyley. The door was open for all of five seconds. And then it slammed shut.

'Goddamnit,' Liza muttered as they both stumbled into the room.

'Oww,' Toby's voice squeaked as one of them obviously stood on him.

'Sorry,' Minnie said, 'are you two OK?'

'Yeah,' Cara said, 'where have you been?'

'Talking to Krotes. If you can believe it, she offered us a job.'

'A job?' Toby said.

'Yep. All those guys out there, our prisoner friends, have already joined Krotes. She has something big planned. Thing is she wouldn't tell us until we said yes.'

'Wait,' Cara said, 'where's Peter?'

A silence. Minnie must have been trying to find the words.

Liza cut in, 'Little Miss Stabby drank the Kool-Aid.'

'What?' Cara snapped.

Minnie sighed, 'Yeah. She, uh, she joined Krotes. I tried to talk her out of it, but . . . well . . . look at us. It's this place, or it's out there. In here with no future or out there with hope and promise. It was hard for me to say no.'

'I'm surprised you didn't,' Liza said.

'Shut up,' Minnie said.

A shifting in the room. Cara had no idea what they were doing.

'So, what do we do now?' Toby's voice came out of the dark.

'Liza has a plan,' Minnie said, sounding just as disappointed as Cara thought she would.

'I do,' Liza said pluckily. 'They didn't search us when we got thrown in here. Lockhart, please tell me you held on to that shiv.'

Cara looked blank, and then felt in her pocket. Her hand closed around the shiv. She felt annoyed with herself that she hadn't thought of it before. 'I do,' she said.

'Yes!' Liza said. 'Nice one, Lockers. So we just have to wait for Moyley to come back. She was talking about coming to get the "other one" when she was bringing us back. We wait, ready, and then when she opens the door, we jump her.'

'What then?' Cara said.

'Then,' Minnie said, 'you end this.'

'Wait, what?'

'Me and Min talked it out,' Liza said. 'We may have underestimated you, Lockhart. You found that room, and you stood up to Krotes. Maybe it should be up to you to end this.'

'I'll go too,' Toby said, 'I need to find some evidence to try and take this whole operation down.'

'So we rush Moyley, follow her out,' Cara confirmed. 'The only plan we'll ever have.'

'OK,' Minnie said. 'Me and Liza will keep everyone else busy. They're all in the dining room. Krotes is in Cara's cell. That's where we met her. The only issue will be the door between the dining room and the Pit. Anyone can get through it.'

'No,' Toby said, 'they slipped up by not searching me either. I have a key card – I'll be able to lock the door so the Cuff lock won't work.'

'Good,' Minnie said, 'looks like we have a plan. Cara?'

Cara thought for a moment. 'OK. Let's finish this.'

And she couldn't see any of them, but she knew they were smiling.

12

It didn't take long for them to hear Moyley coming down the corridor. It was hard to prepare when no one could really see each other. Cara handed Minnie the shiv – it was hers after all, giving it back to her after the attack outside the dining room.

Toby shifted around the room, and she felt him come and stand next to her. Their arms brushed together. And Cara was thankful that he'd be there with her. Toby had been one of the bright spots in the sea of blackness that North Fern and Krotes had brought. If she wanted someone with her at the end, it was him.

'Ready?' whispered Minnie.

Liza grunted, as did Toby, and Cara whispered, 'Yes.'

And the door swung open.

It happened so fast that Cara blinked and almost missed it. Moyley pulled open the door, and Minnie sprang forward. Watching her was like watching someone at work – it was clear she was good at this. She pressed the shiv against the softness of Moyley's neck and slammed her against the wall.

Moyley gave out a soft cry that sounded so feeble Cara couldn't help but feel bad for her. 'You bastards.'

Liza advanced on her. 'No, you bastard. I gave you protection, Sandra.'

Sandra? Liza did indeed seem to have deals with everyone. So much so she knew Moyley's first name, a detail even Cara didn't have.

Minnie glanced at Moyley, then Liza, with trepidation – a look of a person who could hold a shiv but not draw it across somebody's throat. Maybe this situation had changed her as Cara had felt plenty threatened when Minnie was looking to do it to her. Who knew? 'I'm not doing that.'

'Then give me the shiv, I'll do it.'

'No.'

'C'mon.' Liza swiped for it and then Toby stepped forward and got between Moyley and Liza. 'Ah, you spoilsports.'

Minnie turned her attention back to Moyley, and pressed the shiv further and further in to her neck. Until the skin broke. Moyley screamed, and Minnie withdrew the shiv, a slow stream of blood coming out of the wound. Moyley clutched it, moaning and slid down the wall.

Minnie looked at Cara, who was obviously betraying her feelings. 'Sorry, Cara, but she had to be incapacitated.'

Cara stepped out of the Hole.

Moyley lay there, propped up, clutching her neck, which was slowly bleeding.

'Will she be OK?' Cara said. 'She has a family.'

'She'll be fine – nicked a vein, not an artery,' Minnie said, and passed her the shiv.

331

Cara took it, even though she thought Minnie might need it more. She was going to have to contend with a room full of pissed-off prisoners; Cara was set on only one woman, and she had no intention of stabbing her. She didn't know if she had it in her.

They started down the short corridor to the hidden door. Moyley grunted, whether to get attention or in pain, Cara didn't know, but she was the only one who turned to look at her.

Moyley's eyes rose to hers. 'You think you have a chance in hell of getting out of this alive?' She was still clutching her neck.

Cara felt anger towards her, for the first time. 'Why are you following Krotes? What is she offering?'

'Why don't you go see for yourself?' Moyley slurred.

'I might. But I don't think I'll sign up, if it's all the same to you. Krotes killed Barnard. She has us all exactly where she wants us. She has all the power, and you have none. Why can none of you see that? Some partnership.'

'Whatever, Butcher.'

'Why does Krotes think I'd be interested in joining you anyway?'

'What?' Moyley chuckled.

Cara could see that she was wrong. 'You were coming to get me, to take me to Krotes, to try and recruit me?'

'Coming to recruit you?' Moyley laughed. 'Why would we do that? No. I was coming to recruit the Doc.'

And Moyley's laughs were disturbing enough for her to turn away and rush to catch up with the others.

13

It was just like any normal lunchtime in the dining room. Residents were snacking on things they found in the kitchen, and they all looked around, doubtfully, as the hidden door swung open. Then, slowly, but surely, their eyes collectively widened as they saw first Minnie and Liza, and then Toby and Cara.

'Hi, guys,' Liza said, brightly. 'Got any food for us? I'm so hungry I could eat about a hundred back-stabbing slimy little bitches.'

'And I'll wash it down with their blood,' Minnie said, equally brightly.

Liza looked at her. 'Wow, little dark.'

'Eating them's not dark?'

'Well, yeah, but I don't elaborate. I talk in general, broad strokes.'

Cara touched them both on the shoulder. 'Guys, let's talk about this later.'

And Minnie and Liza looked around to see what Cara had already seen. The horde of brainwashed prisoners standing up.

'Well, here we go,' Liza muttered. And, as if that kicked it all off, the scrum began. Women launched themselves at Minnie and Liza. Cara dodged to the side as Liza punched a woman in the face full-force, her features scrunching and blood flying. Minnie was contending with two women, and wrestling one against the other. Cara turned her back on them as women started not only fighting them, but also each other. It seemed that something had broken – the rules of logic. A prison riot tended to be without rules, and it only took one of Krotes' supporters to realise it might be the ideal time to punch that other Krotes' supporter she had some beef with, for others to seize on similar opportunities.

That meant Cara could pick her way through the crowd rather easily, and she saw Toby making his own way too, a few metres in front of her. He got to the wall, and traced it with his hands as though that would offer him some sanctuary as he got closer and closer to the double doors.

Cara watched him, thankfully, and only turned to see who was in her path at the last second. She jumped. Peter was there, standing between her and the door. She looked a little unhinged. In the small time she had been away, she seemed to have grown a wild look in her eyes. 'Cara,' she said, her head tilted slightly like a concerned puppy.

'I don't know what Krotes promised you,' Cara started, walking towards her, 'but she's not going to deliver. I think you know, really, that she is just playing with you.'

Peter looked blank. 'Do you know why I stabbed my boyfriend, Cara?'

'No, no I don't.' Behind them came a yowl of pain from someone – Cara had no idea who or what had happened. She just knew that she had to get out of this room. Behind Peter, Toby had got to the Cuff lock and was looking back through a few sparring purple uniforms to see Cara. He started towards her, but she gave a small, hopefully hidden shake of the head.

'I'll tell you. Why I did it. When I remember,' Peter said.

'You don't remember?'

Peter had started crying. 'Ms Krotes is going to help me remember. Dr Trenner didn't help, so maybe she can.'

Cara didn't know what to say. And she didn't have time to process it right now. 'I'm going to pass you and go to the door. Are you going to stop me, Peter?'

But Peter didn't respond. Instead she erupted into tears, and Cara felt a strong urge to go and hug her. But she knew she couldn't. As Peter sank to the floor, Cara just stepped around her.

What is happening to you?

She sidestepped a woman getting punched in the face and got to the door. She nodded to Toby. 'OK, ready.'

Toby nodded too and put his key card on the Cuff scanner and Cara tried the door. The light above it remained red, but it opened. She slipped through and held it open for Toby.

When they were through, Toby held the key card on the light box on the Pit side and it turned red. Minnie and Liza were locked in. Cara hoped against hope that they would be all right.

'OK,' Toby said, 'I'm going for Anderson.'

'And I'm going for Krotes,' Cara said.

They both nodded. And Toby turned away. But he stopped and turned back. He enveloped her in a hug. She didn't know if it was meant to comfort him or her, but she liked it. She hugged him too. For a long time. And Cara felt tears threaten to spill from her eyes. She realised she hadn't had a hug in two years.

Toby pulled away, sniffing himself. 'Be careful, Cara.'

Cara blinked away the tears. 'Thank you, Toby. Truly.'

And Toby gave one last smile, before turning away and heading up the nearest flight of stairs. She heard his footsteps on the gangway above, but she didn't look after him. She didn't want to think that she might never see him again. But it was true.

She shook herself and made her way across the empty Pit. To her cell. Where Minnie and Liza said Krotes had been. But her cell stood open, empty. She stepped inside. Krotes wasn't here.

Unless . . .

And as she thought it, there was a sound behind her. The door shutting.

And Cara turned to see a flash of Krotes before the back of her head erupted in pain.

And dark snapped on as she fell to the floor.

14

Cara blinked, first seeing nothing through her open eyes, then seeing spots, and then finally her stark reality. She was staring at Barnard's bed, at eye level. She finally remembered why, and went to stand up, her wrists quickly snagging on something and pulling her down. She was handcuffed, her arms behind her back, to her bed frame.

She looked around, trying to ignore the rock that seemed to be bashing about her head when she moved it, and saw the familiar figure of Krotes, sitting there on the stool watching her, leaning on the closed door. She had a pistol in her hand, with a silencer on it. She knew it was a silencer because it looked just like the one that she had seen No-Face carry down the stairs.

Krotes noticed she was awake and smiled. 'Hello, sleepyhead.'

Cara didn't reply.

Krotes didn't seem to care. 'You have a lot of questions, I know. But I promise you, you'll get them answered. I'm afraid our friend Stephanie Barnard slightly accelerated what I had planned, and subsequently shortened her and your life by rather a wide margin. Then I was

337

going to wait until you were,' she made air quotes, '"transferred", but it will all end the same.'

'You killed Barnard,' Cara said, the words grating her throat as they came out. Not a question. A statement. The most resolute and accurate statement she'd ever made.

Krotes sniggered. 'Of course I did.'

She was different from the woman Cara had met in the office all that time ago. But she was still just as unsettling.

Krotes licked her top teeth and they almost shifted. 'It was easy enough to get down here in the middle of the night and override the lock. I popped one into Barnard while you slept like a baby, all drugged up. Just like the wine.'

'Because she found your secret room?' Cara said.

Wait . . . wine?

'Well, that and she had an awful sense of style,' Krotes said, gleefully. 'The goth look is very 2009, don't you think? But I suppose I can't really blame her since that was when she was imprisoned. But, still, look at a magazine for God's sake.'

'What are you talking about?' Cara said. 'That was a woman's life. That was my friend's life.'

Krotes pushed away a stray lock of hair from her forehead with the gun, seeming not to have even heard Cara. 'It all comes down to how you present yourself really. You can be whoever you want to be. I learned that the hard way. But I came out the other side different . . . better.'

'I don't know what you mean,' Cara said.

'Of course you don't,' Krotes snapped. 'You can't see what I am. I am your God right now. I choose whether

338

you live or die. I am the person who made you what you are, what you think, what others think of you. I am the reason you're here. I orchestrated this entire situation – I got you transferred here, I hired the relevant staff, I got you into this unit, I am the mastermind. It's all fallen into place, and North Fern is rolling, it's making, it's manufacturing.'

She wasn't making any sense. 'What is North Fern?'

This seemed to be the right question. Krotes looked smug and leant forward. 'It is an experiment – my experiment. The world out there, Cara, has changed. What is a prison?'

'What?'

'What is a prison? To you? In its basest form, what is it?'

Cara frowned. 'It's a place to put bad people.'

'Bingo! I couldn't have put it better myself. It's a place to put bad people. Criminals, away from innocent people, away from *normal* people, away from the *ordinaries*. So, if everyone outside these walls is ordinary, that means everyone inside these walls is what?'

Krotes was lecturing her like she was in nursery school. Cara didn't answer.

This didn't seem to matter. Krotes was in full flow. 'They're extraordinary. They broke laws, they went against society, they saw how people lived and they said "no, not for me." Whether they murdered, or they stole, or they burned, or they pilfered – everyone here has this in common. Except you of course – you're entirely innocent. But—'

339

'Wait . . . what?' Cara said. Krotes had said it so fast, she almost didn't believe she heard it.

Krotes continued unswervingly. ' . . .the fact they got caught and they got thrown in somewhere like this, means they cannot fulfil their potential. So, and this is a important bit, if someone in a position of power were to see the potential in harnessing that commonality, well, you'd have the biggest criminal enterprise in England. Prisons, by their mere purpose, are flawed, because they put all these like-minded people together.'

'You said I was innocent?' Cara pressed, trying to listen to Krotes but also unable to move on from that.

'Are you paying attention?' Krotes snapped. 'Of course you're bloody innocent. It's not exactly hard to tell. Well, except for the jury and the judge and everyone in that courtroom that day, I guess. So North Fern is . . .'

'A recruitment drive,' Cara finished.

Krotes looked taken aback. 'Wow. Yes. I couldn't have put it better myself. You were listening. I apologise. Yes, North Fern is a recruitment drive. It being the first of its nature, I populated it mostly with my friends – people I already found to join the cause. But I found some guinea pigs, and some other prisons to transfer some actual prisoners to test my hypothesis. Obviously, I didn't tell them my true intentions. To everyone outside these walls, North Fern is just a normal prison and can be easily mistaken for one. But in here, we are criminals for hire on the dark web.

'And North Fern will forever be self-sustaining. A

340

factory. The worst of the worst are sent here and are then persuaded to join the cause. If we get red flags that they won't join, they get transferred back out. But, c'mon, who wouldn't take up the offer of an extremely well-paid job over life in prison.'

'But . . .' Cara couldn't wrap her head around it, ' . . .what about regulators? What about prison inspections? People will come and see this place.'

'Then we play make-believe. This place does look like a prison after all – all we need is everything in its place . . . or everyone, I suppose.'

'I'm not interested in your game,' Cara said, without a thought.

This sent Krotes into hysterics. She wiped her eyes with the butt of her gun. It almost looked comical. 'No, no, no. This venture isn't available to you. You are, let's say, a side project. One that is almost completed.'

'I'm not a jigsaw,' Cara spat, slowly moving around – trying to test the lengths she could go with the handcuffs. She couldn't get far.

'You sort of are, Cara. This moment has taken a lot of pieces to fall in precisely the right order. But here we are, you and me, exactly where the picture on the box predicted.'

'Screw you,' Cara snarled.

Krotes let out a sound like a whistling kettle and thrust the gun at Cara. 'You little bitch. I will kill you. I will kill you right here, in this room.'

'Do it,' Cara said, shockingly calmly. 'You're going to do it anyway. So now is as good a time as any. Just answer – why? Why are you doing this to me? Who are you?'

Krotes calmed down at that. Lowered the gun. Checked her watch. 'No. No. No. Not yet. There's something else first. I need to attend to . . . something else. You're to stay in here for now, until . . .' Krotes was unravelling, and Cara wasn't sure if it was better to press harder on the accelerator or the brakes. Was Krotes more dangerous angry or considered? She wasn't sure.

What was Cara's endgame anyway? She was going to die – she was sure of that. The look in Krotes' eyes betrayed Cara's destiny. And that destiny didn't really work with a plan. She had to believe that she could get out of this – even though the odds were stacked against her – but even if she got out of this cell, what then? She would still be in prison, and she would still be stalked by Krotes and the entire Unit, her only allies possibly already dead. Death waited in every corner.

The lyrics to Eugene's feel-good song from *Rain on Elmore Street* popped into her head.

'The world may seem topsy-turvy, upside-down, inside out
But there's always a good way to look at things
A way to put a smile on your face
So just straighten up your suit and put your tap shoes on
And get ready to put the world in its place.'

How hopelessly wrong Eugene was – or at least the guy who wrote the lyrics. Cara was immediately seized by a scenario where the actor read the lyrics he was about to sing and said 'There isn't always a good way to look at things. What if a woman is accused of two separate crimes, convicted and hated by the whole world, then incarcerated in a closed off pseudo-prison where she is consistently tormented by her demons and a batshit crazy governor, who fancied herself as some crime lord?' Cara almost smiled at this – almost. But she didn't, because there wasn't always a good way to look at things.

Sometimes the world was just topsy-turvy, upside-down, inside out, and you had to grit your teeth and deal with all the shit that was thrown your way. There were so many people in the world, and a limited number of Happy Ever Afters.

Eugene and Giratina could ride off into the sunset, but Cara would still be here, in this room, waiting to die.

And who was to say they had a happy ending anyway? Maybe Giratina would be coaxed back into her rich, promiscuous ways and she would be bewitched by another business mogul who wanted to get into the oil business and promised her more money and had a slightly better singing voice and understood rhyming couplets a little better, and maybe she'd unlearn all the lessons she'd vowed never to forget and maybe she'd leave Eugene, who'd only been able to conjure her up a little flat in downtown Ohio on his pay cheque as a doorman at the city's fourteenth fanciest club. Then, maybe, when she left, Eugene would spiral, longing for his life back in New York and maybe he'd realise that he'd dreamed too big and you could never change someone like his soulmate

– or who he thought had been his soulmate. Maybe he'd start using drugs to get through his long nights at the club, outside in the cold air, and he'd find they dulled the pain of heartache, so he'd use more and more. And eventually he'd turn up to work high as a kite and get fired and lose his pay and then lose the flat and he'd end up on the streets, with his only release looking like it was going to be a noose in a dark alley under a bridge, his final moments serenaded by crackheads, prostitutes, and stray dogs.

Boy, *Rain on Elmore Street 2: A Light Drizzle* was going to suck.

Cara couldn't help it – she let out a small guffaw before she could stop herself.

Krotes' face turned to thunder and she pointed the gun again. 'Is any part of this funny to you, Cara?'

Cara collected herself, still unable to keep a smirk from her face. But she shook her head. No – it wasn't funny at all. But she did feel better. What sweet release she felt being able to laugh while looking into the muzzle of a gun. 'No, I suppose none of this is funny. Or all of it is. I haven't really decided yet.'

Krotes almost stabbed the gun at her. And then she stopped. Her head shot to the side like an alert meerkat spotting a predator. Yes – that was it. That was exactly it. She was listening to something. Cara strained to hear as well, but couldn't hear a thing. All she got was the silence of the empty floor. She looked to where Krotes was looking as if that would help, but it didn't. 'There he is. The loose end.'

Cara strained against her handcuffs. 'What? What loose end?'

Krotes looked back at Cara. She was serenely calm now. 'You must stay in here. And keep quiet, I can't think with your stupid voice going a mile a minute . . . Actually . . .' Then Krotes thought of something and disappeared.

Cara counted ten seconds before she was back, a roll of duct tape in her hands.

'Oh come on,' Cara said, but Krotes was already behind her wrapping a piece of sticky tape around her mouth. She put the tape down on the bed, but it instantly rolled off and fell to Cara's feet.

'That's better,' Krotes said, returning to the door, but not before checking Cara's handcuffs. 'Don't worry, Cara, this is the only other thing I have to do and then you will get the answers you seek. We are so close to the end now. Can't you feel it?' Krotes smiled and then disappeared through the door.

The door started to close. Cara's brain worked overtime, and she didn't even realise why she was doing what she was doing until it worked. She felt for the roll of tape with her feet, which had now fallen onto its flat side. She positioned herself towards the door as fast as she could – the door was nearly closed – and she kicked at the tape. It slid over the floor and stopped in the doorway, just as the door came to rest against it. There was now a crack in the door that she could see through, but, more importantly, she could hear more clearly what was going on outside.

She waited for a few moments – thinking Krotes would surely see what she had done and come back, but she didn't. Krotes obviously either hadn't noticed or was somewhere else.

Cara relaxed on her cuffs, sat back and listened as hard as she could, trying to hear what Krotes had heard. And eventually she heard something. She had to strain her hearing as far as she thought she ever had, but she could just make out a mechanical whirring. And then footsteps – there was definitely more than one set. And they were getting louder. Coming down the Pit.

'Governor Krotes?' a voice called, eager yet drenched in spite. Anderson's voice. 'I caught the quack going through my things. Looks like he thinks I might be shady.' A laugh.

No . . . No . . . Not . . .

But Cara's hopes were squashed before they could even solidify in the first place, when she heard a dreadful shuffling outside, coupled with Anderson's grunts and – another man's.

'Get off of me,' a voice shouted. Another familiar one. Toby's. 'What are you doing?'

There was a hollow THONK noise followed by a cry of pain. And Toby was silent. But it didn't matter if he was talking or not. He was there.

Anderson had Toby, and he had brought him for an audience with Krotes, the mad queen.

15

Cara strained on her handcuffs and tried to bite her way through the tape covering her mouth, but she couldn't. Then she tried to scream and all that came out was a muffled grunt. She had the sharpened shiv in her pocket – the point was so thin that maybe it could slide into the handcuff lock. But what then? She couldn't pick a lock.

'Shut up,' Anderson said outside. They were close – just beyond the cell. In the Pit. Maybe if she could make a sound loud enough, then – what? Then Anderson would hear and – what? There was no help – there was no hero. 'You know, Trenner, you have never, not for one second I've known you, stopped being a pain in the arse.'

'You're going down for this,' Toby said, his voice strained. 'Both of you.'

'In what way could I possibly be going down for this? Look at the situation you're in, dude. If you weren't constantly such a soy-boy beta-cuck, then maybe you'd have survived to see another sunrise. But we are what we are, I guess.' Anderson laughed. 'Ms Krotes?'

Cara slammed against the bar of the bed with the cuffs again – maybe making noise would at least distract them. But it didn't make enough noise to travel, and the cuffs

347

weren't exactly going to disintegrate from banging them against a bar, so she stopped. No – the shiv was the only way. But it was in her pocket, and that seemed like a world away.

There was a scuffling outside in the corridor, but it came from the opposite direction. The snapping foot-steps of heels. It sounded like Krotes was pacing up and down. 'Do you want to be a little quieter, you idiot? I need to think.'

'Ah, who cares,' Anderson scoffed. 'Apart from the Lockhart chick, we're in the clear. Us and the girls and the rest of the guards are all good. Once we find Harper at least. Even Continell came over to our side. So we can shout it from the heavens.'

'Yes, yes,' Krotes snapped. She stopped clacking her heels. She was further away from the cell now– to the right somewhere. But still in the Pit. 'But that doesn't mean you can't use your inside voice.'

'Yes, boss,' Anderson said. 'Here – look what I brought you anyway. I think he's helping the Lockhart chick. God knows why.'

'Hmm,' Krotes mused. 'It's a shame. Really it is. I thought Doctor Trenner might like to join our cause. Crazy people can always use a licensed doctor.'

'Cause?' Toby said, the confusion seeping through his voice. 'You call this a cause? It's a joke, and when I get out of here, this is getting exposed for what it is. And you are going to prison for the rest of your life.'

'Look around, you simpleton. We're already in prison.'

'I mean real prison, you . . . Wait . . . What are you doing with that gun?'

Oh God. She needed to . . .

'Well, Tobias Trenner, because you got bewitched by Lockhart and went snooping around, I'm going to have to shoot you with it.'

'What?' Toby sounded like he was processing the information as slowly as possible as that might prolong his life. There was silence, no doubt as he considered his entire life – and his entire death. And he started begging then (Cara didn't blame him) – unbridled begging that made Anderson laugh and Krotes giggled too.

Cara had to get out – it was her fault Toby was there. She couldn't leave him to die at the hands of two lunatics.

The shiv – she had to get the shiv. She shot up as far as she could so she was almost standing but leaning down to the bar of the bed constrained by the handcuffs. She pulled on them as far as she could and, if she let them cut into her hands, she could almost reach the end of her pocket. She twisted her body around so her hands were as close to the pocket with the shiv in as possible. Her arms sang with pain, as it felt they were pulled as far from their sockets as they could be. She continued and her hands got closer and closer to the pocket. She listened outside and Toby was still begging, and the other two were mocking him. She gritted her teeth as the pain threatened to consume her, but she continued and finally her numb fingers could reach inside the pocket. She felt the shiv, but it took a few attempts to close two fingers around it and pull it out.

She gripped the shiv in her hand, and swivelled back around, sitting down and relinquishing the strain on the handcuffs. She sat there heavy breathing, trying to get the pain out of her head. Her wrists were red raw, and the left one was bleeding – the skin broken. Her arms ached endlessly – like they never had before. But she couldn't stop now.

She shook her hands to get the feeling back in them, then used the shiv in her left hand to manoeuvre it into the lock. It went in, and she felt some resistance, and there was even a little click, but the cuffs didn't unlock. Of course, they didn't. She had no idea what she was doing – she didn't even know if this would work. She tried jabbing it in again – still nothing.

'Sorry, Toby boy,' Anderson said. 'Boss's orders and all that. But then, saying that, if she wasn't going to kill you, then I would.' He guffawed.

'Please,' Toby said, 'I have a daughter. A young daughter.'

Cara tried again. The shiv seemed to jam into something in the cuff mechanism this time, she turned it but it didn't give. 'Come on,' she muttered.

'Oh, come on,' Krotes was saying outside, her voice rising, 'if one gets to this point, one always has a daughter, or a mother, or a grandpa, or a cat to feed, or a cactus to water. You would say anything right now to prolong your stupid little life . . .'

Cara tried again. The shiv clicked in.

' . . .but I'm afraid nothing you can say is going to stop me putting a bullet right between your eyes.

Just like I did to little ol' Stephanie Barnard.'

'So it was you,' Toby said.

Cara turned the shiv. There was a louder click, and astonishingly, miraculously, the cuffs sprang open. Her arms shot up from the bed and she rubbed her wrists. They stung at her touch.

'Yes, of course it was me. You want to know what she felt when I shot her? You're in luck, you're about to find out. Say goodbye, Tobias Trenner.'

No time to recover. Cara jumped up, ripping the tape off with such ferocity that she thought her lips might come away with it. She bounded out of the room, clattering through the door – no plan, just getting between Toby and Krotes.

She emerged into the Pit, almost into the direct centre of the scene. She saw Anderson and Toby to her left first, just because that's the way she'd clumsily stumbled out of the room. Anderson was standing there, with Toby helpless in front of him. He was pinning Toby to his body by holding a baseball bat to his neck with both hands, making a kind of choke lock.

Anderson and Toby had both seemed to start backwards at Cara's appearance, but now they had resumed looking past her. Anderson confident to the point of rashness, Toby scared to the point of inaction.

Cara wheeled around to see what Toby was so scared about. Krotes was standing there, with that crazed look in her eye that was now almost her signature. She was holding the gun up in the air, towards Toby, now with a line of trajectory through Cara.

'Cara?' Krotes said, unable to hide the genuine surprise in her voice. 'Well, you are a plucky young trickster, aren't you? That was a very good party trick.'

'Don't do this,' Cara panted, and she heard Anderson manhandling Toby behind her, and Toby still moaning, pleading. 'He is not a part of this – whatever this is. You want me, so just kill me.'

'Cara, chivalry is soooooo boring.'

'OK then. How about this? He does have a family. He was telling the truth. And if you kill him, there will be questions. They will come looking for answers about what happened to him. Do you really want people coming here – to North Fern, to this unit. You really want people to see what you've done with the place?'

Krotes opened her mouth to say something and then closed it. She seemed to be actively considering what Cara had said. She lowered the gun and then stepped back. 'You know, you're right. I can't have people knowing what happens here.' She seemed genuine, she seemed almost broken. 'I can't have people coming to North Fern. They wouldn't understand – they wouldn't see. Thank you, Cara. I could have made a real mistake there.'

Cara breathed out but couldn't help but nod in appreciation.

Krotes stepped forward to Cara. And smiled at her. Instantly, she rushed her, pushing her aside. Cara went barrelling into her closed cell door and sliding down it, scrabbling around to see Krotes standing there, tall. She smiled at Cara. And Cara knew what was going to happen.

So did Anderson as he instantly thrust Toby away from him – the only person in the Pit who seemed oblivious. Maybe it was better that way.

Krotes gave Cara a wink and turned, raising the gun while Cara could do nothing but watch. And she shot Toby in the head.

'Oops.'

16

'A selfless man obliterated by a Butcher.' Krotes turned and looked to her, even though she couldn't look back. She was too transfixed by Toby's lifeless body. His head had exploded in a spray of blood and chunks of something she didn't really want to think about. He'd fallen to the floor – he wasn't getting up. So why was she still hoping?

The man who had been so kind to her. Gone.

'Very clever, Cara, escaping I mean.' Krotes was speaking and she was listening. But it felt like someone else. 'May I ask how you got out of the handcuffs?'

Cara automatically reached into her pocket and brought out the sharpened plastic weapon. She didn't even think about giving away her final defence – it didn't matter now. Nothing did. Toby had died, just the way Barnard had. Because of Krotes. Because of her. Was she really supposed to walk away, to escape, with all these people on her conscience?

Krotes grabbed the weapon and looked at it in the light.

'What's that?' Anderson said.

'Shut up,' Krotes shouted, 'I don't want to hear another word out of you.'

Anderson shuffled awkwardly on his feet, clearly confused. 'I don't understand, boss. I did exactly as you asked. I brought any loose ends there might be. Here, what's your deal with the Lockhart chick anyway? Pardon for asking, but it's intriguing. I know my connection to her, but what's yours?'

'Didn't I tell you to shut up?' Krotes looked at Anderson, and although Cara couldn't see her expression, it was obviously horrifying enough to shut Anderson up. Then she gazed back to at Cara, and she was the happy and smiling Governor again. 'This will do nicely, Cara. Thank you.'

Cara tore her eyes from Toby to look at her. What did she mean by that?

Krotes gave no further explanation. She left Cara alone, turning her back on her, and focusing all her attention on Anderson. Cara glanced down the Pit to the dining-room doors and then the other way – to the entrance of the Unit. They stood between her and the lift, the only exit blocked by Krotes and Anderson and Toby's dead body. All she could do was watch the scene unfold.

'What did I tell you to do?' Krotes was saying to Anderson as Cara returned her gaze to them. Krotes was advancing towards him. 'What did I tell you to bring here?'

Anderson was looking unsure of himself, but he answered all the same. 'You told me to bring you any loose ends there may be. And I did.'

'Yes,' Krotes said. All Cara could see was her back, but she could imagine her malicious smile. 'Indeed, you did.

355

But did it ever cross your pig brain that the biggest loose end you'd be delivering to me now – was you.'

It was very clear on Anderson's face, that he did not consider that possibility. 'What? I'm not a loose end – you told me to come here, you told me to keep an eye on the Lockhart chick. I'm not a loose end, like the dumb Doc.'

Krotes kept advancing. 'I'm not talking about here, you dolt. I'm not talking about North Fern.'

Anderson was slowly breaking down – his brain looked to be working overtime. 'What do you mean? We don't know each other outside of North Fern. We'd never met before North Fern, before the day I was hired.' But even as he said that, it was obvious he was searching through his brain for any memory of Krotes. 'NO. I don't know you. I didn't, I mean.'

'You did,' Krotes said, 'but you never met me. I was just on the other end of a phone.'

Anderson's face lit up with a foggy realisation. 'You were one of them? One of them who employed me? Well, what happened – I always did the jobs, I always finished them. What can you possibly have to be pissed about? Which one were you? Eh? EH?'

Krotes spoke – but it was different. Her voice was different. 'One went wrong though, didn't it. That one.' The slight French accent was gone, her pitch and tone completely reworked, so now she sounded more like she came from South London. 'How about this? "They're almost ready. Only the room marked Tilly."'

Cara almost recognised the voice and that name – Tilly –

but couldn't think as she saw Anderson's reaction.

He stumbled backwards, his eyes growing five times their normal size. 'You? You're that weird bitch who paid me all that money to kidnap that kid?' Cara's mind swirled. 'Look, I— I thought the main thing you wanted was to frame Lockhart. That happened. Just . . . a little differently. If anything, I did my job better than you ever coulda hoped.'

Krotes scoffed. Almost sounded like she was sobbing. But she kept advancing.

'I said only Tilly's room.'

'And that's exactly what I did . . . but it went a little off script. I was about to get the girl, take her away. The gun was just a precaution, thought if she was awake she might need some persuading to shut up, but . . .' Anderson looked visibly uncomfortable.

Cara had never seen him like that.

Tilly.

Tilly's room.

The image flashed into her mind, flooded what she was actually seeing. No-Face, coming down the stairs – one step at a time.

'I said,' Krotes snarled, 'only Tilly's room. Do you not think that maybe you shouldn't touch anyone else.'

Anderson was gasping at the air. 'How was I supposed to know the hubby took the baby in the lil' bitch's room without you knowing? I talked to you and you knew everything. How come you didn't know that? This isn't on me.

'I was about to pick the girl up. Hadn't seen the crib

in the corner. And there was this deafenin' cry. And I just reacted. I turned and . . . And shot. And then . . . the girl saw . . . and I knew I couldn't . . . So I . . .'

He kept backing up, but Krotes was too quick and grabbed him, dragging him to the opposite side of the Pit and pinning him to the wall with astounding strength.

He realised what was about to happen and changed tack. 'You think it doesn't haunt my dreams? You think I don't see that room every time I close my eyes. You don't do kids and come out the other end the same. I have tortured myself, but sometime you've just gotta move on. Look. I didn't know. But it was my mistake, I'm sorry. I'm very sorry, Ms Krotes. Obviously, it won't happen again. I'm out of that life now, trying to play it straighter. With a little bit of money on the side for helping you. That's what I wanted, that's all I wanted.'

Krotes pressed the point of the weapon to Anderson's neck, just as Minnie had done to Cara, but Krotes pressed harder and, even from her distance away, Cara could see a small trickle of blood flowing down Anderson's neck. 'Stop calling me Krotes. That's not my name.'

He grunted in pain. 'Ms Krotes— I mean whoever you are, whatever you're called, please. Look we can sort this out, can't we? We're a good team, you and me. Me out in the field, you here pulling the strings. That's the ingredients of a winning partnership right there! Isn't it? I thought we were on the same page here. I thought you were happy? Please, Krotes.'

'Not this time, I'm afraid,' Krotes said.

Anderson's eyes widened, and as if it was as easy

as carving through butter, Krotes wrenched the shiv across Anderson's neck, as if she were unzipping it. Krotes pulled the shiv out as Anderson's throat spat with blood. She smiled, Cara could tell from how her wrinkles flexed, as Anderson looked at her and the light started to die in his eyes. She turned to Cara and did a little bow.

The entire scene made Cara feel incredibly sick, and she found herself doubling over and dry-heaving. There was nothing to come out, but she couldn't stop retching until she finally spat something out – it looked like a piece of liver. Her eyes were stinging with tears as she looked back up.

Krotes threw the weapon aside as Anderson spluttered and sprayed down the wall until he came to rest. In a few seconds, it was over. He was dead. And Krotes – or whoever she was – was spattered in blood. She looked at it on her hands and wiped her palms on her torso – although that was equally soaked, so it did nothing to help.

She started towards Cara. 'Well, I don't know about you, but I'd consider those loose ends quite firmly tied up.' Behind Krotes, Anderson's neck gave one last gargle – a spurt of blood jetting out across the Pit. The timing would have been almost comical if it wasn't so horrifying.

'Who are you?' Cara said.

'Hmm?'

'WHO ARE YOU?' she shouted across the Pit, and that made Krotes smile and quicken her step. 'Why are you doing all this? Why are you doing all this to these people? Why are you doing all this to me?'

Krotes looked at her watch as she got to Cara and smiled. 'Hey, look, right on time. Would you believe I planned all this, at short notice?'

'Tell me who you are,' Cara said, trying to sound menacing and not achieving it in the slightest.

'Cara, you know me. You just don't realise it. I left you clues. Clues about that night. Hell, I played that stupid movie over and over again and you still didn't get it. You know, *Elmore Street*. The movie that was on when I came through the door.'

What? Cara couldn't keep up. What . . .?

Krotes sighed. 'OK here, this might help.' She reached up to her fringe and started to pull on her hair. Cara winced, but the hair came away. The blonde hair pulled off – a wig – to reveal short brunette hair. Rough but styled. She tossed the wig behind her. Next, Krotes took her glasses off and threw them at the wall, where they shattered. And then she went to her nose – for one horrifying moment Cara thought she was going to pull that off too, but instead she itched at it with her long nails, almost digging into the skin, carving it. As she did so, a layer of make-up came off, and Cara could see a number of neat, small, but still perceptible acne scars that hadn't healed quite right – most likely because the woman who had them was digging into them with her nails. And her entire frame seemed to slump. Lastly, she reached up and took her top teeth out – they were fake and somewhat too large. Beneath them was a set of grey crooked teeth instead.

When she was done, she cricked her neck and spoke in an ever-so-slight South London accent. 'That's a hell of a lot better. And I can stop talking in that awful accent. Disgusting. Do you remember me, Cara? Do you know me?'

Yes.

She did.

Cara knew her instantly. Didn't know why she hadn't seen it before. Under her nose this whole time. Just a little bit different. And keeping her teeth in with countless licks of her tongue.

Cara was staring at a face that was inexplicably woven into that night. A face she had tried to suppress – a face she associated with pain and grief.

A face she thought – no, hoped, she would never see again.

17

She straightened her skirt. Wondered why she had turned down the offer of a glass of water. Her throat was incredibly dry. All she had worked for, the years she had spent trying to get promotion after promotion – trying to rise up the ranks. All the work, all the toil, all the nights.

The waiting room seemed to be the most ostentatious it could be – prime for making someone like her uncomfortable. In her work, in her environment, she was fierce. But here, she was way out of her depth.

She cleared her throat. And shuffled the thick file on her knee. This was going to work. It was going to be fine. She'd dotted the i's. Crossed the t's. Everything that there was to think of she'd thought of.

A man in a cheap suit left the office. On his iPad. He didn't even notice her as he walked past.

'See you later, love,' he said to the receptionist.

She rolled her eyes.

The phone rang and the receptionist picked it up. After a few curt words, she put it down and said, 'Stellan will see you now.'

362

Moment of truth. The moment this could all come tumbling down. She got up and went through the door.

Into a similarly ostentatious office.

A man, Stellan Tharigold, was sitting behind the desk, on the phone. He nodded to her as she came in. There was no recognition on his face – even though they'd met at least five times at prison events. She was almost glad – a blank slate. Chances weren't swayed.

'I can't deal with this right now,' Stellan was saying as she stood there wondering whether to sit down. 'Since when does the EU . . .? No, I know . . . I understand . . . I get it, I do. Well, last time I checked I was the goddamn Minister of State. I'm hanging up now.' And he did, slamming the phone down.

He tightened his tie and exhaled a long breath of anger.

'Turbulent times,' he said in a strong voice, 'forgive me.'

'Of course,' she said, 'it is for everyone.'

'Still, I don't like losing my cool,' Stellan said, smiling. 'Please have a seat.'

'Thank you.' She did.

'Essie Krotes – I assume that's a professional name,' he said, reading out of his diary.

'Yes sir, it's the name I would assume in this project, if it is greenlit. My real name is Elisabeth Stoker.'

'Stoker. Krotes. I like it.' Stellan laughed. 'Very Agatha Christie. Let's see, you are from the Prism Prisons Group. A very successful organisation. You have a proposition.

Rather a well-thought-out one if the thickness of that file is anything to go by.'

She smiled. He was friendlier than she remembered him. Even if he was only being friendly because he preferred her to the person on the other end of that phone. 'I do.'

She put the folder on the desk – PROJECT N.F. – and slid it over to him.

Stellan smiled.

Took out his reading glasses.

And started to read.

And she knew she had him by page two.

18

That night . . .

'Are you OK?'

Elisabeth looked at him in the passenger seat. 'What?' She was balling her fists into her perfectly ironed dress.

'You just . . . you seem a little off.'

'I'm just nervous,' she said, smiling at David.

'It's understandable,' David said, laughing, 'Not every day you're nominated for an award. You clever girl.' David leant in for a kiss, and she gave him a peck.

He called her a girl. So he didn't deserve anything more.

Girl.

So pitiful.

The girl in the doorway and Kelvin were still watching.

'What's her name?' David asked.

'What?' she said.

'The babysitter.'

She had prepared for this. Thank God David didn't involve himself in the BabysitterVIP service.

'Umm . . .Susan something. Smith, I think.'

'Hmm,' David mused, 'Just looks familiar, that's all. Reminds me of someone.'

She breathed out. It was nerves, but David took it as annoyance.

David took the hint, thankfully dropping it, and started the engine. 'You have your speech?'

'Of course,' Elisabeth said, not bothering to tell him that she'd memorised it. David had been annoying her of late – she knew it was just because she was getting more tetchy as it came closer to the event, but she still couldn't help it. He was being a little overbearing. In a way he'd never been before. Maybe he subconsciously knew what was coming.

Was that good?

It felt good.

Right now, it felt damn good.

Because wasn't this about punishing him too. After all, he'd put it in that whore. He'd made that spawn they called Matilda. Was she kidding herself in thinking that she wouldn't feel some kind of retribution at watching him bawl his goddamn eyes out when they got back?

But against it all, she still loved him. And when he learned what happened when he crossed her (even though it would be a lesson that was learned subconsciously) they would be fine. Because she wasn't just the driving force in her job, she was the driving force in her whole life.

And that felt good.

'Come on, let's go,' Elisabeth said.

She watched the Lockhart girl in the wing mirror as they drove away.

Knowing that nothing would be the same again.

19

That night . . .

The Luxury Grand was buzzing with activity. Countless people in formal dress were pouring through its doors, with some staying outside to chat with people they hadn't caught up with since the last one of these things.

Elisabeth got out of the car. Flipping up a pocket mirror and checking her flyaways. David got out after her, and attempted to link his arm with hers. But she didn't let him, striding towards the entrance independently.

Many people standing outside tried to get her attention, but she just smiled, waved and muttered an excuse. Her mind was on her speech and before she gave it, she couldn't entertain small talk.

She got into the large hall, with countless tables set out for a formal dinner. People were standing and sitting at their places and creating a thrum of noise.

David caught up. 'Hey, slow down.'

Elisabeth looked around. 'Maybe you should speed up instead.' She couldn't take doing anything slowly. That's why she went into David's savings to get the building work finished – not that she told him that of course.

She finally found who she was looking for.

Her one exception for small talk.

Minister for State Stellan Tharigold, in a sharp suit and bow tie, was standing with a gaggle of women around him, as though this were some high-school teen film. The way they were behaving was an insult to her sex, and from Stellan's expression, it seemed like he agreed.

Suddenly, their eyes met, and Stellan extracted himself from the group with glee. Finding his way over to her. 'The woman of the hour,' he said.

David took this as his cue to leave. Thank God. 'I'm going to go and find our seats.'

She didn't even look at him.

'Minister,' she said to Stellan. 'It looks like you have quite the fan club there.'

Stellan laughed. 'They're just trying to get me to fund some projects. I told them all my available funds were tied up in a very secret project.'

Elisabeth laughed. 'I wonder what that could be.'

'I guess we'll find out when you make your speech. They're going to lose their minds over it, you know. Everyone will be eating out of the palm of your hand.'

Elisabeth smiled.

They talked for a few more minutes, before a waiter came round to inform them dinner was about to be served. Elisabeth reluctantly went to go and find David, who was sitting at a table towards the front of the room, by a stage. He was talking with an older woman, who sitting opposite.

368

Elisabeth took a seat. Picked up a glass of champagne and sipped it.

'This is incredible, Lis. Do you know that . . . I'm sorry I've forgotten your name.'

'Continell,' the woman said. She looked out of place in her budget dress.

'Continell is a guard at one of your old prisons.'

'Really?' Elisabeth said, wondering if she could care less.

Dinner was appalling. For starters, she had an under-seasoned lobster bisque. For main, she had Foie de Veau Lyonnaise – basically a fancy type of liver and onions, which was possibly the worst thing she'd ever tasted. For dessert, Eton mess, which probably cost about two pounds to produce but added fifteen pounds around the hips. The entire meal sat in her stomach like a boulder. She felt a little sick.

She didn't know if it was the impending speech. Or the anticipation of what was going to happen at home. But the food tasted like ash.

The conversation was even worse.

David seemed way too interested in this Continell person, even though she wasn't even slightly attractive and was basically double his age.

Maybe it was just that someone was actually paying him some attention.

And the time ticked by so slowly she wondered if the entire concept was broken.

But finally a man in a tux stood up and went over to the stage at the front of the room, standing by a lectern.

The man was Frank Derrington, the general CO of the Prism Prison Group. And he seemed a little drunk.

'Hello, hello, everyone,' he said into a microphone on the lectern, as people sat down. 'OK, quiet down. Now, NOW, haha, we all know why we're here. We're here to honour the special achievement of one of our own. We're here to give out an award, but none of you are aware she is also here to tell us what's coming next. For the company. For prisons. For the country. Please join me in a rapturous round of applause, for our very own Elisabeth Stoker.'

The room erupted.

Eyes on her.

She stood, took her bag, and went up to the stage, wondering whether she liked this attention or not.

She wasn't sure.

She got up onto the stage and shook Derrington's hand. Derrington handed her a controller as a screen descended from the ceiling. He went in for a kiss and she had to let him. Creep. Then he staggered off, leaving her alone.

She put her bag under the lectern.

Her speech was in there. But, suddenly, she decided to wing it.

She spoke into the microphone. 'I am honoured to accept this award. The Prisons and Rehabilitation Centres Group Woman of the Year. Huh. You know, growing up, on my cul-de-sac, I used to love playing one game with all the neighbourhood kids. I honestly turned around and walked back inside if they were playing anything else. That game was Cops and Robbers.

'And I know what you're all thinking. You're visual-ising how this speech is going to go, laid out in some typography-ass-premonition right in front of you. Don't deny it.

'I even see it in the front row. Yeah, I'm looking at you.'

Laughter.

'But here's the thing. I never wanted to be the Cop. Where's the fun in that, right? You've got the Robbers running around the entire cul-de-sac and the Cops are just trying to see them. Because as a cop or a "Cop" or a member of the British Police Force, you have to play by the rules. And as a kid, being faced with that choice – why would you take it?

'I didn't get it. As Cops you had a code, rules. And you had to play by them. You chased after the Robbers, but that was pretty much all you did. Your route was governed by somebody else. You see? But plenty wanted to be Cops. And it was weird. But I had legitimate kids, my age, wanting to be Cops who I know have grown up to be criminals. Career criminals. No black-and-white.

'I didn't know at the time, but that taught me an im-portant lesson. It's good to be bad. Yeah? And we live in a world where that is more apparent than ever. The world has changed. This country has changed. The Dead Room Incident last year has hit the big time. The peo-ple behind that horrific stunt have become rock stars. There isn't a person in the world who doesn't know the inhabitants of that room. And there isn't a criminal who doesn't look at the amount of attention it is getting and see an opportunity. Mark my words, we will see something like that again. Soon. In fact, according to an informant, there is a situation developing in Huddersfield that proves my point.

'Crime has risen by three per cent more than predicted since the Incident. And this has all been down to "showboating" crimes. We're looking at a world filled with villains and no heroes. Heroes don't exist, and if they do, they're the hard-working everymen and women like you and me. But that isn't interesting to the media. Because, in a game of Cops and Robbers, Robbers have the most fun.

'There are more criminals than ever. Prisons are becoming cesspits, idea factories for these kinds of big-deal crimes. We need to solve a problem, we need to show the government we can handle it and, above all, we need to show a united front and take our country back.

'That is the central idea I took to my team. And we think we have come up with a solution. And we thought so highly of this idea . . .' she paused, making the audience hang on every word, 'we already built it and it's already got government approval.'

She pressed the remote in her hand and the screen behind her lit up with a picture of her masterpiece.

'It's called North Fern. A prison for the new age. Where physical imprisonment is matched by a mental one. It may look like a bright and airy building, but, inside, cells are dark and dingy, with no windows other than a hyperrealistic screen that can display whatever we want.

'For too long we have shown criminals too much

humanity – these people are murderers, rapists, serial killers. North Fern is a chance to show the public that we can handle this – we can fight for them and put these bastards and bitches out of the public eye.

'The first North Fern is ready to go in Buckinghamshire and, thanks to the Minister for State, my good friend Stellan sat down there, high-profile prisoners will start to be transferred into the Units.

'If the prison is a success, Prism Prison Group will be adopting the North Fern model exclusively going forward. And maybe state prisons will start to take notice too.

'The big question now is who's with me?'

The clapping started almost immediately when she stopped talking and then the cheering began. She almost didn't hear her phone buzz in her bag.

She went behind the lectern, retrieved her phone and took one quick look.

'It's Done,' said the text.

She smiled.

Yes, she liked the attention.

Elisabeth basked in her applause.

20

Elisabeth Stoker.

Standing there in front of her. It was impossible – but there it was. 'What?' Cara said, 'How? I thought you died. I thought you killed yourself after the children . . . I was told you were gone.'

Elisabeth Stoker smiled. It was not the same as a Krotes's smile. This one was even more considered, even more malicious, even more sure of itself. This changed everything and she knew it.

'No. I would never do such a thing. So pathetic – suicide. Never in a Stoker's blood – that's what my father used to say. "No matter what happens, you have to deal with it. None of this pussy shit, like checking out early." He wasn't a poet, but the meaning got across. And, of course, blood binds.'

'How are you here? How are you here right now? The governor of a prison. And – what were you saying – you – you told Anderson to . . .'

'Just digest it all,' Elisabeth said, absent-mindedly wiping her hand on the only spot of her trousers that wasn't already soaked in blood and then running her hand through her hair. 'We have the time. And I want you to know why you are about to die. But if you think, if you really think, you already know. You have all the pieces. You just need to put them together. Ask the right question.'

'Why did you say all that stuff to Anderson? When you were Krotes. Why did you say "Only Tilly's room"?'

'No,' Elisabeth snapped, taking the gun from her waistband, 'that is not the right question.'

Cara thought. There were so many questions, so many from what she had just seen, so many about her, so many about North Fern itself. But one question stood out among all the others. 'Why me?'

'The blood binds, Cara.'

'Why do you keep saying that?'

'Because did you know that myself and your mother were friends?'

'What?'

'It's true.'

Cara was still muddled. Her thoughts all over the place. 'Why did you say "Only Tilly's room"?'

Elisabeth slapped Cara hard across the face. 'Don't jump ahead.'

Cara's hands immediately shot up to shield her face. Her neck had snapped to the side and throbbed with pain. 'No, I didn't know you were friends.'

'We were firm friends – best friends even. And then one day we met a boy. And everything changed. His name was David – we were at university and I kissed him first, but I knew Martha wanted to as well. I didn't care – David was everything I ever wanted. Smart, handsome, funny, but not in that goofy way that's grating, and then one day, your mother stole him from me.

'I lost contact with them. I had become a little bitter, and I obviously wasn't the easiest person to get on with. I'll admit that – we were still friends but we kept each other at a distance. For example, I didn't know they had children – two little girls, one still a baby.

'They were called Cara, and Matilda. And one day, completely by chance, David and myself bumped into each other at the *CoffeeCorps* in Waterloo Station. We had a conversation, and we parted ways. That night, David showed up at my door with little baby Matilda in his arms. He had broken up with Martha, who knew she couldn't keep two children by herself. So I was to look after her – and I was so besotted with David that I agreed.

'But I knew something was wrong. I couldn't love her. I just couldn't. No matter how hard I tried. And when David proposed to me – and said that losing me was the biggest mistake he'd ever made – I was so happy. But that little thing – that little strange child was there watching me with eyes I thought I knew.

'We married, we had a child of our own – named him Kelvin. But she was always there, with those eyes – a ghost named Matilda – who lived in my house and belonged to my husband but never belonged to me. But those eyes always stared at me. I'd catch her – just staring. It all made sense. Those eyes in Matilda's face – they were her mother's, your mother's, my old friend Martha's. And I had to do something about it.'

Cara looked up at Elisabeth unable to breathe. 'What?'

'David wanted me to adopt Matilda – I thought it might help. I went to your mother and asked, but she wouldn't sign her away. In fact, she wanted to see her. I told your mother to stay away. I told her multiple times, but she didn't. She saw David. And David saw her. He lied to me. He said he was going out with friends, and he left me with her spawn. I knew that they'd started something.

'So I knew she had to go. I crashed into her car, I watched as she burned.'

This was too much to take in. Cara couldn't even think – the woman in front of her, standing in front of her had killed her mother. The car that sped away. Elisabeth Stoker was in that car. Cara opened her mouth and a moan of utter despair came out.

Elisabeth smiled – she was enjoying it. 'I knew when David found out. He stayed quiet for about a week, and then he told me. Sat me down at the kitchen table. Our old university friend Martha Lockhart had driven into a tree on a country road, and her car had exploded. All the authorities found was a burned-out shell of a car, Martha almost disintegrated. David was so damn distraught, he didn't even notice that I didn't cry. Matilda was looking at me from the living room through the doorway. With those eyes. Almost like she knew. That's when I understood my rage wouldn't stop. Not until I got rid of her too.

'It took no time at all for me to actually agree with myself. You might not believe me – but even I thought

I had a limit. I thought there might be another way – other than, well, you know . . . I considered leaving David, but then that would be like your mother won. And I couldn't risk him taking Kelvin as well as Matilda. And even more so, I couldn't risk him leaving Matilda behind.

'One day, David was out of the country on business, I got a little drunk and I got to planning. I hired Anderson, who was a hitman, although he concerned himself with kidnappings as well, on the dark web at the time. I didn't know his name of course – he called himself The Dark Shadow. Can you imagine that? The Dark Shadow. Have you ever heard a name so utterly pathetic?' She sniggered.

'I never met him, only talked to him on the phone. I paid him a lot of money – left it at a drop point in a suitcase. I had to withdraw the money under David's nose – but the thing was we were so soaked in capital, he didn't even really realise. I took as much as I could dare, and I used my parents' inheritance, which I'd put in a separate bank account, for the rest. The number of zeros would make your head spin. It costs extra for a kid – I suppose that's fair enough. So Anderson was meant to kidnap Matilda, take her somewhere and then . . .well . . .

'I couldn't spend another second with Matilda – she was not my blood, and every single time she looked at me, she looked at me with your mother's eyes. I couldn't live like that – can you imagine what it was like? To live with someone who represented the worst moment of your life? If the kidnap went through . . .who knows what I would have done?'

Cara pushed herself off the wall. 'Matilda was still your stepdaughter. You could have raised her. You could have been there for her – taken her to school, watched her go for her first date, helped her apply for university. Been there for her. Blood is not binding.'

'Yes, it is,' Elisabeth said. 'Blood is binding, your mother said it herself.'

'You could have been her mother,' Cara hissed, 'if you wanted to be. Don't hide behind it being some unwritten rule of the universe that you couldn't. You couldn't be her mother because you were stupid scared – that's all you've ever been.'

Elisabeth actually considered this. And shook her head. That didn't work with her world view. She was too far gone to see why she was so completely and utterly wrong. 'Anyway, once I had contracted Anderson, I started to feel better. But that "better" didn't completely manifest itself until I knew she was dead. I knew that I could deal with blood on my hands, from your mother.' She held up her left hand and looked at Anderson's blood on it. She rubbed a finger and her thumb together and when she parted them a sticky string of blood stayed connected to both. 'But . . . Kelvin . . .' She faltered and then continued. 'I knew I liked it though. The power. But this time would be different – I'd have to act like the grieving mother. It would be thrilling, it may sound odd to you, but I was almost looking forward to it. Me and David and Kelvin together forever – all flesh and blood – a fairy-tale ending. All I needed to do was get you in place, and you'd be put away as well.

'It was easy. Especially seeing as you were babysitting anyway. Sometimes things just work out, don't they? It wasn't hard to find you on the BabySitterVIP app. You had a flawless rating – not like those hundreds of babysitters who had reviews like they'd eaten their client's food without asking or stolen something. Your reputation was spotless – almost a hundred reviews and nothing but glowing recommendations. Little Lockhart – doing God's work.'

'You didn't need to do any of this, my mother would have left you alone,' Cara cried, 'I would never have met you. I wouldn't have ever known about you, or my sister. How would I?'

'You misunderstand,' Elisabeth said, 'this was never about worrying you would find us. I just wanted you to pay, because you are hers. And before she died, I told her I would find you. I made her a promise. It was almost like my duty – and the more I focused on it, the more it felt like the promise wasn't just mine, it was like it belonged to a higher power – some higher purpose. And that helped.

'I organised you to babysit on the same day we were going to a dinner, and the same day I contracted Anderson to carry out the hit. I met you and I knew that you deserved what was coming to you. You were a little different back then, if you remember. A little more airy, a little more conceited – a traditional twenty-something I guess. Now, you're strong and brave and you would run in front of a loaded gun to try and save your friend. In fact, that's exactly what you did. Maybe you should be thanking me now. But no, back then, you were soft – a little girl.

'And you had your mother's eyes. You both did. In fact, when you first looked at Matilda, I thought you knew. I assumed you must, because it was so obvious to me. The eyes, Cara. Martha's eyes – your mother's eyes. In both of you. But you didn't see. You were the spitting image of your mother – and I wanted to kill you for that. But I knew what I had planned was better. So I just got dressed for dinner, and we left. And I knew that when I came back, everything would be different – everything would be OK.

'Although things did not go according to plan necessarily. David – the absolute bloody idiot. Putting Kelvin in Matilda's room – he thought that Kelvin would be lonely if we left him in our room, and he was always worried something would happen to him if he was alone. I told Anderson – well, you heard what I said. "Only the room marked Tilly." But David moved the crib into that room.

'Do you remember when I came up the stairs that night? I couldn't help smiling, wholeheartedly. I was happy – maybe the happiest I'd ever been in my life. Because, you see, there had been a problem, and I had worked it out. Alone.

'You were lying on the floor outside Tilly's room, remember? You looked at me through waterfalls. I wanted to taste your tears.

'My grief – that I had practised for so long in the mirror – was genuine, when I opened the door. She was gone – but so was he. And not gone the way I had . . . requested. Actually gone. They'd left. I broke down, feeling every emotion under the sun tenfold. I was impossibly sad, of course – I wanted to cry, I wanted to destroy everything – but I could also not ignore the irony in what had happened. I had ended someone else's child and he had taken mine as well. Anderson. David. Even you.

'David took you into the kitchen while the police came. I doubt you remember that. I barely do. You know why he took you away? Because when he came up the stairs, five minutes after me, I was standing over you holding a pair of scissors. I knew you hadn't killed him, but you could have stopped him. I was a parent then – I had trusted you to look after my boy and you hadn't.

'That's when I knew that I had to get to you too. In the weeks and months that followed, David disappeared into the abyss, finally overdosing in the Holiday Inn just outside of Chelmsford. I didn't even care when I heard. Love was not something I felt anymore. All I felt was anger – towards you and towards the man who killed my boy. Anderson.

'I was always in the prison business – I'm sure you didn't know that. But I was. And I had money. This enterprise was in effect before I even knew what I was going to use it for. My private company was always searching for a contract to revolutionise the prison system – combat overpopulation in prisons across the country. It was an untapped market – if we could approach the government with a foolproof plan then we could stand to make millions. So I got to work and I bought in. And seeing as I'd paid for it, the company saw fit to appoint me as Chief Executive, leader, Governor.

'The contract with the government was actually the easiest bit of the whole plan. They're far too busy at the moment, to be worrying about prison overpopulation – spending hours and days and weeks in the Commons talking about things like deals and tariffs and trade commissions. They passed it, on the condition that they could closely monitor the situation by us sending them daily reports. I've done that – I doubt they've been read.

'I brought everyone here, transferred them. I suppose my intentions were somewhat good at one point. Strange though, I really don't recall.' She seemed to lose herself for a second, and then return. 'But his death . . . when he was taken from me . . . it changes you, you know. And then I started to realise what this place really could be. And how I could get you to come here. You were the one who was most important, after all.'

'So all this . . .' Cara started, her voice fluctuating and moaning at random points, ' . . .all this was just for this moment? All of this was just to kill me.'

Elisabeth smiled, but this time it was sad, and she repeated, 'I trusted you with my child and he ended up dead.'

'You were setting me up with my own sister's kidnap. No, murder. This is all your fault. I didn't kill them, you did.'

'No! NO. Don't you say that. Don't you dare say that! It was Anderson's fault Kelvin died. Loose ends,' Elisabeth said, tears in her eyes. 'I tied them up and I got justice for him.'

'It was your fault,' Cara said. 'It was your fault Kelvin died. How can you not see that? It wasn't Anderson that killed Kelvin and my . . .' her breath hitched, ' . . .and Tilly. It was you. How can you not take responsibility for what you did?'

But Cara answered that question herself. She knew when she looked into Elisabeth's face − at the utter insanity in her features. She couldn't believe that she was responsible because it hurt too much, and her hold on reality was worth less than believing that she killed her little boy. There was nothing Cara could do to get through to her − nothing at all.

This witch had killed her mother and her sister, right in front of her eyes, stalked her through her life and framed her for her own sister's murder all out of some weird presumption that that would make her better − whole. And her mother was in the way.

This was it − the end.

The end of the Lockhart line.

Maybe after Cara was gone, Elisabeth would come to understand that none of it was worth it. Maybe that was the best she could hope for now. One day, all the lies, and the blood, and the death would catch up to her and she'd finally realise all the things she had done in the name of revenge. And she wouldn't be able to live with herself.

'Get on your knees,' Elisabeth said. Her madness was becoming more volatile than ever. Maybe it was best for Cara to go now, before it got worse.

Her mother.

Her sister.

Gone.

Maybe it was time to join them.

'OK,' Cara said, her eyes streaming. 'I won't fight anymore.'

'The final Lockhart,' Elisabeth said, 'the final release. Let this be over. Please.' She started to press on the trigger, and Cara realised she couldn't watch. She couldn't look at the final moment. She shut her eyes, screwed them up, and braced for the end.

There was a sound. Not the sound of a gun. Not the feel of a bullet. A THWACK sound, and she didn't feel anything.

She opened her eyes. Elisabeth was still standing over her, but her eyes were almost spinning. And then she sank to her knees and then to the floor in front of her. A man was standing there, a hulking figure who was familiar. But out of place. Cara's brain was so scrambled she couldn't even remember his name. He was holding a bat. The bat Anderson had used to restrain Toby. He had hit Elisabeth on the back of the head and was looking incredibly confused.

'What in the hell is going on?' Harper said, and dropped the bat with a clatter.

21

Harper looked from Cara to the bodies around her. 'Jesus,' he said. Cara didn't know what to say. Maybe it was possible that Harper wasn't a part of any of this. And the look of utter confusion on his face seemed to prove it.

Cara gave Harper an incredibly quick sum-up of what was happening. Surprisingly, he seemed to take it all in rather easily. The bodies of Anderson, Toby, and Elisabeth seemed to corroborate the story in his mind, as he looked at them all in turn.

'You say Krotes is behind all this? And the other residents are in the dining room?' Harper mused, in a tone that showed he was still processing everything.

'Yes. But she's not Krotes at all. Her name is Elisabeth Stoker. She was the mother and step-mother of the kids that I babysat, the kids who got killed.'

Harper looked at Cara, and she saw something she never thought she'd see in his face again. Compassion. 'And Matilda was your sister?'

'Yes,' Cara said, 'yes.'

Harper clutched his brow. 'This is a little much to take in, all the bloodshed here. Anderson and Dr Trenner too.

It's very distressing, but I cannot unsee what I saw. Kro-tes – or Stoker – was indeed going to kill you, so I had to do something.'

'Thank you,' Cara said, 'oh God, thank you.'

'Of course,' Harper replied, 'this is a prison, and part of the responsibility of a facility such as this is the safety of its residents. Whatever they may have done.'

Cara felt a surge of hope. 'Thank you,' she said again.

'I have to think about what to do next. But you're safe now,' Harper said, 'she,' gesturing down at the uncon-scious Elisabeth, 'will not hurt you anymore.'

A grunt from behind them. They both looked around. Cara had a momentary and ridiculous hope that it was Toby, but it wasn't. Anderson was moaning, and his eyes were open.

Harper ran over to him. Anderson's throat was cut – what looked like his entire body's worth of blood drying around him. There was no way that he could still be alive. 'Cara, come and help me.'

'No,' Cara said.

'Cara,' Harper said, quickly, 'if what you just told me is going to be believed, someone needs to be there to account for it. You're going to have a better chance if this man lives.'

'He's not alive, look at him.'

Anderson moaned again, as if in protest. But Cara could tell there was nothing in it. His eyes were open, yes, but there was no life in them.

'Cara, please,' Harper said, softly.

And Cara sighed. Looked down at Elisabeth, who

hadn't moved an inch. And then went over to Harper, who was holding Anderson by his shoulders. Cara stooped down to them and helped Harper lay Anderson on the floor, next to Toby. Cara tried not to look over to the other body and she tried not to cry.

'You know he's dead,' Cara said, matter-of-factly.

'Yes,' Harper said, placing an open palm over Anderson's face and closing his eyes. 'But I had to try.'

'You know that he was responsible for Dr Trenner's murder? You know that he was responsible for many more – possibly hundreds? You know that he was a monster?'

'Yes,' Harper said, looking down and wiping his eyes. 'I've just never seen a dead body before. Especially one so mutilated.'

Cara couldn't help but feel sorry for him, and oddly for Anderson too.

Harper wiped his eyes again and looked up. 'Wait,' Harper said, pointing over Cara's shoulder.

She wheeled around. The first thing Cara saw was Elisabeth running up the stairs to the gangway and disappearing through the double doors up there.

No – she didn't believe her eyes. And then she looked to where Harper was pointing. A small patch of blood trickling down the corridor. She almost missed what was missing – like an incredibly obvious Spot The Difference.

Elisabeth was gone.

Elisabeth was running.

22

Cara jumped up. 'Oh God.'

Elisabeth must have moved silently, woken up – if she was ever even knocked out in the first place. If she wanted to get out of the Unit, there was only one place she could've gone. The lift.

'I have to go after Stoker,' Cara said, picking up the gun. Harper watched her, but didn't stop her. 'She's heading to the lift.'

Harper nodded, running his Cuff under his nose. 'And my duty is to the residents. I will try to make sense of this mess.' He was being genuine. He really cared for the sanctity of North Fern. 'Don't worry, Cara, I will get help and this will all be over.'

Cara felt a rush of love – all she had to do now was make sure Elisabeth was caught and maybe she would be able to go back to some semblance of a normal life. Would she be released from prison? Would she be exonerated – fully? Would she be able to walk the streets of Britain without being called names such as 'Butcher' and 'Murderer' and 'Child Killer'? Was it really over?

She started away. And then stopped. 'Wait. My Cuff. I'll get shocked if I go out there.'

Harper quickly felt in his pockets for his keys and stepped forward. He put a key into Cara's Cuff and it sprang free. 'Now go.'

'Yes.'

'But whatever retribution you find up there, just know that there'll be people who never believe you. The law judged you, Cara.'

This brought her back. Cara's mind stopped, her hopes dashed in ten measly words. Harper was right. His darn philosopy was right for once. There would always be people who thought Cara was guilty, no matter all the evidence around her. She felt angry at these people – the stubborn and the followers. The hive mind. Just like the prisoners of North Fern and New Hall – all united in their unwavering belief. There were many more out there in the real world with the same kind of philosophy, who would think exactly as Harper said. She wasn't going to change anyone's minds, no matter what she did. She could deliver Elisabeth to every house in England, and the bitch could confess to every citizen, and there'd still be a contingent of suckers who still thought Cara was guilty.

This was all Elisabeth's fault – she had fooled the world. And people would still believe. No matter the truth. And Harper, or Minnie, or Liza, or anyone, would never be able to help her. There was no way out for Cara Lockhart, not anymore. And she saw that now.

She said nothing to Harper – just turned her back and bounded across the Pit, taking the metal stairs two at a time until she was up on the gangway. She ran out of the Unit and around the guards' station, to see that the lift was moving. The light above the lift indicated it was going up.

Up? She was going up? Why?

Cara pressed the call button and waited. Trying not to think about Harper and his blind assumptions. The world was a pushover, a joke – it believed whatever was easiest.

The lift doors slid open, far too slowly – she was in by the time they had fully opened. She looked around for the console, and pressed Up. It whirred and began to ascend.

This was all Stoker's fault.

And one way or another, this was the end.

23

The lift doors opened. Cara felt the wind on her skin. How long had it been since she was outside? It felt like a thousand years – and she had been counting every second. The wind whipped and smacked at her as though it were punishing her for leaving.

The roof. They were on the roof? Why had Elisabeth come here?

Cara ran out, finding herself in a small sheltered outdoor area, with mechanical units all around – air filtration, pooling water ducts, other metal boxes, and misshapen pipes that she didn't know the purpose of. She looked around to see an open mesh gate leading out of the industrial maze and she ran through it.

She was immediately battered even harder by the wind. It threatened to throw her off her feet, take her away and topple her from the roof. And that looked to be incredibly easy as the minimalist design of the walls of North Fern had extended to the roof.

The roof was white stone, slightly uneven but mostly easy to walk on. But there was nothing else on the roof – apart from the industrial section she had just walked out of, there was nothing. Flat, empty, nothing. As

Cara looked around, she saw that there wasn't even a railing at the edge. It just dropped off into nothingness. She felt dizzy thinking about looking over the edge.

She spun around. The building was so large that the roof seemed to stretch as far as the eye could see, but finally it had to end. And far in the distance, she saw Elisabeth Stoker with her back to Cara, standing near – or maybe even on – the edge.

Cara started forward towards her, holding the gun in her hand at her side. As she got closer, it began to rain. She felt the spots of moisture attack her face, but with the gusts, it was almost from the side. They came thin but fast. Not a drizzle but not a torrent either. With the flatness of the roof, however, the water started to pool almost instantly. And Cara found it slippery – with the wind it was deadly. She almost toppled over as she hit a rivet in the roof and slipped down it – but she held her balance, her nerve, her resolve. And carried on walking to Elisabeth. She didn't understand how Elisabeth stood so straight and tall. It was as if she were attached to the building – and in some ways Cara supposed she was. The Governor looking out over her domain.

As she got close, Elisabeth seemed to sense her. She turned slightly. Cara had no idea how she'd been able to tell she was there through the torrential weather, but she had.

'This wasn't supposed to happen,' Elisabeth shouted over the wind. 'I was supposed to kill you in the Pit. Just like clockwork. But then he had to show up, and I must admit he did give me a nasty bump. I mean the back of my head feels like a truck hit it, but you know, that's all fate, I guess. And sometimes . . .' Elisabeth turned on the spot, still staying precariously close to the edge but maintaining her balance as she looked at Cara. 'Well sometimes fate is a bit dramatic it seems.

'So now I'm going to shoot you here. Or maybe I'll convince you to shoot yourself. Or maybe I'll throw you off the roof. I don't really know. Didn't have time to workshop this bit.'

'Really?' Cara shouted, pointing the gun at Elisabeth. It felt alien in her hand, as her finger pressed on the trigger. And it was hard to keep trained on Elisabeth, with the wind trying to pull it away, almost as if it knew. 'It seems like I have the upper hand.'

Elisabeth let out a small giggle that was so high-pitched it managed to worm its way past the whooshing of the wind into Cara's ears. 'Please. We both know you're not going to use that. In fact, we two are the only people in the world who know it.'

Cara kept the gun on Elisabeth, but she knew that she was right. She couldn't do it. She thought she could, but when it came down to it, she couldn't.

Could she?

This woman, standing in front of her, had killed Cara's mother, Cara's sister, Cara's half-brother, and countless others. Was she really going to stand here and debate the moral quandary of shooting this bitch? And, what was more, she stood there and presumed that she knew Cara. But she didn't. She knew Cara as she was, not the woman she had become under all the loss and the torture and the death.

Cara seethed with anger. And she felt her finger on the trigger. But the grip had become hard to hold in the rain. And the slight shuffling she had had to do in her hand to depress the trigger made her lose her grip. The wind pulled the gun from her grasp and it sailed through the air. Cara and Elisabeth tracked it with their eyes, and it momentarily looked like it was going to sail right into Elisabeth's hands. Elisabeth leant for it, trying to keep her feet planted on the ground, but the gun escaped her outstretched hand and went clattering off to the left, until it disappeared over the edge.

Cara watched it go and continued to look – as if it was somehow going to reappear – until she heard a little worried cry. She looked back at Elisabeth to see that her feet were slipping in the rain, and she was so close to the edge that she had no purchase – no chance. Cara knew what was going to happen – and Elisabeth's wild eyes showed that she did too.

With a weak and redundant flap of the arms, Elisabeth Stoker slipped and started to fall backwards into the abyss.

24

Cara acted on instinct. She grabbed Elisabeth by the hand as she started to fall. Elisabeth screamed, scrabbled for Cara's other hand and Cara caught it. But something in Cara slowed. She didn't heave Elisabeth back onto the roof. She just stayed frozen, thinking.

Elisabeth slowly moved her head, looking over her shoulder. Cara could see the fear in her eyes. It was a very long way down. 'Cara, please.' Looking back at her. 'Please, just pull me up. Please, Cara.'

Cara said nothing. She was thinking, but she didn't know what about. The situation was etched in her mind. Her reaching out and holding the woman who put her here. It was almost poetic – she just needed to figure out how it ended.

'You rewrote me,' Cara muttered.

'What?' Elisabeth said.

Cara couldn't think about what was happening down there, about Minnie and Liza and Peter and the others. Because this was all there was. This roof, her, and this woman.

'You rewrote me,' Cara said, her hands grasped tightly around Elisabeth's. 'I told you who I thought I was. And you said no. You rewrote me.' Elisabeth tried to pull herself up without jostling too much, but it didn't work. Cara remained steadfast. 'Some people may have liked that. I mean, how long do you have to live until you really, truly understand who you are . . .'

'What are you talking about?' Elisabeth shrieked, her eyes streaming with tears, filled with fear. 'Pull me up right now. You bitch. You fu—'

'And then you come along and you tell them. Some would find it a relief. This is who you are, this is your life from now on. What a tremendous load off someone's back. To have a life that was defined – devoid of change. Some would love that – change is change however you slice it, and you can't sell change. A life of a revolving door. Peaceful. But it wasn't – not for me.'

'You will not do this. You will not let me go. It isn't you. You're not a killer.' Elisabeth was back to her former self, practically spitting at Cara. Her trembling fear had morphed into unbridled hatred.

Cara laughed, genuinely. 'But I am a killer, remember. I killed your child and the one you couldn't stand. I killed Barnard too – shot her in the head with a silent, invisible gun no less. You told me I did these things. Were you wrong?'

'You know you're not a killer. You know I did all those things – I killed Barnard, I contracted someone to kidnap Matilda, and Kelvin was— They both were . . . You know I did those things. I did them. You're innocent – totally innocent. I set you up, and then I got you here. And your mother. I killed your mother too by my own hand. There you go. A confession. Let me go and I'll tell everyone. I'll tell everyone everything.'

'There's no way back for me now. You made sure of it,' Cara scoffed. 'Maybe I should embrace who I am now.'

The anger subsided in Elisabeth again and the fear came back. Her wide eyes sparked with it, and Cara found it . . . satisfying. 'What? No. You are not the Butcher. You are not a . . .' And realisation blossomed in her face. 'Cara, no . . . Cara, I'm sorry, I'm so sorry.'

'As I said, rewritten,' Cara stated. 'You didn't give me a choice, but I have one now . . .'

'Cara, Cara, please . . .'

'. . . and do you know what, I think I finally know who I am. And I've learnt from the best. Because sometimes Elisabeth, you just have to let go.'

Elisabeth gave out a guttural howl as she understood.

And Cara let go.

25

Cara watched the sky – the real sky, sitting there cross-legged on the roof of North Fern, feeling a strange sort of serene calm. The rain was passing and the sun began to peek out of the clouds. The day continued. Everything continued, always. Whatever happened, there would always be this. The brilliant, brilliant sky. There was a tremendous peace in that.

When she felt brave enough, she looked over the edge just as hordes of police cars and vans crashed through the gates. She thought she could see Elisabeth lying there, a small little stick figure, with some of the sticks at odd angles. She watched as dozens of armed police ran into North Fern, all with their weapons drawn.

She slid back onto the roof and waited. She thought she could hear them inside, hear them running up staircases, shouting at prisoners to get down, and commanding each other to hold fire. But, of course, that was all in her head.

So she just watched the sun.

And by the time it had fully come up to say hello, she heard the roof door burst open, and multiple police officers shouting.

'ARMED POLICE. GET DOWN ON THE GROUND.'

Cara turned to them, her arms raised, her palms out. There were three of them, three of them to take her away from this place, just like there had been three of them to bring her here. Funny how things worked out sometimes.

She got down on the ground.

Epilogue

One month later . . .

She sat in the holding cells of the county court. Familiar surroundings. But this time at least, she had a window. There were guards coming – always coming. And now she was getting used to it – it was almost pleasing. That she could finally just sit back and let them come.

A guard came into view beyond the bars, followed by a man in a rustic suit. Her court-appointed lawyer. What was his name? Something Loamfield? Terry, Terrance. She didn't care. She didn't need to know his name to tell him he wasted his trip. But then she hadn't needed to tell him – all he had to do was look at her to know.

The guard unlocked the door, and stood there in the open doorway.

Cara stood up and held out her hands. The guard put the handcuffs around her wrists. And she stepped forward, led by Loamfield, with the guard behind her. Through the bowels of the court. Loamfield left her with one final look, and went off to the right. Another guard joined the procession instead. Cara just followed, until the guard halted at the end of the corridor in front of a large white door. It looked plastic.

The guard held up a hand, but she had already stopped. The guard behind her stepped forward and unlocked the door, before gesturing to her to go through.

There was a small staircase. She went up it. And emerged into a box surrounded by glass. Beyond the box, a courtroom. She looked down at the lawyers – Loamfield staring up at her with nothing in his eyes. She didn't meet his gaze.

'Miss Cara Lockhart.' A booming voice. She looked directly ahead to see an aged judge, with the funny wig, staring at her with thinly veiled contempt. 'You are charged with the murder of Elisabeth Stoker. How do you plead?'

She found that her eyes started streaming with tears, though she didn't know why. She blinked them away, and then kept her eyes closed.

She was where she deserved to be.

'Guilty.'

And she couldn't help but smile as she answered.

Acknowledgements

Inside Out has been an incredibly odd experience throughout, seeing as the world has changed so much throughout the development of it. I am writing these acknowledgements as Great Britain seems to be coming out of a pandemic so massive that history will remember it forever. So I hope that you found some escapism in what you read here, if even for a little bit.

I would like to thank my agent, Hannah Sheppard, and my editor, Francesca Pathak, who both offered lots of support during the writing of this book. It was a difficult one, and they were always there to help, and at times, push me to keep going. Also, to Lucy Frederick and everyone else seen in the credits of this book just over the page. I couldn't have done this without any of them.

To Daniel Stubbings, who is not just a friend, but also a continued source of positivity and knowledge. Dan is a fantastic beta-reader as he'll tell you exactly what he thinks, and that's exactly what you need when writing. I'm proud to call him a friend.

To the #SauvLife crew – Francesca Dorricott, Lizzie Curle and Jennifer Lewin, who have helped keep me sane during this crazy lockdown with social Zoom calls and a place to chat - not always about books, but always productive!

To the people of Waterstones Durham Crime Book Club, who I really missed during this period.

And finally to the newly formed super-group Northern Crime Syndicate, comprised of myself, Robert Parker, Robert Scragg, Adam Peacock, Trevor Wood and Judith O'Reilly. We were actually meant to kick off our global takeover just as lockdown started at Gateshead Library, but obviously all events swiftly got cancelled. So we picked ourselves up and now host events online – which has really been a Godsend as it means I have something to do. We alternate between panels and more free-form events, and it's a ton of fun. If you'd like to learn more, search Northern Crime Syndicate on Facebook, or Twitter at @northern_crime.

Credits

Chris McGeorge and Orion Fiction would like to thank everyone at Orion who worked on the publication of *Inside Out* in the UK.

Editorial
Francesca Pathak
Lucy Frederick

Copy editor
Jade Craddock

Proof reader
Linda Joyce

Audio
Paul Stark
Amber Bates

Contracts
Anne Goddard
Paul Bulos
Jake Alderson

Design
Debbie Holmes
Joanna Ridley
Nick May

Editorial Management
Charlie Panayiotou
Jane Hughes
Alice Davis

Operations
Jo Jacobs
Sharon Willis
Lisa Pryde
Lucy Brem

Production
Hannah Cox

Finance
Jasdip Nandra
Afeera Ahmed
Elizabeth Beaumont
Sue Baker

Marketing
Tanjiah Islam

Publicity
Alainna Hadjigeorgiou

Rights
Susan Howe
Krystyna Kujawinska
Jessica Purdue
Richard King
Louise Henderson

Sales
Jennifer Wilson
Esther Waters
Victoria Laws
Rachael Hum
Ellie Kyrke-Smith
Frances Doyle
Georgina Cutler

Operations
Jo Jacobs
Sharon Willis
Lisa Pryde
Lucy Brem

If you loved Inside Out, don't miss
Chris McGeorge's epic locked-room mystery:

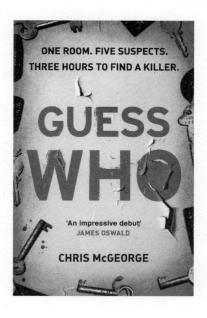

ONE ROOM. FIVE SUSPECTS.
THREE HOURS TO FIND A KILLER.

*'An inventive, entertaining locked room mystery that kept
me utterly hooked'*
ADAM HAMDY

'An ingenious twisty mystery'
CLAIRE McGOWAN

Then jump into this enthralling,
fiendishly clever puzzle...

SIX PEOPLE WENT IN.
ONLY ONE CAME OUT . . .

'*Phenomenal. An utterly compelling read – it blew my
mind ten times over*'
FRANCESCA DORRICOTT

'*Dark and claustrophobic in all the right places*'
ROBERT SCRAGG